STRIVERS ROW

During the 1920s and 1930s, around the time of the Harlem Renaissance, more than a quarter of a million African-Americans settled in Harlem, creating what was described at the time as "a cosmopolitan Negro capital which exert[ed] an influence over Negroes everywhere."

Nowhere was this more evident than on West 138th and 139th Streets between what are now Adam Clayton Powell, Jr., and Frederick Douglass Boulevards, two blocks that came to be known as Strivers Row. These blocks attracted many of Harlem's African-American doctors, lawyers, and entertainers, among them Eubie Blake, Noble Sissle, and W. C. Handy, who were themselves striving to achieve America's middle-class dream.

With its mission of publishing quality African-American literature, Strivers Row emulates those "strivers," capturing that same spirit of hope, creativity, and promise.

D1403512

That Faith,
That Trust,
That Love

That Faith,
That Trust,
That Love

A Novel

JAMELLAH ELLIS

Villard STRIVERS ROW New York

Copyright © 2001 by Jamellah Ellis

Reading Group Guide and A Conversation with Jamellah Ellis
copyright © 2003 by Random House, Inc.

All rights reserved under International and Pan-American
Copyright Conventions. Published in the United States
by Strivers Row, an imprint of Villard Books,
a division of Random House, Inc., New York,
and simultaneously in Canada by Random House
of Canada Limited, Toronto.

Villard Books is a registered trademark of Random House, Inc.
Strivers Row and colophon are trademarks
of Random House, Inc.

An earlier edition of this work was published by
All the While Reconcile Publishing, Bowie, Maryland, in 2001.

Library of Congress Cataloging-in-Publication Data

Ellis, Jamellah.
That faith, that trust, that love: a novel / Jamellah Ellis.
p. cm.
ISBN 0-8129-6656-2
1. African American women lawyers—Fiction.   2. Atlanta (Ga.)—Fiction.   I. Title.

PS3605.L465 T47 2003   813'.6—dc21   2002028884

Villard Books website address: www.villard.com
Printed in the United States of America
24689753

Book design by Jo Anne Metsch

For Alpha Bliss Anderson Robertson:

Nurturer, sustainer, soldier.

I will miss you.

ONE OF MY favorite books in the Bible is the Book of
Ruth. This book tells the story of two women who moved beyond
the limits of their very different backgrounds to develop a mutually
beneficial relationship. Although the relationship developed as a result of a tragedy, these two women decided to allow faith in God to
create a trust in each other that produced unconditional and ever-
lasting love.

Like the Book of Ruth, *That Faith, That Trust, That Love* is about
relationships. It tells the story of three women whose lives are carefully and strategically woven together in the midst of the ups and
downs of life. As you read their story, you will see that their relationships with one another, and the many relationships they encounter, are like a beautifully stitched quilt made of many pieces
and carefully sewn together by the hand of God. It will make you
laugh, cry, and thank God that through faith, trust, and love, we can
enjoy meaningful relationships with others and a life-changing relationship with Him through Jesus Christ.

Throughout our lives, we move in and out of relationships not
always recognizing that whether with family members, friends, as-

sociates, or just casual acquaintances, relationships do not develop by chance—they are divinely orchestrated. It is our responsibility to accept and appreciate God's divine purpose for every relationship. Proverbs 16:9 says, "A man's heart deviseth his way: but the Lord directeth his steps." This verse of scripture describes the sovereignty of God in our lives. It also lets us know that God has a plan for our lives and that He orders each of our steps. *That Faith, That Trust, That Love* shows us very beautifully how God can and will work in our lives.

As you read this book, you will find a familiarity in the characters that will make you feel as though you've met them before. That is because they truly represent real life. This is a real story that teaches a real lesson about life and relationships. It is a story that lets us know that whether we realize it or not, our lives are orchestrated by God and the relationships we establish serve a greater purpose than we know.

Jamellah Ellis is a consummate writer. She writes with clarity and sensitivity that can touch the heart of any reader. In these pages you will undoubtedly find yourself and someone you know. No matter where you find yourself and no matter what you have experienced in life, this is a story that will touch your heart and make you think more seriously about your relationships. It will cause you to consider your past, make an assessment of the present, and change your outlook for the future.

Reverend Willette O. Wright
Temple Hills, Maryland

Part
One

Consider the lilies, how they grow: they neither toil

nor spin; and yet I say to you, even Solomon in all his

glory was not arrayed like one of these. If then God so

clothes the grass, which today is in the field and to-

morrow is thrown into the oven, how much more

will He clothe you, O you of little faith?

—LUKE 12:27−28

SOME WOULD SAY the ending was hard to believe, considering the way it had begun.

The breeze, faint against the warm thickness the sun had cast, gently ruffled the blossoms on the dogwood trees. The scent of lilac and eucalyptus drifted through the air. Butterflies and bees alike visited vibrant May blooms and made their acquaintance. On the lush grounds at Stone Mountain Manor, waiters decked in starched white shirts and black pants scurried about, passing stuffed mushrooms and chèvre filo cups and refilling crystal flutes. Sounds from the Macon Peach Jazz Band wafted through the air like the smell of a low country boil on a stove top in Savannah. And, of course, black folk were talking.

Gathered around over by the tulip beds, next to the stationary hors d'oeuvres, or seated at the forty white linen-covered tables, black folk were talking about how the Shores had once again upped the ante on how a first-rate celebration should be done. And they were talking about the Shores' only son, Gerrard, and his fiancée, Marley. About what a fine boy Gerrard had grown up to be—"fine" having different meanings depending on the gender and age of the particular group doing the talking. And about how his fiancée was both beautiful and outgoing (or stuck-up and pretentious, again depending on the circle that was talking). Theirs would be the wedding of the year, for sure, but for today folk were plain happy and counted it a privilege to have been invited to the engagement party.

They studied, measured, and savored every move the couple made. When the couple wasn't moving but just standing and chatting, the guests soaked that in, too. Gerrard, tall and strapping, was a younger version of his father. His eyelashes, stark against his honey-colored skin, looked as if they'd been hand-dipped in calligraphers' ink. His smile willed you to forget about your bad mood. He strode as if the wind were watching, awaiting his command, pacing itself to follow him. The wind obliged him, until it ran into Marley and stopped. Not on account of her shapely figure, her long, thick hair, or her ample lower lip—traits that came a dime a dozen among the women of Atlanta. Consensus was that it was the mark. That beauty mark, smack dab in the middle of her eyebrows, held court on its own. It seemed, simply, subtly, to say, "Stop." And so eyes, smiles, thoughts, and even the wind obeyed.

Marley's grandmother surveyed the scene, her large, wise eyes sizing up all the characters. "There's got to be more than two hundred people here," Ma Grand said. "Maybe three hundred."

"Probably so," said Pam, Marley's mother, her eyes twinkling with joy at the thought. She tossed her sandy brown hair out of her face and leaned forward in her seat as if she were watching her favorite movie. Pam had just finished making the rounds, greeting the guests, and her feet were aching from all the walking she had done in her open-toed satin-strapped heels.

"Good Lord, Pam, that's nothing to be impressed with! It's a shame before God!" Ma Grand leaned back in her seat and squeezed her thighs together, mainly out of habit—she mostly wore pants these days. Even when she did wear skirts, she made sure they were long enough that she didn't need to worry whether or not her legs were closed.

"Mama, please. Let's just sit here and have a good time. No criticisms, no complaints. Just peace and happiness, okay?" Pam turned her head away quick enough to catch the socially correct smiles from Atlanta's mayor and his wife as they strolled by Pam's table. Following immediately behind them were the presidents of Spelman and Morehouse colleges, managing well the task of chatting while munching discreetly on crab cake medallions. Pam returned their polite smiles, crossed her legs, and fought the urge to squeal in delight.

"What they grinning 'bout?" Ma Grand snapped and cut her eyes at the backs of Mayor and Mrs. Stockton. "Ain't done nothing for the city since he's been elected, except socialize and support his wife's shopping habit. These politicians ain't worth the suits they're wearing. Atlanta ain't been right since Reverend King died."

"Mama, really. Please stop, will you? We're here to celebrate Marley's engagement, not to assassinate the character of every person that passes by our table."

"Why do all these fancy schmancies have to be here in the first place? Is this an engagement party or an inaugural ball? You'd think somebody was campaigning for office or something!" Ma Grand rolled her eyes at no one in particular and shifted her weight in her seat. The cream linen slipcover buckled a bit, and Ma Grand frowned as she tried to smooth the fabric beneath her.

"What are you fussing about now, Ma Grand?" Marley asked, approaching the table. She smoothed a few displaced strands of her grandmother's silver-gray hair and, satisfied, put her hands on her hips and smiled.

"Like she needs a reason to fuss," Pam said.

Ma Grand looked up at Marley and tried her best to maintain a scowl, but her granddaughter's smile broke her every time. She looked away, feigning disgust.

"You having a good time, Gran?" Marley pulled out a chair beside her grandmother and sat. She studied her face—every line, crease, and wrinkle. More than anything, including her own instinct, Marley trusted what she saw in her grandmother's eyes. It dated back to her childhood, when the family had talked in code around Marley to prevent her from hearing more than what they thought a young girl needed to hear. Marley had quickly learned to search her grandmother's eyes for answers. They were a book without a cover.

"Are *you* having a good time?" Ma Grand asked, turning to face Marley. She placed her Parkinson's-afflicted hand on top of the table and grabbed at a silver coffee spoon.

"Yeah. Yes. I am." Marley nodded.

Ma Grand looked at her oddly. "Mm-hm. Well, then, that's all that matters." She stared ahead.

Marley rested her chin in her hand. She glanced at her mother, who was engrossed in a conversation with a distant cousin she had insisted Marley invite to the party. Pam's smile was big and wide, her eyes danced, and her skin glowed. Marley looked back at Ma Grand, who was examining a couple seated to her left.

"Gran," Marley began as she scooted her chair closer to her grandmother. "Tell me what you're *really*—"

Ma Grand elbowed Marley's ribs. Startled, Marley glanced around and saw Ashley and Deanna walking toward her. Her open mouth quickly closed into a smile. Here were her lifelines, of varying degrees. The siblings she had never had. All three girls had grown up in Atlanta and, except for Marley and Ashley, who had been next-door neighbors until the sixth grade when Ashley's family had moved to Dunwoody, the girls had never met until they'd bumped into one another lugging bright-patterned comforter sets and Sam's Club–size toiletries across the Oval on Spelman's campus and through the front doors of Abby Hall.

"Hello, ladies," Pam said after waving good-bye to her cousin. Pam looked the girls up and down. "You-all look gorgeous. Absolutely gorgeous." She beamed as if she had mothered them all. Pam recalled the girls in their late teenage years, with haircuts and boyfriends that had changed like the weather. She remembered the care packages she'd used to take to them on campus and the home-cooked meals she'd occasionally fixed for them on Sundays.

"Not as gorgeous as you," Deanna said, smiling at Pam. The girls had always joked that they would never take Pam out with them because all eyes, young and old, would be on her.

"This is something, isn't it?" Pam grinned.

"It really is," Ashley agreed, taking in the celebration. Chatter filled the air and hovered comfortably like clouds. On a parquet square in the middle of the tables, several couples bopped to an old Smokey Robinson cut.

"Gerrard's family really knows how to throw a party," Deanna added. "I'm so sick of going to functions and eating off of veggie trays, I don't know what to do. Feed me! Know what I'm saying? Don't be serving finger food at five o'clock in the evening when you know people are ready for dinner."

"Really," Ashley agreed, turning to grab a sesame chicken skewer from a tray as a tall, muscular waiter passed by. The waiter paused, ensuring that Ashley got as much chicken as she wanted and also attempting to make eye contact with her. Ashley met his eyes with a flat, toothless smile, and she quickly turned around.

"Marley, Gerrard's family obviously thinks very highly of you, going through all this effort to throw an engagement party," Pam stated as she nodded her head.

Ma Grand chuckled and folded her hands on top of the table. "That's what you think, huh?"

Marley looked askance at her grandmother. "What's that supposed to mean?"

"Honey, just ignore it." Pam waved off her mother's comment. "Just ignore it," she said again, smiling at the Falcons' head coach and his wife, who were seated two tables over.

"This is a fabulous celebration," Ashley said, in part to calm Marley's nerves and in part because it was true. "I'm enjoying myself."

"Good," Pam said. "You should be. And you need to stop ignoring the advances of all these good-looking men out here and find yourself a nice, rich, eligible bachelor."

"Not even looking," Ashley responded quickly. "I'm dating myself."

"Oh, good Lord," Ma Grand said. "How long is this supposed to last?"

"That's the same thing I asked her the other day, Gran," Deanna chimed in. She leaned forward in her chair, her cowry-shell earrings dancing around her cheeks. "But you know, you gotta let Ashley do her thing. Live out her phases. You know what I mean, don't you?" Deanna nudged Ma Grand.

"It's going to last for as long as I need it to last. You-all may find it hard to believe, but I'm actually quite fulfilled with myself right now." Ashley certified her response with a quick nod and turned her head. Her hair, neatly contained in her standard French braid, whipped over her shoulder and lay against her chest.

"You must've just finished a good book," Ma Grand said, looking away. "A good book'll do that for you. But it won't last long. I'll ask you again in another two weeks and see how you're doing."

"My answer won't be different, I promise you," Ashley said.

Marley stared at Ashley, weighing her words. Her straight back and clasped hands were like a fortress around her resolve. Marley wasn't knocking Ashley's decision. She admired it. Envied it, even.

She turned and saw Gerrard striding toward the table, his sandstone-colored linen shirt and slacks flowing behind him. He positioned himself behind Marley's chair, planted his large hands atop her shoulders, and massaged them gently.

"Ladies," he said, his silky mustache rising perfectly above his smiling lips.

Ashley offered Gerrard half a smile and then looked away.

Deanna waved, grinned sarcastically, and said, "Gerrard, we're ab-solutely *thrilled* to see you." Marley leaned her head against her fist and sighed.

"Gerrard, everything is simply beautiful," Pam said. "I told your mother earlier that she did an exceptional job."

"I know that meant a lot to her. But you know she had help. Mom never would have been able to pull this off all by herself." He glanced around quickly. "Anyway," he continued, "I came to get my bride-to-be." He gazed at Marley. "Dad's about to ready to give the toast, so we need to head toward the podium."

Marley rose from her seat slowly. Her rust, ankle-length crepe dress swayed with her body and settled around her hips.

"He's going to want to introduce you too, Pam, so be ready," Gerrard said, smiling.

"Oh, I'll definitely be ready." Pam winked.

"Now look, you tell your daddy he ain't got to introduce me," Ma Grand said and raised her hand in further testimony. "I don't want to be introduced at all, you understand me?"

"Yes, ma'am," Gerrard said and smiled.

"I'm not playing with you, boy," Ma Grand added.

"She's not playing with you, boy," Deanna repeated.

"Dad would've introduced the bridal party as well but for the riffraff," Gerrard said, nodding in Deanna's direction. "Can't be certain Deanna won't get up in front of everybody and start swing-ing from the trees or something."

"Gerrard, walk away with your bride while you still have legs," Deanna retorted.

Pam chuckled deeply. "You-all still go at each other like teenagers! Goodness!" She laughed and shook her head. "It's great you get along so well. Gerrard, you'll become their fourth wheel! The girls'll let you hang out with them, and you'll become a natural part of the crew," she said, winking.

Deanna and Ashley were quiet. Marley said, "Yep."

"Well, baby," Gerrard said, looking down at Marley, "you ready?" Marley stood, wringing her hands.

"Stop that," Pam whispered to her.

"We'll be back." Gerrard winked at the women as he led Marley toward the podium, which fronted a tulip bed. Behind the tulips, sounds from the pebble-lined waterfall trickled and danced in the air.

"You okay, baby?" Gerrard asked as he nodded and smiled at the guests. He continued to massage Marley's shoulders.

"Yeah, I'm fine." Marley gazed ahead.

Gerrard's father was standing near the podium, surrounded by eight or more people, all eager to talk with him. Deftly, he made eye contact with his son while making sure he appeared attentive to the conversation surrounding him. "Absolutely, absolutely," Mr. Shore agreed with one of the men talking to him. "Let's do lunch one day next week and discuss that further," he said, extending his right hand to seal the offer. "Now you'll have to pardon me while I toast the guests of honor." He winked and waved a large, well-manicured, diamond-ringed hand.

Arms around Gerrard and Marley, Mr. Shore glided through the crowd. He motioned for his wife to join them and nodded at a waiter standing nearby, who had already prepared the correct number of flutes on a tray. The waiter approached and handed them each a flute, then quickly disappeared.

Mr. Shore tapped his fingernail against his glass in front of the microphone. "May I have your attention, please?" Within seconds, all conversation and activity ceased.

"My wife and I first want to thank all of you for coming out today to celebrate the coming of what will be the happiest day in our son's life—his marriage to Marley Shepherd."

The applause was thunderous. Marley blushed. Gerrard put his arm around Marley's waist and pulled her closer to him.

"As most of you know, Gloria and I are immensely proud of our only son, as we have been for all his life. I thought I'd seen his finest hour when Shore Development promoted him to assistant chief operating officer. But his decision to marry Marley makes me even more proud, and it shows Gloria and me that Gerrard has grown into the intelligent man we tried to raise him to become."

Ashley leaned toward Deanna's ear and whispered, "Is it just me, or does he sound like he's congratulating his son on a shrewd business decision?"

"Since her college years," Mr. Shore said, "I've had the privilege of watching Marley grow into the fine young woman that she is. I have no doubt she'll be an excellent wife to my son and mother to my grandchildren."

Marley looked at Gloria, whose smile hadn't changed since they'd reached the podium. It was the same smile she always wore, whether she was greeting guests or frying chicken. Marley wondered why, today, Gloria couldn't manage to muster up something more genuine.

"Of course, I can't take the credit for Marley being such a fine young woman. Pamela?" Mr. Shore motioned for Marley's mother. "Come on up and join us so everyone can see where Marley's beauty and brains come from."

Pam smiled and even waved at a few familiar faces as she made her way to the podium. The sun beamed down on her as she walked, glazing her almond skin.

"This is Pamela Shepherd, Marley's mother." Mr. Shore placed his arm around Pam's shoulder. "And I want you all to know that she did one heck of a job raising this little lady. Marley is one of the sharpest lawyers at Morgan & Miller, and on top of that she's one of the most beautiful women in the state! She owes that to her gracious mother here."

The crowd laughed and applauded. "He loves himself some pretty women," Deanna whispered to Ashley, who raised her eyebrows in agreement.

"Now, I promised my wife I would be brief——"

"He lied," Gloria drawled, and the crowd roared. Marley laughed, happy that Gloria had given a glimpse of herself.

"I did indeed," he joked, then quickly sobered. "But in all seriousness, folks, this is one heck of a couple standing here. They did the things they needed to do as individuals, and now they've decided to share the rest of their lives with each other. They're a model of what love and relationships should be. So with all the love, pride, and confidence in my heart, I raise my glass and propose a toast to Gerrard and Marley. May your tomorrows always be as sweet as today!"

"Hear, hear!" the crowd cheered, and glasses touched as the guests joined in the toast. "To the couple of the century!"

TWO WEEKS LATER, after the scent of lilac and eucalyptus had retreated into the atmosphere and the stench of MARTA emissions and urine-stained city sidewalks had claimed the air, the couple of the century rode the elevator to the twelfth floor of the Wachovia Bank building in silence. Marley looked at Gerrard, but he stared ahead, even though he felt her gaze.

"Gerrard, will you try to have a positive attitude about this?" Marley pleaded. She reached for his hand.

Gerrard jerked his arm away. "What's positive about it, Marley? You're dragging me to see a shrink, and I don't even know why."

"She's not a shrink, Gerrard. She's a relationship counselor."

"A shrink, just like I said." Gerrard stuffed his hands into the pockets of his tailored slacks and rested the weight of his body against the wood-paneled elevator.

Marley sighed. "Listen, Gerrard. I know this whole thing is my idea. And maybe you're right—maybe we really don't need to see a counselor. But I will feel a whole lot better if we go in with positive attitudes and make the most of this visit. Maybe we'll both leave feeling glad we saw her."

"If you think we need to pay some third party to tell us about ourselves, then our relationship is not where I thought it was." The elevator doors opened, and Gerrard marched out.

His words stung. Marley closed her eyes, took a deep breath, and followed him.

The walls of the waiting area in Dr. Bell's office suite were painted various shades of yellow, with potted plants filling each corner. One of Mozart's piano concertos trickled out of two speakers mounted in opposite corners of the room. Marley felt the tension in her shoulders begin to tiptoe away. Gerrard sat in a high-backed chair, grabbed a copy of *Sports Illustrated* off the coffee table, and flipped through the pages. Marley signed them in at the front desk and sat on the love seat.

The door adjacent to the front desk opened, and a gangly but large-breasted woman appeared. "Gerrard and Marley?" she called. Her eyes were studious, her smile calming.

"Yes," Marley replied quickly and stood. Gerrard rose, tossed the magazine on the coffee table, and walked toward her.

"I'm Dr. Bell. Very nice to meet you both," she said, smiling and shaking first Gerrard's hand, then Marley's. "Follow me."

Her office was sprawling. Marley counted at least three Turkish area rugs covering the hardwood floor. Varnette Honeywood and Charles Bibbs prints filled the walls, and photographs of a man and two children lined her cherry desk.

Marley and Gerrard gravitated toward the chairs facing her desk. "No, no, over here," Dr. Bell said, closing the door behind her and motioning toward the sitting area. They moved to the oversized couch while she slid into the leather armchair across from them.

"So," she said, suddenly assuming a serious face, "let me see if I understand things correctly. Marley, you initiated this visit, with some reluctance on Gerrard's part, because of some concerns you have about the relationship. Is that right?"

"That's right." Marley nodded and crossed her legs.

"Okay. Gerrard, let's start with you."

Marley and Gerrard looked puzzled. Gerrard's eyes quizzed Marley, then shifted to Dr. Bell.

"Ah, that's fine," Gerrard said slowly, "but I'm not sure exactly what you want me to say."

"Why don't you think you and Marley need to be here today?"

"Well," Gerrard began, leaning back on the couch, eyeing the ceiling, "first of all, I don't believe in shrinks."

"Okay," she said, smiling. "Keep going."

"I believe a man and his wife ought to be able to work through their problems by themselves." He continued to stare at the ceiling, as if the ceiling were asking the questions.

"Mm-hm."

"Second of all," he continued, finally making eye contact with Dr. Bell, "I'm not even sure what the problem is." Gerrard folded his hands behind his head. "I mean, Marley has mentioned some concerns to me, but in my mind they don't rise to a level where we need to seek professional help."

"Okay. We'll come back to that." She looked at Marley. "Marley, why did you want to talk today?"

"Because of things like what you just heard. It's like, in Gerrard's mind, a problem doesn't exist unless he defines it as one. He doesn't validate my concerns, and that makes me feel like my opinion isn't worth anything."

"But Marley, you look for problems in almost every situation," Gerrard said. "Like the hours I work. The amount of time I spend with you. You know how demanding my job is, so what's the issue?"

"Gerrard, don't act like you don't understand what the real problem is," Marley warned, her eyes serious.

"Maybe you should tell him what the real problem is," Dr. Bell interjected, "just in case he doesn't understand."

"The real problem is, he claims to be so busy with work—"

"No, no, don't tell me," Dr. Bell reminded her, "tell him." She nodded in Gerrard's direction.

Marley turned to face Gerrard. His callous eyes silenced her. Weren't those the same eyes that used to dance each time he saw her?

Marley swallowed and began to speak. "The real problem is, you cancel out on me every time we make plans. You claim you're so busy at work, yet you still find time to do the things *you* want to do. Like attending Fulton County Business Association functions, going to Falcons games, playing golf in Ansley Park—"

"And most of the time I'm doing those things with clients."

"Yeah, but some of the time you're not. I think you take for granted that we're going to be together, even if we don't spend time nurturing our relationship, because we've always been together. And because we're engaged. But that's just not good enough anymore, Gerrard. If we're going to spend the rest of our lives together, I need to know that spending time with me will always be a priority in your life."

"Marley, spending time with you will always be a priority in my life," Gerrard said, his tone suggesting she should know better.

"Now he's patronizing me."

Gerrard threw his hands up.

"Okay," Dr. Bell responded quickly, "I think I have a feel for what's going on here." She looked at Marley. "Marley, what's your understanding of Gerrard's work schedule?"

"I know that he works long hours. But I also know—"

"Wait right there. We'll come back to the 'but.' " She looked at Gerrard. "Now, there have been occasions, haven't there, when you've left work at a decent hour to have some non-client-related fun?"

"Well," he began and reclined against the couch. "Sure, sure, there have been a few occasions here and there."

Dr. Bell smiled. "You may not realize it, but you've just taken a critical first step toward understanding and responding to each other's needs. For the rest of our time together, I'd like for each of you to try to think and respond based on what you've just acknowledged about each other and not what you're upset about. Marley, you're thinking and responding based on the fact that you know Gerrard works long hours, and Gerrard, you're—"

"I got you, I got you," he said. He glanced out the window and began to tap his foot on the floor.

"Okay. Gerrard, do you have extra time during the week when you aren't really doing anything?"

"Do I *what*? Are you kidding? Of course not."

"Right. And since spending time with Marley will always be a priority, as you put it, how are you going to make more time for her within the already hectic schedule you have?"

Gerrard stared at Dr. Bell. A grin inched its way to the corners of his mouth. "We're playing mind games, huh?"

"I'm not playing any kind of game with you, Gerrard. I'm just asking a question."

He folded his hands. "Well, I'm going to find the time."

"But how? Doesn't something have to give in order for you to find the time?"

"Yep. Something will have to give. And I can't sit here and say exactly what will have to give because it varies from week to week, you see. One week I might have to skip an awards banquet. Another week I might have to miss a tee time. But I'm going to make more time for Marley." Gerrard smiled, then quickly, as if to ward off another one of Dr. Bell's "don't tell me, tell her" admonitions, turned to face Marley and said, "Marley, I want you to know that I'm going to make more time for you." He took Marley's hand in his and squeezed and patted it.

Dr. Bell shifted her gaze to Marley. "Marley, you understand the kinds of professional obligations that businessmen like Gerrard have to meet in order to be successful, don't you?"

"I do."

✓ "Okay, then. Do you accept Gerrard for the person he is and the career he has chosen?"

Marley sighed. "Yes," she said slowly.

"Are you sure?" Dr. Bell asked.

Gerrard glared at Marley, then looked away.

"Yes, I'm sure."

"Are you going to be comfortable on those occasions when you'd like to spend time with Gerrard but he has to attend work-related functions or simply needs some recreational time?"

"Yes." Marley looked away.

"And what is going to enable you to be more comfortable on those occasions?" Dr. Bell persisted.

"Well, when we start to spend more time together, I'll feel much more comfortable with the times that we can't be together. And I'm also going to remind myself who he is and what things are simply a part of his life and his responsibilities as a businessman."

"Very good, both of you. I know it's probably difficult for you to recognize progress at this juncture, but you've made some. Learning to keep each other's feelings at the forefront of your communication takes lots of time. But it's critical to a successful marriage." Dr. Bell smiled and leaned forward. "After thirty-six years of marriage, my husband and I are still working on it." She chuckled.

Marley picked at a loose thread in her skirt. "Can we end today's session now?" she asked. "I want to digest what we've covered before we tackle new areas."

"Absolutely," Dr. Bell said quickly, rising as she spoke.

"Thank you very much," Marley said, reaching to shake Dr. Bell's hand.

"You're quite welcome, Marley." She extended her hand to Gerrard.

"My pleasure," he said, accepting her hand. "Thanks."

The three walked out of the office, down a short hallway, and returned to the waiting area.

"Let me ask you a question, Doctor," Gerrard said, as they stood in front of the office suite's massive oak doors. "You said you've been married for thirty-six years?"

Dr. Bell's back straightened. "Yes, sir. Thirty-six years next month."

Marley's eyes lingered on Dr. Bell's. "Congratulations," she said softly.

"What's your secret, Doc?" Gerrard pursued.

"Prayer. There's no way in the world Thomas and I would still be married to each other without God in our lives."

"Mm. Okay, then. Thanks again for your time." Gerrard opened the door for Marley.

"Anytime. Take care," she said as they walked away.

Gerrard and Marley were quiet as they waited for the elevator to reach the twelfth floor. Gerrard finally broke the silence.

"What did you think?"

"She was okay," Marley said, staring past Gerrard toward the office suite they'd just left.

"Humph. For her rates, we could have asked each other those questions," he said and laughed.

Marley remained silent.

"Oh, come on, baby." He moved closer to her. "I understand what your concerns are. I really do. And I was serious when I said I'm going to start to make more time for you. Okay? Okay, sweetheart?"

She still would not make eye contact with him, mainly because his effort at emanating warmth had begun to melt her anger away. He had a way of doing that. She had a way of falling for it. Every time.

"Okay?" he said again, moving even closer. Their lips were almost touching, and she felt his breath, warm and moist, against her skin.

She tried to summon up some strength from somewhere inside herself. It wasn't right—his attitude, her reservations, their situation. She saw the wrongness of it all so clearly, but the closer he moved toward her, the more foggy the vision became. The thinner the air became. The weaker she became. The more irresolute her summons became. Weakness—this kind of weakness—was like mid-air suspension with clouds gathered like pillows at her head and feet. It required nothing except to float along thoughtlessly, effortlessly, indeterminately. It was easy, and it felt good.

The elevator bell rang, and the doors opened. "After you," Gerrard said and moved to the side so that Marley could pass.

A chuckle forced its way out of Marley's mouth as she stepped on the elevator. "You're silly," she said, sorry that she wasn't able to suppress her laughter and retain a somber face. Gerrard pulled her toward him and wrapped his arms around her shoulders. He kissed her on the side of her forehead, and she stared ahead as the elevator doors closed.

Dr. Bell's office was a few blocks away from Mickey's, where Marley had agreed to meet Ashley and Deanna for dinner. Marley decided to walk the distance, figuring it would give her time to gather her thoughts. A downy breeze followed her along Peachtree Street. She took several deep breaths and marveled at the notion that each time she exhaled she could chip away at the bundle of nerves that encircled her heart every time she thought about Gerrard.

She stopped to stare at a phenomenal black dress in the window at Ansa's, a boutique she and her mother loved to frequent whenever they had somewhere special to go. As she stared through the window, she caught a glimpse of herself. She saw herself at the elevator with Gerrard. She saw herself, so many times before, letting his soft kisses and sugary reassurances cover his physical absences and emotional delinquencies like square patches over round holes. She saw all this, and she was not pleased with who stared back at her. No mystery it was the reason she had begun to spend so much time grooming herself. Her nails never missed their weekly manicure. She had picked up a shoe and matching purse fetish that was taxing her bank account. And she'd purchased just about every tube of M.A.C. lipstick that had ever been manufactured. But for all the painting she did on the outside, the picture on the inside remained colorless, shapeless—altogether lacking in form.

She reached into the front flap of her ostrich purse and grabbed her white lace handkerchief—her old steady—that Ma Grand had sewn for her when she'd turned six years old. She dabbed at the few tears that threatened to streak her eyeliner. *Who am I fooling?* she thought as she dropped her handkerchief back into her purse. She turned away from the window at Ansa's and quickly walked the last block to Mickey's.

"I swear to God, I'm quitting on Monday morning." Deanna sipped her water, placed the glass back on the table, and picked at her chipped burgundy nail polish. "Swear to God."

"Deanna, you say that every Friday," Ashley said, shaking her head. She downed the last of her orange-cranberry mixture. "If you hate your job that much, why don't you stop talking about it and quit for real?"

"Because," Deanna whined and slumped down in her seat. "I have no clue what else to do with myself."

"What?" Ashley's eyes widened. "Deanna, for the past ten years you've been saying you were going to become an actress. What are you waiting for?"

"Really," Marley agreed. "You're way too creative to sit behind a desk from nine to five."

"Ladies," Deanna sang, "I have bills to pay. Obligations to fulfill." She waved her hands in a circular motion. "What about that?"

"You have habits to support, plain and simple." Ashley reclined in her chair. "Pursuing acting means no more biweekly hair appointments and no more monthly shopping sprees. You don't want to give that up, and you know it."

"Whatever," Deanna said, looping her forty-inch beaded necklace around her index finger.

"Well, it's your choice, Deanna. Take the safe route, and you may never find the professional fulfillment you're looking for," Marley said. She motioned for the waiter to refill her water glass.

"Speaking of professional fulfillment," Ashley said, leaning forward on her elbows, "you'll never believe what my children did in class today. I was reviewing the alphabet with them when Devonne, the little troublemaker I told you about last week, raises his hand. He says, 'Miss Miller, what's gas?' And I say, 'Well, Devonne, there are several different kinds of gases. There's gasoline, which is a fuel we use to fill our cars so we can drive around every day.' He cuts me off and says, 'No, not that kind of gas. How 'bout the gas that comes from people?' And I say, 'Well, Devonne, you're right. There is a kind of gas that comes from people. We get that gas from eating certain kinds of foods. Our bodies digest the food, and gas is one of the ways we pass the food through our bodies.'

"So he says, 'But why does it stink, Miss Miller?' Then Dionne, his twin brother, says, 'Yeah, Miss Miller, why does it stink so bad? My daddy did gas last night and it stinked *real* bad.' Then Devonne says, 'I'ma tell Daddy, Dionne.' To which Dionne responds, 'Do I look like I *care*?' Then Dionne forces out an awful fart. I mean, he forces it out with everything in his little body. And Christina, the sickly little girl who sits next to Dionne, turns red and begins to wrinkle up her face like something died. After about five seconds, Christina yells, 'It's gas! It's very, very bad gas! Run for your life!' And all fifteen of them hop out of their chairs and run out of the classroom, down the hall, and out the side doors into the play yard."

Marley laughed so hard she almost peed on herself. "I need to start dropping in on your class once a day just for entertainment."

"I know you *never* have a dull moment," Deanna said, wiping a tear from her eye. "Maybe I ought to start teaching kindergarten."

"I love it," Ashley said. "I have never been so satisfied in my entire life. I love those children. It's such a mutually beneficial relationship because I get to teach them what they need to know and their innocent little spirits lighten my heart. They really keep me optimistic."

"Do you still want me to be a chaperone on the field trip to the Botanical Garden?" Deanna asked. "I already arranged to take off work, so I can do it if you still need me."

"Oh Dee, that would be wonderful," Ashley said. "And that reminds me of an article I read in the Sunday paper about Bayview Terrace. They've planted weeping cherries near the wedding gazebo, and they are spectacular. I mean spectacular! The branches cascade all the way down to the ground, and they're filled with these beautiful white flowers." Ashley winked at Marley and smiled. "Your Bayview wedding is going to be even more breathtaking than you imagined."

"Yeah, Miss Bride-to-be! Let's talk about you. When do you go for your first fitting? I think we should make a day out of it. You know, have a nice breakfast, go to the fitting, do some accessory shopping, and then go out for dinner that evening," Deanna proposed.

"Sounds like a plan," Marley said quickly and began to eat her fried chicken salad.

"Ugh! What's up with the lack of enthusiasm? *'Sounds like a plan,'* " Deanna mocked and twisted her face in disgust. "*Hello?* This is your *wedding* we're talking about."

Ashley looked at Deanna with raised brows, then looked away.

"I'm not unenthusiastic," Marley said, "just tired, that's all. Planning a wedding can be a draining experience." She heaped another forkful of salad into her mouth.

"Yeah, yeah, yeah, but underneath the fatigue there should still be that special glimmer in your eyes. The glimmer that says, 'I'm so in love.' " Deanna's eyes fixed on Marley's relentlessly, while Marley developed an intense interest in a shred of radish.

"I'm excited, Deanna," Marley finally said, adding a smile for good measure.

Deanna looked at Ashley, tapped her fingers on the table, then leaned forward and looked at Marley again. "Are you *really*?" she pressed.

Marley put her fork down. She looked at Deanna and realized that Deanna was gazing right through her mask. She always had. Marley remembered the time, days after the girls had first met, when she'd walked down three different aisles in Woodruff Library, lost as ever, pretending to be searching for a particular book. "If you're lost, why don't you ask for help?" Deanna had asked pointedly from the end of an aisle. Nothing had changed.

"Well, I'm trying not to get caught up in all the hoopla, you know? A wedding is about more than the ceremony. I'm thinking about the next day and the day after that and the day after that."

"So when you think about the day after that and the day after that, what do you feel?" Deanna asked. "I always wonder about that. Like, will you get tired of doing the same thing all the time? Cooking the same dinner? Seeing each other in the same outfits? Eventually he'll be seeing you in your jumbo purple rollers, girl."

"I imagine things do get very regular very soon," Ashley said. "But I think married couples grow to appreciate that regularity. Like with my parents. They've been together for thirty-two years. I really think the reason they're still married is because they never stopped doing the same old things that caused them to fall in love in the first place. I stopped by their house a few Saturdays ago, and it was pretty late. I expected them to be in bed, knocked out, trying to get their twelve hours of sleep for church the next morning. But when I got to the door and was about to unlock it, I heard this music blasting. Loud as heck! It was Bobby "Blue" Bland or somebody like that. I actually had to stop and consider whether I should knock first to make sure I wouldn't stroll in on something I didn't *even* want to see. I decided to use my key and take a chance. I'm so glad I did. When I walked inside, I saw them cuddled up on the couch. A big bowl of popcorn was on the floor, and boxes of Raisinets and Blockbuster movie cases were on the couch beside them. They looked so adorable I wanted to cry."

The girls oohed and aahed, and they shared stories about the one or two ideal couples they knew. Marley looked hard but couldn't identify herself and Gerrard in a single one of the couples her friends were talking about.

Marley cut her ladies' night out a little shorter than she otherwise would have, mainly because she was hoping Gerrard would call when he finished working and stop by her house to visit. By midnight, however, she realized, as on so many Friday nights before, that Gerrard wasn't going to call. She rolled over onto her back and stared through the skylight in her bedroom ceiling.

It was silly—her not calling him because he hadn't called her. But part of her thought it was best to have a quiet night alone, to reflect on things. Truth be told, seventy percent of the time Marley felt like she was about to make the biggest mistake of her life marrying Gerrard. But the other thirty percent of the time, Gerrard made her so happy. Some things about Gerrard were constant. Like his discipline. In college, Marley had marveled at how Gerrard would manage a morning job and an almost full read of the newspaper well before his eight o'clock class began. Back then, he would call Marley when he woke up and describe the sunrise to her. "There's a purplish orange shade emerging now, Marley. It reminds me of your fiery spirit. And now here comes a softer yellow tone—it's like the love and warmth you project to others whenever you walk into a room." Marley would lie in her twin-size bed in the sophomore dormitory room in Packard Hall and grin herself back to sleep. She never looked at the sunrise herself when Gerrard described it; she wanted to see it and experience it through the colors he painted for her. Nobody else's boyfriend was awake and describing sunrises to them, much less reading the newspaper or exercising. Marley had known then that her future lay with Gerrard.

It didn't matter to Marley when, by senior year, most of her friends believed that referring to Gerrard as overly ambitious was an understatement. Nicknames he'd earned, such as "Wall Street Stallion" and "Won't Stop Climbing Willie," were funny to her, but nothing more. Marley still knew the malleable side of him, even though she was beginning to see it surface less. And it didn't matter that they were not spending as much time together. After all, Gerrard was preparing for business school and Marley was preparing for law school. The bottom line was that Gerrard loved her, so she was willing, for a short time, to accept less than his undivided attention. For a short time.

Still, Marley had learned from watching her parents that a half-hearted relationship dies after a while. She and Gerrard weren't even married, and already their branches were bending. Sometimes Marley wished she could go back to her childhood, when, in her naïve world, she believed love was love with no strings attached. In that world, she'd fully expected to grow up and meet a nice man who smiled a lot and wanted to go to church, which seemed like a nice thing for men and women to do. In that world, broken things could always be fixed.

Then Marley had watched her parents sever the marital cord that held them together. The cord was their lifeline, a strong tie that only God could cut at death—so she thought. But when love is born prematurely, as it had been with her teenage parents who one day had discovered that a child was on the way, the lifeline is weak to begin with. As soon as the Afro went out of style and the dashiki was replaced with a shirt and tie, and the child grew old enough to talk back, and a little too much time passed between the pregnancy and the loss of those extra twenty pounds, and the student loans were repaid, and the raise came, and the extra attention came along with it, the covenant lapsed into code blue. The cord had the marriage by its neck, and it wasn't long before Marley's father broke loose from the grip.

Marley thought no pain could be greater than that kind of death. Surely nothing was worse than entrusting your heart on a promise for life, only to have the promise canceled and your depleted heart handed back to you. Then one day she'd noticed that their living room couch had been placed in front of the window, where it became a watchtower of hope and lost dreams. Her mother would perch there, night after night, staring out the window, waving life on as it passed by and searching the night for a resolution different from what had already claimed her. Marley had become convinced that that kind of pain was worse. And she'd determined she would never know it.

Remembering her promise to herself, Marley pulled her comforter up to her neck, closed her eyes, and welcomed sleep.

Chapter 3

ARLEY HAD JUST finished sautéing the onions, mushrooms, and green peppers for the omelettes when the doorbell rang. She looked at the sunflower clock on her kitchen wall. Gerrard was early. She fantasized that the aroma from her cooking was so inviting, so enticing, that it had snatched Gerrard by the collar of his microfleece knit sweatshirt and decisively aborted his morning jog in favor of the breakfast she was preparing. As she gently folded the vegetables into the cheesy egg batter, she smiled. They had figured this thing out, she and Gerrard. Since neither one's schedule was going to become any less hectic, they had decided—or rather, Marley had suggested and Gerrard had agreed—that they should begin to take advantage of weekend mornings as opportunities for them to spend time together.

It meant that Marley would have to wake up early—something she loathed. As a child, Marley had woken up at seven o'clock every Saturday to do her chores and attend dance lessons with Madame Bofeit. Marley hated France and anything closely related to it because of Madame Bofeit. As it had turned out, Madame Bofeit was really Mrs. Martha Bofaney from Iuka, Mississippi. For Gerrard, though, and for their relationship, Marley would make the sacrifice.

She hopped over the three steps separating the living room from the foyer. Those were the steps she had loved when she bought the house, the same steps Ma Grand had told her would get on her nerves after their novelty wore off. Ma Grand had been right.

She opened the front door to find Gerrard looking like a *GQ* cover model and smelling even better. He smiled and slowly extended his right arm from behind his back. The sweet scent of white calla lilies tickled Marley's nose.

"Thank you, sweetie," she said, hugging him tightly. She lingered in his arms and rested her head on his shoulder.

"My pleasure," he said into her ear, kissing it lightly.

They walked toward the kitchen, hand in hand. Marley smelled her flowers and smiled. "I know you're good and hungry now," she said, bending to get a vase from a cabinet. Gerrard sat at the table and opened the newspaper.

"Mm, a little," he said, his attention already consumed by the front page of *The Atlanta Constitution*.

"A little?" Marley looked at him. "You didn't eat already, did you?"

"No, no. But you know it's hard for me to eat much of anything in the morning." Gerrard flipped to the business section and, once there, crossed his legs and settled in for a good read.

My ambitious man, Marley thought to herself, smiling. Maybe he wasn't so different from the college boy she'd fallen in love with. Maybe this was simply who he was, for better or worse. Surely his ambition would take them far in life, and that was a good thing.

Marley clipped the stems of the calla lilies and dropped them into a glass vase. The stems sprang outward and crashed silently against the vase's walls. Marley's thoughts raced forward through the rest of the day, planning how she and Gerrard might spend it.

Then she remembered that they hadn't really talked about spending the entire day together and felt anxious. Did he have other plans? Would she figure in them? Her thoughts gripped the reins of her mind once again. She always did that—ruined the moment by rushing forward in search of the next one. Right there, at that particular moment, Marley was happy. She willed herself to sit still in it.

"Mmmm," Gerrard said, after she'd set their plates on the table and seated herself across from him. "This looks delicious, Marley."

"Why, thank you," she said, smiling.

Gerrard heaped a forkful of his omelette into his mouth, picked up the newspaper, and continued to read. Marley bowed her head and mumbled a quick prayer of grace.

"Taste good?" she asked.

"Mm-hm," he said from behind the newspaper.

Marley took a few bites of her potatoes, stared at the peeling edges of the wall border, picked at her chipped nail polish, then gave up. She folded her hands and cleared her throat. "Gerrard," she started, "do you mind putting the paper down for a few minutes?"

"Huh?" he asked, his voice muffled by the shifting newspaper. "Oh, I'm sorry." He folded the paper. "I almost forgot. This is my date with my baby." He winked at her, picked up his fork, and continued to eat.

"Did you finish that brief you were working on?" he asked, gulping his orange juice and scooping up some potatoes.

"No. I need to do more research before I can finish the First Amendment section. Right now I need a mental break." Marley tasted her omelette and was impressed. She'd come a long way from the days when hamburgers and pancakes had been the only items in her culinary repertoire.

"Any word on whether you got the Cascade Heights project?" she asked. For the past few weeks, Gerrard had been working on securing the development contract for the new garden apartment complex to be built there. It would be a plum if he got it.

"Not yet. But it's looking good. In fact, I'm meeting Mr. Carter for lunch this afternoon. I'm hoping a little more wining and dining will seal the deal."

It was as if her good feelings were suddenly dumped in a flour sifter and churned out prematurely. Marley continued to eat, failing miserably at trying to mop up the disappointment that by now had spilled out of her face.

"What's wrong?" Gerrard put his fork down. A tiny sliver of orange pulp cupped the corner of his mouth.

"I was hoping we could spend the day together." Her eyes did not leave his.

"Here we go again," he mumbled and reclined in his chair.

She was about to tell him to wipe the pulp off his mouth, but in light of his foul attitude, she decided against it. "I could say the same thing, Gerrard. Not the same old squeeze-Marley-in thing again."

"I have to work, Marley. You know that."

"Do you ever try to schedule these lunches during the week? I mean, I'm busy too, Gerrard. I could be working this weekend, but it's important to me to take a break sometimes so I can spend time with you."

"Don't compare our work schedules, Marley, please." Gerrard folded his arms.

Marley sipped her juice and rested her elbows on the table. Her eyes traveled to the VanDerZee calendar hanging on the wall. "Are you really ready to be married?"

"*What?* Oh, come on, Marley. Really. You're taking this way too—"

"No, I don't think so. I don't think I'm taking this too far at all because my expectations about us spending time together are not going to change. If anything, marriage and family life will make them greater."

Gerrard stood and walked to the sink. He turned to face her. "Marley, you're the woman I want to marry and spend the rest of my life with." Her eyes remained on the calendar. "Look at me, please."

She looked past him.

"I know I'm going to have to make some changes, and I'm willing to do it because I need you. You're my earth. You keep me grounded."

"You're my *what?*" Ashley spat out, while her manicurist oiled her cuticles.

" 'You're my earth,' " Marley repeated in almost a whisper, noticing the smirk on the manicurist's face.

"That's what he said to you?" Ashley looked at Marley with her you-can't-be-serious expression.

Marley rolled her eyes upward and sighed. "Yes."

"Gerrard said that to you?"

"Ashley, cut it out. Who else have I been talking about? Yes, that's what Gerrard said." Marley blew at her fingernails while the pedicurist massaged her calves.

Ashley shook her head slowly and studied the bottle of pale pink polish her manicurist had begun to apply. She was conspicuously silent.

"Just say what you have to say, Ash. Please, spare me the silent treatment."

"Who said I have something to say?" she commented, engrossed in the label on the bottle of nail polish. But she felt Marley's gaze and couldn't ignore it. She sighed. "Look, I think he's whack," she confessed. "I know you don't want to hear that, but I really think he's lame, Marley. He's still talking to you like you're a goggle-eyed freshman who's never met a man with depth and a sense of expression about himself. We're ten years beyond that now; he needs to kick it up a level, in my opinion."

"Ashley, that's how Gerrard talks. He's always been that way. You know he still writes poetry."

Come on, girl, Ashley's eyes seemed to plead. She shook her head quickly. "That's all fine and well, Marley. But I've never been comfortable with guys who speak in metaphors all the time. How in the world will you know what they're really trying to say? That's safe for them. Very unsafe for us.

"And he's always so busy," Ashley continued. "It seems like he's always showing up late, or canceling dates, or getting caught up with work. I know his schedule is demanding, but goodness. He's only going to get busier as he moves up in the company. How's he ever going to have time for you?"

The manicurist looked at Marley as if she were waiting on an answer to Ashley's question. *"Honey,"* she finally volunteered, her English strained at best, "you no want marry man with no time. No, *honey.* No time, not good." She said something to the pedicurist in what Marley guessed was Vietnamese, and the pedicurist snorted.

"Deadbeat," the pedicurist stated in perfect soap opera English, drying Marley's feet.

The following Monday, Marley met her mother for dinner at her favorite restaurant, Bistro Prime. It wasn't that the food was spectacular at Bistro Prime—Pam loved to frequent the place because it was, by all accounts among her peers, the spot to see and be seen. There might have been a time, a long while ago, when Pam would have shunned the notion of going somewhere to watch a performance and, alternately, perform. But a failed marriage and the half-empty bed she'd inherited had changed her convictions.

Pam chatted easily with Byron, the maître d' and an old classmate of hers from Clark College. Byron seated them in the bay window alcove overlooking downtown Atlanta.

"So have you followed up with Kenya about her measurements?" Barely in her seat, Pam fumbled through her purse and pulled out a small spiral notepad on which she'd jotted a wedding checklist. She gently placed her gold-rimmed spectacles on the bridge of her nose.

"Not yet," Marley said flatly. She'd been hoping that wedding plans would not have to be the first order of business that evening. Plus, she'd never wanted Kenya to be in the wedding in the first place. Kenya, the cousin Marley had never gotten along with, had always thought she was better than Marley, at least until she'd turned up pregnant at fifteen and hadn't been completely certain who the father was.

"You haven't?" Pam looked over the rims of her spectacles, her face registering mild shock. "Honey, I don't have to remind you, do I, that Kenya lives thousands of miles away and that you need to be absolutely certain her measurements are accurate before Shirley cuts the fabric? I know Kenya claims to be a size ten, but I don't believe that for one minute, 'cause the last time I saw her she looked like she was barely squeezing into a twelve. I've heard of too many disasters with dresses that don't fit, so you've got to follow up with her soon, honey."

"I will, Mom." Marley looked away and was relieved to see a waiter approach their table. She was quickly disappointed, though, as he took their beverage orders and disappeared sooner than Marley had hoped.

Pam placed her notepad on the table and studied her daughter's face. "Marley, is something wrong?"

Marley twisted the stem of her empty water glass. "No, nothing's wrong. It's just that all the preparations for the wedding have really been wearing on me."

"Oh," Pam said, waving away Marley's comment like a gnat. "That's normal. The preparation gives everyone a headache. But you will forget all about it soon enough." She beamed at Marley, repositioned her spectacles, and busied herself with her checklist.

"Yeah, but I guess it's really making me think about what I'm getting myself into, you know?" There. She'd done it. Taken the plunge. Opened the door. Marley laughed casually, now fiddling with the silver-plated salad fork lying on top of her linen napkin.

Pam narrowed her eyes. "It's awful late for that, don't you think?" The waiter returned with their drinks, and Pam grabbed her ginger ale out of his hand. The waiter smiled nervously, reached for his notepad, then decided against it, backing away slowly.

Pam sipped her soda and glanced around the room. Her eyes lingered upon a couple seated next to her. The man, well groomed and fairly attractive, smiled constantly and punctuated every sentence with a touch on the woman's hand or a light tap on her arm. *He's so attentive,* Pam thought, and wondered why the woman didn't seem to be more appreciative of the spotlight her date was shining on her. *These young women don't understand. They act as if love is promised.* Pam raised her eyebrows and shook her head.

Marley eyed the same couple. The man was leaning so far over the table that his lapel had picked up smears of butter from the butter dish. He looked as if he were ready to slobber on the woman; she looked as if she were prepared to endure the slobbering.

"Mom, I guess what I'm trying to say is I'm having second thoughts. And no, I don't think it's too late to reconsider things, because if it's not meant to be with Gerrard and me, then I'd rather face that before we walk down somebody's aisle."

Pam sighed and folded her hands. Now was the time to try a different approach. What did they say in those how-to-be-a-better-communicator books? Empower the speaker by showing you hear her.

"Okay, honey," Pam said, leaning forward. "Explain to me what's giving you second thoughts about marrying Gerrard."

Marley considered her mother for a moment, then decided to speak. "Well—I don't know, exactly. Gerrard and I have been trying to deal with the same issues for a while now. I guess I'm starting to suspect that the things about him that bother me aren't going to change."

Pam smiled, thinking it was the best disguise for her disbelief. What was this child looking for? A perfect human being? Well, perfect human beings didn't exist—hadn't she discovered that? Hadn't she come to realize that the choice was simple: it was between a flawed man or no man at all?

"Marley, honey, you're engaged," Pam began, eyeing the tablecloth as she smoothed it with her hand. "Haven't you known for years that Gerrard is not perfect and that there will always be issues?" She looked at Marley. "Are these issues new developments, or is it possible that you may have blinded yourself to them in the past?"

"I didn't purposely blind myself to *anything,* Mom. But that's beside the point, because I can't deny what I'm feeling right now."

"And what are you feeling right now?"

Marley sighed. "I question the depth of the love Gerrard and I have for each other. And whether commitment and family life mean the same thing to both of us."

Pam rubbed her temples. God, did psychiatrists have a tough job. Well, she wasn't a psychiatrist, she was a mother. And right now she needed to advise her child the best way she knew how. She'd been down roads Marley didn't even know existed; she wanted it to stay that way.

"Listen, Marley," Pam said, pleased with the firmness of her voice, "marriage is about a whole lot more than *love* and all that touchy-feely stuff. Marriage is about doing and being more together than you would ever do or be by yourself. It's not sentimental, it's practical, you understand? It might not sound all cuddly and cute, but it's reality."

Marley looked at her mother. "That's supposed to make me feel *better*?"

Pam narrowed her eyes. "I'm not trying to make you feel better, Marley—I'm trying to tell you the truth about marriage so you can get this candyland fantasy out of your head and realize that the grass is not always greener someplace else."

Marley sighed and rested her temple on her fingertips. "You know what, Mom? I'm going to be honest with you. And I hope you can take this for what it is." She leaned forward. "I've been hearing your 'truth' about marriage all my life. I realize now that I subconsciously adopted your views as my own. As a matter of fact, they're part of the reason why I'm still with Gerrard today. I try to tell myself he hasn't changed when I know he has. I try to tell myself that even if he has changed, it's okay, when I know it's not. Maybe the grass *is* greener someplace else. I'll never know it if I follow your advice. Now, I'm not blaming you for anything. But I am saying I have a major problem with your outlook on love and marriage, and I'm not going to let it dictate my decisions anymore."

Pam snatched her spectacles off her nose. "You most certainly *are* blaming me. You have your own brain, you're a grown woman, and you can think for yourself. If you made a mistake, don't you *dare* try to use me as an excuse for it!"

"Mom, I'm just trying to share my feelings with you. Please don't get defensive, because I'm not trying to attack you."

"Marley, what do you call what you just said? A compliment? How do you expect me to respond?"

"Mom, just forget it, okay? Forget it."

"I'm not forgetting *anything*," Pam spat. Her eyes bore into Marley's, and Marley looked away. Pam leaned back and realized she was breathing heavily. She glanced to the side and saw the waiter taking measured steps toward their table, his hands gesturing awkwardly toward his writing pad. She motioned for him to wait yet another minute.

Marley had been digging in her purse, and she produced a travel-size bottle of aspirin. "Mom," she announced, not bothering to align the little childproof markers as she popped the cap off, "this is too much for me right now. I'm going to pass on dinner." She dropped a pill onto her tongue and swallowed it with water. "Thanks anyway, though." She gathered her purse, half expecting her mother to ask her not to leave. Pam didn't. Instead, Pam followed suit, grabbing her blazer off the back of her chair and mumbling to herself about needing to get home anyway. She left cash on the table and followed Marley out of the restaurant.

In the parking lot, their bodies hugged good-bye, while their eyes avoided each other.

How often it is that the bodies that hug good-bye and the eyes that avoid each other belong to mothers and daughters. Daughters and mothers. They're an indefatigable institution, cemented together with a biological similitude that lays upon them the weightiest of expectations. The fairness of it all depends on the season. The institutional presumption is an irrational, illogical, laborious sentence for a girl to live under—until, perhaps, she bears her own girl child. The boy child is the one who can conjure up the warmest remembrance simply in the arch of his heel, or the slope of his neck, or the curve of his fingers, or the contour of his thighs. But the girl. The girl is a woman first. A woman at a minimum. A woman if she's to be anything at all, anything worth mentioning, anything that matters in this life.

As far as Ma Grand was concerned, this was the season when the presumption weighed heavily in her favor. It did in most seasons, really. Why shouldn't it, when she'd been here longer, endured more, lost more, and learned more? Take it up with the law of numbers if you didn't like it, but reality was reality: Ma Grand's seventy-eight years had earned her another set of eyes to see contours of valleys and mountains that Pam and Marley couldn't make out with binoculars. Her rhythm was more regular than time; her intuition more precise than a ruler-drawn line. She knew it, Pam and Marley didn't, and it was nothing short of her final duty in life to share her wellspring with her scions before they fell off the deep end of the ocean.

It meant she had to roll up her sleeves and do grassroots work, like calling Pam most evenings to remind her that normal people arrive home from work at five o'clock, period. She absolutely would *not* call Pam at work after five to give her the reminder, for part of the task was accomplished by disregarding the fact that Pam was never at home by five, never had been home by five, and appeared to have no intention of ever arriving home by five. No matter. Instead, Ma Grand opted for leaving curt one-liners on Pam's voice mail every half hour beginning at five and ending when Pam finally answered the phone.

It just so happened that she was absorbed in *Breakfast at Tiffany's,* one of her favorite movies, when she turned the rotary for the last digit in Pam's telephone number and almost missed Pam's "Hello."

"Hellooo?" an agitated Pam repeated into the receiver.

"Pam?" Ma Grand fumbled with the phone as she sat up straight in her recliner and used the remote control to turn down the television's volume. "Pam, is that you?"

"Yes, Mama," Pam replied, her voice suggesting confusion as to who else her mother really thought it could have been.

"I've been calling that house since five o'clock in the evening. Where have you been?"

"Hello, Mama. How are you? I'm doing fine—thanks so much for asking."

"I called you, didn't I? That oughtta let you know I care about how you're doing, and if it don't then I don't know what will help you. What time do you leave that job, Pam?"

"Mama, it varies from day to day. Why do you ask me this every time you call?"

" 'Cause you're never at home when I call! You're gonna run yourself into the ground, working like that. Ain't no job that important where—"

"Mama, I'm not about to discuss my hours with you. Not tonight," Pam said, her words clipped. "Now, did you want something in particular, or are you just calling to talk?"

Ma Grand was a master at hearing what she wanted to hear and ignoring words that lacked appeal. Conversation topics began and ended with her. "Have you ordered the invitations yet? I want to let Sadie know when she can expect to receive hers."

"The invitations to Marley's *wedding?*"

"Yes, Pam! What else would I be talking about?" Ma Grand drawled. "Where is your head? You work so much you can't even think straight no more!"

"Mama, this is June. The wedding is in March. Like I told you last week, we don't send the invitations more than six weeks in advance, so we won't be ordering them for quite a while."

"What? Whose rules are you following? Y'all are crazy. You send those invitations six to eight weeks before that wedding and see if you don't have an empty church. Folks need time to plan for things like that, Pam." Ma Grand managed to file the nail on her trembling index finger. She honestly wondered what had happened to Pam's social skills. She had spent all that money and time carting the child around to Jack and Jill and every other fine organization in Atlanta so that certain rules of etiquette would become second nature to Pam. *What a waste of money,* Ma Grand thought.

But then, those clubs had given Pam and her brother, Steven, the exposure they needed as colored children growing up deep in the throes of dark, white, segregationist Georgia. Those clubs enabled Ma Grand to pull her children out from the snares of bigotry and paint with vivid colors a different, safer portrait of life as a Negro in

America. It was a picture her children could always keep with them, at least in their minds.

Ma Grand glanced at the chipped polish on her toenails, trying to remember the last time she'd had them painted, and reminded herself to ask Mary, the girl who set her hair every other weekend, to paint them for her. Maybe a nice shade of brick red. Something daring.

"No, Mama," Pam said, "it's really only folks like you who need more than six weeks to plan for events, which is the biggest mystery to me because you have all the time in the world to get ready for them. Sadie will get her invitation in January, okay?"

"Marley's not still trying to have that reception on the other side of town, is she? 'Cause folks ain't gonna be up for driving to a church on one side of town, then having to drive to a reception thirty minutes away. They're gonna go home in between, and you're gonna end up wasting your money on all that chocolate fondue and that other fancy mess, all for nothing. What you need to do is go on over to Piggly Wiggly and get some party platters and some punch bowls and a sheet cake or two and call it a day."

"Mama," Pam said steadily, "the wedding and reception will be held at Bayview Terrace."

"Bayview Terrace? What? Is that that boy's church?"

"No, it's not Gerrard's church. It's a private resort in Alpharetta."

"Private resort! You mean to tell me that child is planning to get married somewhere other than church? Great day in the morning! You went along with that foolishness? Pam? What in the devil is wrong with you?"

"Mama, this is Marley's wedding, not yours or mine. You seem to forget that, you know? It's not up to me or you to tell her where she can have her ceremony."

Ma Grand slammed her hand on the armrest of her recliner and got angrier when the action didn't produce much sound. She clutched the television remote control. "I ain't never heard of no such mess as that! Not getting married at church! Well, I know one thing, the good Lord won't be there. Oh, Jesus. Y'all are crazy. I knew I shouldn't have bought a dress 'cause I knew it was gonna be some crazy affair that I don't need to fool with. *Bayview Terrace*. John Brownit! My blood pressure's gone up just thinking about this mess. I'll be! And she ain't serving pork. People gonna leave hungry. Lord have mercy on all of you!"

"Mama, good night."

"What—"

Ma Grand held the receiver in her hand until the phone company recording stated that she needed to hang up if she wanted to place a call, meaning she was an idiot if she still hadn't discovered that the other person had hung up and it was high time for her to do the same. She hung up the receiver, picked it up again, and put her index finger in the loop labeled four, fully intending to call Pam back and finish this thing. But she thought better of it.

"Crazy, just plumb crazy," she said, shaking her head and staring at Audrey Hepburn on the television screen.

After Pam had read all but three sections of the daily paper, she turned on the television. She cased the various networks, as she did every night, desperately hoping she would find some late-night program that would help her forget the drama that had enshrouded her day. There was nothing. Her thoughts seemed to laugh at her ditching attempt, as they resumed center stage. *Your daughter is confused,* one thought touted, as it paraded itself across her brain. *Your mother is insane!* shouted another. *Where, exactly, does that place you on the generational spectrum of emotional well-being?* the thoughts yelled collectively. She didn't know.

Deciding to go to sleep, Pam turned the television volume down low enough to keep her company while she dozed, but after five minutes of tossing and turning, she realized sleep was eluding her. She turned the volume up and watched David Letterman rip some poor guest to shreds in a matter of five words. She laughed, but she still thought about her mother.

⌣ The crisp words she'd spoken to her mother on the telephone that evening had brought with them a sense of both satisfaction and regret. Satisfaction because, quite simply, her mother had annoyed her. But regret because she knew that, underneath all the fussing, her mother was lonely and needed someone to talk to. To check up on. To gossip with. To talk about nothing important with and to know that it was okay. Pam's father had been dead for fifteen years, and Aunt Sarah had died last year. Her mother and Sarah used to talk every hour on the hour about what they had eaten for breakfast, what they were planning to eat for lunch (provided the Tums did their part), why they were taking a unified stand against their bridge club that month, and why they were strongly considering leaving St. Matthias for Bethel Baptist Church. Sarah and Bess, daughters of Cecilia Davis and James Lawrence Abrams, would hardly attend a church where some youngun of a minister saw fit to wear a robe with a patent leather cross embroidered on the chest.

Well, Pam couldn't fill Aunt Sarah's shoes. It was unfair for her mother to expect her to try. Pam was not a retiree with time to spare. She was an interior decorator with contracts to secure. She was a mother who had a thirty-year-old daughter to marry off—a daughter who was, quite frankly, too rational and too emotionally conscious for her own good. In the end, all that rational thinking and emotional intuition would net Marley the grand sum of solitude. Maybe solitude was a worthy and respectable cash prize in the minds of empowerment speakers and women's magazine columnists, but in the mind of one woman who wore the crown involuntarily, there was no merit and there was no pride.

That haunted Pam. It kneaded at the core of her being. Being alone was the worst thing that had ever happened to her. It left her

with the television as her nighttime companion. With gossipy girl-
friends as her source of naughtiness. With a nagging, implacable
mother as her greatest human protector. That haunted her almost
daily, and it rooted out the one thin, honest stem that might have
helped Pam to push past the pain, past the loneliness, and past the
discouragement to find whatever good was located on this side of
circumstance.

She decided to call Marley. She didn't know exactly what she'd
say, but she knew she needed to call.

"Hello," a tired voice, sounding so much like Pam's own, answered.

"Hi, honey," Pam said gently.

There was silence. "Hi, Mom."

Pam sighed. "Marley, I'm really sorry I was so harsh at dinner
tonight, okay? I really am sorry."

"Okay," Marley accepted, yawning as she spoke.

"Weddings can bring on a lot of stress and worry, and I think
we're both on edge these days."

"I know that, Mom," Marley said, her voice scratchy. "But I don't
think you really understand the reason why I'm worried. It's not
about whether to use chiffon or satin. It's about the man I'm planning to marry."

"Oh, Marley, it can't be that bad, can it?" Pam shook her head.
"Listen, I don't want us to argue." She thought for a few seconds.
"Hey, why don't you go to church with me on Sunday? Obviously
you have a lot on your mind, and you haven't been to church in
ages. I bet you'll be able to clear your head after you hear a good
word. I know it'll help me clear my mind," Pam added, already
hopeful about grabbing hold of some good old-fashioned Sunday-
morning endorphins.

"Hear a good word from Reverend Watson? Are you kidding?
His sermons are like personal attacks based on real-life dramas,

Mom. Really—I'll go to church with you on Sunday, but not to Reverend Watson's church."

Pam's mouth fell open. "Marley, the nerve of you to attack Reverend Watson. He's not perfect, but—"

"Far from it," Marley interjected, all traces of sleepiness having vanished from her tone.

"Marley, he is not perfect, but he is doing more than most to improve the community and create opportunities for those in need. He's doing the Lord's work, and you can't take that away from him. He may not be Fred Price, but—"

"Who's comparing him to Fred Price? I know the difference between bananas and cherries," Marley joked.

"That is enough, Marley. That is absolutely enough."

"I'm just playing, Mommy," Marley said, chuckling. "But seriously, I'll go with you. It'll be fun."

"I'm not trying to provide you with Sunday-morning entertainment, Marley. I'm trying to help you hear from the Lord," Pam snapped.

"All right, Mommy. I'll be sure to bring hearing aids for both of us," Marley said, then burst into laughter.

"You're a pathetic child. I swear, I really wonder about you sometimes. Good night," Pam declared, lowering the receiver over Marley's chuckles. Pam fought the urge to laugh for as long as she could, then succumbed. Laughing felt better. It freed her, at least momentarily.

It also empowered her, because when the nagging, nasty little thoughts jumped back onto the stage in her mind, she laughed at them, too, as she pushed her way past them.

Chapter 4

I
T TOOK EVERY ounce of respect Marley had for the sacred to keep a smirk off her face.

If she screams one more time, Marley thought to herself, *I will seriously consider getting up and walking out of here.* The air inside Reverend Watson's church was thick and sweltering, much like the air on a New Orleans trolley headed south toward the hell on Bourbon Street in July. On top of that, women with babies whose diapers smelled as though they hadn't been changed in weeks were somehow all sitting near Marley and Pam, simultaneously fanning the babies and the odor in Marley's direction. And on top of that, this woman—this soloist—was screaming at the top of her lungs as if she'd never have the opportunity to use her vocal cords again. Children were laughing at her; adults were trying to act like adults.

"Oh Lawd! I said, oh Lawd!" The soloist belted out lyrics, then wiped her forehead with a yellow handkerchief she had conveniently stored in the side pocket of her ballooning green, black, and hot-pink floral dress. As the congregation moaned and groaned along with her, she hurriedly grabbed the goblet of ice water sitting

on top of the baby grand, spilling a good bit on the beautifully finished mahogany piano and earning the pianist's furrowed brow.

"Woooh," she let out into the microphone, more as part of her performance than in response to the spill, and replaced the goblet. "Wooh," a child mimicked in the audience, only to get yoked by his mother and scolded on how to behave in church. The soloist paused for about five seconds, seemingly for dramatic effect, and then yelled, "Goin' up yonder!"

"Goin' up yonder," the choir responded, and the piano joined in.

"Goin' up yonder," the soloist yelped again.

"Goin' up yonder-r-r-r!" the choir responded.

"To!" the choir sang, then paused.

"Be!" they sang and paused again.

"With!" This pause was longer than the others.

"My!" This pause was so long that the congregation had time to stand on its feet and clap for a while.

"Lord!" The choir had been instructed during rehearsal to hold the final note for at least ten seconds, but, like dominoes, the sopranos, altos, tenors, and bass dropped out of the note-holding contest, leaving only maybe six or seven obedient choir members. The six or seven who held on were pleased with themselves and their abilities, as evidenced by how they tilted their heads upward and to the side. Yes, *these* were the members who had taken voice lessons when they were younger; *these* were the members who were always on time for rehearsal and certainly never missed one; *they* were the fibers that held this cloth of a choir together, the few chosen among the many who thought they were called.

The director gestured for the choir—or rather the six or seven—to stop singing, and the pianist ended the selection with a melodious recap against a backdrop of applause and funeral-parlor fans waving furiously.

"What a performance," Marley mumbled sideways to her mother. Pam nudged Marley's ribs.

"Mom!" Marley exclaimed in a whisper.

"Behave yourself," Pam whispered back.

"It's the truth," she whispered to her mother, turning to look at her. "You taught me to tell the truth," she said, redirecting her attention to the choir.

"Behave yourself," Pam said again.

After a while, the congregation calmed down a bit and shifted in the pews in preparation for the good right reverend to bring the word. Marley silently thanked the Lord that the song was over. God, how those long solos by screaming women used to grate on her nerves when she was a younger, involuntary church attendee. What irked her the most was that she'd had to endure a good five or six of those selections before the pastor would even approach the pulpit to give his fifteen-minute speech on why the church needed to stop gossiping, or stop backbiting, or stop doing whatever some member had done to him that week. College had freed her from the bondage of mandatory church attendance, and as far as she could see, there was no reason to return. She was an honest, wage-earning citizen. She didn't kill or steal. She wasn't sleeping with someone's husband. She and the church could remain distant relatives—she'd send money or visit when she could, but otherwise the relationship worked best with minimal contact.

Reverend Watson strolled to the podium, nodding his head and agreeing with the lyrics that had been sung. "Goin' up yonder, yes, indeedie. We're all going there one day. I don't know about you, but I'm goin' there for sure! Hallelujah! Praise Him! *I said praise Him!*" He continued to nod and began to wave his handkerchief; then he started a shuffling dance.

The pianist's soft tones broke out into a frantically paced tune that mysteriously, and some would say supernaturally, kept time with Reverend Watson's shuffling. The congregation added its hand clapping and foot stomping, which served to encourage Reverend

Watson further along in his spiritual shuffle. Then Maggie Lou, the third oldest member of the church, hopped out of her seat at the end of the front row and started to do her signature dance. Children continued to laugh, and most of the adults were still trying to act like adults. After a minute or so, the dancing subsided and the deaconesses managed to subdue Maggie Lou at the rear of the sanctuary. They dutifully escorted her back to her seat in the front pew and left her with two extra funeral-parlor fans to keep her cool.

Marley looked at her mother, but Pam refused to acknowledge her. Marley looked around at the faces near her, searching for some indication that others were aware how ridiculous this church show was. She didn't find the consciousness she was looking for, so she faced forward with a frown. She looked down at her watch, then began to tap her foot.

"Today I'm going to preach about alternative dispute resolution," Reverend Watson said, and suddenly, as if on cue, the recessed lights dimmed. "Alternative Dispute Resolution," he repeated slowly, capitalizing each word with his voice, enunciating each letter to the best of his ability.

"Mm," some women in the congregation mumbled, not so quietly.

"You see, y'all walk around here talking about folk, telling their business, gossiping about one another, gossiping about *me*."

"Go on, Rev," one of his deacons shouted. "Tell 'em!"

"You think I don't know it, but I do. You go around—you might be a trustee, or a choir member, or a Sunday school teacher—and you hear something about somebody else, and first thing you do is call up Nancy or Susie and tell her what you just heard!" The reverend paced the pulpit slowly, plucking at a nonexistent lint ball on the sleeve of his robe.

Marley wondered where the good reverend was going with all of this. She noticed that her mother was digging into her purse and pulling out her supertinted spectacles. Pam caught Marley's glance and pursed her lips to hide her smile. Marley remembered those spectacles from childhood; they were the spectacles Pam wore on Sundays only. And not every Sunday, but only the Sundays when the sermons were boring. Marley had been almost a high school graduate when she'd realized her mother was sleeping underneath her tinted lenses.

"So who's he talking about this week?" Marley whispered to her mother.

"Honey," Pam whispered back, shaking her head, "he's just mad because there's a rumor going around that he's hooked on Viagra. He needs to be mad with his wife, 'cause she's the one who started it."

Marley's mouth hung open. "You're kidding?"

"No, honey." Pam positioned her spectacles comfortably on her nose.

Marley stared ahead, deciding that her reasons for not attending church had just been validated. The sermons never inspired her to become a better person. In fact, the sermons didn't seem to have the entire body of believers in mind at all. The pulpit was a sideshow, and she wasn't interested in it.

"That's right, I'ma tell you 'bout it this morning, church. If you got somethin' to say about me, then say it to me! Directly to my face!"

"Yeah, yeah, yeah! Press on, Reverend! Press your claim!" More deacons and deaconesses, and some choir members and congregation members, joined in and offered supportive *yeahs*, *that's rights*, and *tell 'em 'bout its*. Other choir members and esteemed church officers were either quiet or conveniently engrossed in the information printed in the church bulletin.

"That's right! Don't tell Nancy; Nancy don't know nothing. Don't tell Susie; Susie can't help you either! Take it to the source!

In Matthew 18:15—God said this, not me—all right, see, now, right here in this scripture, Jesus said if your brother gets you angry and all worked up about something, then tell it to that brother first. See? Ain't nothing in that scripture about telling Nancy first. You go tell that brother of yours—we *are* brothers and sisters, church—and you tell that brother he offended you. Try to work it out. But give your brother that common courtesy! Give him that respect!" Reverend Watson pushed his fist up into the air and held it there. "Somebody oughtta say Amen!" He shook his fist at the congregation.

"Amen! Amen, Reverend!" many members answered.

Marley leaned over to ask her mother another question, but her mother had already fallen asleep. Had even managed to plaster a neutral, all-responsive smile on her face while she slept. Marley redirected her attention to the sermon but gave up after another minute or so of the reverend's ranting about his personal issues. Marley glanced down at her Bible, still unopened, and wondered why she'd brought it in the first place. And to think she'd gotten a little excited when she'd walked into the sanctuary that morning, hoping that things had changed, expecting that she might hear something from God after all. What an utter waste of time.

The workweek had rolled in like a hurricane, thundering over the freedom of Saturday and raining out the ease of Sunday with one strong bolt. There Marley sat on Tuesday evening, immersed in clients' concerns and partners' demands. She hated the hierarchy; she loved the pressure.

The ringing telephone was an unwelcome distraction. "This is Marley Shepherd," she answered crisply by speakerphone, furiously typing the last paragraph of what she hoped would be the final draft of the brief she had been working on. Bob had been waiting to see the draft since early that morning. It was now six in the evening. Plus, she was meeting Gerrard in half an hour for a much-anticipated dinner date, one they had planned two weeks ago, promising each other that, no matter what, the date would not be canceled.

"Where's the draft, Marley?" Bob barked.

"On its way, Bob," Marley replied calmly, still typing.

"Marley, I told you I wanted to see the draft this morning. It's six o'clock, for crying out loud."

Marley heard what sounded like a desk drawer slam in Bob's office.

"Bob, you gave me the early morning deadline at five o'clock yesterday evening. I've been working on it all night, and I'm almost—"

"Get it to my office now, Marley." Bob slammed the receiver down.

"Argh!" Marley screamed at the top of her lungs, drawing an odd stare from a secretary walking past her office. She rushed to her door and slammed it. "Makes me sick!" she shouted as she thrust the weight of her tired, aching body into her desk chair. She heard the fabric tear near the split in her skirt. She pushed her skirt higher up on her thighs, hoping to avoid another tear and reminding herself that she needed to skip dessert for a while, and sat upright in her chair. She unbuttoned the pearl buttons on the cuffs of her silk blouse, took a swig of Evian, and resumed typing. Another two sentences and she would be finished.

Her phone rang again. She buzzed her secretary, Evelyn. "Yes, Marley," Evelyn answered.

"Evelyn, would you mind holding all my calls, please? I've got to finish this brief."

"Sure thing, honey."

"Thanks."

Ten seconds later, Evelyn buzzed Marley.

"Yes?" Marley answered quickly, trying not to sound irritated.

"Sorry to disturb you, honey, but it's Gerrard. He says it's urgent that he speak with you."

Marley sighed. "I'll pick up," she said, and she grabbed the receiver. "Hello?"

"It's me. Listen, I'm really sorry, but I have to cancel. My dad thinks we lost the Cascade Heights bid, and we've got an emergency meeting with Carter and his boys this evening. It can't be avoided, Marley. I'm really sorry."

Marley rubbed her temples. A full-fledged migraine had surfaced. She was too tired, too frustrated, too spent to protest. "All right, Gerrard."

"Baby, I'm really sorry. I love you so much for understanding. And I promise I'll make it up to you. Okay?"

"All right." She took another gulp of water and rolled her shoulders to loosen the muscles bundled together. She really didn't have time to deal with Gerrard and his excuses. At that moment she wanted, more than anything else, to get Bob off her back.

"I love you, wife-to-be. I'll call you tonight."

She hung up and returned to the computer.

In sum, the Agency's regulation effectively prohibits beneficiaries from protesting against deplorable living conditions. Such protests are the precise conduct the First Amendment seeks to protect, and for that reason this Court must find the Agency's regulation unconstitutional.

Good enough, Marley concluded and printed out her draft. "Evelyn?" she said into the intercom.

"Yes?"

"I've finished my draft. Will you take it down to Bob's office for me? I am exhausted, and I swear I'll die if I hear his voice one more time today."

Evelyn laughed. "Sure thing. Anything else you need me to do?"

"Nope. That's it."

"Go home, Marley. Get some rest."

"I will. Thanks so much, Evelyn," she said, her head having already found a resting place on top of her desk.

Almost twenty minutes passed before Marley realized she had fallen asleep. Had her growling stomach not awakened her, she might well have spent an uncomfortable night at her desk. She packed up her things and decided to stop for carry-out at Prazza, a favorite of Gerrard's and hers because of its dark corners and tucked-away tables.

Smoke, the smell of liquor, and the lure of pretense laid claim to the air inside Prazza. Marley walked into the haze, alongside the eat-in counter, and plopped onto one of the stools. "I'm here to order for carry-out," she quickly informed the waiter. He nodded and took her order.

She reclined against the back of the stool and stretched her arms, relieved she had finished the draft. Although she knew Bob would be hounding her again no later than noon the next day, for the next several hours at least she could divorce herself from thoughts of work. She sometimes wondered whether it was worth it: the constant berating and the virtually nonexistent commendation regarding her work, the long hours, the sacrifices, just to make partner and have her workload and responsibilities increase tenfold. The pay would increase tenfold, too—and that was a good thing—but there was more in it for her than money. She thrived on the analytical challenges she faced each day as she tried to fit her clients' problems into the puzzle pieces of the law. She loved the fact that her final product always reflected the work she'd put into it, for better or for worse. At the firm, her mind was her greatest asset, and no one—not Bob or any other miserable human being like him—could deprive her of it.

"I'm going to the rest room, but I'll be right back," Marley told the waiter and headed toward the rear of the restaurant. Once inside, she splashed her face with cold water and let the air dry it. She stared at herself in the mirror and couldn't help noticing her eyes. They weren't just tired, as she'd thought when she first glanced at them. They were dispirited. Disenchanted. It had little to do with work.

Marley fluffed her hair and added a touch of lip gloss to her lips. She opened the bathroom door and gasped when she saw the door to the men's room open.

"Marley!"

"Gerrard?"

"What are you doing here?"

"Ordering carry-out. What are you doing here?"

"Um, you know, the meeting. With Carter and the group."

"Here? At Prazza? What made you decide to come here?"

A man approached and tried to enter the men's rest room. "Pardon us," Gerrard said, then ushered Marley toward the eat-in counter.

"We should be wrapping up soon. You on your way home?" Gerrard asked quickly.

"Yeah," she said slowly and yawned. Just the mention of home caused her suddenly to long for her bed. "I'm completely exhausted." She reached into her purse for her wallet. By the time she'd pulled out her cash, Gerrard had already given the waiter his credit card and paid for her meal.

"Thanks, sweetheart." Marley rested her head in the palm of her hand.

"No problem," Gerrard said, kissing her forehead. His eyes darted toward the rear of the restaurant. "I need to get back to the meeting. I'll call you tonight."

"Okay. Talk to you then—if I haven't passed out."

Gerrard flashed a smile over his shoulder as he disappeared. Marley watched him, and for that moment she was completely happy with him. He was far from perfect, and their problems were far from being solved, but he was a good man. He meant well. He took care of her. She was thankful.

She was filled, suddenly, with the urge to tell him how she was feeling, and as she rose from the stool, she contemplated searching the restaurant for him. But she decided against it. He was, after all, in a business meeting. She wasn't in the mood to make small talk with Carter and his group anyway. She could save her words for later, when she had Gerrard's full attention.

She picked up her food from the counter. "Sir, did the gentleman give you a tip?" Marley asked before exiting.

"Oh yes, quite a nice one, ma'am," the waiter assured her. He wore an odd expression as his eyes lingered on Marley's.

"Very good. Thank you." She left the restaurant.

Marley had endured one of the worst weeks of her life. After she had given Bob what she thought would be a close-to-final draft of the brief on Tuesday, he insisted she make numerous changes up until Friday afternoon, three hours before she had to file it with the court. She had tried to explain to Bob that many of the changes were plain wrong. "The case law does not support the changes you want me to make, Bob," Marley had told him. "Well, now, we don't want to lie to the court," Bob had responded, then continued to insist she make the changes.

Ashley had promised she had the perfect remedy for Marley's tumultuous week. "Girl, just go with me to my cousin's wedding on Saturday. I promise you'll have the laugh of your life." On the Fourth of July, Shalana, Ashley's "ghet" cousin, as Ashley disdainfully described her, was finally marrying Blue, her high school sweetheart. Shalana refused to let anyone see her wedding dress, but swore to all who asked that Kiki the Cold Cutter had made the dress and it was going to "rock your world." Ashley, who knew her cousin too well, feared the wedding would be along the lines of a Barnum & Bailey's production. "I will die if I have to attend this circus of the ghetto stars by myself," Ashley had whined to Marley and Deanna, knowing full well her complaining was whetting appetites.

Marley had just finished zipping up her chamois sundress when she heard Deanna's car horn honking repeatedly from outside her window. The sound of the horn was as brassy as Deanna, barging through Marley's bedroom windows and demanding to be acknowledged.

"Deanna," Marley called out from the window. "This is Versailles, girl. Try to hide your ig'nance, please, until we leave the neighborhood." She closed the window, grabbed her saltwater pearl clutch purse, and scrambled down the steps.

"Come on, Marley Shepherd!" Deanna shouted as Marley closed and locked her front door. "The wedding starts at three o'clock sharp, and I do not want to miss Shalana walk down the aisle in this showstopping dress!"

"All right, all right," Marley said, hopping down the sidewalk in one sandal. She stopped, dropped the other sandal in front of her, and slid her foot into it. "You're making me mess up my pedicure," Marley fussed, pretending she was irritated. She reached the rear door of Deanna's Explorer and climbed into the backseat.

"Hey, y'all." Marley blew kisses in the air.

"Hey, girl," said Ashley from the front seat. "You look cute."

"You do, too." Marley peered forward and bugged her eyes. "Ash, I can't believe you're not wearing your hair down today? Didn't you just get it done on Wednesday?"

"I didn't like it." Ashley touched up her lip liner.

"All that hair, and she never wears it down." Deanna shook her head.

"I'm not trying to impress anybody," Ashley said, tucking a few loose strands into her French braid.

"If you're not trying to impress anybody, then you may as well make up with Adam and officially pull yourself out of the ring. Unless you've declared yourself Ms. Everywoman In No Need Of Man Ever, this male strike business has gone on long enough." Deanna lifted her cinnamon brown twists off her neck and shook them, oblivious to the hole that Ashley's eyes were attempting to burn into Deanna's head.

"Now, check this out——"

"Excuse me, Deanna," Ashley interrupted, "but Adam and I broke up because of the thousand-plus miles between us, not because of some silly argument that we need to make up over. If I want to be by myself, then let me be by myself. I'm not asking you to join me, 'cause Lord knows you couldn't handle it."

"All right, all right, let's not get testy," Deanna said, leaning over to squeeze Ashley's knee. "You're a strong Nubian queen. Do your thing, girl." She eyed Marley in the rearview mirror and winked.

"Listen to this," Deanna continued, as she turned off the radio and tossed her twists over her shoulder. "I've been dying to tell you this. Remember Ron Wesley, the guy who ran track and was president of Morehouse's business association?"

"Yeah," the girls responded in unison.

"Well, he sells gold teeth."

"Dee, you've got to be kidding. Your stories are getting so outrageous that they're not believable anymore," Marley said.

"Marley, what makes you think I'm making this up? Gold teeth are hot now, and not just in Atlanta. Snap-ons, permanent ones, initial-engraved ones, diamond-studded ones. You name it, folks are buying them. Ron has always been business-savvy. Plus his father and brother are dentists, so even when the trend fades he's safe because he's connected to a profession that uses metals in noncosmetic capacities. At least, that's how he explained it to me." Deanna cut a quick right turn that threw all the girls sideways.

Deanna's informational tidbit ended up leading the girls into a debate about what kinds of business ventures were economically sound, a debate that didn't end until they were walking up the sidewalk leading to Blue's father's house in Austell. There they were greeted by a couple of fourteen-going-on-twenty-four-year-old teenage girls who appeared to be wedding hostesses. Their black satin dresses looked as though they were painted on their bodies. One of the girls had already abandoned her pumps for white bobby socks.

"Welcome to the celebration of Shalana and Blue," the too-grown hostesses said slowly and handed out wedding programs.

"Thank you, girls!" Deanna sang back to them and smiled radiantly. The hostesses looked at Deanna as if she were something out of a rare-species magazine.

"Oh my goodness," Ashley murmured, making three words into three sentences as she examined the program.

Deanna gasped for breath, gripping Marley's arm in the process.
"Ouch, Deanna!"

"No, she didn't," Deanna remarked, staring at the program. On the cover was a collage of pictures of Shalana and Blue. In the center of the cover was a picture of Blue in his high school football uniform, his left arm wrapped around his helmet and his right index finger pointed toward the camera. Superimposed above Blue's head was a picture of Shalana in her cheerleading uniform, airborne in a Russian jump with her hands beneath her chin and a toothy smile slapped across her face. Surrounding these shots were various pictures of the couple, which looked to have been taken mainly at concerts, posed in front of MCM and Mercedes-Benz-sketched backdrops.

"Well, she gets an A for originality," Marley finally said.

More than two hours after the wedding was to begin (the maid of honor's pineapple waves took longer to dry than expected), the guests were still seated in their folding chairs, trying their hardest to fan off the July sun and look good in the process. Finally, one of the too-grown hostesses announced that the wedding was about to begin and asked a group of young men wearing football jerseys to take their seats.

From the stereo speakers situated in the corners of the backyard, a slow, remixed version of "I Don't Wanna Be a Playa" oozed out, dripping on the ears of the guests. Deanna's head was so low that her chin was pushing against her chest, and her shoulders heaved with muted laughter. Ashley's eyes were fixed on the white wicker archway covered with pink carnations, greens, and baby's breath. She shook her head slowly, almost as if in a daze. One of the guys wearing a football jersey began to sing along, loudly, in the kind of voice that suggested that someone, at some point, must have told him he could sing.

The wedding processional began, and the groomsmen, wearing royal blue and white pin-striped suits and matching Stacy Adams shoes, with red carnations adorning their lapels, escorted the brides-maids down the aisle. The bridesmaids were dressed in royal blue-satin fitted gowns and matching satin shoes. The gowns had V-cut backs lined with small ruffles, with another row of ruffles along the side split. The finishing touch was a royal blue ruffled scarf that each bridesmaid had draped loosely around her arms. The couples walked in tandem with the beat of the music as the guests oohed and aahed.

"Did Shalana use these colors in honor of Independence Day?" Deanna whispered to Ashley.

"Very funny, Dee," Ashley whispered back.

An usher dressed in a red suit walked up the aisle, stopping at the first row of seats. He proceeded to light sparklers and handed one to each person sitting in an aisle seat. The sunlight robbed the sparklers of their color, given that it was five o'clock in the afternoon, but faintly visible were traces of red, blue, green, and yellow, and they seemed to emit a Giorgio-like fragrance as they burned and crackled. After each aisle-seated guest was handed a sparkler, "I Don't Wanna Be a Playa" began to fade, and the introductory chords from Prince's "Adore" filled the air. A young lady seated on the groom's side closed her eyes, rocked her body from side to side, and waved her hand slowly.

And then Shalana appeared. Her dress was covered with iridescent sequins and beads. It strapped her right shoulder and cut diagonally across her chest, leaving the left shoulder bare. The dress was form fitting until it reached Shalana's knees, where it flared dramatically in a mermaid cut. As she approached the minister and Blue, miniature S's and B's that were sewn in pearls on her veil became visible. Shalana made eye contact with Marley, and the two women smiled at each other. Marley watched her pass. She would have skipped the pearl lettering on the veil, for sure, and she definitely would not have opted for the mermaid-style dress. But Shalana was smiling, and, despite all the accessory overkill, Marley thought she looked simply beautiful. Blue, who was slapping his best man's right hand and unable to stand still, seemed to agree.

The ceremony was fairly traditional except for the solos, which were sung by people who couldn't sing, people who hummed out the lyrics they hadn't memorized in time for the wedding. Shalana and Blue had written their own vows, and there wasn't a dry eye in the audience after they spoke them. They promised each other unselfish, sacrificial, steadfast, and undying love—love "like the kind Jesus has for us" was Blue's vow. Marley could barely make out their images after Blue spoke, her eyes were so clouded with tears.

"Say what you want about Shalana," Marley whispered to Ashley, dabbing at a tear with a tissue, "but this is a beautiful ceremony." Ashley smiled, and when the sun shone across her face, Marley could see the streak a tear had left on her cheek.

The girls had a ball at the reception, laughing hard at the sequence of events and even harder at the colorful guests. There was the brother with the finger waves and arched eyebrows who approached Deanna, pimping harder than Lenny Who Got Plenty. "Tell me your dreams, baby, and I can make 'em happen," he whispered to her. After Deanna spat out her Coke in laughter, the brother quickly stuffed his money back into his pocket and pimped off. Then there was Ashley and Shalana's aunt Mae Mae, who, with chicken in her mouth and grease on her hands, kept tugging Ashley's hair and asking, "Who did your weave?" The look on Deanna's face was priceless when Blue's father announced that dinner—consisting of several buckets of Kentucky Fried Chicken, troughs of cole slaw, and foil platters stacked with rolls—was served. Shalana and Blue's first dance to "Honey Love" was hilarious. The newlyweds departed the reception executing a precoordinated dance step while the same usher from the ceremony lit firecrackers in the background.

"Ash, I cannot thank you enough for taking me with you to the wedding," Marley said, still laughing as the girls piled into Deanna's truck and headed home. "I haven't laughed that hard in a long time!"

"It was live entertainment, that's for sure," Ashley agreed.

"But you have to admit, Shalana looked really nice," Deanna chuckled, "in spite of the letters sewn into her veil."

"She did. She really did. Her hair was beautiful, her makeup was beautiful. She really was beautiful," Ashley agreed, smiling. "And Blue is at the top of my favorite persons list. Guess what he said when I was leaving?"

"What?" Marley asked.

"He said, 'See you at church in the morning.' " Ashley shook her head.

"Really? As worn out as they're going to be?" Deanna asked.

"Yep. Isn't that something?"

"It really is."

"He's a good brother. Lord knows he's not my type," Ashley said, "but he's still a good brother."

"No wonder Shalana's so happy," Deanna said.

"Mm-hm. She's glowing on the outside because she's fulfilled on the inside." Ashley smiled.

The girls grew silent. Deanna merged onto 20 East. Marley looked down at her hands and began to twist her sapphire ring, a nervous habit she'd developed back in high school. She wondered whether Deanna's comment was aimed at her indirectly. She wondered whether, compared to Shalana, she was lackluster. Transparent.

On the chance her friends hadn't yet figured her out, Marley decided she wasn't ready to divulge. These were her girls, for sure. Still, she wasn't ready to tell them that the thought of marrying Gerrard was starting to keep her awake at night. She didn't like what she saw when she, in her mind's eye, peered into the future she would share with him. She'd be conceding to Ashley that her suspicions about Gerrard being too busy and too self-consumed had been right all along. She'd be conceding to the black elite she'd joined, as Gerrard's fiancée, that she wasn't par for the course, wasn't fit for the game, just wasn't up to it after all. It was a love-hate relationship Marley shared with the black elite: she hated them because they were elite, but she loved them because, well, who didn't desire, in some small but certain space, to be counted among the admired, the successful, the blessed, the beautiful?

But mostly she'd be conceding the failure of her relationship. She wasn't sure, at least not yet, that the relationship had indeed failed. Just the other evening, she'd been thanking God for Gerrard. Sure, he had canceled a dinner date he'd promised he wouldn't cancel, but hadn't he said he would make it up to her? Didn't he always try to make it up to her? And wasn't that what relationships were all about—giving and taking, understanding and accommodating each other? Maybe there had been no failure. Maybe these were nothing more than necessary growing pains.

Marley remained quiet and captive to her thoughts while Deanna passed Six Flags and the Atlanta skyline crept into view.

Chapter 5

ODAY WAS MAKEUP day. Makeup for all the canceled dates, missed events, and misunderstandings. Makeup for all the times when love hadn't been shown, when compassion hadn't been expressed, when sincerity hadn't been felt. Today was the day that would end all prior days of doubt, the day when Gerrard would confirm, once and for all, that nothing—not even work—was more important to him than Marley.

To prove it, Gerrard had cleared his afternoon schedule in advance and had told Marley to clear hers. He had picked her up in his father's Bentley and had driven her to Serenity, an exclusive day spa in Buckhead with a three-month waiting list that didn't apply to the Shores. After he'd helped her out of the car, he'd gone to the trunk and removed two gold foil-wrapped boxes from a shopping bag. "Put these on when you're finished," he'd said, his lips easing into a wide smile.

Marley had blushed, taking the packages from Gerrard, placing them on the hood of the car, and embracing him. She hadn't wanted to let go and would have been satisfied standing there, holding him, for the rest of the day. Finally, he'd loosened his arms from around her waist, causing her to loosen her grip around his neck, and had told her to hurry inside so she wouldn't be late for her appointment. "I'll see you in two hours," he'd said, kissing her on the cheek and hopping into the car. She'd wanted to stand and watch him pull off, but she'd managed to peel herself from the curb and walk inside. Paradise was waiting.

As the masseuse methodically worked the kinks out of her neck, then her shoulders, then her back, Marley had easily slipped into unconscious bliss. She'd let the circular motion of the masseuse's hands purge each of her worries from her mind, movement by movement, knead by knead, stroke by stroke. Later, when her facial had been completed and cold cucumber slices had been placed over her eyes, Marley had fallen asleep. She'd dreamt she and Gerrard were sitting in the middle of an endless, boundless field of orchids. There they'd sat, smiling, talking, dreaming, planning on nothing but being together.

In the herbal bath, she had sipped mineral water with lime, stared at her feet, and smiled. Love had never felt better than this. She had never felt more important than this. She'd decided she would cancel the upcoming appointment with Dr. Bell because there was no need for it. As Gerrard had said, they could work through their problems themselves. They already had.

Inside the dressing suite, Marley grinned as she opened her gifts from Gerrard, slid the sleek black linen slip dress over her head, and slipped her feet into a new pair of Stuart Weitzman open-heeled pumps. She looked at herself in the mirror, eye liner and mascara in hand, and decided she needed nothing. Her inner glow gave her more radiance than any paints and powders could ever give her.

"And how was your retreat, Miss Shepherd?" one of the receptionists asked Marley as she returned to the lobby and sank into a lime green velvet chair.

"Oh, God. It was *wonderful*," Marley said, slightly wobbly, her muscles still loose from manipulation.

The receptionist laughed. "I see," she said. "I've got a message for you from Mr. Shore." She clicked the mouse on her computer and glanced at the monitor. "He asked me to tell you that he'll arrive for you in twenty minutes. Would you like to have tea in the reading room while you wait?"

"Oh, no, I'm fine right here," Marley said. "I don't think I can move right now anyway," she joked. She closed her eyes and rolled her neck from side to side.

Fifteen minutes later, she opened her eyes. She leaned forward and picked up a copy of *Coastal Living* from the marble coffee table. She thought about the glimmer in Gerrard's eyes when he'd recently told her that his parents had decided to give them their first summer home, "just a small place, for starters," in Oak Bluffs. Gerrard had been so proud. "I told you I'd make your dreams come true," he'd said, taking Marley's hand in his and kissing it.

Twenty minutes later, when mild irritation began to surface, Marley decided to visit the reading room after all. "I'm going to go have some tea," she said to the receptionist as she rose. "Would you let Mr. Shore know—"

"Certainly. Just relax and enjoy yourself. I'll send for you as soon as he arrives," the receptionist said, typing as she spoke.

Thirty minutes later, after her second cup of Darjeeling, the muscles in Marley's shoulders were no longer slack. She had to force herself to push her shoulders down, to relax them, to relax herself. *He's coming,* she thought. *Be flexible. Don't ruin this moment,* she told herself, although she couldn't help thinking that if the moment ended up ruined, she really wouldn't be the culprit.

Fifteen more minutes was all she could stand. She pushed her teacup and saucer away, rose from the table, and returned to the lobby. "Would you mind calling a cab for me, ma'am?" Marley asked the receptionist, trying her best to sound restrained and calm. She added a chuckle and said, "I really need to get back to work."

"Certainly. Just wait right there, and I'll have one for you shortly."

Marley couldn't sit anymore. She walked toward the door, returned to the coffee table, walked toward the door again, then positioned herself beside it. She closed her eyes and prayed that Gerrard would arrive before the cab and save them both from the nightmare that was unfolding. *This can't be happening,* she thought, refusing to open her eyes, willing Gerrard to appear. But minutes passed like seconds, despite her efforts to hold back time for him. Her eyelids popped open when she heard the horn, and she almost didn't believe that it was a yellow-and-black cab, not a silver Bentley, waiting at the curb. Not trusting her voice, she waved at the receptionist and left.

She climbed into the backseat and gave the driver the address of her office building. Just as the driver was about to pull away from the curb, the Bentley pulled up, its tires screeching as Gerrard brought the car to an abrupt halt. He hopped out, leaving his door open as he rushed toward the cab and opened Marley's door. Avoiding her eyes, he pulled out his wallet, leaned inside the cab, and handed the driver a twenty-dollar bill. "I apologize for the inconvenience, sir," he said, guiding Marley from the car. Still avoiding Marley's eyes, he led her to his car, opened the passenger door, and ushered her inside.

They rode in silence for several minutes. Finally, Gerrard cleared his throat. "Baby," he began, then stopped, as if he weren't sure what to say. "Listen. I know you've had it with me and my schedule. I know it's not fair for me to continue to expect you to understand my work conflicts."

Marley stared out the window.

"I feel silly even trying to explain what happened this afternoon, because today was supposed to be about me making up for all my broken commitments, and I turned around and broke another one." He looked at Marley, seeming to search for a hint of softness. She continued to face the window.

"We didn't get the Cascade Heights project." Gerrard gripped the steering wheel and picked up speed.

Marley's eyes dropped. She hated to hear that. She knew how hard Gerrard had worked to secure the contract, his father having entrusted a lot of the negotiations to him. It had been an opportunity for Gerrard to shine and prove himself, and apparently he hadn't.

"Sorry to hear that," Marley said, still looking down.

"Yeah. You and me both." He drove on in silence. "I tried everything, short of outright begging, to get Carter to reconsider, but he wouldn't. Said he had the utmost confidence in Shore Development but thought it was best to stick with a developer he'd used before. 'But don't worry, Shore, because there'll be plenty more contracts like Cascade Heights, and you'll always be on my shortlist of candidates,' " Gerrard huffed, mocking Carter. "I almost slammed the phone in the man's ear. Man, days like this make me wonder."

Marley reeled around to face him. "Wonder about *what?*" she snapped. "Not about whether you're happy doing what you're doing? We all know you're *ecstatic*." She faced the window again.

They endured the rest of the drive in silence. Gerrard pulled up in front of Marley's office building and turned off the ignition. She found it interesting that he'd taken her back to work without asking her whether she'd wanted to return. Sure, she was fuming, but hadn't they planned to spend the afternoon together? Why was he voluntarily terminating the rest of the day's plans?

He turned to face her. "Marley, all I can say is that I sincerely apologize. You have every right to be angry. I got caught up trying to put out a fire, and in the process I neglected you. I'm sorry."

"Why am I always the one who suffers? Why am I always second to work?" She pressed her index fingers in the corners of her eyes, mashing away the moisture.

"Baby, you're not second. You're really not. But tell me, what should I have done differently? Honestly?" He reached for her hand, but she snatched it away.

"What are cell phones for, Gerrard? It didn't occur to you that 'Hey, it's probably not cool to leave Marley waiting *an hour* for me, so let me just handle my business with Carter from the car?' " She stared at him. "You just can't see beyond Shore Development?"

Gerrard was quiet. He rubbed his forehead, his eyes closed.

"I've gotta go." Marley reached for her purse and bags.

"Can we go and grab something to eat?" He turned to face her. "Let's make the most of the time we do have, Marley. Please?"

That was better, but still not good enough. "I'm really not hungry," she said, looking out the window. She turned to face him. "I think it's better if I go inside and get some work done. I need to think some things over." She twisted her ring.

"Are you free for dinner?" he asked.

"I'm going to Ma Grand's for dinner." She looked at him. "Why don't you come with me?"

Gerrard tapped his fingers on the steering wheel. "I'll see. I'll give you a call around six or so."

Marley shook her head. "A minute ago you asked if I was free for dinner, but now that dinner is at my grandmother's, you have to 'see'? Unbelievable," she said, opening the car door and climbing out. The pedicurist had been right: he *was* a deadbeat.

Gerrard frowned, his eyebrows furrowed. "You know," he said evenly, "it seems like I can't ever do anything right in your eyes. Ever." He stared ahead. "Like I said, I'm sorry about today. And I'm sorry you're not hungry now. But I have to get back to you about this evening—I need to check on a few things before I commit to going to your grandmother's—and it would be nice if you could understand that."

"I understand perfectly." Marley slammed the door and walked away.

That evening, Marley showed up at Ma Grand's an hour late and un-apologetic. "Hey," she said blandly, kissing her grandmother on the cheek as she squeezed by her and headed for the bathroom.

"Lord, Lord, Lord," Marley heard her grandmother say as she closed the door and locked its five bolts. But "hey" was really all Marley had to give at the moment. She hadn't wanted to show up at all; she'd wanted to go straight home and mull over Gerrard. Tough questions had forced their way to the surface of her consciousness and fixed themselves there. Was Gerrard ever going to change? Would work always come first in his life? Should she just accept it and be grateful for the benefits—the day spas, the summer homes, the clothes she *knew* she loved to wear? Was a little time together better than nothing? She had to come up with answers.

Get yourself together, she thought, flushing the toilet and washing her hands. *Get it together.*

She left the bathroom, walked into the kitchen, and surveyed the scene. "Hi, Mom," she said, sounding more like herself as she kissed her mother on the cheek.

"Hi, honey," Pam answered, opening the refrigerator. "Long day?"

"Yeah." Marley sat at the kitchen table and grabbed the news-paper, quickly deciding it would be her weapon against any unwel-come conversation.

Leaning against the sink, Ma Grand eyed Marley. "Girl, I know one thing—you better get yourself together, walking in here an hour late talkin' 'bout some 'hey,' 'hi,' and 'yeah.' Shoot." Ma Grand rolled her eyes, pursed her lips, and looked out the window.

"Mama, do you mind rinsing the beans for me?" Pam asked from the refrigerator. "They're on the counter."

Ma Grand's eyes cased the counter and bugged when they settled on the package of beans. She picked up the package, and a look of horror came over her face. "Pam, where did you get these butter beans from?"

"Gourmet Grocer," Pam replied, bending over the vegetable bin.

"Gourmet who? Is that the fancy grocery store that charges an arm and a leg for that ragweed they call lettuce? How much did you pay for these beans, Pam?" She looked at Pam as if she had committed a federal crime.

"Mama, what difference does it make? I mean, really?" Pam rose from the vegetable bin and walked toward the kitchen sink, cucumbers and tomatoes in hand. She was sniffing a bit, probably on account of the cool air October had ushered into town without warning. And she looked as though the day had drained her. Probably working too hard again.

"Makes a whole lot of difference. I have always used Mattie's beans for all my bean dishes, Pam, and you know that. Mattie's beans cost forty-five cents a bag, and they're better than all of that new mess you go out and buy for two dollars a bag. I wonder where your head is sometimes. I really do," Ma Grand said, moving away from the sink. "Now, I'm sorry, but I ain't never made butter beans with this, this Provincial brand or whatever the bag says. Can't half read it 'cause I lost the left lens to my eyeglasses and that's the eye that needs a lens the most. But I have never used this brand, and I'm not about to use it tonight. No, ma'am. We'll just have chili."

Ma Grand stumbled toward the pantry, where she kept cans upon cans of chili in all its varieties: chili with kidney beans, chili with whole tomatoes, chili with diced tomatoes, chili with stewed tomatoes—as if the Depression had never ended and each and every can of that chili would one day be her saving grace and prove her wisest purchase.

"Ma Grand, I don't eat canned chili, remember? I don't eat beef anymore," Marley said from the kitchen table, scanning the *Journal*. She would have tried to broker the battle over the beans, as she did with most of her mother's and grandmother's disputes, but she thought it best to lie low.

"Oh shoot, child. Been raised on beef all your life, and now you won't eat it. What's wrong with it? I bet you'll eat it tonight," Ma Grand snapped, hobbling toward the pantry with even more vigor.

"Mama, do you hear yourself? You're being irrational. You refuse to cook beans you've never seen before, and as a result you're going to force Marley to starve? She doesn't eat beef. Let's just follow through with our original plan and have the butter beans, corn bread, and salad, okay?" Pam moistened a paper towel under the faucet and wiped her forehead. She pushed her hair out of her face, all but the short strands around the edges that perspiration had already set into curly motion.

"Oh, the devil," Ma Grand huffed. "What in the world was I thinking, agreeing to have dinner with you two on a Monday night? Shoot! I don't even dress on Mondays, and here I am fooling around with you. I'm missing *Bonanza,* and if I had any sense, I'd walk out of this kitchen right now and go sit myself down in my quiet room and watch my show in peace!"

Nevertheless, Ma Grand returned from the pantry with two bags of Mattie's butter beans, extra large, and tossed them onto the counter. She grabbed her colander from the lazy Susan that Pam had installed for her last Mother's Day and poured the beans into the strainer. She rinsed them well, plucking out the bad ones, commenced her quick soak, then leaned back against the kitchen counter and looked first at her daughter, then at her granddaughter. Marley glanced up and returned Ma Grand's gaze with a toothless smile. Ma Grand shook her head and rolled her eyes as hard as she could without straining the sockets.

"How much money have you-all spent so far on that wedding, Pam?" Ma Grand ate a forkful of butter beans. She leaned forward and plucked a wilting leaf off the wildflower arrangement in the center of her dining room table. Aaron, the Jamiesons' grandson from down the street, had brought the flowers to her that morning. "Picked 'em mahself, Mrs. Franklin," he'd told Ma Grand. *Stole 'em yourself is more like it,* Ma Grand had thought, as she smiled and patted and pushed Aaron's backside out the front door.

"I hope I don't need to remind you," Ma Grand continued, "that it's only one day and nobody will remember half of what you're going into debt to buy. Lord knows, I never would have believed people would spend the kind of money on weddings that they're spending now. Sinful, really. And Pam, don't go out and buy the most expensive dress you see. You don't need a thousand-dollar dress to look nice, plus you have enough clothes hanging in your four or five closets to last you a lifetime. Half the people you invited have never seen you wear all those nice clothes, so I truly hope you use some sense and save your money. I know one thing, I'll be wearing that silver pantsuit that's hanging in my closet right now." Ma Grand bugged her eyes, punctuating her declaration.

"Mama, does that suit even fit you? Didn't you buy it almost ten years ago for Aunt Faye's seventieth birthday party?" Pam nibbled on her last bite of corn bread. "I thought you were going to wear the periwinkle dress we got at Rich's last month."

"Yes, the suit still fits," Ma Grand drawled. "I have not gained any weight over the last ten years—well, I'll say this—if I have, it's because of these doggone water pills they have me taking." Ma Grand grabbed a handful of cashews from a glass leaf dish.

"Mama, I know Dr. Bailey restricted you from eating nuts. Why do you keep them on the table if you know you can't have them?"

Ma Grand stopped chewing and looked at Pam. "Do you really think I won't eat them if I hide them somewhere?"

The half-chewed nuts were plainly visible on her tongue, and Pam found it difficult to swallow her own food. "Mama," she began, intending to remind her mother to swallow before she spoke, but Ma Grand kept talking.

"I'll know where I hid them. I will always want them, and I'm not going to stop buying them." She finished chewing the nuts. "Marley, you haven't said one word. What's wrong with you?"

Marley averted her eyes from Ma Grand's gaze and picked up her fork, figuring she could dodge the question by stuffing more beans into her mouth, but her plate was empty. "Uh, I don't know, Gran. Just reflecting on things, you know?"

"No, I don't know. You spend more time reflecting than any child I know. Why so much thinking lately? You're a bride. Not supposed to be so pensive at such a carefree time in your young life."

Pam's and Marley's eyes met, then they both looked down at their empty plates. Their eye contact did not go unnoticed.

"What in the devil is going on? Something wrong with you and that boy? Don't you sit there and try to hide it. I am seventy-eight years old, and I might be losing it, but I done sho' 'nuff been around this block before."

"It's nothing, Ma Grand." Marley pushed her plate away. "I just—" Marley looked at Ma Grand, then at her mother. "Nothing. It's nothing." Marley looked down at her hands and began to twist her ring. She wished her grandmother would get back to fussing with her mother or do something, anything, other than sit there waiting on her to speak. Marley's face got hot, and before she knew it a tear had formed in the corner of her eye. She wiped at her eyes, which only served to burst the dam that had welled up inside her.

"What is *wrong* with you, girl?" Ma Grand fussed, struggling as she stood and grabbing a few tissues from the kitchen. She hobbled back into the dining room.

"Look," she said, her shaking hand extended toward Marley, "if that boy is making you cry like this, you need to run for your life." Her voice quivered. "Ain't nothing in this world more important than your happiness, do you hear me?" She shook the tissues at Marley until Marley took them.

Heaving her body back into her chair, Ma Grand sighed and shook her head. She looked at Pam out of the corner of her eyes. Pam was quiet, her face blank.

"Wasn't my favorite anyway," Ma Grand said. "Come in my house like he's king of something. He ain't king here. His daddy ought to take all that money he's making and put that boy in obedience school with the dogs."

"Mama! Stop it!" Pam caught herself and lowered her voice. "All you're doing is agitating the situation. Stop filling her head with that foolishness. You barely know Gerrard, yet you think you have the right to sit here and bad-mouth him. You spend more time finding fault with people than getting to know them. It's almost like you prefer to dislike people."

"I do. Especially the false people you-all take up with. I can see through that boy like a three-dollar bill. I don't know why you can't." Ma Grand leaned back in her chair and folded her arms.

"Ma Grand," Marley said, sniffling, "that's not fair."

"Oh shoot, child, don't talk to me about fair. Talk to me about truth!" Ma Grand snapped.

Pam's eyes were on fire as she stared at her mother. "Nobody is ever good enough for you! There's something wrong with everybody!"

"Oh stop it, Pam. Stop that nonsense. If you're talking about that fool you decided to marry, don't blame it on me. I told you thirty years ago that he was a slickster. A slickster with a handful of sense. Little bit of education. He thought he was somebody's king, too, strolling in here and throwing all that sugar on me like I'm some child wanting candy. Even Rowland saw through him."

"Don't you dare bring Daddy into this! Daddy never once spoke against my husband! All Daddy ever did was support me!" Determined to burn through Ma Grand's words, Pam's eyes hadn't blinked.

"Your daddy did not want to hurt your feelings," Ma Grand said. "He could see you were head over heels in love with Silas. But what you will never understand is that your marrying Silas made your father feel like a failure. You grew up in this house, and you had an example of a real man right in the flesh. You saw how he did for me and how he did for you and your brother. Good as he was, he did *not* stroll around this house like some king. He was too busy making sure we felt like queens. Maybe we didn't have a whole, whole lot of money, but we had enough. And maybe his clothes were not the fanciest, but they were clean. And taking care of his family was the most important thing in the world to him. He came home *every* night, on time, and took us everywhere with him. He *served* us.

"But then you go off to school," Ma Grand continued, her voice suddenly lower, angrier, "and bring this slickster back into this house, and the first day we meet him you tell us you're going to marry him. And he just sits there, letting you do all the talking, thinking his smiles and his high-and-mighty educational talk are going to fool us. It didn't fool us one bit! It broke your father's heart, that's what it did."

Pam's eyes were glassy. She slowly rose from her chair at the dining room table, where generations before her had sat and had similar weighty conversations, and walked to the bathroom. Marley heard the latch on the door click into the hole. She couldn't help but think that her mother's heart had just broken and that, if a breaking heart had a sound, it would have sounded like the latch clicking shut.

Marley looked at her grandmother, years of questions running through her mind.

"Don't say one word to me, Marley," Ma Grand said. "Not one word. You don't know." Ma Grand rose from the table. "You just don't know."

$\mathscr{M}$ARLEY DROVE HOME from Ma Grand's that night with a heavy heart and dim prospects. Her mother was hurting, and her grandmother was angry. In many ways, what they had perceived as dramatically different life paths had, ultimately, led them to a common destination: they both felt abandoned.

Marley didn't want to feel abandoned. She didn't want to be hurting at fifty-two and angry at seventy-eight. She wanted to lie snuggled up next to her husband, the father of her children, the man who had kissed her chalky mouth in the mornings and held her unbathed body in the evenings. She wanted that so badly that almost no cost was too great to pay for it.

I'm tripping, she thought to herself. She decided to call Ashley from the car.

"Hello?" Ashley said, sounding as though she'd long since settled in for the evening.

"Hey, girl. I know it's way past your bedtime, but I really need to talk."

"Don't worry about it," Ashley said, yawning. "What's up?"

"Ohhh, where do I begin? I don't know. Gerrard is constantly flaking out on me, and my mother and grandmother are constantly going off on each other. It's just too much for me right now."

"Girl, your mother and Ma Grand will be all right. That's how they are. Just let them work through their issues and stay out of it—stop trying to be the referee all the time," Ashley said.

"I don't always try to referee—"

"Marley, please. Trust me on that," Ashley said. "Their situation will work itself out. I'm more concerned about you and Gerrard."

"Yeah, well, me too." Marley turned on Cascade, slowing her speed.

"What's going on with you two? Weren't you supposed to be doing something special today?"

Marley sighed. "Yep. We were supposed to spend the afternoon together. It started out perfectly, Ash. He picked me up from work in the Bentley and dropped me off at Serenity."

"Mm," Ashley said.

"And gave me a new dress and a new pair of shoes to put on after my massage."

"Nice," Ashley responded.

"But it went downhill from there. He said he'd be back in two hours. I sat a whole hour waiting on him to show up."

"Are you serious? He didn't call?"

"Nope. He'd left a message just before I finished up, letting me know he was running a few minutes late. But then I didn't hear from him again and ended up having to ask the receptionist to call a cab for me."

"Oh, God."

"Do you know how *embarrassing* that was? I mean, here I am strolling in there, all smiles and giggles, like I'm the Queen of Sheba, and then I end up having to pass an hour in the reading room because Mr. Big Spender hasn't come back to pick me up."

"Mmm-mmm-mmm. I know, girl."

"So then, out of nowhere, he comes flying into the parking lot, pulling up next to the cab, right when I'm about to leave."

"No way."

"Yes. Gives the driver some money and pulls me out of the cab."

"So what did he *say*? What in the world *happened*?" Ashley asked in a high-pitched voice.

"What else? It was *work*. It couldn't be *avoided*. He didn't get a contract, and the world was about to end."

"Mm. I don't know," Ashley said.

Marley paused. "What do you mean?" she asked. She pulled up into her driveway and turned off the ignition.

"Just seems like there could have been another way for him to handle the work situation without leaving you waiting a whole hour."

"That's exactly what I said."

"I mean, you-all are about to get married," Ashley said.

"Exactly," Marley agreed.

"Marley, do you think he's being straight with you about everything that's going on in his life? I know he's busy and everything, but do you think work is the only thing keeping him so busy?"

Marley's eyebrows furrowed. "What do you mean?"

"I don't know," Ashley said, "nothing particular. I'm just wondering why he's so unavailable all the time. It's a little strange, don't you think?"

Marley forced out a chuckle. "I really don't know what you're trying to say, Ashley. Are you trying to suggest something?"

"No, not really. Just raising a question."

"Well," Marley said quickly, "it seems like you're trying to suggest that I should be suspicious about something. What, you think he's selling drugs in his spare time? Or paying visits to a mystery wife and child? Come on, Ashley."

"I'm just raising a question. You're the one going to the extreme with it," Ashley said.

"Well, thank you for raising the question, but we don't need to go there. Really." Marley got out of the car and walked to her front door. "I'm at my front door now. I'll call you back once I get inside and get situated."

"Okay. Talk to you then," Ashley said, hanging up.

Marley turned off her cell phone and tossed it into her purse. "Sheesh," she said, opening the front door. "Who wants to hear all *that?*"

She climbed the stairs, dropped her purse onto the floor of her bedroom, and threw herself across the bed. What a day. She felt like lying there until morning, but she had to meet Bob in New York the next day to prepare for a deposition, and she still had to pack her clothes. She glanced at her answering machine. The red light was blinking. She pressed the play button and tried to listen to the messages casually, as if she really weren't waiting to hear his voice.

Three messages in, she felt her heart drop. He hadn't called, and it looked as if the tape was at its end. But then, just when shame was about to claim her, she heard his voice.

"Hi, baby. It's me. Just missing you, wishing I could be with you at your grandmother's, wanting to talk to you. I learned a valuable lesson today. It won't happen again. I hope you forgive me. I love you, Marley."

Before she had time to think, to weigh the sincerity of his message, to ponder its meaning and determine her response, the telephone rang. She couldn't deny that she hoped it was Gerrard. How she hoped it was Gerrard.

"Hello?"

"Hi, baby."

Marley sighed while her eyes closed. "Hi."

"It's so good to hear your voice," he said.

"Yeah," she responded, ashamed to admit it was good to hear his, too.

"You forgive me, sweetheart?"

"I'm still thinking about it," she said halfheartedly, knowing she'd already forgiven him ten times over.

"Good enough. So," he asked, "you're leaving me tomorrow?"

"Yeah. The deposition is Friday. The clients are totally unprepared and will need every bit of assistance they can get. But I'll be back Friday night."

"And I'll be waiting for you," Gerrard said.

"You will?" Marley twirled the telephone cord with her finger.

"I will. And I'm gonna beat up Bob for you, too."

They both laughed. After four or five rounds of "I love you" and "I love you too," they hung up.

That night, Marley made up her mind that there would be no concessions. There would be no failures. She would not take a seat alongside her mother and grandmother on the throne of abandonment. The roads that lay in front of her were unobstructed, their destinations as clear as her choice: solitude or companionship. She would choose companionship.

Marley ran down the corridors of Concourse B like Flo Jo going for gold. The zippers, clasps, and other metal objects adorning her purse and her carry-on bag were hitting against the outer sides of her thighs like a barrage of intentional inflictions all aimed at punishing her for cutting it so close yet again. She'd sworn at least ten times in the past, when she'd had to run for her life to catch an airplane and, in the process, drench a newly dry-cleaned suit with sweat, that she'd never again arrive less than one hour prior to departure. And she'd meant it. But this time she'd overslept—she'd accidentally set her alarm clock for five in the evening rather than five in the morning.

Her loose curls flew wildly in and around her face as she approached the ticket counter at Gate 16. She gasped for breath as she patted one of the outer pockets of her bag in search of her ticket. "Are you still boarding for the six-thirty flight to LaGuardia?" Marley asked, almost begging.

"Oh, so sorry, dear. We just secured the door," the ticketing agent responded. She turned to remove the placard displaying the recently departed flight number. "Would you like me to book you on the next flight?"

"What time does the next flight depart?"

"Eight o'clock. Gives you time to have some *real* coffee if you want," the agent offered politely, hanging a new placard on the board. "I wouldn't drink this airline's brew if they paid me," she joked.

Marley ran her hand through her hair. She couldn't believe it. The thought of having to call Bob and explain to him that she'd be arriving more than an hour later than scheduled made her want to hurl herself out a window. That trauma would be far more bearable than Bob's mouth.

"Yes, I guess so. Thanks," Marley said, handing the agent her ticket.

"We'll begin boarding about thirty minutes prior to departure," the agent said. "Go rest yourself for a while," she said, smiling.

"Thanks," Marley said.

Witnessing the sky transform from dreamy shades of navy blue and violet to brighter promises of orange and yellow, Marley decided she was glad she'd missed the first flight. It had enabled her to absorb this small, daily miracle that she took for granted and rarely experienced. The spectrum in the sky invited her to escape the confines and limitations of the natural world and explore the realm of human impossibility. Even as a child, Marley would often stand on her front doorstep and stare out into the endless sky, believing it held all life's secrets and offered higher roads to greater destinies for those who dared to reach for them. And now, standing on her thirty years of safe travels upon reasonably attainable paths, the quickly evolving sunrise reminded her that a higher level awaited her should she decide to reach for it.

A loud thump in the jetway drew Marley back to earth. She peered down the jetway but could see only the back of a man holding two large boxes with "Reap the Harvest Food Services" emblazoned on them. When the man turned around and placed the boxes on the floor, Marley saw his face.

It was like a dream. Every feature seemed divinely crafted and perfectly woven together to create a masterpiece Bearden and Barnes together could not rival. His brows and mustache were thick, dark, and striking. His full lips were so perfectly shaped that they seemed specially carved. Marley could barely make out his eyes, but she sensed an intensity behind them that somehow commanded her attention, even at a distance.

"This is the final call for all passengers boarding Flight 777 to New York's LaGuardia Airport. Please proceed to Gate Sixteen." Startled by the announcement, Marley grabbed her carry-on and made her way down the jetway. Her ears grew warm, and she began to feel guilty for admiring—well, gawking at—another man the way she had been. She was engaged, for goodness' sake.

As she approached the plane, the door at the end of the jetway opened and the same man appeared, holding more boxes in his arms. They stood inches apart. Their eyes locked, and he offered her a smile warmer than the Johannesburg sun. She smiled, too, betting that from the way her lips curled, it was a really goofy smile she had managed to produce.

"Have a good flight," he said, still smiling, and attempted to move. Marley was somewhat dazed, finally realizing that the only reason he was still standing there was that he couldn't maneuver around her with the boxes in his arms. She tried to step forward but stumbled over her foot in the process. She heard the giggles of aircraft personnel behind her and felt the burn of their amused eyes tingling down her back. Then the seat of her slacks began to wedge up her behind, and she was overcome with the urge to pull it out. She hurried onto the plane and took her seat, rocking from side to side, trying to dislodge the wedgie with grace and discretion. When the rocking didn't work, she yanked her slacks out of her behind, not even bothering to see if anyone was watching, then rested her head against the spongy leather seat. She closed her eyes, deciding that sleep would make her forget the way the morning had begun. She'd step off the plane in northern territory, a new creature with a new beginning.

The wait was unbearable. Pam was dying to know the outcome. Either they liked it, or they didn't. Neither feeling was hard to identify, so what in the world was taking them so long?

Pam straightened the papers, paperweights, pens, and desk blotter on her desk for the third time, then folded her hands and waited. She opened her drawer and grabbed her mirrored compact. Peering at herself, she touched up her forehead and cheeks with Sierra Sand pressed powder that was really too dark for her face, closed the compact, and tossed it nervously back into the drawer. She glanced at the still lights on her telephone. Realizing that even her burning glare would not cause them to flash with the news of an incoming call, she hopped out of her chair and walked to her window to take in the beginnings of downtown Atlanta's kaleidoscopic sunset.

Aside from the nerves eating at her stomach, Pam felt great. She hadn't felt this good in a while, actually. It was Friday, and if Bethany phoned in with the decision Pam had been praying for, she fully intended to have herself a good time all weekend long.

Her body jumped at the sound of the ringing telephone. She charged back to her desk, paused and took a deep breath, tucked her hair behind her ears, and picked up the receiver.

"Pamela Shepherd," she said, trying her best to sound busy and slightly bothered. Anything to shield the eagerness and excitement that was threatening to spill out of her mouth.

"Hi, Pamela, it's Bethany from Mr. Cochran's office. How *are* you?" she sang into Pam's ear.

"I'm fabulous, Bethany. And you, dear?" Pam could turn on the charm herself when she needed to.

"That makes two of us!" Bethany beamed. They laughed together, and Pam sensed that the conversation was headed precisely where she had hoped.

"Well, I'm gonna get right to it. Mr. and Mrs. Cochran have completed their interviews of prospective interior designers for their new home in Atlanta, and they have enthusiastically decided to accept your proposal."

Pam gasped. She covered her heart with her hand, closed her eyes, and quickly mumbled thanks to God.

"Bethany, I am absolutely *honored* that they have chosen me. Please give them my warmest regards, my sincere thanks, and tell them they will not be disappointed."

"I certainly will, Pamela. Your work is awesome, by the way. I flipped through a few pages of your portfolio and thought, my God, if I ever make as much money as Mr. Cochran, I swear I will hire you to decorate all of my houses." Bethany and Pam laughed.

"Bethany, you have my word that I'll stand ready to help you when that day comes. Thanks again, and give my best to the Cochrans."

"Will do, Pamela. You'll be receiving the signed contract and other documentation in the mail, and Mr. Cochran's assistant in Atlanta will contact you shortly to begin scheduling."

Pam hung up the phone and screamed. She kicked off her shoes and ran in circles around her office. She threw her arms up over her head and screamed some more until she felt a sharp pain under her arm and remembered she was no spring chicken and probably hadn't stretched her arms that high in more than twenty-five years. She plopped down on the love seat and reached for the telephone. She had gotten the coveted Cochran contract, a deal for which at least four other interior designers had competed. The commission would be outrageous. Pam had to share the news, and with excitement brimming, she deliberated whom she would call first.

She wasn't going to call her mother. Pam still was not speaking to her mother. Ma Grand's words at the last Monday-night dinner had bruised Pam, causing damage she wasn't yet willing to try to repair. Plus, her mother's brand of enthusiasm about good news was like humidity on a new hairdo.

She couldn't call Marley—at least not yet. Marley was either still in New York on business or on her way home. Pam figured she would have a better chance catching Marley the next morning.

She decided to call Ava, her best friend of more than forty years. Ava and Pam had grown up together in Atlanta, gone to Clark College together, married roommates who had both turned out to be less than husbands and more than heartaches, and ended up nursing their wounds and carrying on with life in suburban Atlanta. Ava was someone Pam could always turn to, someone who understood Pam's pain and allowed her to talk around it ("No, girl, nothing's wrong, I'm just tired.") or feign its nonexistence ("Child, his leaving was the best thing that ever could have happened to me."). Ava gave Pam a zone in which she could say or do whatever was necessary to make it through.

"Ava?" Pam inquired eagerly into the telephone.

"Hey, girl," Ava replied, sounding happy to hear her friend's voice.

"Ava, you have got to meet me at Bistro Prime tonight. I have some news that you will not believe."

"Say you do?" Ava was always ready to hear news of any kind about anything or anybody.

"I do. Can you meet me there in an hour or so? I need to run home and change first."

"Yeah, I believe I can pull myself together by then. You want me to call Byron and tell him to save our favorite table?"

"Yeah, would you? That would be *fan*-tastic. I'll see you there."

"Okey-dokey, then. See you in a bit."

Pam drove so fast that she made it from downtown to the Roswell Road exit in half the time it normally took. Her excitement, coupled with one of the Spinners' old hits playing on 107.5, seemed to add wings to her tires. Pam was flying high. It seemed as if things were finally coming together. She'd faced her share of stumbling blocks, if not boulders, but she'd always known that greater things were in store for her.

Pam sang along with the Spinners, slapping the steering wheel and not caring, for a change, whether other drivers were staring at her. She laughed when she saw old Mr. Hickson from across the street widen his eyes horrifically and cover his ears. "You're *accosting* my *decrepit* eardrums," he mouthed at her slowly. It was all he ever said to anyone on the street—be it the Cobb County Girl Scouts selling Trefoils or the Dickinsons offering Jehovah—before he snatched up his green-and-white plaited lawn chair with the American flag taped to the plastic arm cover and huffed inside his door.

She skipped up the front steps, scooped up the mail lying on the floor in the foyer, and made her way to her bedroom to change. Her first thought was to leave the mail alone until she got back from dinner, but, having glanced at the already growing stack of unopened envelopes on her dining room table, she felt a twinge of guilt at the thought of adding to the pile. Flipping through the envelopes and circulars, she came across an invoice from her doctor's laboratory. She opened the envelope, irritated at the prospect of having to pay for any shortage her insurance hadn't covered. What good was insurance, if it didn't cover routine examinations?

Glancing halfway down the page, she realized she was not holding an invoice.

The results of your mammogram were abnormal and indicate the presence of a solid mass in your left breast. Please contact your physician immediately to schedule a biopsy.

Pam lowered herself on the bed and stared at the words on the page until they blurred together. She folded the letter and closed her eyes. She remained still and tried to think clearly. Absent was the feeling that this was nothing to be concerned about, that this would turn out to be nothing. After all, this was her third abnormal mammogram.

Pam took a deep breath and lifted her arm. She placed her right hand inside her bra and ran her fingertips over the outer contours of her left breast. Almost immediately she felt a sizable lump near her armpit. It was the same lump she'd been dismissing as bone tissue—so hard to the touch, so foreign from her muscle tissue. After two abnormal mammograms, she should have known better. Maybe she *had* known better.

Pam rushed over to the telephone on her nightstand. She prayed that Ava hadn't left her house yet.

"Hello?" Ava said breathlessly.

"Ava, glad I caught you. Listen, now that I'm at home, I'm not feeling up to dinner after all."

"Say you're not? What's wrong?"

"I'm just tired. I went into the office really early this morning, and I think it's catching up with me now." Pam hoped Ava wouldn't ask many more questions.

"Well, what about your news? You had me all worked up to hear something good."

"I got the Cochran contract."

"Wow! Pam, that's wonderful news!" Ava said. Pam was silent. Ava frowned. "Goodness, you must really be tired."

"Yeah," Pam said, her voice cracking.

"Pam?"

She tried to remain quiet, but her muted sniffles burst into audible sobs.

"Pam, what's wrong? Do you need me to come over?"

"No, no. I'm fine. My mammogram turned up a lump in my left breast, so I've got to have another biopsy," she said in between sniffles.

"Oh, my Lord." Ava took a deep breath. "Pam, you listen here. Everything is going to be okay. You know that, don't you?"

"Yeah, I do," Pam lied.

"We've made it through a whole lot, and we're going to make it through this, too. You hear me?"

"Yep."

"I'm coming over, okay? I'll pick us up some dinner, and I'll be over shortly."

"Okay." Pam wiped her eyes.

"See you in a few."

"Okay."

Chapter 7

"I DON'T KNOW WHY I let you talk me into this," Ma Grand mumbled to Marley as they walked through her front door. Marley helped her grandmother remove her coat. "I swear I don't know what in John Brownit's name possessed me to do this." Ma Grand stood in the middle of the foyer as if she were contemplating turning around and walking away. Bewilderment, mixed with fear, coated her face. "We ain't done these Monday-night dinners in a month. Been the most peaceful month of my life." She tried to straighten a slightly crooked frame hanging on the wall but gave up in midair, not willing to fight the spasms.

Marley couldn't help but laugh, as she had since she was a child, at the sight of Ma Grand working herself up into an unnecessary fit.

"What in the devil is so funny to you?" Ma Grand snapped.

"You are," Marley said, hugging her with one free arm and ushering her into the living room.

"Humph," Ma Grand grunted. The stargazer lilies on the rattan coffee table had quickly claimed the better part of her attention.

"Gran, we're going to have a good time tonight. It's ladies' night.

We're going to forgive and forget, and then we're going to celebrate."

"Don't you know by now that forgiving and forgetting are like oil and water? I don't know why people always lump them together, 'cause they don't mix. Ain't nothing I need to be forgiven for anyway, and I sure ain't forgetting the fact that my mother taught me to always speak the truth."

"Gran, come on," Marley pleaded with her from the kitchen. She pulled out her skillet and heated a few tablespoons of olive oil. "No one is perfect. I just think—"

"And I never said I was perfect. No, ma'am. I have never thought more highly of myself than I ought." Seated on the couch, Ma Grand folded her hands on her lap and pressed her thumbs together.

"*What?*" Marley said, cracking up. Ma Grand's head had always been above the clouds. That fact was at once her virtue and her vice.

"What you mean, 'what?' " Ma Grand leaned forward slightly, fingering one of the lilies.

"Anyway, Ma Grand. All I want to say is that, yes, the truth should always be spoken, but there's a way to do it if your goal is to make sure the other person hears you. No one likes to be beat upside the head with the truth."

"Oh, shoot," Ma Grand responded, rolling her eyes and dismissing Marley's comment. "You can't tell me I beat your mother upside the head with the truth. I didn't tell Pam anything she doesn't already know for herself, and I've been telling her the same thing since she met that rascal almost thirty years ago."

"Gran, that's exactly what I'm talking about." Marley placed the chopping knife on the counter and walked around the breakfast bar to face her grandmother. "You may not think very highly of my father, but calling him a rascal doesn't make me want to listen to the truth of what you're saying."

"Well, it's the truth," she said under her breath as the doorbell rang.

"All right, Gran." Marley waved her grandmother's comment away with one hand and opened the front door with the other. "Hi, Mommy," she said, helping Pam remove her coat and noticing she felt warm, almost overheated.

"Hi, sweetheart." Pam sounded drained. Walking up the steps, she looked to her right and saw her mother seated on the couch. "Hello," Pam said, and kept walking toward the kitchen.

"Hello." Ma Grand rolled her eyes and folded her hands in her lap.

"What are you cooking?" Pam surveyed the sea of vegetables on the counter.

"It's a surprise. Now please leave the kitchen." Marley's eyes were firm. Pam stared blankly at her, then walked away without protest.

Ma Grand eyed Pam peripherally as Pam eased into the cranberry oversized chair. "Did you come here from work?" she inquired stiffly.

"Yes." Pam fished out the latest *Essence* from Marley's magazine rack and flipped through it.

"Mm." Ma Grand looked in the other direction and twiddled her thumbs. "Do they give you vacation on that job?" she asked, looking at Pam again.

Pam raised her eyes above the magazine's rim and stared at Ma Grand. "Mama, what kind of question is that? You know I take four weeks of vacation every year."

"Well, no, I don't know really. I mean, sometimes I wonder. Maybe the vacation policy has changed."

"The policy hasn't changed."

Marley drained and rinsed the linguine. Things hadn't gotten off to a promising start. But in their family, a good meal always broke the ice, and Marley was quite confident she had put her foot in the primavera sauce.

"Well, you look tired, Pam. I sure wish you would take some time off to—"

"I *am* tired! I am *very* tired!" Pam threw the magazine down on the table. "Do you want to know why I'm tired, Mama? *Do you?*"

Ma Grand jumped in her seat and gripped the armrest with one hand. She didn't answer Pam.

"I'm tired because I have cancer! I have cancer in my left breast, and if I don't start chemotherapy right away, then I may as well dig my own grave and go lie in it!"

Marley's single favorite serving piece was a handmade mosaic platter of rust, alabaster, and teal blue bone china chips. The chips had been placed together to form a breathtaking picture of southern Italy's countryside. Gerrard had given it to her after his trip to Rome. The platter slipped from Marley's hands, and she heard it shatter beneath her. She felt some of the tiny fragments pierce the tops of her feet. Or at least she felt the moisture from the blood that had been drawn. But all of it—the sound of the platter against the tile, the feel of the chips against her skin, and the blood that held them there—all of it was numb against the words her mother had just spoken.

"What did you say?" Marley whispered.

Pam rubbed her forehead. Then she began to weep. "I said I have cancer."

"Oh, boy." Ma Grand shifted her weight on the couch. Each wrinkle on her face worked together to constrict the pools of tears that filled the corners of her eyes.

The room was deathly quiet until Marley's great-uncle's splintered oak grandfather clock struck eight. And when it struck, she realized time was no longer willing to wait patiently for her to catch up with the news she'd just heard. There were too many issues to resolve. "How long have you known this?" Marley asked, walking into the living room.

"I had a biopsy two weeks ago. I found out shortly after that that the lump was malignant."

The three were quiet. Marley lowered herself slowly on the couch. Myriad questions swarmed her brain. Why hadn't her mother told them earlier? How had she kept her biopsy a secret? Were there other things—worse things—she wasn't telling them?

"So what course have the doctors recommended?" Marley swallowed, trying to force back down her throat the lump that had risen.

"A mastectomy, then chemotherapy." Pam wiped her eyes.

"Have you scheduled the surgery?" Ma Grand asked.

"Next Monday." Pam fidgeted with her tennis bracelet and noticed a diamond was missing. Gray, crusty matter had collected in its stead.

"And the treatment starts after that?"

"Yes."

"Well, all right, then. We'll make it through. It'll be all right." Ma Grand looked away and nervously patted her right hand on top of her left.

"What do you mean, 'We'll make it through and it'll be all right?' " Marley asked incredulously, tears dripping on the collar of her white oxford shirt. "How can you say that? You don't know that."

"No, I don't know," Ma Grand said. "But I do know one thing. It doesn't do us any good to sit here and cry about what already is. There ain't nothing you or I can do about your mother's cancer except support her and encourage her through it. But I'll tell you what I'm *not* going to do," she said, her voice cracking, "and that's to sit here crying and helpless."

"Why are you so desensitized, Gran? How can you be so cold about this? This is her life!"

"I *do* have feelings about this, Marley! Don't you dare sit there and tell me about my own attitude. I don't care how many tears I cry, not a one of them is going to wash away the cancer inside her body!"

Marley stared at her grandmother, a woman who had dealt with more grief in her life than Marley and her mother combined. She'd lost her husband and her son. To Ma Grand, her husband had been the ocean and her son the river that flowed from it. Marley considered all these things. But still.

"You can sit there and mope all you want, but I will be no part of that foolishness," Ma Grand continued. "I am going to spend my energy on things that I *can* control. Now, your mother needs help, and she needs support. She does not need a bunch of sop that's going to make her weaker than she already is."

Marley decided she didn't want to hear any more of what Ma Grand was saying. She went and sat at her mother's feet and looked up at her. "Mommy, are you okay?"

"I'm fine, baby," she responded from behind her hands.

"How do you feel right now?"

"I feel fine."

"Do you have a headache?"

"Yes, I do."

"Okay, I'll get you some aspirin. Are you ready to eat?"

"Mm-hm."

"Okay, well, why don't you go on into the dining room and get comfortable, and after I get the aspirin I'll fix our plates. Okay?"

"Mm-hm."

"Mom," Marley said, standing up and grabbing her mother's hands. Marley winced in pain from the china fragments still stuck to the tops of her feet. Pam looked up at her. "I can't imagine what you're feeling right now. I won't even try. But I know we'll get through this. And you will be stronger for it. I know it."

Pam's lips managed a smile, and she squeezed Marley's hands.

Marley went upstairs, feeling a sense of achievement. She went into her bathroom to get the aspirin. By the time she reached the medicine cabinet, she reflected on the vacant look in her mother's eyes and realized the smile had been for her benefit. It hadn't come from within. Marley didn't *know* anything, contrary to the representation she'd just tried to make to her mother, and Pam would have been a fool to find solace in anything Marley had said.

These were the issues that led folks to down entire bottles of pills, Marley thought, taking a bottle of aspirin from the cabinet, imagining herself passed out on the bathroom floor. She closed the cabinet door and stared at herself. She was fresh out of hope, of joy, of strength and resolve, of determination. None of it was within her grasp. There were no bandages for these kinds of cuts, no salves for these kinds of wounds. Mommy couldn't help her; she needed help herself.

There, in the confines of her bathroom with the water running and the fan on high, Marley tried to muffle the sounds of fear flooding her eyes.

"I'm glad you finally told them, Pam," Ava said, and sipped from her cappuccino mug.

Pam looked out the window of Java Jive. She knew she had upset her mother and Marley by waiting so long to tell them about the cancer, but initially she had been more concerned about getting herself together. After she'd learned the news, she'd been a wreck. She'd called in sick at work the next day and never left her bedroom or changed out of her pajamas. Not that she didn't intend to handle the news like a big girl, a grown woman. She did. But a grown woman's shoes are large: they're hard to fill and even harder to walk in. She'd look like a twelve-year-old in stilettos if she tried it right now. So not yet—not until she could walk straight, and walk big, and walk right.

"I think I should call Silas." Pam slid a small jar of honey back and forth between her fingers.

Ava processed Pam's comment. "Okay," she said, her tone inviting further explanation.

"Ava, I could be dead next year. That means my child would be parentless unless Silas decides to get involved in her life. His periodic phone calls and holiday care packages won't cut it anymore."

Ava nodded. "Pam, you've done an excellent job raising Marley. She's a mature woman who is strong and who knows how to survive. If she's made it this far without Silas, she'll continue to make it without him, even if she doesn't have you."

Hearing those words stung Pam to the core. It was one thing for Pam to talk about the future in terms that might not include her. She still had some measure of control when she was the one constructing the hypotheticals. But it was something altogether different, and altogether frightening, to hear someone else refer to a future of which she might not be a part.

"Ava, he needs to know." Pam's voice cracked. She stared at Ava, then looked away.

Minutes passed and neither spoke. The gray sky finally burst forth with the plump drops of rain that had been swelling the clouds all morning.

"This is not about my getting pity from Silas, if that's what you're thinking," Pam finally said.

Ava sipped her cappuccino.

"I just firmly believe that, as Marley's father, he needs to know. He deserves to know, not because he's so great but because he is her father, he is alive, and he is at least half interested in her life." From the window, Pam watched a young couple walk down the street, hand in hand. She wondered what their future held. Whether, twenty years from now, they'd still be holding hands, grinning as if their Virginia Highland world was all that existed and all that mattered.

Pam knew she wasn't being completely honest with Ava, but she figured Ava already knew as much. Anyway, what could Ava say? Pam remembered several occasions when Ava had gotten in touch with her ex-husband and, in Pam's opinion, sought the same pity: when Ava's mother had died, when Ava had been mugged at gunpoint, and when Ava's son had been sent to the Persian Gulf War.

Maybe it wasn't pity that either of them was seeking. The need for pity was just another one of love's aftertastes given a bad name. Pam had loved Silas with every muscle in her body; he'd inhabited every blood vessel. And then, one day, he'd left. He'd just walked away. Left his keys, garage opener, and AAA membership card on the kitchen table.

"I know you'll do what's best for Marley," Ava said, reaching out to touch Pam's hands.

Pam forced a smile and stared out the window.

It was Thursday night, and Marley couldn't sleep. She lay in her bed and stared at the wall, feeling like a body without limbs. Never before had she had to cope with her mother being sick. Sure, she'd helped nurse her mother through common colds and influenza, but those ordinary occurrences could hardly be considered bumps in the road. This, though—this was cancer. This was serious. This could be fatal.

Like every child, Marley had experienced fleeting moments of thought about life without her mother. But she'd bulldozed those thoughts, laden with pain and a frightening sense of emptiness, out of her mind. Her mother had been the one sure thing in her life. Sacrificing, toiling relentlessly—almost slaving—to make sure Marley enjoyed a perception about her life and her circumstances and her fortune that was far greater, grander, comfier, than the story reality told.

As a grown woman, Marley knew her mother had put herself second so that Marley's needs and wants could be first. That knowledge bound her even closer to her mother, converting her resentment toward her father into rage. Silent rage, but rage nonetheless.

How dare he just leave the scene? Was he really at peace with himself when nothing short of lust had tricked him into walking out on his family, making him believe he was being "true" to himself? Did he think his bimonthly telephone calls, Valentine's Day roses, and holiday gifts filled the hole he'd left?

Marley propped herself up on her elbow and grabbed the telephone off the nightstand. She needed to talk to Gerrard. She needed to hear his voice.

"Hello," Gerrard whispered into the telephone. He was very clearly asleep.

"Hi, sweetie, it's me."

"What time is it?"

Marley glanced at the clock on her nightstand. "Little after one," she said, feeling slightly guilty.

Gerrard yawned. "What's wrong?"

"Nothing. *Everything.* I can't sleep. I keep thinking about my mother."

"Yeah," Gerrard said, sounding more lucid. "I know it's tough." He yawned again.

"I can't imagine what I would do without her, Gerrard." Abruptly, she stopped speaking. She felt a lump forming in her throat, and crying was the last thing she felt like doing.

"Don't imagine it. Don't even think like that. It'll be okay."

Somehow his response wasn't satisfying. In fact, it made her feel worse. "But what if it isn't? I mean, women die from cancer all the time."

"Yeah, but that doesn't mean you need to worry about it. Use positive thinking, Marley. Think positive thoughts, and you'll have a positive outcome."

Not only was he not making her feel better, but now he was irritating her. His transcendental motivational attempt wasn't giving her an ounce of encouragement. She sighed. "Fine, Gerrard. What are you doing this weekend?"

"I'll be tied up with my dad all weekend."

Marley rolled her eyes. He was unavailable. Again. "I thought we were going to start our registry on Saturday."

"I'm gonna leave that to you and your mom. Okay, baby? I trust your taste. That's why you're going to be Mrs. Shore."

"Yeah, but my mother is not going to be Mr. Shore. And she's sick, Gerrard. I wanted us to do the registry together." She paused. "This is getting really tired, you know."

"Look, let's not argue. It's one in the morning. Let's get some rest, and I'll call you at work, okay?"

"Good-bye, Gerrard."

"Good night, Marley. I love you. Oh, and don't forget to tell your mom and grandmother about my mother's Thanksgiving dinner invitation."

She hung up the telephone, sucking her teeth and shaking her head. She stared at the wall again, replaying her conversation with Gerrard and growing angrier. She felt like calling him back and telling him that she'd already mentioned the Thanksgiving dinner invitation to her mother and grandmother and that her grandmother had said she wouldn't be caught *dead* at the Shores' house for Thanksgiving even if the *Pilgrims* showed up to carve the turkey. She picked up the phone, then slammed it down and thrust her body against the mattress.

Across the world, children were starving. Downtown, not ten miles away, people were sleeping on grates. There were girls who had never known their mothers, boys who had never known their fathers, children who had never known love. Yet to Marley, nothing was worse than her trials and tribulations: her mother had cancer, her father was absent, and her fiancé didn't care. She tried to care more for the struggles of others' lives, but she couldn't. They were powerless; so was she. They needed help; so did she.

Chapter 8

"I'M SO GLAD you convinced her to go with us," Deanna said. She leaned forward on Marley's couch, rested her arms on top of her long, slender thighs, and clasped her hands together. Her Nefertiti bangles and gold bracelets jingled.

"Well, it wasn't easy," Ashley confessed, shaking her head. She put her index finger to her lips, reminding Deanna to lower her voice. "She's been very, very upset about her mom," Ashley added.

"Of course," Deanna said softly. "I can't even imagine how I would feel. She's doing much better than I would be, I know that."

"We should go visit Pam," Ashley said. "Not right now, of course, because we don't want to make her feel like she's on her deathbed. But in a few weeks. For now we can send her some flowers, and maybe a good book with psalms or daily motivations."

"That's a good idea," Deanna said. "I'll take care of it."

"Hey, you know what? I'll make her a quilt," Ashley said. "It'll be from both of us, of course."

"Oh, that would be wonderful." Deanna clasped her hands together hopefully.

"It'll take me a while, though. At least two months. Maybe longer."

"That's fine. Pam will appreciate it no matter when we give it to her," Deanna said.

Ashley's eyes traveled across the room as she looped several strands of hair around her finger. "Seems like Marley's been dealing with all of this by herself. That fool Gerrard certainly hasn't been any help."

"Ooh, he makes me sick," Deanna tried to whisper back.

Ashley shushed her again. "If she hears you, she will go ballistic, Deanna," Ashley reminded.

"Okay, okay, sorry, sorry," Deanna said. "Where is he this weekend?" she asked.

"Off handling business with Daddy, where else?" Ashley rolled her eyes.

"Have you had that talk with her yet? You know, about Gerrard and the relationship?"

"We talk about it all the time, Deanna," Ashley said, waving one hand in the air dismissively. "Marley knows how I feel about her relationship. She knows how both of us feel, so at this point all we can do is support her."

Deanna shook her head. She raised her finger and began to speak, with a neck roll to back it up, but Ashley quickly elbowed her.

"Whoa! Look at you, Marley! You look fantastic!" Ashley's grin was wide.

They turned to face Marley as she made her way down the steps. She smiled at them.

"No she didn't bust out with the silver shimmy-shimmy dress and silver shimmy-shimmy shoes," Deanna teased.

"That dress is gorgeous, girl," Ashley added. "You're gonna hurt the brothers tonight."

"Just trying to keep up with you, Ashley," Marley replied, only partly joking. Ashley was herself a knockout in her black off-the-shoulder form-fitting gown. Her hair was loose and combed straight back, revealing the new ruby-and-diamond earrings her father had bought her.

"Well, Marley wins tonight's award for quickest dresser. I sat at Ash's house for over an hour waiting on her to get ready." Deanna pulled an emery board out of her red-and-gold beaded purse and began to file vigorously at one of her nails.

"You're exaggerating terribly, Deanna. You hardly sat thirty minutes waiting on me." Ashley leaned back on the couch, her tresses landing softly on the sides of her arms.

"But you act like thirty minutes is thirty seconds, Ashley. I just don't understand why it always takes you, like, fifty hours to dress when we have somewhere to go. Most of the time you've thought all week about what you're going to wear, or you've gone out and bought something, so it's no big mystery. What happens between that point and the actual putting on of the clothes, I will never understand."

"Deanna, just because you dress like you're changing costumes between performances doesn't mean the rest of us have to dress as fast," Ashley said.

"Whatever," Deanna mumbled and tossed her freshly twisted hair—this week ash blond—in Ashley's direction. "We need to get going. The banquet starts in fifteen minutes, and the hotel is all the way in Buckhead."

Believers' Temple, the church to which Ashley and her parents belonged, was holding a banquet to celebrate their hundred-year anniversary. The girls had promised Ashley's mother months ago that they would purchase tickets to the banquet, never planning to attend until Mrs. Miller had called each of them last weekend to give them a "loving reminder." Marley had backed out and Mrs. Miller had understood completely, but Ashley had not let up.

"Let's go." Marley held her front door open as her friends walked out. "By the way," she said, locking the door behind them, "you-all really should talk a little lower the next time you have a conversation about Gerrard and me in my own living room." She turned around and walked past them.

Deanna and Ashley stared at each other.

They began the car drive in silence. Deanna glanced at Marley through the rearview mirror. "Marley, you know we didn't mean any harm—"

"Of course you didn't." Marley folded her hands across her lap.

"Seriously," Ashley said, feeling the worst. "All we were saying was that—"

"I know what you were saying. I heard it all, remember? And I know you didn't mean any harm. But how do you think it makes me feel to know that my friends don't like my fiancé? I'm marrying him, for goodness' sake. I know he's not perfect, and believe me, there are things about him that I would like to change. But the worst I can say about him is that he works too much and that affects the time he spends with me. I'm not pleased with it, but it's certainly not grounds for calling off the wedding."

"You're right, Marley. His working too hard is not the worst thing that can happen in a relationship. But it could lead to other, bigger problems down the road. That's all we're concerned about," Deanna said.

"Deanna, it took you two months to break up with Keith after Ashley saw him at the movies with another woman, so I'm having a *really* hard time hearing you," Marley snapped.

"Hey, hey, let's not get ugly here," Ashley intervened. "We were wrong for having that conversation without you, Marley. I understand how you feel, and I apologize. And you're right—Deanna of all people should be a little more sensitive to your situation." Ashley looked pointedly at Deanna.

Deanna sighed. "Sorry, Marley."

"Sorry, too," Marley responded.

"Good, we're all in love again," Ashley said, turning to face Marley. "Friends have a right to be concerned about one another," she continued. "And all we meant to say is that we want to make sure Gerrard's work, or whatever, doesn't get in the way of him being there for you—especially now when you need him the most."

"I understand your point," Marley said. "And I appreciate your concern. I really do."

The band was playing a rendition of "That Sunday, That Summer" when the girls arrived at the Grand Ritz Hotel. Buffet tables lined the walls inside the banquet hall. Crowding the floor was a sea of black faces adorned in tuxedos and bow ties and dresses of every imaginable fabric. Sisters' curls were tight; brothers' waves and kinks were neatly patted or matted into shape.

Mrs. Miller spotted the girls immediately. "Ashley! Over here, sugar!" she called from table ten.

The girls approached. "There they are," Mrs. Miller beamed. "Look at 'em. Aren't they something?"

"Yes indeedie," said one of Mrs. Miller's friends, who wore a flamingo pink feathered hat and a fuchsia sequined floor-length gown. The sequins were stretched so far out of place across her bosom that the black nylon lining was no longer lining anything.

"Ashley, you remember Mrs. Ainsley, don't you? She was your Girl Scout troop leader back in—oh goodness, how long ago, Dorothy?"

"Seventy-eight," Mrs. Ainsley said in between bites of buffalo wings. "Nineteen seventy-eight."

"I sure do remember," Ashley said sweetly. "How are you, Mrs. Ainsley?" She hugged her.

"Just fine, baby. You're looking mighty good. Mighty good," she said and suctioned a piece of chicken from between her front teeth.

"Thank you." Ashley looked Mrs. Ainsley up and down and

smiled. She'd have been lying if she returned the compliment because Mrs. Ainsley looked awful, just downright awful. "Thank you
very much," Ashley said. "It's so good to see you." That was the
truth.

"Let me introduce you to my friends," she added, putting her
hand on Mrs. Ainsley's shoulder.

"All right," said Mrs. Ainsley, her voice rich and creamy like
cheesecake.

"This is Deanna, and that's Marley."

"Nice to meet you," the girls said in unison.

"Mm-hm. And you." Mrs. Ainsley grinned, and the dentures at
the top of her mouth fell off her gums. With a swift click of her
tongue, Mrs. Ainsley locked them back into place. "That dern
generic brand of denture gook my husband bought me don't hardly
keep 'em in place right," she drawled, her eyes wandering across the
room without a trace of embarrassment. "Why ain't none of you
girls wear Thanksgiving colors? It's right 'round the corner, you
know." Mrs. Ainsley picked at her front teeth.

Deanna's eyes widened, and her mouth threatened to burst open
with something disastrous. "Mama," Ashley said, "we're gonna go
fix our plates." She nodded toward the buffet tables.

"Oh, absolutely, sugar. Go right ahead while everything is nice
and hot. Come on back and sit at the table with your father and
me," Mrs. Miller added and waved them off.

"Oh-my-goodness oh-my-goodness," Deanna mumbled in a mono-
tone voice as soon as they reached the buffet tables. "Don't look
now," she whispered, while she busied herself in front of the macaroni and cheese. Marley turned around and looked, and Deanna elbowed her firmly in her side.

"Ouch, Deanna! That hurt!"

"Why did you turn around and look? I told you not to look,"
Deanna whispered. "Now, I mean it this time. Don't look. I think
that's Pablo Hall over there in the far right corner."

Ashley turned around and looked in the far right corner. "You mean the guy in the checkered sports jacket?"

Deanna threw her hands up in the air. "I don't believe you-all. I say don't look, and what do you do?"

"Oh, get over it, Dee." Ashley put a roll on her plate.

"That *is* Pablo Hall," Marley whispered to Deanna, still looking in the far right corner.

"Marley, why in the world are you whispering?" Deanna bugged her eyes. "Everybody standing near us knows what we're talking about, and he already knows we're staring at him."

"He's much cuter in person than he is on TV," Marley said.

"He's my brother's favorite baseball player." Deanna tried to steal another glance across the room.

"You should go ask him for his autograph," Marley teased.

"Ha ha ha," Deanna said.

"Matter of fact, I think I'll let him know that we require his services."

"Marley, don't you dare—"

Deanna turned to see Marley waving Pablo over. He smiled and eagerly left the group of older women with whom he was talking.

"Thank you for saving my life," he said, approaching the girls and flashing teeth that were whiter than a Ken doll's. "I'm here with my grandmother, and I've been talking to the women in her bridge club for the last ten minutes. Not that I have anything against bridge."

Marley laughed. "Pablo, I want you to meet my girlfriend Deanna." Marley swept her right arm to the side, as if she were presenting Miss America.

"Hi, Pablo," Deanna said nervously and reached out to shake his hand.

"Very nice to meet you, Deanna." He took her hand in his, shook it, then pulled her closer and hugged her. Deanna blushed.

"We're all fans of yours," Marley continued, "but Deanna's little brother Marcus is probably your biggest fan ever. Would you mind giving Deanna your autograph for Marcus?"

"Not at all," Pablo said. "How old is Marcus?"

"Ah, he'll be, ah, twelve—no, thirteen, yeah, thirteen, um, next month."

Pablo chuckled. "You should bring him by Scout's Alley next Friday afternoon. We're doing a little meet-and-greet session with the Fulton County Science Fair winners. I'll put your brother's name on the list if you think he can make it."

"Really?" Deanna's eyes widened. "I'm sure he can make it. He won't believe this."

"Will *you* be able to bring him?" Pablo smiled. It was clear that he was hoping to see Deanna again.

"Me? Ah, yeah. Yes, I can bring him. Definitely."

"Good." He finished writing his message to Marcus on a banquet program. "I'm looking forward to meeting him. And I'm *really* looking forward to seeing you again."

"Likewise," Deanna said, her overstated confidence finally surfacing. "It's a date."

"It sure is." Pablo and Deanna locked eyes, temporarily oblivious to everything surrounding them. "Ladies," he said, breaking away, "it was very nice meeting you. Enjoy the banquet." He waved goodbye and then walked across the room and sat at a table next to an older woman, who patted him on his head and pressed it down on her small shoulder.

"You can thank me at your wedding," Marley said.

"Whatever you do," Ashley said, "don't break up with him before the World Series. Atlanta's got a good chance of making it this year, and you need to get us tickets if they go."

"Can you let the brother ask me out before you start scheming on how to hit him up for World Series tickets? Goodness!"

The girls made their way to the table where the Millers were seated. "Hey, save me a seat," Marley said quickly, handing Ashley her plate. "I need to run to the rest room."

"Hurry up," Ashley said. "Mama will have a fit if you miss any part of the keynote address. Reverend Baldwin's been working on it all year, you know."

"How old is that man?" Deanna asked. "Looks like he's pushing ninety."

"Ninety-two," Ashley said.

"Oh, Lord. He'll still be acknowledging the distinguished guests by the time I get back," Marley teased and waved at them as she walked away.

Making her way down the marble-tiled hall, Marley noticed the pictures hanging on the walls. They depicted battle scenes from the Civil War. Marley studied the pictures closely and wasn't surprised that no black faces were included. She sighed, wishing she were roaming the halls of a black-owned hotel, where portraits of Frederick Douglass and Harriet Tubman would hang in place of Stonewall Jackson and Robert E. Lee, where Monk, rather than Mozart, might drift from the recessed speakers overhead. "Makes no sense," she said out loud, wondering what was wrong with black people, when suddenly Ma Grand's voice cut through her self-righteous scolding. "How many times did you patronize Paschals?" Ma Grand had grilled her when the news had broken that the hotel's ownership had changed hands.

Marley spotted an exquisite walnut bombé chest and thought about her mother. For months, Pam had been searching for a piece to replace the mahogany console with the broken leg that stood crooked in her foyer. Marley decided she'd bring her mother by the hotel in a few weeks, after the surgery, to show her the chest. In fact, she'd call her tonight, as soon as she left the bathroom, and tell her about it. That would cheer her. Take her mind off things. She'd call even though Pam had told her to stop calling two and three times a day. Said Marley was making her feel as though she already had one foot in her grave. The chest would be an exception, Marley figured. Her mother would want to know about the chest.

Seeing no signs that pointed in the direction of the rest rooms, Marley walked to the front desk and stood behind a woman who appeared to be checking in to the hotel. Marley started to bounce and bop to the imaginary music in her head, the music she played when she had to fight the urge to pee on the spot. *I wish this woman would hurry up and get checked in,* she thought, leaning to the right to peer over the woman's shoulder and determine whether she was almost finished with whatever she was doing.

"We've put the champagne and the chocolate-covered strawberries in your suite as you requested," the concierge said.

"Thank you, sir." The woman tossed her long ringlets over her shoulder. Marley admired the woman's hair, how it shone under the light the way the Pantene Pro-V models' hair did on the commercials. She gave her own strands a critical, compassionless tug. She'd been letting her hair "grow out" for years, but it seemed as though it was still hanging at the same length, somewhere near her shoulder blades—and maybe in the middle of them on a good day. *No more trims,* she declared to herself. Then she realized she was being ridiculous. *I'll just hold a mirror in my hand and watch Lucy's scissors very closely,* she thought, satisfied.

"That will make things perfect," the woman said. Marley smiled. The woman was obviously about to share a romantic evening with someone she loved. Marley thought about Gerrard and suddenly felt alone. Maybe she would call him on his cell phone and tell him she missed him.

The woman turned and began to walk away. Her eyes met Marley's, and the two shared a smile. A kindred smile, which vanished without warning when the woman stopped in her tracks as if she'd forgotten something.

"Everything okay, ma'am?" the concierge asked.

"Yes," she said quickly, not bothering to turn around. "Everything's fine, thanks." She walked away quickly, her Via Spigas click-ing rhythmically against the marble floor.

The concierge shrugged and looked at Marley. "May I help you, ma'am?"

"Yes. Where is your rest room?" Marley bounced on one leg.

He smiled. "Emergency, I see. It's around the corner, just past the main entrance, and to the right of the elevators."

"Thank you." Marley practically ran around the corner, making it just in time to avoid major embarrassment.

As she left the rest room and walked past the elevators, she smelled a familiar scent. It lingered around her senses like clean linen, like an herbal bath. Such a sweet, sweet, familiar smell. It embraced her, welcomed her, reminded her of old, good times.

She heard low voices inside the elevator to her far left. She quickened her pace and reached the last elevator just as the doors were beginning to close.

There was the woman. The one with the Pantene hair and the feisty Via Spigas. She was being held and kissed on the forehead. A deep dimple surfaced on her cheek as she smiled. Marley's eyes traveled from the dimple to the cheek of the man she was embrac-ing. She knew that cheek. That skin. Those lips. That smile.

"Gerrard?" Marley stared blankly inside the elevator. Gerrard turned his head, and his eyes bolted wide. Marley charged forward and tried to put her hands inside the elevator doors, but they had shut. She pressed her hands against the doors and banged on them. "Gerrard! Gerrard!" Her voice echoed inside the elevator bank, au-dible only to herself.

Marley rested her face on the steel doors. She swallowed hard, trying to slow down her breathing. She stepped backward, looked up to see which floor number was illuminated on the panel, and saw that the elevator was going to the fifteenth floor. The top floor. Marley pounded the up button and hopped frantically onto the middle elevator. She wrapped her arms around her waist as the elevator rose, rocking herself back and forth, still trying to slow her quickening heart rate. She coughed and patted her chest. The elevator doors opened, and she stepped off.

Marley looked around. She saw Persian rugs, French Provincial sofas, Louis VIII armchairs, and Monet replicas—but no Gerrard. She yelled his name several times but got no response.

She sunk onto a settee, rested her head in her hands, and waited on the tears to come, but they wouldn't. She rewound the scene she'd just witnessed, hoping and praying that her eyes had deceived her. But she knew they hadn't. She had seen Gerrard. Her fiancé. The man she had loved since she'd become a woman. The man she was to marry. It was all true—all of what was happening in her life. Today, she'd seen her fiancé behaving as if the name *Marley* meant nothing to him. As if he didn't even love her. As if he didn't even know her.

"Marley."

She looked up. Gerrard was standing in front of her, his hands in his pockets, his head hung low, his eyes avoiding hers.

"Please listen to me," he began, his voice hoarse.

Marley jumped out of the settee and lunged forward. The Persian rug slipped underneath her feet, and Gerrard caught her. Marley collapsed into his arms and cried while he held her tightly. She caught her breath and began to pound ferociously on his muscular shoulders, trying to fight her way out of his tight grip. "You bastard! You trifling, lying—"

"Shh," Gerrard said as he tried to rock Marley back and forth, but she kneed him in the groin and broke free.

"You lying bastard!" She dropped her arms beside her waist and wiped her hands on the sides of her dress. The moisture left two indentations in the silk fabric. "You've been lying to me all this time." She covered her mouth with one hand.

"Marley, listen." Gerrard limped toward her, his face contorted.

"Stay the hell away from me, Gerrard," she cried, stepping back. "You're a liar. A cheating, low-down, trifling dog of a liar. How could you *do* this to me?"

"I'm sorry. I'm so, so sorry, Marley." His eyes were red. "I've been so selfish and so wrong, and I never, ever wanted to hurt you." A tear dropped and he slapped it away.

Marley sat down, wiped her eyes, and looked squarely at Gerrard for the first time that evening. All she could see was a lie. A perfect well-groomed lie.

"You've been wasting my time. Wasting my mother's money. You couldn't just be a man, Gerrard? You couldn't just say you weren't ready for marriage?" The tears continued to flow.

Gerrard sat on the couch across from Marley. He put his hands over his face, then rubbed his temples. "I was trying to be a man. The man I was raised to be. The man my daddy raised me to be."

"*What?* You don't have enough sense to realize that you don't have to do everything your father does? You can't just draw the line at the point of decency and decide not to cross it, even if it means you won't please your daddy?"

He sighed and leaned back on the couch. "I know, I know. I realize now how wrong I've been. You have to believe me, Marley."

She glared at him. "I will never believe another word you say." She stood and walked to the elevator. She pressed the down button and faced the elevator doors, tapping her foot, waiting on the doors to open. *Open, open, come on, please open.* The elevator arrived. She stepped on, and for a minute her heart really stopped beating and air really seemed to have escaped her lungs when she turned and saw Gerrard still seated on the couch.

She stared at him. Her voice was a hoarse whisper. "You're actually going to *stay* here?" She already knew the answer.

"I need to talk to Angela. I need to explain to her that—"

"You lying dog! You lying, lowlife—"

"Marley, no, wait!" Gerrard hopped off the couch. He tried to catch the elevator doors, but he was too late.

It was a long ride down. Nothing seemed clear to her. The numbers on the panel inside the elevator, the green wool threads in the carpet—all of it was a blur. She couldn't deny what she had seen. No way she could deny it. It was so horrible, such an awful, awful truth, that she wished to God there was a possibility she had misread the situation. Assumed too much. It hurt so badly that she began to wish, shamefully, she hadn't seen Gerrard in the hall. If he hadn't come out to talk to her and if he hadn't said what he said, then she could have continued to be the same Marley she'd been when she'd left her friends in the banquet hall. She would have said anything, done anything to change the fate she had just confronted.

The elevator reached the lobby. She pulled herself together well enough to slip into the rest room without anyone noticing her swollen eyelids. She splashed cold water onto her face and stared at her reflection. She didn't recognize herself. The woman in the mirror was pained, shaken, desperate. She was heavy, much too heavy, for Marley to wear.

How in the world was she going to tell her friends? She couldn't. The pain was too intense, the incident too fresh, the embarrassment too great. Maybe tomorrow, after she'd gotten some perspective on the situation. Tonight she needed to go home, get in her bed, and be alone.

The keynote address was well under way when Marley returned to the banquet hall. She eased up the right side of the room and caught Ashley's eye. Her eyes widened when she saw Marley, and she furrowed her brow. Marley motioned her outside.

"Where have you been?" Ashley whispered, as soon as she opened the doors. "You know my mother is having a fit." Ashley's hands were on her hips.

"Girl, I gotta go." Marley looked at her friend, and she couldn't fight back the tears.

"What's wrong?" Ashley moved closer to Marley. "Is Pam okay?"

"She's fine. She's fine," Marley said, sniffling. "Everything's fine. I can't go into it now, but I'll call you tomorrow morning."

"Marley, what's wrong?" Ashley's tone was serious, and her eyes were concerned. "I can't let you leave like this, at least not without knowing whether you'll be okay."

"Ashley, trust me. I'll be fine. You know I would tell you if I weren't okay. I promise I'll call you tomorrow. Right now I just need some space." Marley sniffled again and dabbed at the corners of her eyes with a tissue.

Ashley stared across the room, contemplating what Marley had said, deciding whether to accept it. "How are you going to get home?"

"I'm gonna take a cab."

"What? And spend all that money?"

"Ashley, really, it's not a problem. I want to do it. I don't want to interrupt Deanna. Plus, I need the time to myself. Okay?"

Ashley was silent, her forehead wrinkled. "You leave me a message on my machine as soon as you get home so I'll know you made it. Okay?"

"I will," Marley agreed. "I will."

"All right. I'll talk to you tomorrow. I'll come over," Ashley added, staring at her friend.

"Okay. I'm gonna run now. See you tomorrow." Marley gave Ashley a quick kiss on the cheek and walked away.

She searched the shelves in her pantry frantically. She knew she'd stashed them in there somewhere. She knocked over boxes of microwave popcorn, Honey Nut Cheerios, and Wheat Thins until she found them: two bottles of Merlot one of Gerrard's French business associates had given them as an engagement gift. She grabbed them both, along with a goblet, and went into the living room.

Several minutes passed. She stared out the window and listened to Sade sing "Is It a Crime?" It was a crime, Marley thought, that Gerrard was such a lowlife he'd cheat on her four months before their wedding. A week before Thanksgiving. Didn't he have any measure of loyalty to the holidays, if not to her?

Marley poured wine into the goblet and stared at it. It was a crime that his unfaithfulness had never occurred to her. She gulped down all of the wine and poured another glass. She reclined on the couch. The Italian leather was stiffer, colder than normal. Her tears rolled easily, and she tasted their salt in the corners of her mouth.

It's a crime that I've been so stupid, Marley thought, and she sat up quickly. She gulped down the second glass of wine and stared at the table. She felt her empty stomach knot up, and queasiness began to set in. *Crime that I thought he loved me.* She wept silently, holding the glass to her cheek. *Crime that I'm all alone. Just like my mother.*

She filled the glass again, drank it all, and tossed herself back on the couch. The room had begun to spin, but she didn't mind. No physical side effect could match the emotional nausea that had subsumed her. Indeed, she welcomed it all and hoped it would distract her somehow. But fifteen minutes later it hadn't. The images of Gerrard and the woman in the elevator were, it seemed, even more vivid in her mind. And even more painful. "Angela," he'd said. *Angela.*

She poured another glass and gulped it down, then wiped her mouth firmly with the back of her hand, hitting her bottom lip with her sapphire ring. She barely felt the throbbing in her lip, and she certainly didn't taste the blood the stone had drawn. She felt good and dizzy now. Good and unstable. Good and numb. Her mind raced back to images of her father retreating to the living room, late at night, after yet another argument with her mother culminating in a slammed bedroom door. She saw him holding a brandy snifter in his hands, smiling at her with glassy eyes, assuring her that Daddy was fine, was just relaxing, and telling her to go back to bed. She wished, now, for the same relaxation—the same fix that had enabled her father to smile through his pain.

"All a crime. It's all a crime. All is," she slurred and climbed the steps to her bedroom. She managed to peel all her clothes off before she collapsed into her bed. "And I don't care no more," she mumbled, thankful that inebriation and drowsiness had blunted her pain, even if only for the moment. If they could shield her long enough to allow her to fall asleep without the image of Gerrard in her head, she would be thankful forever more. "I'll be thankful," she said, talking to God, then laughing, deciding He was ignoring her. But she kept talking. "Please, please, just keep the image away, please," she slurred. "Greatly appreciate if you do."

Chapter 9

THE NEXT AFTERNOON, Marley pulled up in front of Ashley's house, turned off the ignition, and stared at her dashboard until it, the steering wheel, and the windshield become one big amalgamated haze. This was not going to be an easy conversation.

Marley took a deep breath and knocked on the door. She had a major headache, no doubt from the shameful amount of drinking she'd done the night before.

"Marley?" Ashley said from behind the door.

"Yeah, it's me."

Ashley opened the door. "How *are* you?" Her face was twisted with concern.

"I could be better," Marley said and unzipped her FUBU windbreaker. She flopped on Ashley's couch and kicked off her tennis shoes.

"You know I would have gone to your house if you had let me."

"I know, but I needed to get out." Marley got up and walked into the kitchen. "I'm gonna fix myself some tea. Do you want some?"

"Yeah, chamomile, please." Ashley sat in her rocking chair and folded her hands on top of her knees.

Marley returned to the living room with two mugs and set one in front of Ashley on the distressed wood table. Marley sipped her tea. "Well, what can I say? It's over with Gerrard and me." She stared at the rim of her mug.

Ashley reached for her tea and took a sip. Figuring that Marley needed a minute to pull herself together, Ashley fought her inclination to go hug her. Instead she remained silent.

"I caught him cheating on me."

"Are you serious? When?" Ashley asked, setting her mug on the table.

"Last night." Marley smiled as a tear cascaded down her cheek.

"Aw, sweetie." Ashley walked over to the couch and sat beside Marley. She rubbed Marley's back gently. "It's all right."

Marley leaned back on the couch. Ashley scooted to the other side, folded her legs, and faced Marley. She started to speak but stopped herself. Trying to teach her kindergarten class to be better listeners had shown her some things about herself. She pressed her lips together.

"When I left to go to the bathroom, I saw him in the hotel. On the elevator with another woman. They were——" Marley shook her head and covered her mouth.

"It's all right, sweetie, it's all right," Ashley reassured her. "You talk whenever you're ready to talk."

"They were hugging, embracing, or whatever. I don't really know what I saw, but I know I saw them all over each other. I prayed it wasn't really Gerrard, but I knew deep in my heart that it was. I followed them up in another elevator, and he came out into the hallway."

"How'd he know you were in the hallway?"

Marley paused. "I think I might have screamed his name a couple of times." She looked at Ashley sheepishly, and Ashley tried but failed to suppress a grin. "I was screaming like a madwoman, to tell the truth," she said, and they laughed. A little. That little laugh was like a droplet of water against a dry throat. Barely soothing. Soon forgotten.

"Anyway, he came out into the hallway and tried to explain himself. Talked about his understanding of manhood, which he claimed he'd learned from his father. Then he tried to apologize and tell me how he'd never meant to hurt me. All that standard crap."

"Where was the girl during all of this?"

"I guess she was in their room. I don't know." Marley sipped her tea.

"So what happened after that?"

"I left." She stared ahead, avoiding Ashley's eyes. This part was the most embarrassing, in her mind, because it was the part where Gerrard could have tried to save himself if he really wanted to. But he hadn't. He'd stayed where he was. Hadn't gone after her. Hadn't even tried.

"And what did Gerrard do?" Ashley asked, her voice louder, her tone questioning.

"He stayed at the hotel, I guess." Marley shifted in her seat and began to twist her ring. She looked at the beige carpet. Except for the shadow of the stain the brown hair dye had left when Deanna had spilled it on her way to the powder room one Saturday, the carpet still looked brand new.

"Has he called you today?"

"Nope."

Ashley picked up her mug and took another sip of tea, even though she didn't want it. Sipping the tea was all she could do to hold her tongue. Given the opportunity, she thought to herself, she could actually kill Gerrard for this.

Marley sighed. "But there's so much more to it, Ash. Things haven't been perfect. I've had some concerns for a while, mainly because he wasn't spending a lot of time with me. It was bothering me so much," Marley said, "that I convinced Gerrard we should see a counselor." She tried to read Ashley's initial reaction, but Ashley's face was blank. *Had she already known?*

"Did you know about the counseling?"

"No, Marley. Just go on."

"Well, the counseling didn't change anything. Granted, we only went once, but still. He acted like it was the biggest waste of time, like everything was completely fine with us and I was overreacting. And now I find out he's been dogging me the entire time." Another tear streamed down her face. "Ashley, I know I haven't been talking to you about everything that's been going on with Gerrard and me. I've been trying to work through it all, to sort it out, you know? It has nothing to do with our friendship." She looked at Ashley.

"Girl, you know you don't need to feel bad about that. This isn't first grade, when I used to catch an attitude with you because you didn't tell me what color ribbon you were going to wear to school. True friendship is elastic. Plus, I respect the sacredness of the bond between a man and a woman—at least in marriage. I wouldn't ever want to interfere with what's between Gerrard and you.

"At the same time, though," Ashley continued, leaning forward and placing her mug on the table, "true friends always keep it real with each other. And true friends have an obligation to speak openly and honestly when they sense change. I would be less than honest if I didn't tell you that it was obvious something was wrong with you and Gerrard."

Marley's stomach turned a little, and her muscles tensed up, but she listened.

"One of the most obvious signs was that you never wanted to talk about your wedding. Getting married and planning a wedding is a girl's dream, Marley. So there was no way you could fool anybody into thinking everything was peaches and cream when you were dodging questions about the wedding. Talking 'bout, 'I haven't planned that part yet,' when people had basic questions about things that you should've planned a long time ago. I didn't know the details of your relationship, but I know you well enough to know that something was wrong. I knew the relationship was not inspiring you to be a better person."

"Wait a minute, Ashley. Don't make things out to be worse than they really are. Things haven't been spectacular, but my relationship with Gerrard is not *that* bad."

"I was talking about you, not the relationship. But since you've brought up the relationship, explain to me how it isn't *that* bad? Explain to me how cheating is not *that* bad, Marley."

"Like I said, things haven't been perfect. But how many men do you know who haven't cheated when times got rough? I'm not making excuses for him, and I'm certainly not justifying cheating. A dog is a dog. But I'm asking you to be honest. What men do you know who haven't cheated during hard times?"

"Real men don't, Marley. And *why*," she asked, nearing exasperation, "are we talking in the present tense when your relationship with Gerrard is now a thing of the past? It's over, right?"

"Look, cheating is bad, okay? But our foundation was strong. I can't imagine that we couldn't restore it if we really wanted to." Marley hoped Ashley wouldn't press her, again, to answer the question whether the relationship was over. It *was* over, in a sense. It was over because it had to be over, at least for now. But deep inside, Marley knew she couldn't quite will herself to say that it was over for good, forever, if Gerrard came running back and promised her that things would change.

That's why Ashley's words were idealistic as far as Marley was concerned. They sounded good; they sounded like words to live by. They sounded like the words of a woman operating under a self-inflicted decision to "date herself." But standing in the thick of it, in the thick of the real world of men rather than the world of real men like Marley was, Ashley's words were just that: words.

"The question is," Ashley said, "is it a 'we' thing or a 'you' thing?

I see you making an effort—you know, cooking breakfast and all that stuff—but someone who cancels dates with you on a regular basis doesn't sound too interested in restoring a foundation." Ashley leaned forward, arms resting on her thighs, and folded her hands.

"Listen, it's not my place to judge how strong your foundation is—or *was*—with Gerrard, or whether it can ever be restored. But let's really consider the foundation. He was dating Shelley from Georgia Tech when he hooked up with you. That's cheating. From what I remember, he strung Shelley along for quite a while before he broke it off and started seeing you exclusively. That's dishonesty. I know he was charming and kind and thoughtful and deep, and he used to make you feel beautiful and like you could conquer the world and all that, but cheating and dishonesty are still parts of your foundation with him. I know he used to encourage you, but how's he been making you feel lately, Marley?"

Marley looked at Ashley and smiled. Ashley simply wasn't equipped to grasp the total picture. This wasn't a high school "I quit you" thing. This was her future marriage on the line.

"Ash, I appreciate your candor. I really do. It's one of the things I love most about you. But these are serious issues I'm facing right now, and I can't just walk away overnight from my history and my future with Gerrard. You can't do that when you're married, you know. You can't just walk away when things get bad."

"But you're not married yet, thank the Lord. And a man who's ready for marriage doesn't behave like this."

Marley sighed and rested her head on her hand. "I can't help but feel like it's easy for you to sit there and say what you're saying."

"I don't deny that it is. I'm not even pretending I have the hard part in this. *You* do. It is very easy for me to say what I'm saying and very hard for you to actually put it into practice. But that doesn't change the fact that you have to do it."

"I don't want to talk about this anymore." Marley rubbed her temples.

"No problem," Ashley said quickly and hopped off the couch. "You hungry? I'm starving. Let's go to Buster's Kitchen." She took their mugs into the kitchen.

Marley stood and stretched her arms. "Did you go to church this morning?" she asked, knowing that Ashley rarely missed a Sunday.

"Yep," she said, turning off the faucet. "You would've flipped out at the subject of today's sermon. It was about faithfulness."

"Humph." Marley rolled her eyes and bent down to tie her shoelaces.

"You really should go with me next Sunday. I think you'd be pleasantly surprised. You'd leave feeling much better than when you arrived, I promise."

The thought of Ashley's church made Marley want to laugh. It was worse than Pam's church, with the four offerings it took per service, the raffle tickets it was always selling for some cause that could never quite be explained, and the greasy fish fries that lit up all of Edgewood Avenue and made Sweet Auburn smell sour. All these churches that were so busy being about everything except God had worked Marley's last nerve. She'd simply seen too much, and felt too little, to be bothered with them.

"I'll think about it," Marley said. "You ready?"

Chapter 10

AM WAS DOING well, considering the circumstances. Her surgery was the next morning. She was packing her bag for the hospital, handling the preparations as if she were going on a five-day, four-night Caribbean excursion. But when she heard Marley's car pull into the driveway, she got emotional again.

What scared Pam most of all was the possibility that she would not be around to watch her only child complete her transition into womanhood. There were so many things still undone. There was the wedding she was planning for Marley, the wedding she'd determined would be the one she'd never had, even if she had to spend her last dime. Not that it would be the first time Pam had spent herself to within one step of the poorhouse on Marley's account. Ma Grand's favorite pastime during Marley's childhood had been telling Pam how absolutely stupid she was being for spending more on Marley than she could afford. The piano lessons, the dance costumes, the debutante gowns, the quality clothing—all of it had added up to more than she could reasonably handle on a single income. She'd had to jump through some hoops, take out some loans, make ends meet in ways even Ma Grand didn't know. But given the chance, Pam would do it all over again—and not out of obligation or a sense of pride or pretense, those superficialities she suspected had often motivated her own mother when Pam was coming of age. She would do it all over again because Marley, her princess, deserved no less.

"Hey, Mom," Marley said from the foyer, keys and bags jingling and rustling.

"Hey." Pam closed her armoire doors. "Be down in a minute."

"Okay, but hurry up. I brought you some food, and I don't want it to get cold."

In the midst of all the packing, Pam hadn't thought about eating, which wasn't good because the hospital staff had instructed her not to eat after five o'clock. It was half past three, and she was hungry. She quickly made her way downstairs.

"How you feeling?" Marley asked, hugging her mother tightly.

"Not bad. Not bad at all." She did well at smiling.

"Good. You hungry?" Marley busied herself setting a place for her mother at the kitchen table.

"Yes. Thank you, honey." Pam sat down and watched Marley spoon pasta onto a plate.

"What time do you have to be at the hospital in the morning?" Marley sat down.

"I've got to be at the admissions desk by eight o'clock."

"Okay. I'll just stay over tonight instead of coming back in the morning to pick you up."

"Oh, no, honey, you don't have to do that. Ava can take me."

"Ava?"

"Yeah. I already asked her. I didn't want to impose on your schedule, knowing how busy you are. You know it's easy for Ava to do it because she makes her own hours during the week. It's okay, honey, really." Pam tugged at the fringes of the table runner.

"Mommy, why would you ask Ava to take you when I can easily do it myself? Why are you always asking Ava to do things and not telling me about it?"

This is about the biopsy, Pam thought. Marley still had not gotten over the fact that Pam had asked Ava to be with her through the procedure. "Marley, really, I was just trying to consider your schedule. But if you can do it, that's just fine. I'll tell Ava not to worry about it. I didn't know, that's all."

"Yes, I can do it. And what about Gran? Have you talked to her? I'm sure she wants to get to the hospital at some point tomorrow."

"I talked to her earlier this morning. She wants to go whenever someone can pick her up and take her. She was talking about having Sadie drive her over, and I reminded her that Motor Vehicle did not renew Sadie's driving license because Sadie can't see well. Of course that threw Mama into a tizzy, and she started telling me how Sadie can see better than you and I put together, even with her bifocals, and that Sadie was the safest driver she knew, and if she had her way then Sadie would be the only person she'd ever get into a car with."

Marley laughed.

"So I said, 'Fine, Mama, let Sadie drive you over. I hope the police don't stop you because I'll be in surgery and I won't be able to bail you out of jail when they lock you and Sadie up.' "

"That's your mama," Marley joked. "I'll call her and let her know I can pick her up after I get you situated."

"Good." Pam ate a few forkfuls of her pasta. "So how'd it go with the registry? Did you and Gerrard decide on Macy's?"

"Ah, yeah, we did." Marley stood abruptly and looked at her watch. "I'm going upstairs—I need to make a business call."

"But aren't you going to eat some of this pasta?"

"I ate earlier," Marley called back, already on her way upstairs.

*   *   *

The sound of the shower in the hall bathroom startled Pam from her nap. She glanced at the clock on her nightstand and realized she had slept much longer than she'd planned. She still had a few things to put into her suitcase.

She walked toward her bathroom and waited to see what emotion had come to visit her that hour. It was like a roller-coaster ride, this cancer thing. One minute she was fine; the next she felt like jumping out of a twenty-story window. She sat on the toilet and felt fear, so familiar, caress her shoulders. She wept a little, thinking about all the women she knew whose lives had ended with breast cancer. Aunt Sarah had died from it just last year. The nasty thing had taken Silas's mother at an early age, after three long, battling years. And it had killed Clarise, Pam's and Ava's college buddy, about five years ago. The only breast cancer survivor she knew was her mother, who was an exception as far as she was concerned. Her mother had simply dealt with too much grief in her life for God to take her out on account of cancer. Her mother deserved, more than anyone else, to die peacefully in her sleep.

The lyrics to a song on the radio caught her attention. "God has not given us a spirit of fear," the choir belted out. *Humph,* Pam mumbled to herself. If that were true, why was she so afraid?

And who wouldn't be afraid? The next morning, Pam was scheduled to lose a breast—part of the essence of her womanhood. A pillar that supported her self-worth. What kind of woman would she be after that? She knew that married women who had mastectomies often were concerned about whether their husbands would still desire them. Well, she didn't have a husband, and after this she'd have a snowball's chance in hell of finding one. Sure, she could wear a breast form like her seventy-eight-year-old mother, who had no desire ever to have sex with a man again, much less to have her breasts touched or her nipples kissed. She could have a new breast created from the fat in her stomach, but she'd heard too many horror stories about how the re-created breast gains weight on its own and can become twice the size of the normal breast. How grand it would be, the day her oversized breast busted out of one of her V-neck blouses and slapped an innocent client in the face as she bent over a conference table to point out fabrics and wallpaper samplings.

Soon Pam would start to lose her hair. Next to her breasts, her hair had truly been her crowning glory. Her hairstylist had been trying for years to coax her into posing for some of the trendy hair magazines because her hair was so "perfect." People constantly commented on the luster and body her hair retained, whether in a short bob or a long, layered cut. It had been that way since she'd been a child. Little boys had pulled on her ponytails at the playground, and during beauty parlor time at her childhood slumber parties, the girls had always wanted to do Pam's hair first. Now, though, she would be reduced to wearing wigs. Women would publicly pat her on the back and tell her she still looked good; secretly they would pity her for such a shameful loss.

Then her eyebrows would thin, and she would have to draw some on her face, which would be bloated along with other parts of her body. And she would often be constricted by pain and fatigue. That was what awaited her. And after enduring all of it, she very well might die. This was the existence, the reality that, according to the song on the radio, Pam was not supposed to fear.

She crawled back into bed and fell asleep, clutching her pillow to her chest.

Ma Grand was sitting on her front porch, on her favorite rocking bench with the gardenia-print cushions, when Marley turned onto Waterford Drive and parked in front of the tan brick, pink-shuttered house. It had belonged to Rowland's parents, but they had given it to Rowland and Bess as a wedding gift in the spring of 1941. Rowland had built the front porch and the rocking bench himself, not long after Steven had been born. He'd said his wife and child deserved to sit on the porch and breathe the great outdoors whenever the wind so moved them. Many a morning, like today, Ma Grand sat and lost her eyes to the sky. Searching for Rowland. Searching for Steven. Searching for answers. Screaming for peace.

"Hey, Gran," Marley said, kissing her on the cheek and sitting beside her.

"Hello." Ma Grand continued to stare at the sky.

"You're not cold out here?" Marley asked, rubbing her hands together. "It's chilly."

"No, I'm not."

"How you doin' today, Gran?"

"How do you think I'm doing today, Marley? Not good."

"I know. It's hard for all of us. But we've got to be strong, especially for Mommy."

Ma Grand looked at her. "Don't tell me I've got to be strong, Marley. Especially when I can look at your face and see the swelling in your eyelids from all the crying you've been doing. I am going to be strong. I *am* strong. I been strong for this family all my life. But I have a right," Ma Grand continued, her voice cracking as her hand pounded the armrest, "not to be doing good today." She pushed her weight down on her heels and forced the bench into rocking motion.

"I dealt with breast cancer when I was sixty-five years old. It was hard enough then, but Lord knows it can't compare to your mother having to deal with it at fifty-two." She took a deep breath, tinged with the rasp of asthma and age, and continued. "Pamela has been through more than one person should have to deal with in a lifetime. That no-good cheating fool she married. The sacrifices she made so he could get ahead in his career—that was the most important thing to him. The struggles she faced after he left her without a dime and didn't even have the decency to provide for you on a regular basis."

"Ma Grand, that's enough," Marley interrupted. "I'm not going to listen to this today. Not today, okay?" Marley's eyes began to water.

"You don't have to listen to it. But it's the truth."

"It's *not* the truth, Gran. You don't know everything, even though you think you do. There are things my father did for me that you'll never know about."

"That doesn't change what he did to your mother, which I do know about. I'm not going to talk about this with you anymore. You're too young and naive to understand. Come on here and take me on to this hospital right now. You're making my blood pressure go up." She stood and grabbed the overnight bag she had placed beside the rocking bench.

"I'll carry it," Marley said, reaching to take the bag from her.

"Girl, leave this bag alone and come on now. I'm ready to go. Been ready since six o'clock this morning when y'all were just turning over in your beds. Come on here and carry me up to this hospital. Let's go."

Marley followed Ma Grand as she hobbled down the steps with her cane in one hand and her overnight bag in the other.

"Gran, do you mind if we stop at Lenox before we go to the hospital? I want to pick up a nice gown and robe for Mom to lounge in." Marley looked over at Ma Grand, who was staring out the car window.

"Naw, I don't mind. I wanted to get her some more house slippers myself. Lord knows the ones she's been wearing look like a dog's had at them for a good while now."

Marley laughed, and they drove on in silence. "Gran, I didn't mean to insult you earlier." She kept her eyes on the road. "It's hard for all of us, and honestly, I can't imagine what it feels like for you to watch your daughter going through this. I know it's painful, and

I didn't mean to belittle that or to try to tell you how to handle the situation."

"Child, I don't pay you no mind. You should know that by now. You'll learn to listen to me one day."

"I listen to you now, Ma Grand." Marley was happy that her grandmother was her snappy, witty self again. "You know," Marley said as she drove, "I do wonder a lot what it was like when you were raising Mom."

"What do you mean, 'what it was like'?" Ma Grand snapped.

She wanted to know what kind of mother Ma Grand had been and how her child rearing had shaped her daughter into the woman she was. Marley wanted to know why Ma Grand and her mother weren't very close, yet were there for each other at times and in ways no one else would be. That was what Marley meant, but she needed to figure out how to put it to Ma Grand diplomatically. Ma Grand was no fool.

"I mean, did you and Mom do a lot of things as mother and daughter, or was it more that you-all did things as an entire family, with Grampy and Steven?"

"We did both. I took your mother to her various classes and group meetings. I was a leader or teacher at many of them, like the Girl Scouts. And Rowland took Steven to Boy Scouts. We also did things as a family. We went to church together. We did what most families did, I guess you could say." Ma Grand looked down at her hands, then stared out the window.

"Would you say that you and Mom were close when she was growing up?"

"What do you mean, 'close'?" Ma Grand snapped back in the same defensive tone she'd used a few minutes before. "If you mean was I telling her I loved her all the time and such nonsense as that, no, I was not!" Ma Grand rolled her eyes. "I hear all these mothers running 'round today talking 'bout 'I love you' and 'I'm your best friend' and all that foolishness. And that ain't helping the child one bit. I was not trying to be a *friend* to my children. I was trying to be a mother. Of course I *loved* my children. I got up and went to work every day, came home and cooked every night, and got up every weekend morning to cart them around town to where they needed to be so they could have opportunities in life. If that's not love, then I don't know what is."

Marley pondered Ma Grand's words. She was right that a bunch of talk about love, with no corresponding action, made for an impotent parent. But the ideal situation was a balance of both. She knew her mother in a way that Ma Grand did not, simply because she was Pam's child. And she knew that her mother suffered most from feeling, somehow, that she could use a little more love.

"Were Great-grandma and Great-granddaddy happily married?"

"Well, they were married. That's about all I can say. Happier when they were both working and running around town trying to save the world. When they retired and were at home, I don't much remember a time when they stayed in the same room together unless they had to. Daddy sat on the porch reading his newspaper and smoking his pipe. Mama stayed in the front room playing her piano and reading her cookbooks like they were novels. 'Course, when Mama took ill and couldn't do for herself, well, Daddy didn't handle that too well. Pushed himself even further away. Then he died one week after Mama died. So what do you make of that?" Ma Grand stared out the window.

"But they didn't show affection 'round us children. No, sir. Mama didn't think it was proper for young children to see a whole lot of kissing and hugging 'cause Mama didn't want the headmaster from school calling to tell her that her boys or her girls were hugging up on someone of the opposite sex. Told us that would be the worst degradation we could commit on ourselves—to act like dogs in heat and give white folk reason to think they were right about black folk being sexual creatures with no brains and so forth. Mama knew this was so 'cause her own mother was white and disowned Mama when she married Daddy, you see."

"Wow," Marley said quietly. "I never knew that."

"Yeah, well, for my brothers and sisters and me," Ma Grand continued, "life was about learning and being obedient. Making something of yourself and making your family proud of you. Turns out we all did that, one way or another. We never shamed Mama and Daddy's name." To this Ma Grand slowly nodded her head.

Pam found it difficult to open her eyes and even more difficult to swallow away the scorched sensation in her throat. It took her a few minutes to make sense of her surroundings. The tall pole to her right side, from which multiple plastic bags of fluid were hanging, quickly reminded her that she was in the recovery room.

She opened her mouth to call for a nurse, but no sound would come out. There was probably a call button on the side of her bed, but she decided against searching for it. She lay still and stared at the ceiling.

It had been done. Her breast was gone. And soon she'd find out whether the cancer had spread to other parts of her body. Slowly, she lifted her right arm and placed her hand where her left breast had been. Her stomach knotted as she gently canvassed the bandages covering the flat surface underneath her hospital gown. She felt a lump form in her throat but refused to cry. She was tired of crying.

"Hey, there." A soft voice floated inside the room from the doorway. Pam turned her head and saw Dr. Croskey, her surgeon. He smiled and walked over to the bed.

"How are you feeling, Ms. Shepherd?"

"Fine," Pam whispered, still unable to find her voice. Dr. Croskey poured water from the pitcher on the tray beside Pam's bed and handed her the cup. She took a few sips and thanked him.

"Everything went really well. We were able to remove the entire mass, and we took out a number of lymph nodes as well. We're running tests now, and we'll have more information for you very soon. You did a great job," Dr. Croskey concluded, touching Pam's hand and turning to leave the room.

"I'd like to see it," Pam whispered.

"I'm sorry?" Dr. Croskey asked, halfway through the door.

"I said," Pam repeated, her voice stronger, "I want to see it."

"What would you like to see, Ms. Shepherd?" Dr. Croskey wore a soft but confused expression.

"My chest."

"Your chest? You mean where we just performed surgery?"

Pam nodded.

"Oh no, I'm afraid we can't do that. It's been bandaged, for one thing, and it needs time to heal.

"Then let me see the bandages."

"Ms. Shepherd, I'm not sure I understand—"

"I want to see my chest, Doctor. Sit me up in the bed"—her voice croaked—"hand me a mirror, and let me see my chest." Pam's eyes penetrated Dr. Croskey's like burning coals. He remained still, then left the room.

He returned with a small mirror and held it up in front of Pam. "This is completely out of line with protocol, Ms. Shepherd. I just want you to know that. And in my professional opinion, I—"

"This isn't professional, Doctor. It's personal." Pam pushed the elevation button on the side of her bed and, once upright, stared into the mirror. She was silent as she took herself in. She touched the bandages. She avoided her eyes for fear that their reflection would scare her more than the bandages.

"Well," Pam finally said. She placed the mirror on her lap and pressed her fingertips to her eyes. "I guess that's that." She thanked Dr. Croskey, handed him the mirror, reclined against the pillows, and closed her eyes.

* * *

Pam was grateful for the solitude that greeted her in her private room. On her nightstand, she found a note from Marley and her mother. "Stepped out for a few. Be right back. XOXO."

"You're quite a popular patient, Ms. Shepherd," the nurse said, helping Pam from the bathroom into her bed. "We've been holding several flower deliveries at the nurses' station until we found out what your room assignment was going to be. Gorgeous arrangements," the nurse added.

Pam's mouth formed a smile. "How 'bout that," she offered dryly.

"Yes, ma'am! Believe it or not, many patients stay in the hospital several days, sometimes weeks, and never receive flowers or visitors. You're blessed, honey." The nurse fluffed Pam's pillows and helped her recline into a comfortable position.

"Now, you just buzz me with this button right here if you need anything, sugar. Anything at all, you hear?"

Pam nodded and thanked the nurse as she left. Pam thought about the nurse's comment that she was blessed, and for a moment she tried very hard to focus on all the things she had to be grateful for. She could be dead. She could have had surgery to remove an arm or a leg or to transplant her heart. For sure, things could be far worse than losing a breast to cancer.

And even if her cancer would ultimately be diagnosed as terminal, Pam thought, she should be grateful for having lived a relatively full life. Her life had certainly been longer than that of Steven, who had been killed by a drunk driver when he was twenty-one, engaged to be married, two months before he was to graduate from Howard University. Steven had never known what it was like to be married, so who was Pam to complain about having a marriage that hadn't lasted?

She drifted off, and in what felt like hours but was only minutes, awoke to the sounds of her mother's and Marley's voices entering the room. Their laughter quickly subsided when they saw Pam lying in the bed.

"I'm awake. Don't stop talking on my account." Pam felt around the side of her bed for the elevation button.

"Hey," Marley whispered and kissed Pam on the cheek. She looked at her mother and smiled, stroking her hair.

Ma Grand stood at the foot of the bed. "Are you okay?" She placed a shaking hand on Pam's leg.

"I'm fine. Feel just fine," Pam said to both of them. "My left side is pretty sore, especially my arm. But I feel fine."

"Well, that's to be expected," Ma Grand said, stumbling toward the window. "Just be sure you don't overdo it in this hospital. Let the nurses take care of you, and don't you be climbing out of the bed trying to get things for yourself." She stared out the window, then turned and heaved her weight into a chair.

"Look at all these beautiful flowers!" Marley walked over to one of the arrangements on top of the dresser and searched for a card.

"They are beautiful," Pam agreed, taking them in for the first time. "The nurse must have brought them in while I was—Marley, stop being nosy!"

"What? I was just looking for the cards so I could give them to you. How else will you know who sent them?" Marley laughed. "Seriously, though, who sent you this gigantic arrangement in the center of the dresser? This thing is incredible!" It was an aromatic display of orchids and stephanotis at least four feet tall. Marley dug out the card and read it: " 'We appreciate all your work and wish you a relaxing recovery. Don't rush back. We'll wait on you. Cochran & Company.'

"Goodness, Mommy! What did you do to them? You've got them hooked! Holding up their house decorations for you? Go on with your bad self."

Pam couldn't hold back her smile. She shook her head and raised her eyebrows. "Isn't that something?" It made her feel quite good. Wanted.

"Why can't he wait just like everybody else?" Ma Grand interjected. "Cochran ain't special. He's a human being with flaws, just like the rest of us. All that matters is that you take your time, Pam, and recover. And do what the doctors tell you to do. And don't worry about that job, 'cause it will be there when you're well again, and so will your clients."

"Oh, stop fussing, Gran. Mom is going to take care of herself, and I'm going to help her. And there's nothing wrong with her thinking about her clients while she's away. She does have some pretty impressive ones." Marley winked at her mother, then replaced the card from Cochran & Company.

"Oh, child, hush! You sound silly, talking 'bout some clients when your mother just had surgery and has to fight cancer." Ma Grand glared at Marley, then stared out the window.

"All right, both of you. Please, that's enough. Mama, I'm not going to rush back to work." Pam looked at Marley. "And *you* should know by now when to respond to your grandmother and when to be quiet. It's not always worth it, okay?"

She settled herself against the pillows, folded her hands, and grinned. "Now read me the cards from the rest of my flowers, please."

Chapter 11

ARLEY WAS PROUD of herself. She had managed, all week long, to pull off an Emmy award–winning performance in front of her mother. One evening at the hospital, she had spun a massive, most impressive tale about how Mr. Shore had deployed Gerrard to South Africa for an indefinite period of time, and as a result they had decided to postpone the wedding—which was for the best because they both had been feeling that they needed some time away from each other. And no, they hadn't come up with a new date just yet, but not to worry—they would. Soon they would.

Ma Grand had eyed Marley as though she were an imposter and looked away, her lips mashed together.

Marley's mother—her touchstone—had no idea Marley's life had been turned upside down. She had no idea that Marley's smiles were plastered and painful, that they were replaced with a mouth that involuntarily fell open from shock as soon as she left her presence. Pam had no idea that Marley was out of groove just as much as she was.

That Friday evening, Marley dropped her grandmother off and went home, anxious to change out of her panty hose and into some sweats. She thought about Gerrard the whole way home, but for the first time that week she didn't cry. She didn't know whether it was progress or numbness. Either way, it felt good to have a clear throat and a dry eye. Until she turned on St. Marteen and saw the black Range Rover in her driveway.

Her heart dropped. The only thing that saved her from an on-slaught of tears was her anger at Gerrard's nerve. *Who did he think he was?*

She got out of her car and slammed the door. "What do you want?" she snapped as Gerrard climbed out of his truck and began to walk toward her. She didn't bother to look in his direction and instead walked quickly toward her front door.

"Marley, please wait," he said softly, almost tripping over the monkey grass lining her sidewalk. She kept walking. She reached the front door, but her hands were shaking so badly that it seemed an hour passed before she found her door key. By that time, he had joined her at the front door. She felt his fingertips on her shoulder, and part of her inner wall began to crumble. She wasn't even aware of her tears until one fell on the hand that held her keys.

"You don't even have to turn around. Just listen to me, please. I am wrong. There is no excuse. I won't even stand here and try to offer you one because there is none. You could hate me for the rest of your life if you wanted to, and I couldn't say one thing about it. And I'm not here to convince you not to hate me. I'm just here to apologize. You mean more to me than anyone else in this world, and I've hurt you. And I can't live with myself unless I tell you how sorry I am. You don't even have to forgive me, Marley. Just know that I am truly, truly sorry."

The tears continued to fall, but she refused to turn around and allow him to see her upset again. She'd unleashed on him at the hotel like a Chicago snowstorm, and every time she replayed the scene she wished she could take it all back. He wasn't worth all the emotion she'd spent on him. He didn't deserve it.

"Only a lowlife could do what you did to me, Gerrard," she said, unable to control the cracking in her voice. "You scare me."

He was quiet. His hand was still on her shoulder.

"Get your hand off me," she hissed, jerking her shoulder. She turned to face him. "I heard what you had to say. I appreciate the fact that you felt like you needed to come here and say that. But it's been a week, and I needed to hear those words Saturday night when your tired behind stayed at the hotel and let me leave by myself. I don't need to hear it now."

He looked down and stuffed his hands in his pockets. Even then, he looked good. Perfectly groomed and impeccably dressed. Maybe if he'd looked a little disheveled, Marley would have felt better. Maybe if he'd looked like she felt, she would have believed he was sorry.

"Don't come back, Gerrard. Do you hear me?" The tears had begun again. She fumbled with her house key, hurriedly put it into the lock, and opened the door. She slipped inside and slammed the door, leaning against the wall while her tears washed away the centimeter of progress she'd made over the last six days.

Why is this happening to me? Marley thought. She began to question God, wondering what she had done to deserve a cheating fiancé and a cancer-ridden mother all at the same time. She wrapped her arms around her shoulders. It would have been so much easier if Gerrard had simply stayed away. She glanced at the door. Now he was back, begging her to believe him. Her heart was begging her mind for the permission to believe.

It was as if Gerrard could sense that she needed someone. As if he knew she simply could not carry all her pain by herself and that at that particular moment the weight was so unbearable, and her soul so buckling, that she would gladly share the load with anybody, even him. So he knocked on the door, and she opened it. And she fell into his arms, and he held her as she cried.

First he said nothing. He just kissed her forehead. And rubbed her neck. He stroked her hair. Then he told her that everything would be okay. He mumbled apologies into her ear, and she clung to his taut body and to his soothing words.

Then he began to kiss her lips. Gently at first, but before she knew it, they were moving frantically, knocking hanging pictures off balance. A sepia four-by-five of Silas, Pam, and three-year-old Marley—the only family picture she had—crashed against the ceramic tile, shattering the glass in the maple frame. Marley heard the glass, but then she didn't. She felt Gerrard's hand slide up her skirt and caress her thigh, and for a little while she didn't do anything to stop him. That was when she knew she was in trouble.

"Gerrard," she said between kisses, "wait a minute." He stopped kissing her mouth and nibbled at her neck.

"Gerrard." She grabbed his face with her hands. He stared at her with bottomless eyes of onyx, the eyes that had stolen her heart so many years before. He lowered his gaze and took her hands.

"I know we're moving too fast, baby," he said softly, still not looking at her. "I'm sorry. We have a lot to work through, and I want us to take things slowly."

"Who said we were taking things *anywhere*, Gerrard? You think we're back together or something?" Marley stepped back. His presumptuousness inflamed her. Insulted her. Made her feel cheap.

"Shh," he said, tracing his finger around her mouth and pulling her close to him. "Of course I don't think we're back together, sweetheart. I just meant that I don't want us to let our feelings get in the way of us working through all that we need to work through. I love you with everything inside of me, Marley, and I want you to know that. I want you to see it and believe it for yourself, and I don't care how long it takes for me to prove it to you."

They sat on the steps. The foyer was cold and Marley was freezing. But she didn't invite him into the living room. Certainly it would have been more comfortable; yet it was easier to deal with him near the door. A false sense of distance came along with doorway dealings, and Marley, unable to draw her own line in the mud, clung to it like her last hope.

"Marley, I really don't know where to begin, but I want to tell you everything so that——"

"Please," she whispered, still staring ahead. A single tear streamed down her cheek. She shook her head and closed her eyes. "I don't want to know right now." More tears fell. "I really don't want to know."

"Well, okay," he said and moved closer to her. He put his arm around her shoulder and squeezed her. "I just want you to know that I'll do whatever you want to do. I'll listen, I'll talk, I'll leave, I'll stay. Whatever you want, at your pace, until we get this thing right again." He squeezed her again and stared ahead.

Marley didn't believe him, but it was okay. That night she needed for everything to be okay, in spite of everything. And so it was.

And so it remained, for as long as reality cooperated. Saturday, he asked for her car keys, disappeared for two hours, then returned, leaving her with a kiss on the cheek and a fully detailed automobile. Sunday, he took her to Buster's Kitchen, then sat next to her on a bench in Piedmont Park and let her cry on his shoulder until her ducts dried out. He called her twice on Monday and sent a dozen long-stemmed roses; she called him three times on Tuesday. Wednesday, they played phone tag; Thursday, he didn't return her phone calls. He wasn't in his office on Friday and didn't contact her until three in the morning on Saturday to let her know that he was out of town on business with his father. Marley knew he was lying. And even if he wasn't, she was not willing to spend any more energy confirming the truth. Gerrard—the one she dreamed of futures with, the one she had passed up others for, the one she had accommodated, even at her own expense—was gone. Had been gone.

* * *

On Thanksgiving, no one was thankful.

Marley and Ma Grand had started cooking at Pam's the night before and had finished their preparations by early afternoon on Thanksgiving Day. Ma Grand had brought over her signature wax turkey centerpiece and had placed it on Pam's dining room table, and Marley had gathered leaves and acorns from the yard and crafted several basket displays for the downstairs windows, but it still didn't feel like Thanksgiving.

After removing all the food from the oven and pulling the Lenox out of the china cabinet, Marley left Ma Grand to set the dining room table and went upstairs to get her mother.

Pam was lying on her back, staring at the ceiling. The television was off, and the curtains were drawn. "Mom, you okay?" Marley asked from the doorway.

"Yes," Pam mumbled, eyes still fixed on the ceiling.

"You ready to come down for dinner, or would you be more comfortable eating in here?" Marley wiped the sweat from her forehead.

"I'd rather stay in here, if you don't mind," Pam said.

"Okay, then. I'll bring the plates up in a minute." Marley turned to walk away, then remembered what she had wanted to forget. She looked at the tube hanging out the side of her mother's chest. "I better drain the tube now."

Pam was silent, motionless, as Marley tried to replicate the procedure the nurse had shown her. "It looks worse than it is," the nurse had said, trying to console Marley. "Just watch out for her arm while you're doing it," she had advised. Pam's left arm had swelled, and the nurse had taken to massaging and exercising it at least three times a day.

"We'll do some more arm exercises after dinner," Marley said, replacing the cap at the end of the tube. She might as well have been talking to herself. She removed a moist rag from a covered plastic container near Pam's bed and blotted Pam's forehead.

"Wasn't so bad this time, huh?" Marley asked, not really waiting on a response. She did well at smiling as she helped Pam recline against the pillows. Pam shifted sideways and lay flat on the mattress again. Eyes on the ceiling again.

"Okay. Be back up in a minute," Marley said, standing. "Want anything special?"

"No. Thanks." Pam blinked.

By the time Marley made it downstairs, Ma Grand had finished setting the table and had returned to the kitchen to begin transporting the food to the dining room.

Marley poked her head inside the kitchen doorway. "Gran, Mom wants to eat in her room, so I'm going to get some TV trays and take them up for us."

Ma Grand stood still at the stove and stared at Marley. "In that *bedroom*? Oh, the devil," Ma Grand snapped, her hands a shaking frenzy as she struggled to carry the stuffing from the stove to the counter. She stared at the stuffing, her knuckles knocking against the sides of the dish, then left the kitchen.

Marley tried to think of nothing except dinner as she grabbed three TV trays from the family room closet and carried them upstairs. She set them up in the bedroom, then went to her mother's side. "Mom, you ready to sit up now?"

Pam ignored Marley, still staring at the ceiling.

"Mom?" Marley rubbed her mother's shoulder.

"When is the nurse coming back?" Pam asked, her tone sharp.

"Uh, not until tomorrow, Mom. Today's Thanksgiving and she—"

"I know what day it is! I'm not senile, Marley. Goodness!" Pam rolled to her side, away from Marley.

Marley sighed and rubbed her forehead. "I'm going to bring our plates up," Marley said quietly, turning to leave the room.

"Please don't," Pam responded. "I'm not hungry right now."

Marley's legs carried her downstairs, while her mind departed to foreign places and explored their sensations. The feel of light rain along the Nile. The color of the reefs adorning Curaçao's aquatic terrain. In the kitchen, she began to hum as she fixed plates for her grandmother and herself. Humming marked the beginning of losing your mind and fighting to keep it, she thought, piling the macaroni and cheese high on her plate, not caring whether she overate. She left the kitchen with plates in hand and hunted her grandmother down in the family room.

"If that's for me, I don't want it," Ma Grand said, sitting motionless in the rocking chair.

"Gran, please," Marley pleaded. The plates suddenly became heavy. "We didn't have breakfast, and we've been cooking all morning. We've got to eat. Please eat with me."

"Marley, I said I don't want anything right now. Don't hassle me," Ma Grand warned, looking away.

"But this is Thanksgiving! Can't we just eat together and try to be happy about *something*?"

"What in the *world* do I need to be happy about? What kind of sitcom do you think this is? You think things are supposed to be perfect just because it's Thanksgiving?" Ma Grand glared at Marley. "We live in the *real* world, Marley, and it ain't perfect. Just because the government decided this day was special doesn't mean I got to be happy. *I* decide what days are special. This ain't one of 'em."

Marley walked away before her grandmother had finished her sentence. In the kitchen, she pulled plastic wrap from the pantry, covered the plates, and sat them on the stove. She transferred the food from baking dishes to plastic containers, ignoring the steam that was still rising from the food and the fog that immediately coated the sides of the containers. She put the food into the refrigerator, tuning out the admonitions her mother had given her over the years about refrigerating hot food before it cooled. She eyed the turkey, which Ma Grand had stuffed and baked, and decided to finish carving it. She bagged the meat and carried it out of the kitchen.

"Be back shortly," Marley called to Ma Grand from the foyer, grabbing her wool-lined windbreaker from the coat closet, exiting without waiting on a response. She placed the bag on the passenger seat of her car and drove five miles to the park on the Chattahoochee River.

No one was there. Normal families were eating dinner, playing cards, watching football, finding things to be thankful for. Marley walked along a bank, bagged turkey in hand, eyes fastened on the leaves that coated the ground. She heard branches crackling overhead and glanced upward. Two squirrels were fighting over a small object, and after a few seconds of vigorous gnawing and pawing, one gave up and hopped away. Just like that. For the first time, Marley envied the apparent simplicity of a squirrel's life. The squirrel had its problems: occasional food shortages, less-than-desirable weather, hostile and even violent neighbors. Through it all, though, the squirrel's countenance was steady. Its eyes were bright and wide. Its vigor was restored daily, and it moved on, no matter what the circumstances. Even death didn't rob a squirrel of the determination that framed its eyes; they still seemed to look onward.

Marley walked to the edge of the bank and sprinkled chunks of turkey along its slope. There was plenty to share. Maybe the surplus Marley was adding to the environment would enable one of the animals on the low end of the food chain to live a day longer. Maybe there would be fewer fights, more contentment. Maybe there would be an air of gratitude among the wild. For them, maybe today would be a happy Thanksgiving.

Part
Two

He that findeth his life shall lose it: and he that loseth
his life for my sake shall find it.

—MATTHEW 10:39

Chapter 12

ROM THE FIFTEENTH floor of the One Peachtree Center building, Marley could see daffodils and red coral bells blooming in the garden plots on the corner of International Boulevard. Just five weeks ago, the plots had been bare. Just five months ago, she had seen Gerrard with Angela, watched her future slip out from beneath her, felt her eyes grow as vacant as the plots. Because, after all, just one year ago it was Gerrard and *she* the world had been celebrating.

But the promise of spring, so faithful, with its clearer skies, its softer breezes, and its newer blooms, had given Marley fresh air to breathe. New horizons to witness. New chances to take. She floated through the air, drifting through the possibilities, until the ringing telephone yanked her away from her mind's eye and back to her office desk.

"Marley Shepherd," she said into the speakerphone. She heard static on the other end and guessed that it was Bob calling from his cell phone.

"Yeah, Bob here. Listen, I've gotta head to New York for the hearing a day earlier than I'd expected, so I've called a meeting with the team in an hour. Tell Evelyn to get a conference room for me. And get the poster boards from duplicating and bring them along with the draft oral argument I asked you to do. I'm on my way back to the office from Marietta." Bob hung up the telephone, the thought of saying good-bye or thank you never even crossing his mind.

Marley sat at her desk and fumed. She picked up the receiver and slammed it back down again, even though Bob had long since disconnected himself from the call. "He thinks I'm a slave girl!" She shook her head in disgust, fed up with Bob and his unilateral order-issuing sessions disguised as phone calls. Even the customers at PoJo's, the restaurant where she'd waited tables in high school, had treated her with more consideration and respect.

Get a grip, Marley told herself. She swiveled in her chair to face the window again and tried to return to the daydream Bob had yanked her from. But all she could see were buses, taxis, cars, and pedestrians clamoring for coveted positions on the street.

She thought about it but decided against it. *Should she?* Of course not. Why in the world would she? What in the world would she say?

She rocked back and forth in her chair, but she couldn't push it from her mind. She should do it. *Of course she should.* She certainly was strong enough to do it. Once upon a time she hadn't been so strong; back when Gerrard had apparently found his mind and started to call her every day, leaving messages at her work and her home, pleading for forgiveness. She had had enough sense not to return his calls. Not a single one, because back then she'd vacillated worse than a pendulum: one day she'd hated his guts; the next, she'd wondered whether more counseling might enable them to start over. But five months had passed. She wanted to know how he was doing. What was wrong with that?

She could even handle seeing him. She was wearing a brand-new ice pink linen dress trimmed in tiny pearls. The dress hugged her slim waist and made her body look rounder and firmer than it really was. It was one of those dresses that made you want to skip out for lunch, or go out for dinner—anywhere but straight home—just to see *somebody* while you were wearing it, so *somebody* could confirm that you looked as good as you believed you did. How much sweeter it would be if that somebody was somebody who used to want you. Somebody who would see what he was missing, who could not hide the glimmer in his eye, whose glimmer would be all you really ever needed to move on for good. It all boiled down to fair farewells.

She picked up the phone and dialed the number. Her heart felt as though it were forcing its way up her throat; her cheeks felt like furnaces. She closed her eyes, inhaling and exhaling silently.

"Shore Development, how may I direct your call?"

"Hello, may I speak with Gerrard, please?" Marley grabbed a pen off her desk and clutched it in her fist.

"Surely. Is this Angela?"

"Is this—what—*pardon me?*"

"Ah, excuse me. Excuse me, please," the receptionist stammered. "Please hold the line."

The reason Marley hated the roller coasters at Six Flags was because the first hill—the first big dip on the ride—made her stomach feel like a bottomless pit. Here she was in her office, miles away from Six Flags, with the same sinking feeling in her stomach. On top of that, she was hot. Unbearably hot. With no extra layers to peel.

She hung up the telephone, wiped the sweat from her forehead, and closed her eyes. She had set herself up for this. Who could she blame? She couldn't blame Mary, the receptionist, for not recognizing her voice. Obviously Mary knew only Angela's voice these days.

Evelyn buzzed her.

"Yeah," Marley said, feigning normality.

"Honey, it's Gerrard on the line."

"Oh, okay." Her attempt at sounding surprised wouldn't have fooled a fly. "I'll pick up. Thanks, Evelyn."

"Mm-hm," Evelyn said, her tone confirming that Marley's attempt had failed.

"Yes?" Marley's crispness rattled the receiver.

"Marley." He sounded apologetic. Pathetic. He took a deep breath and released it slowly. Heavily. "How are you?"

"Fine, and you?" She stared at her computer and tried to read her e-mail.

"Ah . . . well, okay . . . I guess. Listen, Mary told me what happened. I'm really sorry about that. She had no business——"

"So you're with *Angela?*" She couldn't help it. She hadn't planned to ask it. She had promised herself she wouldn't, not just for the sake of pretending she didn't care, but also because she was inviting another, different answer from the one Mary had already given her. What would she do then——choose the one she liked best?

The silence that passed was much too protracted for Marley to handle with dignity. "Gerrard," she began, her voice already cracking, "you're still the same *dog* you were when——"

"Wait a minute, wait a minute. You can't just call me out of the blue and then go off on me, Marley. We haven't talked in months!"

"So what does that mean? That gives you a license to forget that we were getting *married?* That we were supposed to be in *love?*"

"Marley, I called you a million times, and you never returned my calls! What did you expect me to do? Sit around and wait on you to decide to talk to me? Gimme a break!"

"You know, you're right. What was I thinking? You don't need to wait on *anybody*. You're Gerrard hot-diggity Shore. I was lucky to get multiple phone calls in the first place 'cause that's way over your quota. Pardon me——I must've bumped my head somewhere."

"Look, Marley. The last thing I want to do is argue with you. Please. Let's call a truce and be friends. Can we do that? We should be able to do that, after all we've been through."

She laughed. One of those laugh-to-keep-from-crying laughs.

One of those helpless, speechless, humiliating laughs. "I refuse to give you the satisfaction of a truce, Gerrard. You might not be feeling it now, because you're all wrapped up in *Angela*," she said, rolling her head wildly and feeling nauseated from the aftertaste of that name on her tongue, "but one day you will. One day you're going to feel the pain of what you did to me. And you'll want to appease your conscience, and a truce would allow you to do that. I'm not giving it to you. Find another way to justify your tired, trifling self."

She slammed the phone into the base and bent over, holding her head and her tears in her hands. The truth and the reality, so hollow and unsatisfying, had come to rest with her. There was nothing more to expect. Nothing more to hope for. Returning his calls was the last card she'd had to play. That was it; completely it.

She heard a light rap on her door and ignored it.

"Marley?" she heard Evelyn inquire from outside as she peered through the glass beside the door and saw Marley wiping her face. "Honey, is everything all right?"

"Just a minute," Marley said, standing up and smoothing her dress. She opened the door for Evelyn. "Sorry, I was just—" She couldn't continue, the tears having stolen her words.

Evelyn scooted inside the office and quickly closed the door behind her. "What's wrong?"

Marley sat in her chair and rubbed her temples. "I just got off the phone with Gerrard. I hadn't talked to him since I broke off the engagement, so there were still a lot of unresolved issues and, well, it was, you know, it was painful. Really painful." She sniffed and wiped her eyes.

"Oh, absolutely. Of course." Evelyn slid into a chair, her face as pain-stricken as Marley's.

"But it was good we talked. It really was. I needed to have that talk. To bring, you know, closure to everything."

"Yes, yes. Definitely." Evelyn was professional even then, her hands folded and her short legs squeezed together. Her straight, jet-black hair was tucked neatly into a bun, and her faux-pearl studs sat proudly on her large earlobes.

"But I still feel this big weight. I feel worse than I have in months. I thought I was over this," Marley said as tears streamed down her cheeks. "I don't know if I can handle this pain again."

"You don't have to, honey. You really don't have to."

Marley shook her head quickly. "Believe me, I wouldn't be dealing with it if I didn't have to—if I had a choice in the matter." She sniffed again.

"You do have a choice in the matter. This burden is not yours to carry." Evelyn crossed her legs and leaned forward. "You know, it's funny we're having this conversation because I've been meaning to ask you to go to church with me."

Marley reclined in her chair. She was not at all interested in a sales pitch on how church is the Band-Aid of all Band-Aids. She'd heard enough of that from Ashley on a regular basis. "I don't know, Evelyn. I'm sort of fed up with churches these days. I'm just not getting anything from them, so I feel like I'm better off staying at home."

"Oh, I know what you mean. I felt the same way for a long time. Figured I knew how to be a good person so I didn't need to sit in some sanctuary while another human being took my money and told me how to behave."

"Exactly!" Finally, Marley thought, here was someone else in the world who understood how she felt. Someone whose head was not in the ecumenical clouds.

"But then I started to realize that being a good person wasn't enough. Being a good person wasn't saving my marriage. It wasn't helping me to be the kind of mother I wanted to be to my children. And it wasn't giving me the peace I wanted in my life. Then, one Sunday, some friends of ours invited us to church with them. For the first time, I didn't hear a bunch of Bible verses about what *thouest shouldn't'est doeth*," Evelyn said.

"Yeah," Marley added, shaking her head. "Who talks like that, anyway?"

"God surely doesn't," Evelyn said, moving to the edge of her seat. "And that's the thing. He's not some abstract, foreign-speaking spirit beyond our reach. That's what I used to think. But that Sunday, at church with our friends, the sermon was about God's patience. It was about how He loves us even when we turn away from Him, because He already knew we'd turn away. And how He knows what our futures hold, and He waits on us, hoping we'll return to Him."

"Mm," Marley said, looking at Evelyn intently.

"Isn't that something? That He loves us, knowing we're going to reject Him?" Evelyn's eyes were wide.

"Yeah, it is," Marley said quietly. She looked at her hands.

"So anyway, Johnny and I kept going back. We had to hear more. Finally we joined the church. For the first time in our lives, God became a part of our marriage and our family. Things started to change, Marley. We talked to each other differently. We talked to our children differently. The spirit of the Lord got inside of us, and we changed."

Marley nodded. "That's good. That's really good. But that doesn't change the fact that we all have the same problems. I mean, honestly, Evelyn, I see church folks facing crises just like everybody else."

"Of course they do," she said, her brows so furrowed that they met in the middle of her forehead. "That's part of living in the world, and God never promised that life would be easier for those who know Him. The difference is that those who know Him and know His word know how to *handle* life's problems. Despite what's challenging them on the outside, God's children have peace on the inside—or at least they *should*. They know God is always in control.

"Like with your situation today. You're sitting here trying to handle it on your own while God is waiting, just standing by, ready to take your burden from you. It's already in His hands. All you have to do is release it to Him. It really is that simple."

Marley nodded, twisting her ring. Evelyn's words sounded good, almost too good. If life with God was so much better than life without Him, why were so many people passing it up?

Yet there was something about Evelyn that had always intrigued Marley. Evelyn very clearly knew peace. She wore it like a tailored overcoat. Marley had never seen Evelyn go off on Bob when he ordered her around as if she were his second secretary. Many a day, when Marley's anger had driven her right up to the line where she could have crossed over, cursed Bob out, and lost her job, she had regretted her behavior and wished for a temperament like Evelyn's. But she never held out much hope, figuring Evelyn was one of those lucky few who had been born into some predetermined state of calm.

"All right. I'd like to visit your church."

"Oh, praise the Lord!" Evelyn clapped her hands together like a nursery school teacher. "It will be wonderful, I promise you," she said. "Let's talk on Saturday, and we can plan to meet somewhere before the service begins."

"Okay. I'll call you Saturday evening." Marley smiled. If nothing else, she was happy that Evelyn was so pleased. "Evelyn, thanks for talking to me."

"Oh, anytime, honey." She stood, walked over to Marley, and hugged her shoulders. "Buzz me if you need me." She left, then opened the door and stuck her head back inside.

"Oh, and Bob called me right after he spoke to you. I got the conference room for the meeting, and I asked Tony to bring the boards up from duplicating so you wouldn't have to worry about it." She winked and closed the door behind her.

Marley smiled, thankful for Evelyn. Then she turned to her computer and stared at the draft oral argument on the screen. It stared back at her with so many gaps left to fill. Much like her emotional resolve. Much like a purse with too many holes. You think you're on your way somewhere, and all the while stuff is falling out and you're losing things, valuable things. You could try to patch it up, but would you ever really trust those patches? Would you ever really rely upon their strength? They would, after all, be just patches. Just substitutes, fill-ins for the fabric that had been torn away.

She erased Gerrard from her mind. She erased the draft argument from her screen. She made up her mind. She was starting over.

Chapter 13

WHILE IT HELPED somewhat that Marley had set her alarm clock to "tune" instead of "buzz," the music that moseyed into her dreams at half past six on Sunday morning was still an unwelcome intrusion. She rolled over, eyed the alarm clock as if it were a burglar, and not-so-gingerly hit the snooze button with the palm of her hand.

Last night, she had actually been excited about going to church. She had agreed to meet Evelyn at the eight o'clock service, even though Evelyn had warned her that she might appreciate the extra few hours of sleep she could get by going to the later one. Marley had taken the time to pin curl her hair, wash her panty hose, and iron the few wrinkles in the plaid suit she was planning to wear. But now, on Sunday morning, something was on her back, zapping her desire to follow through with her plans.

She was tired. She even suspected a mild headache was surfacing. She rolled onto her back and stared out the window, thinking it really didn't make a difference whether she went to church or not. The weeds that had grown in her front yard were atrocious, and she'd promised herself she wouldn't let another spring season catch her with the worst-looking lawn in Versailles. No way she could compete with the Rudolphs, who paid a landscaping service to trim their shrubs into those weird geometric shapes, but the least she could do was whack her weeds and plant some bulbs.

These were the kinds of things she needed to take care of in the morning rather than later in the day. So she decided to listen to some gospel music for a little while, maybe even find a good tele-vangelist on one of the networks, and then take care of business. She couldn't think of any scripture that said she had to go to church every Sunday anyway. Evelyn would understand.

Marley wrapped herself up in her favorite pink terry-cloth robe and skipped down the steps to the kitchen. The vision of a spinach and mushroom omelette was dancing in her head, and she eagerly opened the refrigerator to pull out all the ingredients she needed to make it. Her eyes widened in disbelief when she saw that her spinach had wilted into oblivion, her one remaining egg had already been boiled, and her mushrooms had browned beyond recognition. She tried to shake it off, pretending it was no big deal, while her stomach growled in defiance.

Munching on an apple, she went into her garage to organize her yard tools. Her fertilizer, weed whacker, hoes, and yard gloves were all missing from the shelves. She stood with her hands on her hips, racking her brain to figure out where the equipment could be. Then she remembered she had loaned them to Ashley.

"This is a trip," she said, shaking her head and chuckling. She went back into the kitchen and tried to call Evelyn, but there was no answer. The sunflower clock on the wall read a quarter past seven. It was too late for her to make the early service. She decided to take a quick speed walk around the neighborhood, shower and dress, treat herself to a good breakfast at Buster's Kitchen, and ar-rive on time for the next service.

*   *   *

Gilead's Balm was a relatively small church, with roughly five hundred people at each service, much like Marley's childhood church. The feeling inside was familiar, probably because one big family had gathered together to celebrate their love for the guest of honor, whom they loved in different but equal ways. It didn't matter that people like Marley, who knew little more than the Lord's Prayer, were joining the family every Sunday. It was still a family, God was the father, and all His children were welcome.

The few remaining vacant seats were close to the pulpit. A big-bosomed woman with stunning gray hair and a steady smile ushered Marley into the fourth row next to two elderly gentlemen. Like grandfathers, they smiled warmly and wished her a good morning, making her feel even more at home. She got situated in her seat and glanced around, and suddenly she became embarrassed. Everyone around her had Bibles in their laps, opened and displaying highlights, pen marks, and dog-eared pages. Marley's cheeks turned red when she eyed her old Children's Bible, the only one she owned. She had never been embarrassed to tote that Bible to church before. Ma Grand had given it to her when she'd been baptized at the age of nine. The pages were crumpled and stuck together from water damage and general lack of care. The once gold trim around the edges had turned a nasty creek-water brown. Marley felt ashamed, felt as though the elderly men sitting next to her would take one look at her Bible and see right through her sinful self.

She knew it shouldn't matter what kind of Bible she had or what condition it was in; she knew that none of it mattered in God's eyes. Still, she was embarrassed. She leaned forward and put her Bible under her seat, deciding she would pull it out only when she absolutely needed it, praying to God that the smell of mold and mildew would not leap from the pages when she finally cracked them open.

The pastor and the youth choir entered the pulpit, and the congregation stood on its feet and began to sing. Marley didn't know the song, but the words—"Jesus is my help"—struck her, washed over her consciousness like rain on a mud-streaked window. "Jesus is my help." Marley searched her purse for her white lace handkerchief. She lowered her head and dabbed discreetly at the corners of her eyes. Then she stared at the choir. These children—the oldest of whom looked to be about seventeen—already had such a heartfelt testimony to God's grace. She began to thank God. For knowing her and loving her in spite of herself. For loving her enough to make it almost impossible for her to miss church that morning, because He knew how much she needed it. That same patience Evelyn had talked about had been extended to her—to Marley Shepherd. *Why?* she wondered.

After the invocation, one of the ministers sitting in the pulpit approached the podium. Marley was struck by how young he looked; she was accustomed to seeing older men hold all the clerical positions.

"Praise the Lord!" the young minister bellowed into the microphone, his voice like Paul Robeson's.

"Praise the Lord!" the congregation responded.

"I'd like to ask all our visitors to please stand for a moment. Please stand for just a moment—we won't bite you!"

The congregation laughed, and Marley summoned the courage to stand. It felt as though ten thousand eyes were burning holes through the plaid in her suit. Though the eyes belonged to smiling faces, she felt like a spectacle nonetheless.

"All righty, then. Young man in the sharp blue suit, what's your name?"

Marley glanced over at the first victim, a man who looked to be about thirty or so, standing in the row in front of her. All she could think was that she was next.

"Ah, yes sir, ah, my name is, ah, Felton Machesney."

"Machesney? Is your daddy's daddy from Birmingham?" the minister asked.

"Ah, yeah, actually, yes he is, sir." Felton was surprised by the minister's ability to connect the Machesney paternal lineage.

"Brother, you and me are like family. Our granddaddies taught music together at Parker High School. My granddaddy used to talk about your granddaddy all the time, and to this day he's got a picture of the two of them in his living room."

"What's your last name, sir, ah, if you don't mind me asking?" Felton inquired nervously.

"Ainsworth. I'm Reverend Kelly Ainsworth the third, my daddy is Kelly Ainsworth the second, and my granddaddy is the alpha."

"Oh, wow! I know exactly who you are! I think we met when we were children!" Felton responded eagerly, stumbling over his words far less than before.

"Yes, yes, yes!" Reverend Ainsworth responded. "Well, listen, brother, we welcome you to Gilead's Balm with all the Christian love in the world. We want you to make yourself right at home, sign our guest book in the vestibule before you go, and be sure to give us enough information to keep in touch with you. Well, I'll be! Boy, the Lord works in mysterious ways. I'll catch up with you after service, Machesney. God bless you, now," he concluded, obviously wishing he could go and call his grandfather.

"All righty, then, let's see. Young lady standing to my right, what's your name?"

It was Marley's turn. She cleared her throat. "Hi, I'm Marley Shepherd." Her cheeks turned red. She had sounded like a game-show contestant. *If I could kick myself in my own behind,* she thought, *I would.*

"Marley Shepherd? You any kin to the Shepherds from Mobile?"

"Ah, I don't think so." Marley hoped her smile concealed her shame at not knowing her roots. *Not your fault you don't know, Marley. Not your fault. Now pay attention to Reverend Ainsworth, and don't sound so stupid the next time you open your mouth.*

"Well, with a name like Shepherd, you don't have a choice but to do God's work, now, do you?"

The congregation laughed. "I'm starting to think you're right," Marley answered.

"You have a church home, Marley?" Reverend Ainsworth's voice was warm, his smile reassuring.

"Ah, well, not exactly. Yes and no."

"Yes and no? Yes and no? Girl, you a lawyer?"

This time she laughed with the congregation. "Actually, I am."

"I knew it! I knew it! Okay, now," he said, leaning on the podium, "tell me 'bout the 'yes and no.' "

"Well, I grew up in a Methodist church in College Park. Technically, I'm still a member there since I never officially left. But I guess you could say I'm looking around."

"I understand. Completely," he said. "Marley, with all the Christian love that exists, we welcome you to Gilead's Balm. We pray that the word you hear will encourage you and ignite you, and we pray you'll come back to worship with us real soon. God bless you real good, now, you hear?"

"Thank you." Marley took her seat. She must have sighed her relief louder than she thought because one of the elderly gentlemen smiled a toothless grin and nodded at her while the other said, "Wasn't so bad after all, was it?"

"Boy, we sure is happy to have you visitin' wit' us. Mighty happy to have you," the toothless gentleman said.

Marley thanked him. She felt close to him, all of a sudden. She wanted to hug him. Instead she smiled. "Thank you *so* much," she said, leaning sideways to touch his hand. He grabbed hold of her hand as if it were a promise of longer life, and he squeezed it until her knuckles began to hurt. "Mighty nice, child. We love you, child." With watery eyes, he loosened his grip.

After the choir sang another song and the ushers took the offering, Pastor Woods walked to the podium. His simplicity startled Marley. He didn't *look* like a pastor. Absent were the common trappings of ecclesiastical success: the two or three diamond rings whose brilliance was blinding if the light hit them at the right angle, the two or three diamond bracelets that jingled and crashed against the microphone each time it was touched, the expensive cologne that could be smelled all the way in the vestibule, and the swagger—that hard-learned, hard-earned swagger—that seemed to surface like clockwork not long after the trustees agreed it was indeed time for two services instead of one. Pastor Woods didn't have any of it. Instead, he had these eyes. These remarkable eyes. Marley had never seen humility bleed forth the way it did from his eyes.

"Church," he began, clasping his hands, "I want to talk today about something that might seem elementary to you. It may seem like a foregone conclusion, may sound like a total waste of time, but just trust me. Stay with me. For you may find that you don't know all you think you know. You may find that you're doing what you're doing for all the wrong reasons. You may find that until you hear God's word, you're simply going through the motions."

"Well, Lord," a middle-aged man in a tweed suit sang out from the third row.

"I want to talk today about Christian responsibility. We as Christians have several responsibilities, but key among them is our responsibility to attend church. Now, turn with me to Romans, Chapter Twelve, and while you're finding that scripture, let me tell you what should *not* be motivating you to come to church. You should *not* be motivated by a guilty conscience. Don't come 'cause you think God is gonna get you if you don't. Don't do all the dirt you can possibly do Monday through Saturday, then apologize on Sunday, and start up with the same mess on Monday. God knows your heart."

He paced the pulpit. "You should *not* be coming to church to hear the choir sing your favorite song, or to sit next to your best buddy, or to wear your white uniform, or to show off your new suit. Nor should you come because it's Easter or Mother's Day. Y'all are laughing," he said over the uproar and raised his voice, "but you know good and well you ain't seen some of our members since last Christmas."

"Well, Lord," the same middle-aged man from the third row shouted. He stood up, hopped on one leg while he thrust his arms in an upward arch, and slipped back into his seat.

"Church, let's look at Romans Twelve. God is telling us here that he needs us, each one of us, for a unique reason. In Verse Four, God compares the Church to the human body. The body has several members, or parts, and each part serves a different function. The Church, which is the body of Christ, is the same way. We individuals are part of a whole. The whole will never function at full capacity if it's missing one of its parts."

Marley shook her head, amazed at the topic of the sermon. Was coincidence this good? She grabbed a pen from her purse and began to jot down a few notes on the back of her program.

"Why?" Pastor Woods asked. "Because Verse Six says each part has a specific and unique contribution to make to the whole. Every time you stay away from the Church, it suffers. There's something that you as a member are supposed to be doing. There's a gift you have that you're not sharing. A purpose for your life that you're not fulfilling. God didn't put us here for entertainment. He didn't put us here so we could spend our lives doing whatever makes us feel good. How *dare* we think a power as awesome as God has nothing better to do with His time than create us and watch us live purposeless lives? How *dare* we think we can stay away from God all our lives and still fulfill that purpose? How *dare* we think we don't need the Church when we're the very members of the body? Ain't no such thing as a perfect Church, and that's 'cause we're in it! If the body ain't acting right, fix it! Get it in shape. It's the body God gave us! Don't bash it and then abandon it! How could we?"

Marley hung her head. She was one of the holiday Christians, the halfhearted, sometimey, iffy, opportunist believers, and suddenly she felt uncomfortable. She wasn't a part of this body of Christ that Pastor Woods was talking about, and for the first time she felt left out.

At the end of the sermon, when the pastor announced that he was giving a call to Christ, Marley felt a tugging at her heart. She hesitated. She wanted to make changes in her life, but she was nowhere near ready to join anybody's church.

"The call to Christ is not an invitation to join the Church," he said. "It is an invitation from your heavenly Father, asking you, pleading with you, to start all over and give your life to Jesus Christ." The pastor's arms were outstretched as he spoke. "Getting out of your seat may feel like the hardest thing you've ever had to do in your life. But hell will be harder."

Marley trembled. Tears began to flow, and she tried her hardest to will herself out of her seat. She felt as though a ton had been dropped on her thighs. Never had she felt a heavier weight.

"You may think you're not ready. You may think you need to get your life together, clean up your act, before you go to God. Don't you realize that your life would already be together and your act would already be cleaned up if you could do it on your own? Jesus died so you could have power to overcome all the obstacles in your life. Put your hands in His. Stop trusting yourself. Trust in the one who made you."

Before she could think further, she shot out of her seat and made her way down the aisle. The pastor hugged her like a long-lost daughter. She cried so much she barely heard what he was saying.

"Welcome to your new life," Pastor Woods said and smiled. She looked around her and saw two women and four men standing at the altar with her. It felt so good not to be alone. It felt good to see she was not the only one with a soul in disrepair.

"Now, I want you all to say this prayer with me. Father God," he began, and Marley and the others repeated after him. "I come to you in the name of Jesus. Lord, I'm tired of doing things my way. I realize that my way is not Your way. I realize that my way is not leading me where I should go. My way is not giving me the peace Jesus died for me to have."

Marley sniffled and repeated the words of the prayer. Another tear streamed down her cheek. All she could see was the turbulence she had lived through. The mornings when she awoke and felt as if she hadn't slept at all. The mornings when she wondered how she would make it through an entire day.

"Forgive me for the arrogance of my ways, Father. Forgive me for believing I could live my life apart from You when You're the one who gave me life. I realize the way to You is through your Son, Jesus Christ, and I accept Him as my personal Lord and Savior. I'm now a new creature in You. My sins are forgiven. I've been washed by the blood of the Lamb. I've been made whole. I thank you for it, in Jesus' name. Amen."

Marley lifted her head and took a deep breath. She felt better. But she didn't feel different. Her heart still hurt when she thought about Gerrard. Her mind still wandered to scary corners when she thought about her mother. She stared at Pastor Woods, her eyes imploring, asking something she couldn't quite name.

"Now, let me caution you all about something. You're a brand-new person. But don't expect to feel like one overnight. Don't be surprised when a war rages on the inside of you because part of you wants to keep doing the same old things you used to do. You're going to feel like you want one more drink. One more smoke. You might feel like you need to lie down one more time. That's because we're made of flesh. Flesh knows nothing except to seek pleasure. That's all it knows to do, and you must understand that. Don't beat yourself up for that. But now the spirit of Jesus lives inside you. That's the difference you'll begin to see and feel in your life. You'll begin to feel your spirit pulling you in the opposite direction of your flesh. You have the power to go the other way and stay there. That's why Jesus hung on the cross—to set you free from addictions, free from obsessions, free from bad choices and bad situations, free from all the weights in your life. Now you have the power to overcome, and more importantly, to have peace in the process. Amen?"

"Amen," the congregation said.

"Amen," said the men and women at the altar.

"Amen," Marley said.

When the service was over, Marley walked into the vestibule and received hugs from at least five members of the church.

"Welcome home, sugar!" said an elderly woman with a cane.

"Ain't nothing greater than giving your life to Jesus," said a grandfatherly man with silver hair that stood proudly around his leathery face.

Marley felt good. Energized. Challenged. She had heard from God that morning. She was on her way. As she walked toward the doors, a familiar face caught her eyes. She stopped and studied the face for a moment. Where had she seen it before?

Then she remembered. How could she have forgotten that face? Those eyebrows that seemed somehow to seal strength. Those lips that sculpture could not craft. He was talking to a group of people, and when he turned he saw Marley staring at him.

She tried to divert her eyes to the bulletin board hanging near his head, but she knew she was busted. She began to fish through her purse in search of nothing and felt her ears grow hot. When she looked up again, he was still staring at her, and he was smiling. He said something to the group of people he was standing with and made his way over to her.

It *was* him—the guy carrying the boxes of food at the airport a few months ago. The guy she'd practically gawked at until she'd re-minded herself she was engaged.

"The airport, right?" He was still smiling.

"Yeah." Marley blushed. "I remember you." She smiled and real-ized she was nervous. She gripped her purse.

"I definitely remember you." He offered no more than those words, a steady smile, and unwavering eyes that gripped her soul at its root. He didn't seem at all uncomfortable with the silence that ensued. She tried to hold his gaze, but knowing that she contained emotions about as well as a shook-up soda bottle, she looked away.

"I'm Lazarus," he said, reaching for her hand and holding it with both of his. They were warm, yet so unimposing. She couldn't re-member the last time she'd held hands that felt like his, and she hoped, for a minute, that he would never let go.

"I'm Marley. Nice to meet you." She wondered who would let go of whose hand first.

"So this is your first time visiting Gilead's Balm?" He was still holding her hand.

"Yeah, it is. My secretary is a member. We were supposed to meet for the early service, but I sort of got a late start."

"Who's your secretary?"

"Evelyn Gillespie."

"Evelyn's your secretary? Get out of here!" He released Marley's hands.

"Yeah." She wished he was still holding them.

"Oh, man! Her older sister was my baby-sitter! Wow." He rubbed his hand down his nape, his smile still wide.

"It's a small world," Marley commented.

"It's a divine world. It still amazes me how interconnected we all are." He shook his head, and Marley couldn't help but notice that he was even more attractive than she remembered. His skin was like henna, looked as though it were silky to the touch.

"So. I take it you liked the service?"

"I loved it. It was just what I needed."

"Well, praise God," he said.

Marley smiled too. It felt weird hearing him say that. Praise God. She wasn't used to hearing people—especially brothers—express joy about God so openly to people they didn't know.

"Welcome to Gilead's Balm. Hope the word was good enough to make you want to visit again."

"It definitely was," she promised him. "Seemed like the message was aimed directly at me," she laughed.

"I know. It always trips me out when that happens to me. That's how you know God is talking to you," he said. "Well, let me give you a visitor's welcome hug—this ain't a pickup hug, now."

They laughed. Then they embraced. It was warm and affectionate; it was brotherly. Marley wished it were more than that. Then she reminded herself that she was in church.

"Well, Marley. I would offer to walk you to your car, but I have to fold the chairs in the Sunday school classrooms." Lazarus's thick eyebrows wrinkled. He rubbed his neck again.

"Oh, no, don't worry about it," she said, trying to hide her disappointment.

"It was my pleasure to meet you, though. I really hope to see you again one day soon."

"Me too." She smiled.

"God bless you." He gave her a quick squeeze and walked away.

Marley watched him walk down the hall, then she left. On her way to the parking lot, she realized she was feeling empty all of a sudden. She wanted more from her exchange with Lazarus. There was something distinctive about him, and it obviously had to do with his love for God. Yet a part of her wanted Lazarus to be typical and maybe ask for her telephone number the way most men did when they were interested. He hadn't. The fact that he was willing to walk away and risk never seeing or talking to her again was a novelty.

Then she started to focus on the reason why she'd come to church in the first place: because she needed to hear from God. She had. And until she'd bumped into Lazarus, she'd been feeling good. Full. Content.

Marley opened her car door, slid into the driver's seat, and anxiously reread the notes she had jotted down on her program during the sermon. As she allowed her eyes to take in the words, she felt that sweet stirring in her soul again, and the emptiness began to disappear. She knew she'd have to fight to maintain the peace she had found that day. It surely had not come easy, and it felt too good to lose. No anger, no excitement, and certainly no man would get in the way of it. She was determined.

Chapter 14

*P*AM'S EYES WERE on the framed photographs that covered her end table, but her mind was still at the doctor's office. She'd thought she was going to be liberated today. She'd thought she was going to be relieved of the cancerous weight she had been carrying since her surgery back in November. She'd thought, today, that she would receive clearance to stop worrying and start living. Instead, she'd been effectively put on hold. Forced to dwell in uncertainty a little bit longer.

Her last chemotherapy session had been in March, and today she had seen her oncologist for her one-month follow-up. He had examined her chest, heart, lungs, and lymph node areas. He had drawn blood to check her kidneys, liver, and bones. She had expected him to tell her that she had been healed, but he hadn't. Said he couldn't. Said it was too soon to tell much of anything. Said he'd know more at her next follow-up visit in July. "See you then," he had said, as the papers on his clipboard fluttered and he followed her out of the examination room.

It made no sense. For three months she had put her body through a liquid hell, trying to get better—banking on getting better. Each session, she had listened to the nurse talk softly while she pushed hard red fluid through the intravenous needle, followed by white fluid. She had watched the drugs enter her body, and she had drifted along with them into a chemical underworld until her eyelids had grown too heavy to support. She had taken the Zofran for three days after each session, just as the doctor had told her. She had done everything the doctor had told her; she had done more. She had gone out and found an expensive nutritionist to help her reconstruct her entire lifestyle. All of this, and she knew nothing. Wouldn't know anything for another three months. This was worse than the sickest mind game anyone could ever play on her.

She heard keys unlock her front door and sat upright. She pretended to adjust one of the frames on the end table as Marley walked in.

"Hey, Mom." Marley dropped her keys into her purse and tossed it on the couch. "Whew—is it a gorgeous day outside or what? Don't you just love April? Not too hot, not too cold, not too green, and not too pink. It's just right."

Pam looked at her daughter. She was beautiful. More beautiful every day. Words couldn't express the hopes and dreams for her child that she had tucked away in her heart.

"Yeah, April has always been one of my favorite months. Revitalization . . . in April." Pam stood, placing her hands on her hips.

Marley went into the kitchen and opened the refrigerator. "Mmm, this tuna salad looks good." She pulled out the container and stuck a fork in it. "I'm glad to see you're eating well, Mom." She heaped a forkful of tuna into her mouth. "Like your nutritionist said, garbage in, garbage out; nutrients in, nutrients out." She grabbed a box of crackers from the pantry and dug her hand inside.

"Mm-hm," Pam said. She was not going to discuss her cancer with Marley. Not now. Hearing Marley's "Fight, fight, fight" mantra would give her a sure-enough nervous breakdown.

"Oh, before I forget," Pam said quickly, enthusiasm suddenly stepping into the shoes of indifference as she walked into the foyer, "Ava told me about an incredible string quartet she heard at one of her office parties. I thought we might call their agent and get some information—you know, for when you and Gerrard start planning the wedding again. You know, when you're ready to do that." Pam dug out her spiral notepad from the console drawer and returned to the living room. Pen in hand, spectacles on nose, she was ready to talk about things that mattered.

Marley walked into the living room with the plastic container of tuna and the box of crackers. She put them on the coffee table and sat on the couch. Pam was standing by her Queen Anne chair flipping through the pages in her notepad.

"Mom, sit down for a minute."

Pam smiled, her eyes still on the pages in her notepad, and raised a finger. "Okay, just a minute, honey." She mouthed a few words, nodded, then sat in the chair and looked at Marley.

Marley rubbed her eyes, then sighed. "Gerrard and I are not getting married, Mom. Ever."

The smile slowly faded off Pam's face, carrying with it the enthusiasm that had been sparked only moments ago. "Why?"

"I caught him cheating on me." There. No sense dancing around it. Now she found it hard to look at her mother. She was embarrassed—that was a large part of it. Humiliated and bruised, too, because confessing that your man had been cheating on you always took a huge chunk out of your ego. No one—absolutely no one—was immune to becoming a victim, but a part of her still wanted to believe she was beautiful enough, lovable enough, valuable enough that *her* man wouldn't chance it and risk losing *her*.

Pam reclined in the chair and took a deep breath. She folded her hands in front of her mouth. They sat, neither feeling compelled to speak.

"You're certain?" Pam asked.

"*What?* Of course I'm certain, Mom. I saw him with my own eyes. Please don't try to clean this up. It can't be cleaned up, all right?"

"No, no, I'm not trying to do that. I'm just—" Pam stopped speaking. She looked at Marley, and she fought back tears. Tears that foreclosed any possibility of a genuine conversation. There was no way Pam could be honest, come clean, and tell her child that some of her nights were so lonely she would have traded them in for more days of denial with Silas. Pam couldn't bring herself to share that. She could only trust that her daughter was stronger—more self-confident—than she had been. She could only encourage her daughter to use that strength and self-confidence to stay away from Gerrard and know that something better would come along. Or maybe it wouldn't. But either way, Marley would be a better woman for it. These were truths that Pam had been too fragile to embrace. She could only pray her daughter would step into them and walk in them, as if she already knew them.

"If he wasn't treating you right, then you had to break it off. You didn't have a choice," Pam said, looking down. She fiddled with her fingers. "You really didn't have a choice."

Marley looked at her strangely.

"Well." Pam stood up. "That's that," she said, and dropped her spiral notepad on the coffee table. It smacked against the glass surface.

Marley looked down. "Mom, is something wrong? For some strange reason, I feel like you're angry with *me*."

Pam busied herself at the window, fussing with the curtains, fastening and refastening the tiebacks. "No, of course not." She tugged at the sheers. "I just wanted something different for your life, that's all."

"Different from what?" Marley stood, hands on her hips.

"Different from my life." Pam turned around to face Marley. "I wanted you to be married, happy, and taken care of."

"How do you know I won't have that? Gerrard isn't the only man out there, you know. And I can be happy by myself."

"I know that. And you're right. Don't pay me any mind, hear? I'm just—I don't know. You did the right thing, honey." Pam walked past Marley and went upstairs.

Chapter 15

ARLEY STOOD OVER Evelyn's shoulder as they tried to decipher the handwriting that covered Marley's draft brief.

"You *know* I wouldn't dump this job on you if I had time to do it myself, Evelyn. No one should be expected to translate this man's chicken scratch."

"Marley, how many times do I have to tell you that it's not your job to enter a partner's edits to your drafts? You should know that by now. I've been dealing with old men like Bob Billows for twenty years. If I can't figure out what he's written, I'll call him myself and make him translate it for me. Just let me do my job, and you do yours, all right?"

Evelyn shooed Marley away and redirected her attention to the sea of comments in red ink on the paper in front of her. "He needs to leave your drafts alone anyway. Don't know why he doesn't realize he's just messing up the good job you've already done. Good Lord," she mumbled to herself, making the changes faster than Marley ever could have. A CeCe Winans CD was playing on the compact disc player Marley had given Evelyn for Christmas.

Marley's extension rang as she walked away from Evelyn's desk. "Marley, it's Bob," Evelyn called out, still typing.

Marley walked back to Evelyn's desk. "I'll take the call here." She picked up the receiver. "Hi, Bob."

"Are the edits done yet?"

"Ah, no, Bob. You just gave me your changes thirty minutes ago. There appear to be roughly forty pages of edits, so it will take longer than thirty minutes to get them all in." Marley bugged her eyes at Evelyn, and Evelyn shook her head.

"Don't lose your temper with him," Evelyn whispered, squinting to read a comment.

"Well, how much longer is it going to take? I'm leaving in half an hour to catch a plane, and I'd like to take the revised draft with me."

"Evelyn is working as fast as she can. If she can have it done in half an hour, I'll bring the draft to you."

"See that she gets it done, Marley. I'm in a rush, and I need the revised draft." Bob hung up the phone.

Marley stared at the telephone. "He hung up on me."

"Marley, that man is miserable. Don't you know that by now? Don't pay him any mind. Get on back to the work you were doing before he interrupted you. Leave him to the devil." Evelyn took the receiver out of Marley's hand and shooed her, again, to her office.

"Oh, Marley, before you go, I meant to ask you whether you wanted to go to Bible study with me tonight. Seven-thirty. I'm working overtime, so we could follow each other over to the church. How 'bout that?"

Marley hesitated. "Well, I was planning to visit my mother for a little while."

"Why can't you do both? Visit your mom before we go? Bible study will do you good, honey. You've been under a lot of pressure lately between these fools here at work and everything in your personal life. You need to nourish your soul. Going to church on Sundays is wonderful, and I'm so happy you've been going regularly. But you'll find that you really start to learn the word at Bible study. Give it a try. I promise you'll feel better afterward."

"Well, all right." The thought of being at Gilead's Balm, in the company of all those people who loved God, was soothing. In a matter of weeks, Gilead's Balm had become Marley's second home, her respite. "I do want to go by my mother's house first, though— she was sort of down when I stopped by the other day. So I'll meet you at church?"

"Yep," Evelyn responded, chipping away at the keyboard. "In the lobby at quarter past seven. We'll get seats together."

"Sounds good. Thanks for thinking of me, Evelyn."

Marley saw Evelyn as soon as she walked into the vestibule. And when Evelyn stood on her toes and waved Marley over, she saw someone standing next to her. It was Lazarus.

Suddenly, the ten-foot distance between the door and where Evelyn and Lazarus were standing seemed like a swimsuit pageant runway. Marley abhorred being watched as she walked, which was exactly what Evelyn and Lazarus were doing. She managed to make it over without stumbling over her heels or otherwise draw-ing more attention to herself. Her cheeks were burning when she reached them.

"Hey, sugar," Evelyn beamed, hugging Marley. "You remember Lazarus, don't you?" she asked innocently, a knowing glance ema-nating from her eyes.

"I do. How are you, Lazarus?"

"Doing good, doing good. And you?"

"I'm doing really well. Good to see you again."

"Even better to see you," he said. "Have you been going to the early service?"

"Um, actually, I've been switching between the two. My work schedule has been pretty hectic lately."

"Mm-hm. So that's why I've been missing you." He smiled.

Marley's stomach dropped. Had he said what she thought he'd said? He'd been "missing" her? Hoping to see her? "Really?" she heard herself say.

Evelyn chuckled. "Well, let's head on inside and see if we can find seats together." Like a chaperone, she led them into the sanctuary.

Marley tried to stay focused on the message, but the first ten minutes of what was said did not make it through one ear. She could not believe she was sitting next to Lazarus. She had not expected to see him.

He was gorgeous. But more than that, warmth radiated from him. Marley couldn't help but let her mind run wild with thoughts about what it all might mean, her meeting Lazarus after such a chance encounter at the airport. Maybe their meeting wasn't by chance after all. Maybe they would go out on a date. Maybe they'd end up in a serious relationship. Maybe they would get married. Maybe, maybe, maybe.

She got a grip on herself and tuned in to the message. Her concentration lasted all of forty seconds. She was dying to know whether Lazarus was equally excited about sitting next to her. She tried to sneak a sideways glance at him. She noticed his long, thick eyelashes, how they complimented his brows and mustache, and the butterflies began to turn in her stomach. She was so caught up in her sideways glance that she didn't notice Lazarus lower his eyes and return the glance. His huge smile surfaced, and Marley realized she was caught. She immediately turned her attention to her Bible—a new one made of genuine leather—and fumbled with the delicate pages. She silently thanked God when she heard the pastor repeat the scripture from which he was reading, and she quickly flipped there. She immersed herself in the message, not realizing until her jaws began to hurt that she had not stopped smiling. Neither had Lazarus.

"The word was right on time, as usual," Evelyn said to Lazarus and Marley as they walked toward the parking lot.

"Wasn't it?" Lazarus said.

"It's amazing how I feel like Pastor Woods is speaking directly about my problems every time I come," Marley said. "I've heard so many people quote the scripture that tells us to be still and know that God is God, but before tonight, I never really understood what it meant. I'm always on the verge of going off on my boss," she added, glancing sheepishly at Evelyn and chuckling, "and I'm always thinking that something I say or do will cause him to change. I can't change that man. And now I realize it's not my job to change him. God can handle that."

"That's right, sugar," Evelyn said, smiling. "God is a big God. You just sit still and let Him do His thing." Evelyn reached into her purse and pulled out her keys. "Well, this is me." She unlocked the driver's door. "Thanks for walking me to my car, babies. Now you-all be good boys and girls and get in your cars and go on home." The three shared a laugh, and Lazarus closed Evelyn's car door and waved her off as she drove away.

"I'm glad you enjoyed Bible study," he said, turning to look at Marley as they walked toward her car.

"Yeah, I really did. Although I have to confess that I sort of missed the first ten minutes of what Pastor Woods said."

Lazarus laughed. "Tell me about it." It grew comfortably silent as they walked.

"The Bible has never made so much sense to me before. This might sound sacrilegious to you, but I never really used to look forward to reading the Bible, much less studying it. Now I find myself excited about it. My mother used to have to drag me out of bed to go to church on Sunday mornings. You never could have told me the day would come when I would have my own desire to go."

"That doesn't sound sacrilegious at all. I went through the same thing, and I'd be surprised if most people don't go through it at one point or another. Your parents can take you to church all they want, but it's not until you establish an independent relationship with God that things begin to mean something to you. The Bible is just another book written by men until you know God for yourself."

Marley nodded. "So you've been a member of this church for a long time?"

"Yeah, pretty much all my life. My family used to go to another church not too far from here, but Pastor Woods and my father went to high school together, played football together, and all that. When he told my father he was going to start Gilead's Balm, our family was one of the first to join."

"Wow. Deeply ingrained," Marley commented, half impressed with Lazarus's established relationship with the church and God—and half envious.

"Mm, well, I wouldn't necessarily say that. I love this church. But I'm not here because of it or the pastor. I keep coming because of the word. If I ever stop hearing the word—I mean the real word, not some sugar-coated prepackaged message that comes from everywhere but the Bible—then I'm gone. 'Cause I'm only a man. And the minute I'm separated from the word, I'm in trouble."

Lazarus's humility struck Marley. She wasn't used to hearing a man acknowledge his weaknesses so openly. Gerrard was the exact opposite. Talking to Gerrard, one would think there was no being higher than him. Yet Lazarus seemed to put all his confidence in God and absolutely none in himself. That was strange to her, different. Even she was guilty of acting as if every great thing she did was a result of her own talents, her own skills, her own abilities. She seethed when Bob took all the credit for work that she did, stamping his name on it and deleting hers. It had not occurred to her that

God was the real author and it really should not have made a difference whether or not she got recognition.

"Yeah," was all she could manage in response.

"Do you travel a lot on your job?"

"Well, it depends on the client I'm working with. When I saw you at the airport, I was on my way to New York to defend the deposition of a vice president of one of my corporate clients. But a lot of clients are local, so I don't have to travel much to do their work."

"Evelyn said they work you pretty hard. You know that means you do good work, right? They wouldn't be hounding you otherwise."

"If you say so." Marley smiled. "So you've been getting the four-one-one on me from Evelyn?"

"Oh, *yeah*," Lazarus sang. "Brother's gotta do his homework." They had long since reached Marley's car and were standing in front of her door. She climbed into the driver's seat.

"Mm-*hm*," Marley said as Lazarus closed the door for her. She was silent. She knew Lazarus was different from other men she had met in the past and that this was not going to be the part where he would ask her for her phone number or come up with some smooth line to ensure things would move forward. She knew this, but part of her still desired it.

It was as if he could read her mind.

"Let me be straight with you, Marley. I want to get to know you as a friend. I'm not going to kick a lot of game to you the way I might have back in the day, because that's not how God wants me to behave toward women. I'm a take-it-slow, get-to-know kind of man. I know it's old-fashioned, but trust me when I say that the old-fashioned me is a much better person than the cool, hip, and down me."

"That's completely fine with me, Lazarus." Which was mostly true. But impatience was one of Marley's biggest shortcomings.

"You play tennis?"

"Tennis? Well, not really. I mean, I've been trying to develop a game for a while now. I know some of the basics, but I have no skills to speak of."

"What?" Lazarus said, feigning surprise. "You mean you can't beat Venus?"

"Hah! Venus could be blindfolded and still whip me."

"Well, what are you doing this Saturday?"

"Nothing much." The butterflies had reclaimed her stomach again, and she had no clue what Lazarus was going to say next.

"Why don't you and some of your friends come out to White Park in the morning to hit some balls? I teach a tennis clinic to some of the Beecher Hills kids from nine to ten, and after that I'm going to help my brother and his wife and her sister with their backhands and their serves. Actually, they're going to need help with more than that, based on how they were doing the last time we met on the courts."

Marley smiled. She could not believe he hadn't proposed the same dinner-and-a-movie plan that almost every other man in Atlanta would have offered like a two-carat diamond ring. Nor had he come up with a plan for the two of them to be alone on a "first date," when expectations would be high and the potential for disaster even higher. What if he didn't have an interesting bone in his body? What if he was one of those Holy Rollers, always toting a Bible and quoting scripture and mentioning God every third sentence? What if he had halitosis like Glenn Jerome Harris from Mayes High who had been so fine and so perfect that something *had* to be wrong with him, and it had turned out to be his breath? This tennis plan of Lazarus's made it very easy for either one of them to check out early if things began to head south.

"I'd love to."

"Cool. Ten o'clock at the park?"

"Yep."

"The park is just past West End. You know how to get there?"

"What? I went to school in West End. Don't play me like I don't know about the 'hood!"

"Where'd you go? To the Gated Community at Spelman?"

"Why do I have to be from Spelman?" Marley asked, barely able to contain her laughter.

"What? You went to Mo' Brown? Huh? I got it wrong?"

Marley doubled over. "Whatever. I'll see you at ten o'clock on Saturday, Lazarus."

"Cool. See you then. Drive safely."

"You, too."

"God bless you."

Marley smiled. Those three words sounded better than any three she'd ever heard a man speak to her in her entire life. They gave her a new perspective.

"God bless you, too."

"Girl, what took you so long to get home? I've been calling you for the past hour!" Marley was bursting with excitement. "I *have* to tell you what happened tonight!"

"All right, all right! Goodness!" Ashley said. "What's it about?"

"This guy I met at church."

"Oh, Lord."

"Seriously, Ashley!"

"All right, all right, what's his name?" Ashley had this thing about needing to know someone's name before she could process anything else about the person. She liked to fit people into boxes that already existed in her mind.

"Lazarus."

"Mm-hm. Okay, go ahead."

"Okay," Marley said, grinning. "The first time I saw him was at the airport last year on my way to New York to defend a deposition. Girl, it was like a movie. The sun was rising, the leaves were rustling in the wind—"

"You're crazy."

"I'm serious! All this was really happening when I met him."

"But you were at the airport, not strolling through the park!"

"But I was looking out the window! Would you let me finish, please! Like I was saying, I was watching the sun rise and the leaves rustle from the *window* at the airport. I started walking down the jetway, and I saw him carrying a large box to the plane."

"Mm, a handyman. Well, all right now," Ashley said, pleasantly surprised. Ashley was biased in favor of blue-collar brothers; Ashley's father, her poster man for male perfection, was a mechanic.

"Yeah, girl. You should've seen him carrying that box. Biceps busting out all over the place. But seriously, Ashley, there was something really different that I sensed about him. Something very peaceful and good."

"I believe you. I think that's totally possible. You don't have to be able to pinpoint a specific source to know that your senses are right."

"Exactly. So anyway, I ran into him just as I was boarding the plane, but nothing happened. We exchanged a few words and that was it. But you know how you get hot all over when you know someone is watching you?"

"Oh, yes. That is the worst!"

"Isn't it? I was on fire when I walked away. Then I got a wedgie. Then I almost tripped and fell inside the plane."

"Why does that always happen when you see someone you like? I mean, of all times, why then?"

"*Really.* So anyway, I thought about him a few times here and there, but not too much because I was still with Gerrard. Then, remember the first time I visited Gilead's Balm?"

"Yeah."

"I ran into him after the service."

"Get out of here! You didn't mention that before."

"I know, I know. Because I was really excited about the service, and I didn't want to confuse the two, you know what I mean? He just wasn't the significant thing about that day, so I didn't think it was worth mentioning."

"I'm so proud of you, Marley. Imagine how proud of you God is."

"Yes, yes, yes. So anyway, I ran into him and we talked for a few minutes."

"Did he remember you?"

"Oh, yeah. He made that very clear. But we didn't talk for long, because he had to fold chairs after the service."

"Aw. He's active in the church? That is *so* good."

"I know, isn't it?"

"Yes, girl. It really is."

"So anyway, that was that. I was kind of mad that he didn't ask for my number or anything, but—"

"Ha. Hurt that ego a little bit, huh?"

"Well, you know, a sister *was* looking good that day."

"Rocking one of your side-split suits?"

"You know I was."

"Yeah, that steps on the toes a bit. But then he would have been a typical brother, and that's the last thing you need."

"Lord knows I don't need that. But the ego was slightly black and blue as a result."

"Okay, so keep going."

"Right. So I didn't let that faze me. I had gone to church for a reason that day, and it had nothing to do with Lazarus because, remember, I didn't even know he was there. I needed God in my life in a major way."

"Right, right. I hear you."

"So anyway, I went to Bible study tonight and saw him again. Girl, girl, girl."

"Did he see you?"

"As soon as I walked in the door. He was standing with Evelyn. We all sat together. It was like sitting next to my teacher and a boy I have a crush on. I felt like I was in third grade, Ashley. All silly and giddy."

"Mm. I remember the last time I felt that way around somebody. Adam." Ashley sighed. "He definitely brought out the inner child in me."

"Yeah, he was a sweetie," Marley responded in a chiding tone. For three months after Adam had left Atlanta for business school in Pennsylvania, he and Ashley had tried to maintain a long-distance relationship. Adam had asked Mr. Miller if Ashley could live with him until they got married two years later, and Mr. Miller told Adam that planes would still fly from Atlanta to Pennsylvania in two years and she could go then. Two years had come and gone. Adam was still in Pennsylvania, Ashley in Atlanta, each hoping the other would come around.

"Yeah, yeah, yeah. Back to Lazarus. Did you exchange numbers this time?"

"Actually, we didn't. But we did make plans."

"Plans? What kind of plans?"

"Well, he invited me to play tennis this Saturday."

"Are you serious?"

"Yeah."

"Does he know you can't play that well?"

"Of course he knows that. He's going to help me along with some of his family members. He told me to bring my friends."

"Hm. He sounds really decent, Marley. Not the typical first date at all."

"I know. I don't think I could handle a typical first date right now."

"Exactly. The whole Gerrard thing was a serious chapter in your life, and even though time has passed, you still need to heal and be with yourself."

"You're preaching to the choir. Believe me, I can't even imagine myself in a relationship with someone else anytime soon. A good friend is about all I need."

"Have you told your mother what really happened with Gerrard?"

Marley sighed. "Yeah, finally. I'd been trying to tell her for a while, but every time I got myself ready to do it, something seemed to go wrong—she was nauseated, or her blood count was low—it was always something."

"How did it go?" Ashley asked.

"Mm, okay, I guess. At first she was hoping there was some kind of mistake."

"Oh, goodness."

"You know? Like I really hadn't seen him with my own eyes—I'd just seen somebody who walked, talked, and sounded like him."

"Mm-mm-mm," Ashley said.

"Eventually she came around. She even said I'd done the right thing. But she seemed so hurt, Ashley. Like she had nothing left to hope for."

"Mm. That's understandable. Think about all she's been through. Just continue to stick close to her during this time."

"I will. I'm going over Friday after work. Are you and Deanna still planning to go over, too?"

"Yeah. In fact, I'll probably get to her house before you because I'm leaving work early that day. Oh, and wait till you see what we're giving her. It's incredible."

"If you-all put your heads together, then I know it is," Marley said.

"So . . . tennis Saturday morning, huh?"

"Yep." Marley was smiling again. "You have to go with me, Ash. I don't care what you have to do. Nothing is more important than helping me out. Plus, I want you to meet him."

"I'll go. It'll be fun. Don't be mad when I flex my skills, though. You know I'm about to turn pro."

"Whatever. I'm gonna call Deanna and see if she can go, too."

"You know Deanna wouldn't miss this kind of high drama for the world."

"All right, girl. So I'll see you Friday?" Marley asked.

"Yep. See you Friday."

"All right. Ash? Thanks, girl."

Marley hung up and lay flat on her bed. She kicked off her shoes, lifted her legs, and stared at her feet. The daisies the pedicurist had painted on her two large toes seemed to smile and wave at her. She smiled and waved back. "Hi, daisies," she said, wiggling her toes. "You-all had a good day today?" She chuckled. "Me, too."

Chapter 16

PAM WAS LAUGHING at one of Deanna's jokes when Marley walked through the door on Friday evening. Everyone was in good humor—even Ma Grand was chuckling.

"Hi, honey," Pam said to Marley, lifting her cheek for a kiss. "Your friends are crazy, that's all I have to say." Pam reached for her water. She was sitting in her Queen Anne chair with a colorful quilt draped over her knees.

"Wow! That quilt is beautiful! Where did you get it?" Marley inquired, making her rounds to hug and kiss everyone.

"The girls gave it to me. Isn't it the most precious thing you've ever seen?" Vines with oval leaves and burgundy square patches with coral and mauve flowers were sewn onto a deep beige background. Pam smoothed it admiringly.

"Very nice, ladies." Marley winked thanks at her friends. Ashley was sitting on the floor in between Deanna's legs while Deanna oiled her scalp.

"I know one thing," Ma Grand said. "You better not call that boy again."

"Call what boy?" Marley asked, sitting next to Deanna on the couch and pulling off her block-heeled pumps. "Who are you talking about?"

"Pablo," Ashley answered. Pablo and Deanna had begun to date shortly after they'd met at the Believers' Temple banquet last winter. But once the Braves' season had begun, Pablo had managed to call Deanna only twice.

"In my day it was unheard of, strictly unheard of, for you to call on a man. You're supposed to let him pursue you. You ain't supposed to chase after him like you're in heat."

"Yes, Ma Grand, but it's a new millennium. Things aren't the way they were back then. Today women are progressive. There's nothing wrong with a woman calling a man for a change."

"Some things should never change, Deanna. That's why all these sorry men are walking around here today, unemployed, sitting up, and being taken care of like little girls while the women are going out every day earning a living. 'Cause y'all want to be aggressive with them and do all the things they're supposed to be doing. You need to let a man be a man, honey."

"Ma Grand, I said *progressive*, not *aggressive*," Deanna corrected.

"I know what you said. And I know what I said. *Aggressive.* Fast. Hot pants. Fire burning between your legs."

"Deanna," Marley said, "you can't win this battle with her, so you may as well cut your losses."

"All of you need to listen to me," Ma Grand said, wagging her finger. "I've been here much longer than you have, and certain things just don't change. Now, if you want to earn any kind of respect for yourself as a woman, you sit still and be patient and let a man express some leadership and direction about himself. If you don't ever hear from him, forget about him and move on. I don't care what kind of ball he throws around in the air for a living. Football, basketball, baseball, ain't none of it nothing but a game, and ain't none of them nothing but imperfections on legs, just like the rest of us."

"Well all righty then." Marley stood up to go to the kitchen. "I guess you told us."

"I can't argue with that, Ma Grand," Deanna said. "I'm going to try your way and just sit still and be patient." Ashley stood and began to brush her hair, and Deanna crossed her legs and wrapped her arms around her knees. She wiggled her toes, eight of which were adorned with silver rings.

"You do that," said Ma Grand.

"In fact, I'll resort to extracting my pleasures vicariously. Maybe I'll meet some nice old-fashioned man when I go to play tennis with Marley and her new friend tomorrow."

Marley almost dropped the glass she had removed from the kitchen cabinet. She had specifically told Deanna—or at least she had intended to tell Deanna—not to mention Lazarus and the tennis date in front of her mother. Her mother was not at all prepared for that.

"Say what?" Ma Grand asked.

"Uh-oh." Deanna leaned sideways for a glimpse of Marley in the kitchen, to find out whether she had just stuck her foot in her mouth. "I'm rambling again. Just ignore me." Deanna waved her hand in the air and with it tried to dismiss the valuable piece of information she had revealed.

"You and your mouth," Ashley mumbled, brushing her hair more vigorously.

Pam stared ahead, sipping her water.

"You have a new friend?" Ma Grand asked Marley. Marley pretended not to hear Ma Grand. "I know you heard me!" Ma Grand bellowed.

"That's right, I have a friend. Period." Marley returned to the living room. "Deanna is making it sound much more involved than it is. He is simply a friend I met at my church, and a *group* of us, not just he and I, are going to play tennis tomorrow. He is not a love interest." Marley sat back down on the couch and purposefully caused most of her weight to land on Deanna's thigh. Deanna winced, contorted her upper body in trademark dramatized pain, and gave Marley a light shove.

Ma Grand examined Marley. "You sure have been spending a lot of time at that church lately." She looked away, then looked squarely back at her and whispered, "Have you taken up with a cult?"

"No, Gran, I have not taken up with a cult."

"Well, all right, then." Ma Grand picked up *Better Homes and Gardens* from the coffee table. "He asked you to go, right?"

"Yes, ma'am."

"Yeah, well, that's all right, then. You can go." Everyone laughed at the notion that Marley would need Ma Grand's permission to play tennis with Lazarus. Everyone except Pam, who remained conspicuously silent.

After another hour of chatter, Deanna and Ashley said their good-byes and left. Marley stayed behind and regretted it the moment her mother began to speak.

"So who's this young man you're seeing?" Pam asked, picking at a loose thread in her new quilt.

"I'm not seeing anyone, Mom. A friend from church invited me to play tennis, that's all." Marley pretended to be preoccupied with an article she wasn't reading in the newspaper.

"It's good to know that that's all there is to it. Just a few months ago, you were planning to marry Gerrard. Even though you're angry with him, you still need to give yourself time."

"Angry with him? You think I'm *angry* with him? I'm not angry. I'm *disgusted*. He makes my *skin* crawl. There's nothing I need to sort out. The way you make it sound, I'm just temporarily upset with him over something trivial."

"No, I'm not saying that at all. I'm just advising you not to let your

feelings toward Gerrard drive you prematurely into another relationship. That can happen, you know, without you even realizing it
until later." By now Pam had made the loose thread considerably
looser and had begun to wrap it around her pinky.

"Look, I appreciate your advice. And I'm not rushing into anything. But I'm through with Gerrard, and I want to be very clear
about that. No amount of time in the world is going to make me
change my mind, okay?" Marley stared at her mother, awaiting
some form of acknowledgment.

"I understand you, loud and clear," Pam responded, still looping
the loose thread around her pinky.

"That's the smartest thing I've heard you say in a long time," Ma
Grand said, not looking up from her magazine. "Boy ain't no good,
never was no good, never gonna be no good. You just saved yourself and us all a lifetime of heartache." Ma Grand turned the page in
her magazine.

Pam stopped looping the thread. "Mama, are you implying
something?"

"I ain't implying nothing, Pamela. I'm stating a fact, which is that
she had no business marrying that boy in the first place, and she
made the right decision to cancel that thing before it was too late."

"No, I mean the comment about a lifetime of heartache. Were
you implying something about me?"

"No, I was not. I don't need to imply things. I'll say them directly. You know how I feel about your marriage, Pamela, so why
would I imply it? You had no business marrying the man you married. And that man gave me heartache, for sure. But I'll say that directly. I don't need to imply it."

"You know what? I'm really, really tired of your comments,
Mama."

"Mom, don't—"

"Marley, hush. Just be quiet, you hear?" Pam looked at her
mother. "I have listened to you bad-mouth my decisions since child-

hood. From the friends I chose to the instrument I wanted to play in high school to the major I selected in college. I could have married Jesus Christ, and that still would not have been good enough for you."

"Don't you dare bring the Lord Jesus Christ into this, Pamela! You better watch yourself, young—"

"No, no, I'm not going to watch myself. I'm going to say what I have to say, in my house, and you're going to listen to me. Nothing I did was ever good enough for you. The fact that you think marrying Silas was a mistake doesn't mean much, because just about everything I do is a mistake in your eyes."

"Pamela, do you hear yourself? You're talking crazy. That medication must be affecting you, 'cause you're not making any sense at all right now. I was pleased with a lot of things you did. Maybe not everything, but certainly with a lot of things."

"Oh, really? Like what?" Pam let go of the loose thread. The quilt began to slide down her knees.

"Mom," Marley interjected, beginning to fear the outcome of the conversation. Ten minutes ago, they had been laughing. How had this happened? "Let's just—"

Ma Grand ignored Marley. "Pam, this is ridiculous. I'm not going to sit here and name all the things you did in life that made me happy. That's ridiculous. You're taking this too far." Ma Grand patted the arm of the love seat. "Now just stop it and calm yourself down."

"I'm calm, Mama. I'm simply asking you a question that you can't answer. You know, I'm learning a lot about myself and about you right through here. And I'm not going to continue to carry around all this guilt about the choices I've made in life. If I made bad choices when I was younger, it's not just a reflection on me. It's a reflection on you as my mother. You're the one who was supposed to teach me everything I needed to know as a woman."

"Oh, no, you will not! You most certainly will *not* sit here and blame me for your bad decisions. I taught you what you needed to know, and you still went out and did what you wanted to do. You ain't gon' blame me for that!"

"Oh, yes. Yes indeed. What's your role in all this, Mama? What did you ever teach me about finding a husband? When did you ever pull me aside, sit me down, and tell me what you thought I needed to know about men and about marriage? All you ever did was turn your nose up at everyone I dated or had any interest in. That's nothing but passive, negative feedback. What did you do to teach me what you thought I needed to know? Huh?"

"Why are you-all arguing about the past?" Marley whined, slamming her hands on her knees. "Please! Stop it!"

"Marley, shut your mouth!" Ma Grand snapped, then turned to face Pam. "Pamela, you had a daddy that was the perfect role model for a husband! No words I could have ever said to you would have been better than the living example you had in your own house when you were growing up."

"Yeah, Mama, but that's just not enough. That's your perspective, not mine. In my view, Daddy put up with a whole lot of crap from you, and most times I wished he would put his foot down and not let you dominate him. I can't say that I was looking for someone just like Daddy."

"Your father was good to me, Pamela! Don't you ever forget it! I did not mistreat him. He loved me, and I loved him, and we understood each other. And that's what marriage is about."

"Yeah, well, maybe that worked for you-all, but I wanted more. Maybe Daddy understood that your way of showing him you loved him was by fussing at him and telling him what to do all the time. I decided that I wanted to express love differently in my marriage. But when I got married, I realized I didn't really know how to do that. Because I had never seen it done in my house. I wanted to kiss my husband a lot and tell him that I loved him, but it was hard to do. I felt awkward and silly when I tried to express my emotions. So I started doing other things. Like baking cakes. But my husband didn't need baked goods."

"Well, that's not my fault! Maybe your childhood wasn't perfect, but you did not want for anything and you had—"

"There you go again, Mama. Talking about what I had and what I did not lack. There's more to childhood and parenting than that. It's so easy for you to tell everybody else what's wrong with them, but you can never accept the fact that maybe you didn't always get it right."

"I won't stand for this! I will not. You say whatever you want about me, but don't you say one unkind word about your father to my face ever again! You hear me, Pamela?"

Marley hopped off the couch and walked toward her grandmother. "Gran, *please,*" she begged, touching her shoulder lightly, "don't get upset." She squeezed Ma Grand's shoulder, trying to subdue the tension in it with her fingers.

Pam looked past Marley, past her attempts to soothe Ma Grand and calm the situation, and continued. "I didn't say an unkind word about Daddy. I loved him just as much as you did. I'm talking about you, not him. And what I'm saying is not unkind. It's the *truth,* as you so often characterize it." Pam bent over and picked up the quilt.

"Ain't no truth in none of that!" Ma Grand's voice cracked. She lifted herself up by the arm of the love seat, shaking Marley's hand off her shoulder in the process, and made her way out of the living room. Pam sat quietly as her mother passed. Ma Grand continued to mumble to herself as she walked up the steps to the guest room.

Marley's eyes followed her grandmother out of the room, then rested on her mother. She ran her fingers through her hair and dropped her weight onto the love seat. Sighing, she rested her face in her hands.

"Mom," Marley began, her face still covered, her voice muffled, "maybe the three of us should go to church together on Sunday. I think it would be good for us." She rubbed her eyes, then looked at her mother.

Pam narrowed her eyes. "Marley, church is not the answer to everything. Stop talking to me about church. I know about church. I've been going to church much longer than you have. Church does not hold the answers to all of life's problems."

"No, it doesn't. But God does."

"Fine, then you talk to God about your problems and I'll talk to Him about mine. Okay?"

"Okay." Marley stood up and stretched. "I'm gonna head on home now. Get some rest, Mom." She leaned over and kissed her mother on the cheek. "I'll call you tomorrow. I love you."

Marley walked toward the front door. "Bye, Ma Grand," she called up the steps but didn't get a response. Ma Grand either couldn't hear her or didn't want to hear her, either of which was fine with Marley. She understood. "Tell Ma Grand I said bye." She walked out the front door.

Pam yanked the loose thread from the quilt. The central stitches began to unravel.

Chapter 17

THE GIRLS MET for breakfast at Buster's Kitchen early on Saturday morning. For different reasons, they were all intrigued by the day's coming events. Deanna had been dying to wear the tennis dress she had bought on sale at Parisians almost two years before. Ashley wanted to meet this Lazarus and get a feel for the kind of man he was. Marley just wanted to see his smile again.

"Good morning, beautiful ladies," Deanna sang, swishing her hips from side to side as she approached the table. Everyone had a good laugh as she turned around and modeled her outfit.

"Look at how her tennis shoes match the stripe on the side of her dress," Ashley observed. "Very cute, very cute. But the question is," she said, eyes wide, "can you play as good as you look? 'Cause, see, you can't be out there looking like a million bucks and playing like ten cents. That's why I refuse to buy anything that remotely resembles a tennis outfit until I can legitimately call myself an intermediate player."

"I'll have you know that I actually have game. I don't know why you assume I don't. I played tennis throughout high school. Granted,

I've let my game slip a bit over the past few years, but the kid still has skills."

"Okay, Deanna. We'll soon see," Ashley said.

"Morning, ladies." It was Kendall, a waiter who had attended Emory while the girls were at Spelman.

"Hey, Kendall," they sang in unison.

"How you doin'?" Deanna asked, happy to see him. They knew each other well because their paths had crossed in the undergraduate thespian world.

"I'm fantastic, Deanna. And you?"

"I can't complain." Deanna had a way of making even simple statements sound seductive when she wanted to.

"You certainly can't. Hey," he said, sliding an empty tray under his arm, "I've been meaning to ask you why I haven't seen you at any of the SAG meetings? Don't you still want to act?"

"Of course I do, Kendall," Deanna replied with widened eyes, lightly touching his hand with her fingertips. "I've just been sidetracked lately. I got bit by the corporate America bug, and I ended up allowing my car note and shopping sprees to become higher priorities than starving to make the big time. I have allowed myself to become a true sellout, Kendall. *Whatever* are we going to *do* with me?"

"I'm not mad at you," he said, smiling. "You gotta take care of business, and sometimes it means putting your dreams on the back burner. But you need to be saving that money you're making instead of spending it. That's the only way you'll be able to go for it when you're ready."

"True indeed," Deanna agreed.

"So what can I get you ladies?" He winked at Marley and Ashley.

"We're eating light, Kendall," Marley said. "We're playing tennis this morning, and we don't want to be all big and bloated on the courts."

"I ain't *never* seen you ladies eat light! This will be a first."

They laughed, and Kendall took their orders and politely excused himself.

"He is a chocolate morsel from heaven. A chocolate morsel, I tell you," Deanna said.

"Yes, he is," Ashley agreed.

"Does Lazarus look as good as him?" Deanna asked.

Marley smiled. "I'm not even going to hype him up. You'll see. But I was serious when I told you that this is not a typical physical attraction kind of thing. He looks good, for sure, but it's his spirit that is really attracting me and making me want to get to know him. Just having him as a friend would be enough for me right now."

"Whatever," Deanna said, smirking.

"I'm serious, Dee. Why is that so hard to believe?"

"Because you can't tell me that you'd be playing tennis with him today if you weren't physically attracted to him. Spiritual attraction alone will not do the job."

"That's true, Deanna," Ashley added, "but if all she's looking for is a friend, then she doesn't need anything more than spiritual attraction to spend time with him. That's totally possible."

"Yes, but that's not the situation here, Ashley. Can't you see? Look at Marley. She blushes whenever you mention the man's name. She has that unintentionally beautiful look going on this morning—you know, diamond studs in her ears, hair sort of pulled up but sort of hanging in all the right places. Lip gloss a-shining. She knows exactly what she's doing, and it *ain't* about no spiritual attraction."

Ashley looked at Marley, then laughed. "She sort of has you pegged, sweetie."

"I never said I wasn't attracted to Lazarus. I'd be lying if I said I wasn't. But I'm not looking for a relationship, Deanna. Not right now." Marley looked at her hands. "Honestly, the most important thing to me these days is getting my inner self together. I have been spending more and more time with God, and I cannot tell you how much happier I am." She smiled. "I am amazed with God right now. If I'm in love with anyone, it's Him."

Ashley grinned, her cheeks bloated with pride. "I've noticed a change in you, too," she said. "And I want to tell you publicly that I am *so* proud of you. You've always been a beautiful person physically. But since you've been going to church, Marley, you've become a more beautiful person spiritually. You've found God, and He is making such a difference in your life."

Marley hugged Ashley and felt a lump forming in her throat. "That means so much to me, Ash. It has not been easy. I had hit a very low point. There was just so much pain in my life—with Gerrard, with my mother—and I really didn't know how to deal with it. But I feel like God literally picked me up out of the middle of a storm. I know I sound like I'm testifying or something," she added, laughing awkwardly and looking down.

"That's okay, keep on," Ashley said.

"But God is good," Marley continued. "I can say that and really mean it. You know, they say that things change in your life when you've really made a commitment to God. It's amazing, but the first thing that changed with me is that I can't even imagine drinking anymore."

"You mean drinking *alcohol?*" Deanna asked.

"Yeah." Marley leaned forward and whispered, "Do you know that the night of the church banquet, when I saw Gerrard, I drank a whole bottle of wine by myself?"

"What's wrong with wine?" Deanna asked loudly. "Shoot, *Jesus* drank wine. I mean, I can see why you shouldn't get drunk, but are you saying you think there's something wrong with having a little wine every now and then?" Deanna's eyes were wide and disbelieving.

"I think there's something wrong with it," Ashley said. "But you know I've felt that way since forever. There's a scripture in Romans that we studied recently in my Bible study, and it confirmed exactly what I had been feeling. Basically, if you're a Christian you have a responsibility to live upright in front of your brothers and sisters so that you don't cause them to stumble in their Christian walk. Not everyone can handle drinking, so, basically, your drinking could cause someone else to stumble.

"Like my Aunt Joyce," Ashley continued. "The whole family knows she's an alcoholic. She had finally stopped drinking and was starting to get herself together. Then she went to a card party at Uncle Raymond's house. Uncle Ray has everything from Alizé to Johnny Walker Red, and not only that, but his bottles are in a revolving glass case he locks when he leaves the room. It's better than the corner liquor store. Aunt Joyce left the party early because she just couldn't stand it. The next week my dad found her in her living room passed out from a binge."

Deanna cocked her head to the side. "Why should your uncle have to change his lifestyle on account of your aunt's weaknesses? That doesn't even make sense. She's a grown woman, responsible for herself."

"Why did Jesus need to die for your sins? You're a grown woman, responsible for your own actions. Right?" Ashley asked. "It's all about sacrificing for someone else's sake, Dee. It's about living for reasons other than doing what makes you feel good."

Deanna raised her hand. "All right, all right, all *right*." She guzzled the orange juice that Kendall had dropped off. "But I need to see that scripture for myself. That might be one man's interpretation of it. And I bet you ten other people would interpret it differently."

"Well, find out for yourself. You're a Christian, Deanna, so you're obligated to do that—now that I've told you about it. See whether God convicts your heart one way or the other." Ashley winked and sipped her juice.

*　　*　　*

When they arrived at the park, Marley's stomach began to hurt. She twisted her ring.

"You nervous?" Ashley asked.

"It's the weirdest thing! I feel like a child. I can't remember the last time I got butterflies before I saw a man."

Deanna patted Marley's hair and grinned.

"That's precious. Really, it is. It's innocent. Hold on to that." Ashley climbed out of the car and grabbed her racket and balls from the trunk.

They walked toward the courts, where nine or ten children sat in a semicircle facing Lazarus. Marley could not hear what Lazarus was saying, but the children were nodding and laughing and seemed to agree with all of it. She got closer, and suddenly the group turned quiet. She squinted and realized that Lazarus and the children had bowed their heads. They were praying. She heard Lazarus speaking softly, and heard him conclude with a resounding "in Jesus' name."

"In Jesus' name!" the children shouted, lifting their heads and opening their eyes in excitement. "Amen!" They hopped up and scattered like marbles.

"I like him already," Ashley whispered to Marley and shoved her on the arm.

"Hi." A soft voice traveled up to Marley from several feet below. A delicate voice. Marley looked down and saw a little girl. Her hair was unruly, and the crust in the corners of her eyes suggested that her face had not been washed since she'd woken up that morning. Still, she was beautiful.

"Well, hello there," Marley said, squatting so their eyes could meet. "What's your name?"

"Aiesha," she sang, and she swayed her body from side to side. Then she smiled a huge smile, revealing two missing front teeth.

"Aiesha. A pretty name for a pretty girl. You played tennis this morning, Aiesha?"

"Yeah. Mr. Lazarus showed me how to use my backhand to hit the ball."

"Did he really?"

"Yeah," Aiesha said dreamily. "And I did it right, too. And I got a star for doing good—wanna see it?"

"Aiesha! Get on over here and leave that woman alone," a voice growled from behind Marley and Ashley. They turned and saw a woman approach. She looked like Aiesha, only harder. Much harder. She looked as though life had thoroughly beaten her behind.

"Leon, get your sister and come on. What I tell you 'bout leaving her alone and letting her bother strangers, huh?" She popped Leon upside the head and shoved him forward. Leon ran up to Marley and Ashley and gently took hold of Aiesha's hand.

" 'Scuse us," he whispered, pulling Aiesha speedily toward the woman. She snatched Leon's hand and pulled them away.

"Good Lord," Deanna said, shaking her head. "Poor things. Thank God they get a chance to leave the house and get away from her."

Lazarus smiled at the girls when they reached the courts. "Good morning," he said, then gave Marley a brief hug and turned to face Ashley and Deanna. "I'm Lazarus Jacobs. How you doin'?"

Ashley smiled. "Ashley Miller," she said, extending her hand.

"And I'm Deanna," Deanna said, waving. "Nice to meet you."

"I'm glad y'all could come out this morning," he said. "My brother and his wife and her sister will be here any minute. I'm going to help them with a few techniques, and I told Marley I'd be happy to help you-all as well. Or we can play a few games. I love tennis, so I'm happy doing anything as long as I'm hitting the ball." He smiled again and wiped his forehead with a white towel that had been hanging over his shoulder. His movements were more fluid than the water he drank.

Marley looked at her friends, who were smiling and openly admiring Lazarus. She chuckled. "Well, Deanna is probably the only one who can actually play a game with you. You can consider the rest of us on the same level as your students who just left."

"Don't sleep, now. Some of my students are pretty skilled."

"Well, consider us worse than the worst one in your class," Ashley said, and they all laughed.

"Not a problem. We're gonna have fun. Wait until you see my brother and his wife. They're funny because they think they can play and they really can't. My brother tries to teach me, and he just learned how to play last year."

"Well, we know how you men can be," Deanna said.

Lazarus smiled. "Actually, in this case it's not a macho thing. It's that he's my older brother and he thinks he knows more than me by default."

"That must be him," Marley said, pointing to a man and two women hurriedly approaching the courts.

"Morning, everybody," Lazarus's brother said quickly, as if the morning bell were about to ring and he wasn't in his seat. "I'm Paul," he said, nodding and pushing his glasses high on the bridge of his nose. "This is my wife, Sheila, and my sister-in-law, Lisa," he added, giving a perfunctory nod in their direction while he and Lazarus did the fingertip-grabbing, hand-gripping, back-patting thing.

Sheila smiled warmly and said hello to the girls while Lisa offered a plastic smile and extended her fingertips to be shaken. Then she swung her hair over her shoulders and placed a hand on her thigh. Deanna raised her brows at Marley.

"Ah—okay, then," Lazarus said. "Why don't we set up like we're playing doubles. We'll warm up with some volleys, and then we'll start to work on technique."

Paul and Sheila faced Lazarus, Marley, and Ashley on one court. Next to them, Deanna faced Lisa.

"Let's just start volleying from half-court. Don't worry about serving unless you just can't help yourself," Lazarus joked.

Lisa laughed loudly and, within seconds, served a seventy-mile-per-hour ball in Deanna's direction. Deanna dodged to the side of the court.

"What are you *doing?*" Deanna cried out, trying her best to maintain a smile.

"Oh, my gosh, I'm so, so sorry. I thought you were ready." Lisa smiled at Deanna and grabbed another ball from the pocket of her exceedingly short tennis skirt. "You just let me know when you're ready, hon." Lisa dribbled the tennis ball on the court with the flat of her tennis racket.

"Know what? Let's hold off on playing and just work on volleying back and forth for now," Lazarus said diplomatically. He looked at Marley and smiled. "You ready?" His voice was deep and soft.

Another butterfly began to stir inside Marley's stomach. "Yeah, I'm ready."

"Ready, Paul?" he barked.

"Yeah, man, let's get it on." Paul's knees were bent as he swayed from side to side. "And I apologize in advance for the butt whipping I'm gonna give you in front of all your friends."

Lazarus hit the ball firmly over the net, and Paul returned it with equal force. Lazarus's next stroke was tilted slightly, causing the ball to drop in front of the net unexpectedly. The ball bounced twice by the time Paul attempted to return it.

"That's just so you know what's what, bruh," Lazarus joked, returning to half-court and bouncing another ball. Sheila and Marley looked at each other and laughed.

Meanwhile, Deanna and Lisa had begun a vigorous volley and were totally oblivious to everyone else. Both were impressive players. Deanna won the volley, and she looked quite pleased. Lisa turned red and fiddled with the sweet spot on her racket.

"Thanks for the warm-up," Deanna said to Lisa and smiled. Lisa smirked, tossing her hair over her shoulders.

After several rounds of basic volleying and technique review, Sheila, Marley, and Ashley joined together on a court to practice what Lazarus had taught them. Lazarus and Lisa teamed up against Paul and Deanna on the neighboring court, and war broke out. After Lazarus served an amazing ace, his fifth in four games, Lazarus and Lisa emerged as the victors.

"Yes!" Lisa ran over to Lazarus and hugged him. Jealousy bolted through Marley's body as she observed Lisa's short skirt rise to ridiculous heights while she stood on her toes with her arms wrapped around Lazarus's neck. Ashley raised her eyebrows, then looked at Marley.

"You go, champ," Lisa cooed at Lazarus. Lazarus chuckled politely and wiped his forehead. Then Lisa bent over, directly in front of him, and began to pick up tennis balls.

"Oh, my God," Deanna whispered. Marley fumed. There were so many other honorable ways that Lisa could have bent over to pick up balls, none of which would have included flashing her behind in Lazarus's face. Lisa wanted Lazarus; it was clear.

But he doesn't want that, Marley convinced herself. The flashiness, the overt seductiveness—he didn't, couldn't want any of it. She cleared her throat and walked toward the edge of the court with all the confidence she could muster.

Lazarus quickly followed her, reaching out to touch her elbow and slow her pace. "You did well. *Really* well," he said, smiling.

Minus Lisa, who had another engagement, the group ate lunch at Conked Out, a new Caribbean restaurant in Little Five Points. The restaurant owner was a good friend of Lazarus's and Paul's and had seated the group at a choice table beside an open window fronting Highland Avenue.

"So how do you know the restaurant owner?" Deanna asked, seeming pleased with her surroundings and the friends in high places that Lazarus and Paul seemed to have.

"He was a classmate of ours," Paul said. "For years he dreamed of opening an authentic Caribbean restaurant in an artsy section of the city. He's finally done it. I'm proud of the brother."

"Me, too. Especially because so many people tried to convince him to start with a franchise," Lazarus added. "But that brother stayed focused. I think it took him all of a year and a half to pool together the initial investment for this place."

"Hm," Deanna said, nodding. She was impressed by Lazarus's entrepreneurial knowledge, given that he was simply an airport boy.

Secretly Marley was, too. The appeal of dating someone who hadn't obtained some sort of graduate degree was tempered by the subconscious condition that he be significantly intelligent and at least as knowledgeable as she about the world. Marley, and most women in her position, were doubtful such a combination even existed—at least to the degree a professional woman needed to be comfortable at obligatory dinner parties or Saturday-afternoon sporting events with their bosses and colleagues. And if it did exist among black men, the women were nevertheless doubtful that the combination existed in bulk supply, sufficient to satisfy the demand.

"Did you go to high school with the owner?" Marley asked. An attractive, island-flavored waitress placed glasses of lime water and flutes of papaya juice in front of them and promised to return shortly.

Paul looked at Marley oddly. "No. We went to B school together."

"Business school?" Deanna asked incredulously. Marley kneed her under the table.

"Yeah," Lazarus said. He looked amused.

"Oh, oh, okay. Which school did you-all go to?" Deanna tried her best not to sound completely shocked. But her effort failed, and Lazarus began to laugh.

"Y'all are funny," he said, laughing even harder. "Marley must've had y'all thinking I cart luggage at the airport." He laughed again. "Don't try to play it off."

Paul still held a puzzled look, and his gold-rimmed glasses illuminated the confusion in his eyes. "I'm lost, guys."

"When I first met Marley—or saw her, rather—I was at the airport. It was right after we started the trial contract with US Airlines, Paul. Remember?"

"Oh, yeah," Paul said slowly.

"Now I'm confused," Marley said. "And not ashamed to admit it."

"Paul and I own a commercial food supply business. The day I saw you at the airport was the first day we supplied food to the airline. So I was there supervising our delivery guys, making sure the airline received the food in the same packaging condition as when it left us. And making sure the airline personnel knew I was there watching everything. I didn't want to hear a word about five missing cookies or ten smashed sandwiches 'cause you know The Man is quick to think brothers are trying to get over."

"It has happened before," Sheila added. "I have always told Paul and Lazarus that they need to take extra precautions because they're newcomers to the business and need to establish their reputation."

Deanna shook her head. "Mm, mm, mm," she mumbled. "That's really something."

Lazarus looked at Marley. "So I guess I'm not what you expected," he teased.

She blushed. "Much more," she said, looking down.

"Wooh. Heavy, heavy, heavy," Paul said and fanned himself. Sheila elbowed her husband.

The island-flavored waitress reappeared, pen and pad in hand. "Welcome to Conked Out, an experience that is guaranteed to exceed all your expectations. What can I get for you today?"

No one realized that almost two hours had passed since they'd sat down to eat. Their bellies were undeniably full by the time the waitress brought them plantain pudding, but they gobbled it down without shame.

"So much for our tennis workout," Sheila said to the girls. "I feel like I've gained five pounds since we sat down. I'll be doing good if I can get up from this table and walk out the door."

"I know that's right," Ashley added. "Thank God my shirt overlaps my shorts because right now my stomach has picked up an additional roll of fat that would love to show itself."

"How long have you and Paul been married?" Marley asked Sheila. Lazarus and Paul were caught up in an intense conversation about their business.

"It'll be ten years in December," Sheila said proudly.

"These days five years of marriage is a blessing for young couples," Deanna said, scooping up the remnants of her pudding.

"You're right about that," Sheila said, nodding. "Not that Paul and I have not had our difficult times."

"If you don't mind my asking," Ashley said, "what has kept you-all together? Being able to communicate?"

"Yeah, but more important than that is that we've kept God in the center of our relationship. Without God, even good communication skills won't save you."

"It's so refreshing to hear you say that," Ashley said. "My parents have been married for thirty-two years, and they always give God credit for their marriage, but I rarely hear younger couples say the same thing."

"Well, for me and Paul, God gets all the glory," Sheila said, smiling, as she leaned in closer. "I remember what it was like when we slipped up and let God become an afterthought in our lives. We had moved from Atlanta to New York about a year after we got married because Paul had gotten a great job on Wall Street."

"Did you and Paul meet in college?" Ashley interrupted.

"Yeah. He was at Morehouse while I was at Spelman."

The girls screamed in delight at the revelation. Finding fellow

Spelmanites was like finding treasures on an ocean floor. Their over-and-across-the-table hugging drew Lazarus and Paul out of their conversation.

"Oh, Lord," Paul said, looking at his wife. "She must've found some Spelman sisters."

"We're gonna be here all night, man." Lazarus shook his head.

"Oh, hush," Sheila said to Paul, rolling her eyes playfully. A smile grew out of the corners of Paul's mouth, and he kissed his wife softly on the lips.

"Honey, I was telling the girls about our experience in New York."

"Whew," Paul said. "An experience it was."

"They were asking why I thought our marriage has been successful, and I was telling them that—"

"Jesus is the answer." Paul finished Sheila's sentence.

"Exactly."

"Laz and I grew up in a strong Christian family," Paul said, twisting the stem of his empty flute between his fingers. "We couldn't have asked for better parents in that regard. Of course, as an adult you can't survive on the strength of your parents' relationship with God, so we've all had to grow up and find our own way to the Lord."

"It's five boys in their family, you know," Sheila added.

"Really?" Marley asked. "You-all have three more brothers?"

"Yep," Paul answered. "Beanie's the oldest. Then Jeremi, then me, then Isaiah, then Laz."

"You're the baby," Marley said softly, gazing at Lazarus. He blushed.

"We're still praying for Beanie," Paul said, shaking his head. To Marley, Paul sounded more like the eldest son, the one who carried his home training like a baton, ran his leg of the race with ease, and tapped his foot as he waited on the younger ones to catch up and carry on.

"He's sort of out there right now," Paul continued. "But if God saved us, we know He'll save Beanie, too."

"Is his real name Beanie?" Ashley asked. Marley wanted to know too, but was too scared to ask. Beanie was, after all, a weird name. Especially compared to names like Jeremi and Isaiah, which were so meaningful. Maybe being named Beanie was part of his problem.

"Oh, no," Lazarus laughed. "His name is Abraham. I could never say Abraham when I was young, and the closest I came to it was Beanie. The family has been calling him that ever since."

"Anyway," Paul continued. "Sheila and I had known the Lord all our lives. But when we moved to New York, we fell off the wagon big time. We stopped going to church—"

"Which was mistake number one," Sheila said, leaning closer to Paul. "Actually, it was mistake number two. Mistake number one was not finding a church before we made the move in the first place. It's like finding a school for your children. Good parents won't sacrifice their children's education and development simply for a higher-paying job in another city if there are no good schools for their children to attend. We needed to have the same mentality about finding the word, but we didn't."

"Exactly," Paul agreed, rubbing Sheila's shoulder. "We got caught up in the glitz and glamour of life in the Big Apple. Started sinking into debt, trying to keep up with the Joneses and live a lifestyle that any fool off the street knew we could not afford to live. We stopped looking for a church and convinced ourselves we were strong enough Christians that we could feed ourselves. We went from praying together every day to praying together on Sunday mornings only to never praying together except to bless the food."

"It was an awful downward spiral," Sheila said, shaking her head slowly. "We had begun to lose the peace that had always surrounded our marriage, and stupid as we were, we couldn't figure out why." Sheila and Paul looked at each other and laughed.

Marley stared at them. The depth of their intimacy seemed to tower above the table and linger there, like the promise held by a lighthouse in the fog.

"Sheila and I started to argue almost every day," Paul said, patting the table for emphasis. "About toothpaste. Toilet tissue. How to fold the linen. Where to buy gas. It was ridiculous. The devil was whipping our behinds with his pinky."

"And it sounds silly, but it's the little things that start to add up," Sheila continued. "Without the peace of God, those little things become big things, and they can tear a marriage apart. Christians have the advantage. We know that the name of Jesus is above every name. It's above insecurity, doubt, fear, need, and confusion. But once you stop exalting the name of Jesus, you're in a rut right along with the rest of the world, trying to solve problems the way the world solves problems. We were about to start seeing a marriage counselor that one of Paul's colleagues referred him to. This man has been divorced three times, mind you."

"And Sheila happened to mention it to Mama on the telephone one night, just before our first appointment." Paul shook his head.

"That was the talk of the family," Lazarus added. "Matter of fact, I was at Mama's house when Sheila called. Mama said, 'You're gonna do *what?*' " Sheila, Paul, and Lazarus laughed at the shared memory.

"She asked me whether we had gotten counseling from our pastor," Sheila continued. "I told her we didn't exactly have a pastor at the time. She told me she could save us the time and money we'd spend seeing the marriage counselor. She told me we needed to get back in church, study the Bible, pray together every day, and think about Jesus every time we began a serious discussion. Then she asked to speak to Paul, and I think she gave him a piece of her mind for a good hour or so."

"Sure did," Paul said, nodding. "Told me I should have been ashamed of myself for allowing my family to stray away from God.

Told me I was not fulfilling my role as a husband and that God would hold me accountable for every day Sheila and I lived apart from Him. Told me I knew better and I was without excuse."

"They packed up and moved back home within two months," Lazarus said.

"To make a long story short," Sheila said, lifting one hand, "we realized that without God we are absolutely nothing. Nothing but warped human beings with tons of faults that we impose on each other on a daily basis, and the only way to live a peaceful and enjoyable life with an imperfect person is to keep God in the center of it. The fact that God forgives us is what reminds Paul and me that we have no right to stay angry at each other for the mistakes we make. With all the mercy God shows us, we have no choice but to show each other that same mercy and love." Sheila looked at Paul, and he squeezed her shoulder.

"That's something to strive for," Ashley said softly, staring at the couple.

"Really," Deanna agreed. The table was quiet.

"Thanks so much for sharing that," Marley said. All she could think about was the fact that but for what she once had thought was an incidental twist of fate, she would have married a man whose views of marriage did not at all resemble those of Paul and Sheila. Gerrard and Marley had never even attended church together as a couple, except on holidays, "the majors," as Gerrard had said, and even then he would fall asleep. Marley had been saved from a disastrous marriage. She was overcome with gratitude and emotion.

"Excuse me, please," she said and went to the rest room.

Ashley excused herself, too, and followed. She opened the door to the rest room and spotted Marley at the sink. "You all right, sweetie?" She wrapped her arm around Marley's shoulder. "I know it can get rough sometimes. But you have to remember it hasn't been that long since you broke up with Gerrard. It's going to be painful at times. Don't beat yourself up for that. Just be thankful you're not married to him now."

"I am, I am," Marley said, wiping her eyes. "It's just that I feel so disgraceful when I think about the fact that I was going to marry him in the first place, knowing he wasn't the man he should have been. I mean, what does that say about *me?*" Marley sniffed.

"The same thing it says about all of us. That we're not perfect. And without God, we're walking disasters. You weren't following God then, Marley. But you are now. The choices you make from this point on will be so different. And they'll be blessed."

Marley and Ashley hugged tightly.

"And honey," Ashley added, "if that Lazarus isn't a blessing, with his fine self, then I don't know what is! *Good Lord Almighty!*" Ashley threw her arms up in the air.

They doubled over in laughter, and this time Marley wiped tears of joy from the corners of her eyes.

As they left the restaurant, the group lauded Conked Out's owner for a splendid dining experience. He promised Lazarus and Paul that they'd always have one of the best tables in the house whenever they came to visit. Deanna told him she'd be back to visit and asked whether he would give her one of the good tables, too. He told Deanna he'd give her whatever she wanted, and three minutes later they had made plans to go out the following weekend.

"You need to slow down, Dee," Ashley said. "Seems like you're out on a date every weekend."

"And what's wrong with that? I'm young, and I'm getting to know men. I'm certainly not having sex with them, so what difference does it make? At least I'll know exactly what I want in a man before I settle down."

"That's fine. Just make sure you spend some time getting to know yourself as well. That's just as important," Ashley said.

"Yes, mother."

"You ladies feel up to a stroll through the park?" Lazarus asked, catching up with them. "I, for one, need to work off some of this Caribbean weight I'm carrying," he said, chuckling.

Marley looked at her friends and wished with everything inside her that they would go home.

They followed cue. "No," Ashley began slowly, eyeing Marley. "I don't think so. I have some errands I need to run before the entire day gets away from me. Thanks anyway, Lazarus. It was wonderful hanging out with you and your family. I look forward to all of us doing it again soon."

"Me, too," Deanna said and walked over to hug Sheila.

"Will you be able to drop me off at my car after we leave the park?" Marley asked Lazarus. "It's at Buster's Kitchen."

"Of course." He looked at Ashley. "Ashley, you seem like the type that likes to write down license plate numbers when your friends ride with strange men, so let me give you a pen and a piece of paper and let you handle your business."

"Actually," she said in between chuckles, "I wrote all that information down when we left the tennis court, so I'm straight."

"Marley, come here for a sec," Deanna said once she and Ashley had distanced themselves from Lazarus.

Marley walked over, grinning from ear to ear. The three stood close, almost in a circle, and tried their best to appear composed.

"Girl, he's the *bomb*," Deanna whispered in delight.

"He's such a gentleman, Marley," Ashley added.

"We are very impressed, and we give you permission to have a good time, okay?" Deanna said.

"What do you mean, 'a good time'?" Ashley asked, head cocked to one side.

"I mean she should have fun. Walk through the park with him. Heck, go get ice cream if she wants. He's a nice guy, and she deserves to have a good evening."

"Okay, just wanted to make sure we were on the same page."

"For goodness' sake, Ashley, did you think I meant she should go to the Motel Six with the brother?"

"Anyway, Marley, have a wonderful, wonderful time," Ashley said. "Call me as soon as you get home."

"Me, too! Wait—no, I might not be at home, now that I think about it," Deanna said. "Pablo gave me two tickets to tonight's game, and—"

"Oh, so he *finally* called?" Ashley asked.

"Yeah, girl. He was feeling all bad, making guilt offerings, which I have no problem accepting. Anyway, I promised Marcus I'd take him. But still, call me and leave a juicy detailed voice mail so I can get a capsule summary as soon as I walk in the door."

"I will," Marley agreed, still smiling. "I love you-all."

"We love you, too." They hugged, and the girls left.

"You ready?" Lazarus asked. It was something about the way he spoke to her that caused her body to tingle from her toes to the hairs on her head. He was so sure. So steady. So solid.

"I'm ready," she said.

"Paul, we'll follow you there."

Lazarus exhaled deeply and smiled wide as he and Marley started down a path in the Botanical Garden. The air, warm and moist, sneaked up on their skin and coated it.

Marley looked at him and grinned. "I had a really good time at lunch, Lazarus. And I *really* enjoyed meeting Paul and Sheila. They are truly special." She glanced at them, walking several feet ahead, their arms linked.

"They are. Paul and I have always been the closest of all of us boys. I've always looked up to him."

"When did you decide to go into business together?"

"Well," Lazarus said, sighing, "we'd been talking about it for a while, but the timing wasn't right until about six years ago. I was ready to start as soon as I graduated from college. But Paul refused to start a venture with me until both of us finished B school. I respected his decision, but I never quite agreed with it, mainly because my dad is a businessman and he doesn't have any academic training."

"What does your dad do?" Marley asked, trying not to sound panicked, fearing that she'd run into another ~on of a wealthy man.

"He owns an apartment building." Lazarus brushed his fingertips against the leaves that draped the path they walked. He began to smile. "You thought I was making five dollars an hour carrying boxes at the airport, didn't you?"

"Of course not!" Marley laughed. "I thought you were making *ten* dollars an hour."

He laughed, looking down. Then he looked at her. "There's nothing wrong with that, you know. I respect the brothers and sisters who do it in the face of all the opportunities for illegal gain, that's for sure."

"Oh, I do, too."

They walked in silence. Marley inhaled deeply and savored the crisp air filling her lungs. "And to be honest," she continued, "I was sort of hoping you might be one of those brothers."

Lazarus raised his eyebrows. "Why?"

"Because my ex-fiancé was the opposite, and I think his wealth had a lot to do with his hang-ups."

Lazarus shrugged. "Maybe so. But it's not money in and of itself that ruins a person. It's the person's attitude toward money."

"True, but I think that because he's had it so easy all his life, his worldview is completely different from an average person earning a modest living."

"Why is he your *ex*-fiancé, if you don't mind me asking?"

Marley smiled nervously. "Well, I'm not even sure how to answer that."

"Oh, no problem. Don't feel like you have to——"

"No, no, it's no problem. It's not that I mind sharing it with you. Actually, it feels good to talk about it. It's just that the answer I would have given you a few months ago is far more simplistic than the real answer. I called the wedding off after I found out he had been cheating on me."

"Mm," Lazarus mumbled, eyes wide. "I know that was rough."

"Yeah, it was. But I also realized that marriage meant different things to us. To him, it was a necessary next step. I mean, he loved me enough to choose me as the one to marry. But he didn't honor me. He honored his career. And I don't think he ever believed he had an obligation to be faithful to me. Only to provide for me, which he knew he could handle."

"How long had you been together?"

"Since college, basically."

Lazarus nodded. They walked in silence.

"You're probably wondering why in the world it took me so long to figure him out, huh?"

"No, not at all. You could say the same thing about me. It took me three years to realize that the last woman I dated was completely wrong for me."

"Really?"

"Yeah. Of course, hindsight is twenty-twenty. And if I had paid more attention to the signs God was showing me all along, I could have saved myself a lot of time. But I didn't. Wanted to do things my way and make things work. 'Cause, you know, I'm the man and I can do that."

They laughed.

"Naw, it never would have worked. She wanted me to be someone I wasn't and never would be. The plain old me wasn't good enough for her." He bent down and examined a small patch of perennials that resembled dandelions. "I think she thought she could mold me into a new creature if we got married. But my parents have been married for almost fifty years, and one thing I know from watching them is that grown folk don't change. What you see is what you get. Your attitude in marriage has to be that at ninety years old, your spouse will still have every single fault he had when he was twenty-five years old, but you will love him for exactly who he is, regardless. I realized I would never have that commitment from her. And that's a tough situation to be in because part of you wants to try to be that person you aren't, just to make it work. I tried to do that for a while. But I wasn't being true to myself. So we split."

Marley looked at Lazarus. Her eyes traveled to Sheila, who was resting her head on Paul's broad shoulder as they walked. They were almost out of sight.

"Do you miss her?"

"No, not really. Come smell these," he said, reaching for Marley's hand. She bent down beside him and smelled the flowers. "Mmm," she said.

"Don't they smell good? They're not even that pretty," he said.

"They look wild. But they do smell good."

He stood, then helped Marley up. "I miss sharing that kind of closeness with a woman. Because underneath it all we were really good friends. I lost a friend when we broke up. But in all truthfulness, I don't miss *her*. She had started to wreck my nerves, for real."

Marley laughed, and Lazarus joined her.

"What about you? Do you miss your fiancé?"

"Ex-fiancé."

"Excuse me," Lazarus sang. "Your ex-fiancé."

"No, I don't miss him. He became another person, the kind of person who's not worth missing. I was looking forward to marriage, though. Just the concept of it, which I realize never would have been enough to keep us together. But I was ready for the commitment. Part of me misses that."

"Well, you know it's all in God's hands. We make it so much

harder than it has to be. We try to work things out the way we think they should go, and we end up messing up the whole program and missing our blessings."

Marley looked at Lazarus, then looked down at her feet. "I know." They walked in silence. "But sometimes," she continued, stopping to touch a hydrangea bloom, "I just don't feel worthy of any blessings. I feel like I haven't done anything to deserve blessings."

"You know what, Marley? We'll never be worthy of God's blessings. We'll grow and become better people and God will see that He can trust us more, but we'll never, ever be worthy of His grace. He doesn't bless us because we're so good to Him. Matter of fact, we disappoint Him probably every day. He blesses us because we're His children and He loves us, plain and simple. It's just like how your parents took care of you even when you disobeyed them. Multiply that by ten thousand, and you'll get an inkling of the kind of love God has for us."

Marley sighed, still touching the hydrangea. She smiled. "God is something, huh?"

"Yep," Lazarus agreed.

An hour later, Lazarus had returned Marley to the parking lot at Buster's Kitchen. They stood beside her car.

"I had a good time," Lazarus said. "Thanks for spending the day with me. It was cool getting to know a little bit about you."

"Me, too. I had fun."

It was awkward. They stared at each other, then both looked down and could find nothing else to do except shuffle their feet and jingle their keys.

"Well, let me head on home. I've got to set up chairs at the early service tomorrow."

"Do you?" Marley asked, not really seeking an answer.

"Yeah. Which service are you going to?"

"I hadn't decided yet. I like both of them, but I guess it's about time I picked one to attend on a regular basis."

"Why don't you meet me at the early service? We could sit together."

"Okay," Marley said, smiling. "I'd like that a lot."

"Me, too."

Another awkward moment passed.

"Well, I'll see you in the morning. Quarter to eight in the lobby?"

"Yep," Marley agreed.

"Okay, then. Thanks again for spending the day with me."

"No, thank *you*."

They laughed at themselves.

"Good night, Marley." Lazarus leaned forward and embraced her. But he didn't let go as quickly as he had in the past. Nor did she. She felt the sweetest current shoot through her body, tingling her nerve endings, weakening her muscles, and she could not pull herself away.

He kissed her on the cheek. Then, abruptly, he stepped back. "Go on and get in the car so I can see you off safely," he said, his voice husky, his eyes averted from hers.

She climbed inside, fastened her seat belt, and rolled her windows down.

"See you tomorrow morning," she said, smiling.

"See you then. God bless you."

There were those words again. Still, and every time, the sweetest words a man had ever spoken to her. They made her tremble with a brand of passion she had never known before. "God bless you, too," she whispered, barely making eye contact. She drove off, and he stood in the parking lot watching her disappear into a stream of moving cars.

Chapter 18

I T WAS MAY, and Pam's hair had still not grown back. The wisps that had resurfaced took the form of clustered patches in indiscriminate places across her scalp. She longed for the days when she could pull her thick, soft hair into an elegant bun at the base of her neck. Today, there was nothing elegant about Pam's hair.

Right after Pam had begun chemotherapy, she had spent considerable time shopping for the best, most natural-looking wig she could find. Nothing had suited her taste, and during her last phone conversation with Clifford, her hairstylist, in which she had canceled her appointment for the third time in a month, she had complained to him about the poor selection of wigs in the beauty supply stores she had visited. Not three weeks after she had spoken with Clifford, a large hat-size box had been delivered to her front door. Inside was a custom-made wig. Clifford had sent the manufacturer a picture of Pam, along with her hair color, texture, length, and other specifications. That lifted her spirits until she noticed that her pubic hair—which, two months prior, had started to turn gray—was falling out, too. These days Pam chose to look past herself in the mirror.

She knew she would have to discuss her feelings today during her appointment with Richard, her nutritionist. Richard absolutely refused to begin a session without asking Pam how she was feeling about herself. All the fruits, vegetables, and whole grains in the world would not improve Pam's overall health, Richard said, if a poor self-image and low self-worth were eating her alive on the inside.

To ward off Richard's psychological delving, Pam put extra effort into her appearance. She wore a scoop neck mid-calf-length black dress made of cotton and spandex that hugged her torso nicely and gave no hint that one of her perfectly shaped breasts was a lie. Though her eyebrows had thinned, a brow pencil helped make them look fairly normal. She dusted her cheeks a sandy brown and painted her lips a glossy mocha. In fact she looked quite stunning. Not at all like a woman who wondered every day whether she would ever be attractive to anyone else, much less herself.

"Well, well, well, we're not having a low-self-esteem day today, are we?" Richard said, eyeing Pam as she stood in his doorway. "Look at that hair! And look at that dress! Just look at you!"

Pam could not control the smile that spread across her face. "Well, I try," she said, feigning bashfulness.

"You look wonderful, Pamela. How do you *feel* today?" Richard asked warmly, looking directly into Pam's eyes.

"I'm doing pretty good, Richard. I really am. I've had some low points recently, mainly in coming to terms with the fact that I'm still, well, bald. My body is just so different. But today I decided to go all out and dress up as if nothing had ever happened to me. And I must admit, it feels pretty good." She smiled and crossed her legs.

"Excellent, Pamela. Remember that beauty starts from within. No matter what you do to yourself on the outside, you've got to maintain a clean house on the inside in order for beauty and health to radiate through your body."

"Yes, sir," Pam teased.

"Let's take a look at your diet chart."

Pam removed some papers from the woven handbag she carried and handed Richard the chart on which she had recorded her food intake for the past seven days. She had stuck to Richard's recommendations, for the most part. She had not recorded the hot fudge cake she'd eaten yesterday, though.

"This is good, Pamela," Richard said, still reading the entries. "Excellent job staying away from all the partially hydrogenated and monosaturated foods. Not as much leafy green intake as I'd like to see in one week, but certainly a significant improvement from the week before." He stroked his goatee, still studying the chart. "Very, very good," Richard concluded, smiling.

Pam smiled, too. It felt good to receive positive encouragement and specialized attention.

"Okay, here's what we're going to do over the next two weeks. I need you to increase your leafy green intake by one cup per day. You've got to do this, Pamela. You can't skimp in one area and still achieve the optimum benefit we're striving for, okay?"

"Okay," she agreed.

"Also, we've got to step up the omega-three fatty acid consumption. Did you find the flax seeds yet?"

"No, but in all honesty I haven't looked that hard for them," she said. "If I don't find them at Sevananda, I'll let you know. You can pick them up from your co-op for me, and I'll reimburse you."

Richard hopped out of his chair and walked over to a closet. As he opened and closed several cardboard boxes, Pam couldn't help but notice the well-developed muscles in his arms. The ones in his shoulders and back were plainly visible, even through the thick, cotton polo shirt he wore.

Inside Richard's closet was a miniature GNC, a storehouse of nutritional goodies. "While we're waiting on you to do that," he mumbled from inside the closet, moving boxes around, "I'm going to give you a small pack of seeds to hold you over. I don't want another day to pass without you using the seeds." Richard returned to his desk with a small bag.

"See, it takes time to develop both the habit and the attitude of need. Every day that passes in which you don't consume the flax seeds or some other nutrient that you're scheduled to consume is a day in which you have not begun to develop the habit of consumption. And unless you have an independent appreciation of the need to consume these things, you won't even develop forced appreciation until you develop a habit of taking it. Does that make sense?"

"Yes, it does," Pam agreed, nodding. "And I don't want you to think I'm not taking this seriously. I am. It's just that it requires radical changes on my part, and I can't help but move a little slower than either of us would like."

"That's fine, Pamela, that's fine. I'm extremely proud of the progress you've made so far. Let's not sweep that aside, because we have to celebrate each and every achievement you make. But I don't settle for anything less than excellence. I want you to achieve optimum health. I want you to realize that you have the power to heal your body and the only thing standing in the way of that healing is you."

"Understood."

"Very good. Now let me see your exercise chart."

The whole chart-keeping task was unnerving to Pam, mainly because she wasn't doing everything Richard required. It would be so much easier to sit in his face and answer questions about what she had or had not done over the past week. But the fact that Richard insisted on the additional layer of keeping a chart, forcing her to pull it out and look at it with him during consultation, made it a tight situation. Confession was unavoidable, and the repeated embarrassment of not having done what Richard asked and what Pam was paying to be done was enough to shame her into doing it. Or stop using Richard altogether, which really would render Pam trifling.

"I don't have an exercise chart, Richard," Pam said quickly. "I'm sorry, but I'm not going to sit here and lie. I didn't start this week, and I realize that that's not good, okay? I am going to start tomorrow."

Richard's face was austere. "Pamela," he sighed, folding his hands on top of his desk, "this is serious business. Either you want to beat the odds, or you don't. Either you want to live in fear of a recurrence and rely on body-shocking drugs to stabilize you temporarily, or you want to heal your body on the inside and develop an illness-defensive lifestyle. You're walking the line, and it's just not acceptable. Think about what you went through over the past few months. Do you want to do it all again in two or three years?"

Pam was embarrassed. Again. She'd sworn, after her last visit two weeks ago, when Richard had chastised her mildly because she hadn't begun to exercise, that she would not show up at another consultation without beginning her regimen.

"I don't want to go through this again," she answered, and without warning a tear fell from her eye. "I'm not a weak person. You're dealing with me at a weak time in my life, but I'm not a weak person, and I want you to know that." She wiped her eye quickly.

"I know you're not a weak person," Richard said softly. "There's no doubt in my mind that you can do this, Pamela. That's why I'm so hard on you. That's why I've put you on an aggressive program, and that's why I increase your responsibilities every time we meet instead of decreasing them. I know what you're made of, and I'm going to help you bring it out again. Deal?"

"It's a deal." Pam looked down at her hands.

"I've got an idea. Something that will help you get a jump start on your exercise regimen, since that seems to be your biggest problem area."

"I'm all ears," Pam said pitifully, beginning to doubt herself.

"Why don't you sign up for a few personal training sessions at a fitness center? That way, you've committed time and invested money in exercising, so it will be a lot harder to blow off your sessions. How about that?"

She liked the idea. She hated the fact that she needed to build in so many obstacles and mechanisms to prevent herself from failing, when all she really needed to do was honor the commitments she'd made once she'd learned she had cancer. But she was desperate and constantly doubting her willpower. The idea of having to keep appointments with someone was appealing.

"That sounds good," Pam agreed. "Except that I have no idea which fitness center to join. There are so many of them, and I don't need all that fancy equipment most of them have. Nor do I want to be in a facility with a lot of teenyboppers. You know what I mean?"

Richard laughed. "I know exactly what you mean. We don't need those naturally healthy young people around us to remind us how old and decrepit we are." They laughed together.

"You know," Richard continued, "you might like my gym. It's a regional chain with locations all over Atlanta and the surrounding suburbs. I know where the teenyboppers frequent and which locations we older folks hobble into."

"Well, you need to give me that information right away, 'cause I refuse to bounce around next to a twenty-year-old."

"You'd have the twenty-year-old beat by a mile, Pamela." He stared at her. "The sooner you realize that about yourself, the sooner you'll leave your cocoon and fly."

"Thank you, Richard. I always feel uplifted after our sessions. I'm on my way. You'll see."

"I know you are. And I see it already."

* * *

Ava eyed Pam suspiciously as they sifted through the spandex and stretch cotton exercise gear hanging on the racks at Macy's. "I can't believe you," Ava said. "Really, Pam, what has gotten into you?"

"Like I said, Ava, I'm joining a gym." Pam pulled a canary yellow leotard off the rack, eyed it closely, frowned, then hung it back up. "I'm getting serious about my health and fitness. I have *cancer,* Ava," Pam said, suddenly distracted by a violet-and-black two-piece outfit. "Can't you understand that?"

Ava was about to tell Pam about herself, really help her see that she was suffering from a major midlife crisis, when she saw Dottie Westmoreland moseying her way over. It was too late for Ava to warn Pam, too late for them to turn around quickly, too late for them to pretend they hadn't seen Dottie approach.

Pam looked up from the rack, and her eyes widened. "Dottie!" She plastered a perfect, steady smile on her face. "How nice to see you," she said, making sure she sounded charmed.

"Pamela Shepherd! Even better to see you!" Dottie beamed, doing a much better job than Pam of sounding genuine. "And Ava, my goodness! It's been almost two years since I've seen you! You're looking, ah, goodness, you're looking like yourself!"

"Thanks," Ava said flatly, refusing to join the game. She returned her attention to the spandex and stretch cotton.

The best you could say about Dottie Westmoreland was that she was tolerable. Not that it was personality or generosity or sensitivity that made her tolerable. It was respect for the past that made folks pause when they otherwise would have opted to give Dottie a piece of their minds and be through with her. Dottie was the grandchild of Atlanta's first black funeral parlor owner, a man whose charitable heart and love of community had made him a hero among his people and a legend among later generations. He had worked every day of his life, amassing a sizable fortune that had eventually landed in Dottie's lap.

Everybody knew Dottie's fortune had officially been depleted. She'd been through three husbands, none of whom had stayed with her for longer than three years and all of whom had left in a better financial condition than they'd been in before the marriage. But even though the fortune was squandered, the trappings remained. The minks, the cars, the diamonds, the holiday parties. And here Dottie was, browsing through hosiery, wearing a beaver stole in May.

"Pamela, I've been meaning to give you a call, dear, and ask you whether you needed anything, anything at all, as you plan for this wedding of Marley's. Especially with your cancer and all." Dottie smiled even bigger than she had before, her bright pink lipstick staining one of her front teeth.

Ava's mouth fell open. She looked at Dottie as if she might pounce on her. Everybody in the city knew the engagement had been called off. Everybody knew, and Dottie was certainly no exception.

Pam stared at Dottie and swore she could see a glimmer of willful intent in her eyes. Pam nervously touched the side of her head. She remembered she was wearing a wig, and her cheeks flushed. She straightened her back and cleared her throat. "You haven't heard, Dottie? The wedding is off." Pam tried to turn around, but Dottie grabbed her arm.

"You're *kidding*! Pamela, that just cannot *be*!" Dottie cried, her eyes wide in feigned shock. "Oh, dear, I am so *terribly* sorry to hear that." Dottie shook her head and lowered it, as if she were honoring a moment of silence for the dead. "Is your Marley faring well? We all know how much she simply *adored* that young man, and understandably so. He was quite a catch." Dottie nodded knowingly at Pam.

"Dottie, you know, I could slap you," Ava said, stepping toward her. "I'm sick and tired of your mouth, and I have a mind to—"

"Ava!" Pam grabbed her by the arm and pulled her back. Dottie's mouth flung open.

"Dottie, we'll see you later." Pam steered Ava away.

"I don't care who her granddaddy is," Ava mumbled as she and Pam walked away. Dottie pulled a tattered, collapsible Simpson's Funeral Home fan out of her purse. She fanned herself, dabbed at the sweat on her forehead with a handkerchief bearing the Simpson monogram and left Hosiery.

Chapter 19

MARLEY HAD READ the same paragraph so many times she'd stopped counting. She rubbed her temples and gave it one more try.

When attempting to undertake an analysis of the precepts of privity of estate, it is necessary that one keep distinct two kinds of privity of estate: (i) a specified relationship existing between the original promisor and promisee (known as horizontal privity), and (ii) a specified relationship between an original party to the contract and an assignee (known as vertical privity). While it is true that both may be required for the burden of a real covenant to run to an assignee, it must be noted that only the latter may be required for the benefit to run.

She gave up. Half an hour earlier, her brain had simply shut itself off from the world of real property. The sun was shining, Peachtree was bustling, and she wanted to be in and among them both.

More than that, she wanted to call Lazarus. Truth be told, he was the main reason she could not finish reading the case. She couldn't stop thinking about him. About his patience and gentleness, which, since their first tennis date last month, she had observed almost every Saturday morning at the clinic, as he never tired of answering every "why" question the children posed. "But why don't the ball keep bouncing?" "Why come I have to swing all the way through?" "Why we gotta use a backhand, huh, Mista Laz?"

She thought about his humor, which had given her bellyaches during their Sunday-afternoon brunches. When he'd stood up in Buster's Kitchen and imitated Michael Jackson's infamous "Billie Jean" performance on the Motown Twenty-five television special— all to prove he'd been the bigger Michael Jackson fan growing up— Marley's ribs felt like they were collapsing. He was *so* comfortable in his skin. He forced her, without intending it, to be more comfortable in hers.

She turned off her computer, grabbed her attaché, and walked out of her office.

"Evelyn," she said, "I'm out of here. Today is just too pretty for me to stay cooped up in my hole until dark. Will you forward all my calls to voice mail, please?"

Evelyn stopped typing and looked up at Marley with raised brows and a closed-mouth grin. "My, my, my. Don't we have a new attitude?"

"We sure do. I think I'll walk through Macy's for a little while and let the traffic die down. Oh, and if my mom calls, tell her I'm going to stop by her house later on."

"Will do, sweetie. Enjoy yourself."

"I will. See you tomorrow."

Marley stood in the elevator bank and began to feel guilty, albeit only slightly, about going home without a single case to read. As she stepped onto the elevator, Evelyn breezed through the doors.

"Whew! Glad I caught you," she said, tucking loose strands of hair back into her bun. "Make sure you go straight to the lobby. You've got a visitor waiting." She winked, spun around, and darted off as quickly as she had come.

Marley tried to suppress the grin that had taken her mouth captive. She didn't want to look like a cheerleader when she stepped off the elevator, but she couldn't help it. She knew it was Lazarus; she felt it. And as soon as the doors opened, her eyes confirmed it. He was standing in the middle of the lobby, with a smile wider than hers, holding two ice cream cones. She walked up to him, not worrying anymore how goofy she looked.

"I just left a contract negotiation in Midtown and said to myself, 'Self, there's no way you can go back to the office today. Too nice outside.' So I picked up some cones next door at Mae Bell's House of Cream and decided to drop in and say hi to this beautiful woman I know. Man, she's beautiful. Inside and out. Never met anyone like her. Have you seen her?"

She couldn't stop grinning.

"Seriously, have you seen her? 'Bout five feet seven inches, two gold teeth, a long blond weave?"

"Okay, I'm going to call Security on you now and tell them there's a lunatic on the premises." Marley gripped his arm playfully.

"Hi, Marley." Smiling, he handed her strawberry ice cream in a waffle cone.

"Hi, Lazarus." She took a lick and felt like skipping through the lobby.

"How was your day?"

"Too long. I didn't get a thing done," she said.

"You on your way out?"

"Yeah. I was going to run to Macy's for a few minutes."

"Really? I need to get a few pairs of socks. Somehow I'm missing one of almost every pair of brown ones I own. For the life of me I cannot figure out how I keep losing my socks."

It was unreal. She had been thinking about him. He had been

thinking about her. They shared the same space with no effort, no pressure, no prying or prodding, no whining or coaxing. They were just there, comfortably. As though it were the only place for either of them to be.

"Can I pick them out for you?"

He smiled. "I was hoping you would."

"Mom?" Marley called from the foyer. She heard music playing upstairs but didn't hear her mother respond. "Mom," she called out again, walking toward the foot of the steps. "It's me."

"I'm Every Woman" was blasting from the ministereo in Pam's bedroom. Pam thought she heard a voice. "Who's that?" She rushed over to turn the volume down. "Marley?"

"Yeah, it's me." Marley made her way upstairs.

"Whew! You scared me." She turned the volume back up.

"Check you out, having a party in your room." Marley grinned, relieved to find her mother in such high spirits. Finally, then, she could tell her about Lazarus. She was *dying* to tell her about Lazarus. She was, at least, until she caught a glimpse of her mother's outfit and had to grip the molding around the doorway for support.

Pam was dressed in a black spandex tank top and black spandex biker shorts that stopped at the upper middle of her thighs. Neither the bottom of the tank top nor the top of the biker shorts covered Pam's midriff, so a nice portion of her waistline and her belly button was on display. She wore a pair of purple-and-black Air Jordans. She had even managed to pull a section of her wig hair into a ponytail, leaving several pieces hanging to camouflage the fake scalp-colored material.

"Mom, what are you doing?"

"Huh?" Pam half replied, preoccupied with her eyeliner and her image in the mirror.

"What are you doing? Where are you going dressed like that?"

"What do you mean, where am I going dressed like this? Where does it look like I'm going? I'm going to the gym."

"The gym? What gym? You don't even have a membership at a gym."

"I certainly do," Pam mumbled between pursed lips, as she applied lip liner.

"Since when?" Marley folded her arms across her chest.

"Why?"

"Mom, really. What's going on?"

"What do you mean, 'What's going on?' Why does something have to be *going on,* Marley? And why are you interrogating me like a criminal?"

Marley sighed. "Okay. Mom, when did you join a gym?"

"Recently."

"When did you buy those gym clothes?"

"There you go again." Pam squinted, trying to determine whether the edge of the wig was visible from the side of her head.

Marley rolled her eyes upward and sat on the bed. "How was church Sunday?" she asked, plucking a lint ball from the sleeve of her suit.

"I didn't make it." Pam fluffed her ponytail. She hadn't been to church the last three Sundays. She was sick of hearing the same dull sermons from Reverend Watson and the same dull solos from Shirley.

Marley chuckled. "Guess what the topic of the sermon was at Gilead's Balm?"

"What?"

"It was about how Christians become too comfortable," she said, and laughed again.

Pam eyed Marley from the mirror. "And did *you* learn something from that sermon?"

"Oh yeah, definitely. I realized it's easy for Christians to be content simply with being Christians, because we think that makes us good people and that's all we have to worry about in life. And that's how we become comfortable. And then we start skipping church, praying less often, reading the Bible less often. You know, those sorts of things," Marley said, gesturing with her hand. "And then we look up and realize we're far, far away from God." Marley smoothed the wrinkles in her skirt and leaned back on her elbows.

Pam stared at Marley through the mirror as she continued to fix her hair. All this terminology Marley had picked up was unsettling. She sounded like a missionary who'd slipped into Pam's house to begin a conversion speech. *Who did this child think she was?* Pam had taught her everything she knew about God and Christianity, and here the child was sitting on Pam's bed telling her, twenty years Marley's senior, why she needed to make sure she wasn't a too-comfortable Christian.

"You know," Pam began, hands on her hips, "you don't need to warn me about becoming too comfortable as a Christian."

"Huh?"

"I *said,* you don't need to give me a sermon on what happens when you become too comfortable as a Christian. In case you've forgotten, I have not only been a member of the same church for the past twenty years, but I am also on the board of advisers."

"I know that, Mom."

"Good. Then you know you don't need to preach to me. Now, I'm happy you've found a church you're interested in. That's really great. But the fact that you've attended this church for ten whole Sundays in a row does not make you holier than thou and qualify you to tell me what I need to do in my spiritual life."

Marley's mouth hung open. She stared at her mother, then cleared her throat and stood. "The only reason I was telling you about the sermon was because it really taught me something I didn't know. I was thinking about me and the things I need to learn, not about you."

Pam digested Marley's words. "Okay, sorry. I snapped at you, and I shouldn't have." She offered a smile.

"All right." Marley sat for a moment, deciding whether to let her hurt feelings go. Pam tugged at a few strands of her hair, the way she used to do when Marley was a little girl with long pigtails and shiny satin ribbons. Marley smiled, then giggled and reclined on her elbows again.

"Mom," she started, "I think it's wonderful that you're going to start exercising."

"Thank you, honey. I do, too." Pam returned to the mirror.

"It's really great, really it is. I can't help but notice, though, that you're wearing an awfully revealing gym outfit. It looks like you're trying to impress somebody."

Pam turned to face Marley. "What?"

Marley instantly wished she could take the words back. She had only been joking, for the most part. She decided to push a little further, albeit gingerly. "I mean, it's not that you don't look nice. It's just that I've never seen you—"

"You've never seen me *what*? I'm entitled to change my wardrobe. I'm entitled to wear spandex. And I *am* trying to impress somebody. Myself." She faced the mirror again.

Marley didn't believe her. Marley was her child, but she was also a woman. And women are onto other women, always. "That's all?" she asked, looking at the wall.

"What?"

"You're just trying to impress yourself and nobody else?"

"Marley, I don't know where you get off asking me all these questions. They're inappropriate. I am your mother, not your child."

Marley shrugged. "I think my questions are appropriate when I see my mother acting out of character. Mom, I think this is about your nutritionist."

Pam reeled around.

Marley did not flinch. "I do. When you first told me about him, you said he was an exercise freak. That was one of the reasons you liked him, because you figured he could motivate you to start exercising. The next time I asked you about your session, you talked more about him than you did the diet-related things you're seeing him for. Now you've gone off and joined a gym and bought a tight-fitting outfit and new tennis shoes. A week ago you wouldn't even walk around the block. Now you look like you're ready to do the StairMaster at level twelve for an entire hour."

"You think women your age are the only ones who have the right to wear gym clothes?" Pam snapped.

"No, but—"

"Okay, then. Leave me alone. I happen to look nice in these clothes, and that makes me feel good." Pam's voice cracked. "After all I've been through," she said, then shook her head and frowned.

"I'm not saying the clothes look bad on you, Mom. I'm saying they don't look *like* you. That's all. But if those clothes make you happy, I'm happy. Okay?"

Marley stood and walked to the door. "Anyway, I just stopped by to see how you were doing. I see you're on your way out, so I'll check with you later on."

She went downstairs. Pam stared at herself in the mirror, then quickly ran to the top of the steps.

"Marley," she called. Marley turned away from the door and looked up at her mother.

"Thanks for stopping by, honey. I appreciate it." Pam smiled.

Marley tossed a waving hand in the air and left.

The music was blaring inside the gym. After Pam and the receptionist yelled information over the volume in order to complete Pam's registration, Pam made her way to the stretching mats where Richard had said he would meet her.

Richard had offered Pam a free personal training session of sorts so she could get acquainted with the equipment before she met with her trainer for the first time. Mainly, he had said he wanted to be sure that Pam started going to the gym right away and didn't use the personal trainer's unavailability until the following week as an excuse not to start exercising.

"Hey there," came a familiar voice. Pam turned around and saw Richard. She almost gasped and tried her best to stop her eyes from bugging out of their sockets. Richard wore a red tank top that made his dark chocolate skin shine like a polished sculpture. A spray of curly black hair dusted his chest. His black biker shorts accentuated the bulging muscles in his thighs and calves.

Pam had not seen a body like his in years. Not since college, when she'd been a majorette watching the football players tough it out at Herndon Stadium. Even then, Pam had beheld such physiques only from afar. Silas, a basketball player, had been much more slender in build. And Silas was the only man Pam had been with. Ever.

"Richard! Hi, how are you?" Pam said in her best professional voice, reaching out to shake his hand.

"I'm doing great. How are you doing today?"

"I'm doing well." Pam smiled and felt around for something to grasp. Her arm missed the side bar on the treadmill near her, and she lost her balance.

"Oops, you okay?" Richard grabbed Pam's arm.

"I'm fine, thanks." Pam took a deep breath. "Here I am, in a gym, and I have to say, I feel like I'm in a strange land."

Richard laughed. "That's okay. Everybody feels that way the first time, so don't knock yourself. Before you know it, you'll be an old pro."

"Humph. We'll see."

"Let's get started," he said. "We always begin every exercise session with stretching, and that's because we need to loosen our muscles before we pull and challenge them in our exercise routine. Okay?"

"Makes sense."

They positioned themselves on a mat, and Richard began to

demonstrate a series of upper-body stretches that Pam followed with ease.

"Excellent. See, you're a natural. Your body is already inclined to do the right thing," he said. "You're going to be a workout addict, I can see it."

"Ha." Pam raised her arm and leaned to the side.

They stretched their legs. Every time Richard bent a knee, it looked like a string quartet gearing up to play a concerto on his thigh. He demonstrated a side lunge and stressed the importance of maintaining proper back alignment to avoid pulling a muscle. But Pam kept bending her back improperly.

"Let me show you," he said and stood behind Pam. She felt her body heat up, and she became nervous. He was standing so close she could smell him faintly, the way the scent of autumn sort of sneaks up in October.

He placed his hand in the small of her back. "When you're doing this stretch, you should not feel any pressure at all in your lower back. In this area here," he said, circling her back lightly with his hand.

"Okay," Pam said nervously, trying to straighten her upper body.

"In fact, your upper body should remain perfectly straight. The stress should occur in your upper thigh and nowhere else. Do you feel it?"

"Mm-hm." Pam nodded quickly. Richard stepped back and watched her.

"Excellent," he said.

They completed their stretching and then toured the cardiovascular section of the gym. Richard identified all the equipment, ending with the treadmill.

"Okay, let's start our cardio workout here," Richard said. "You can walk at a very slow pace, or you can run. You can walk on a flat surface or against an incline that simulates a hill. Or you can do a combination of all of those things. You can walk for a certain time period or for a certain distance, like a mile. You can gear all of these things to a target heart rate, which is probably what the personal trainer will teach you to do. Maintaining a lower heart rate during exercise will help you burn fat, while maintaining a higher heart rate will help you tone muscle."

"Let's program it for a lower heart rate, then. All this fat I've got," Pam said, frowning as she looked herself over.

"I sure don't see it," he said, looking at Pam. "All I see is a body most women would love to have."

Pam looked away. Before Richard, she could not remember the last time a man had complimented her on her physical appearance. Since the cancer, she had begun to ignore her body. She had stopped looking at anything past her left breast. None of the rest of it mattered to her.

Pam climbed on the treadmill. "I'm ready."

"Not yet," Richard said and laughed. "Put both your legs outside the belt. When that belt starts to move, the last place you want to be is on it. You never know whether it will begin slowly or malfunction."

Richard showed Pam how to select the program she desired and match it to a targeted heart rate, and Pam commenced a brisk walk. He jogged on the treadmill next to her. Every few minutes, he would look over at Pam, smile, and tell her she was doing a wonderful job.

An hour later, a completely sweaty Richard and a slightly moist Pam trudged out of the gym. Richard wiped his forehead with a towel.

"Compared to you, I don't feel like I did a thing," Pam said.

"Aw, that's okay. I didn't want you to overexert yourself on your first day. That's a guaranteed way to pull a muscle. Then you'd have a legitimate excuse for calling me and saying 'Richard, I just can't make it to the gym this week, or this month for that matter. I think

I've broken my body.' " He mocked Pam's southern drawl and had them both doubled over in laughter.

"You're wrong," she said and pushed him lightly on his shoulder.

"Well, I'm glad you made it to the gym today. Congratulations on the first day of the rest of your exercise life."

"If it weren't for you, I wouldn't have come. I don't know why I've been lacking the drive to get going with a routine. But I'm excited now. Thank you so much."

"De nada," Richard said.

"No, it is something—to me, at least."

They walked on in silence.

"Let me repay you," Pam said quickly.

"Oh, no. You don't need to repay me, Pamela. It was my pleasure to help you. My repayment will be seeing you on a self-sustained regimen in the very near future."

"Yes, but I'd still like to do something for you. What you've done today is totally outside the scope of what I'm paying you to do, and you've taken your personal time to do it. I really, really appreciate it. Why don't you let me fix you dinner? You've got to be starving, after that ferocious workout you just had."

Richard was silent. "You don't have to do that, Pamela. I appreciate the offer, but—"

"I insist." In Richard's company, Pam always felt as if she were ridding herself of the clutter in her mind. She felt as though every corner and crevice had been swept, the old, useless thoughts packed away, the spots bleached and surfaces scrubbed.

"All right," he said slowly. "I'll go home and shower, and then I'll stop by. But not because you owe me. Only because I'm starving."

"Oh, wonderful, Richard! Very good. And don't worry, the food will be healthy!"

* * *

All sorts of questions raced through Pam's mind as she tore off her clothes and ran hot water in her shower. Was this a date? Was Richard attracted to her? Or was he just being kind, the way he always was? Was this proper, given that they had a sort of doctor-patient relationship? Did he spend extracurricular time with all his vulnerable breast cancer patients who weren't feeling particularly good about themselves? Was she throwing herself at him? Was she desperate?

Pam didn't have answers to her questions. But it didn't matter. She was excited. It felt like a date, and she hadn't had one in quite a while. Someone seemed to be interested in her, at least enough to share a meal with her. With *her,* despite her fake breast and her bald scalp.

The phone rang, and Pam's mind told her not to answer. She was floating on the outer edges of reality and didn't want to be drawn in by anyone. It rang again, and she grabbed it.

"Hello?" she panted into the receiver.

"Mom, what's wrong?" Marley asked. "You sound out of breath."

"Oh no, I'm fine." Pam tested the water temperature in the shower with her fingertips.

"You sure? You sound weird."

"No, no. I'm fine. How are you?"

"I'm okay. Just checking on you. We didn't really get a chance to talk earlier, you know, with—"

"Yeah, I know. Listen, I'm sorry for the way I acted. I really am, hear?"

"Don't worry about it." Marley paused. "You in a rush?" She was hoping not. She really wanted to tell her about Lazarus.

"Ah, well, sort of, yeah."

"Mom," Marley laughed, "what is going on? What are you up to?"

Pam loosened a bit. Maybe Marley could handle it after all. Pam sure was bursting to tell somebody the exciting news. "I'm having a friend over for dinner."

"What?"

"Yes," Pam squealed, "I'm cooking dinner for Richard."

"Richard, your *nutritionist*?"

"Yeah."

"Mom, you can't be serious. Richard's not a friend, he's an adviser! You're his client. That's ridiculous! You barely know the man." She lowered her voice. "This is a very fragile time for you, Mom."

"Look. You are *not* going to ruin my mood. For once in I don't know how long, I am happy and I feel good. I am *not* fragile—I reject fragility. I choose happiness. Do you understand me?"

"Yes, but Mommy, all I'm saying is—"

"Honestly, Marley, I'm not interested in hearing what you have to say right now. It's not positive. I'm a grown woman, and I am enjoying my life. Now, let me—"

"But this is not you! This is so different from who you—"

"It *is* me! I'm changing, don't you understand that? I mean, good grief, Marley! Things aren't always cookie-cutter simple, okay? I know your life has turned out that way, but mine is different. Now please, back off with the pressure and the accusations. That's not what I need right now."

"Okay, Mom," Marley mumbled, her voice cracking. "I'm going to pray for you because—"

"You're going to do *what*? Child, have you lost your mind? You don't need to pray for me! I'm not a heathen off the street! And you're not Holy Mary Mother of God!"

"All right, Mommy. Good-bye."

Pam sautéed scallions and garlic in a skillet while Betty Carter crooned in the background. She had decided to make shrimp linguine, one of her specialties, figuring Richard wouldn't mind the cholesterol too much. Pam's homemade spinach and artichoke dip was nestled in the middle of a smattering of tortilla chips circling a saffron platter. It looked and smelled perfect.

The telephone rang, and, thinking it was her doorbell, Pam jumped. She laughed at herself and picked up the receiver.

"Hello," she sang.

"Pamela? Hi, it's Richard."

"Hey." It was half past seven, the time they had agreed upon for dinner. "You lost?"

"No, I'm not lost. Actually, I was calling to let you know that I'm not going to come after all."

Disappointment rose up in Pam's belly and quickly spread through her veins. She could taste it, coating her throat like chalk.

"It's not that I don't want to come, believe me. It's just that, well, we have a professional relationship, and I don't think I'd ever have peace of mind if I allowed our relationship to exceed those bounds. At least not at this time."

Pam was quiet.

"Pamela, please don't get quiet on me. This is not easy for me to do. I owe you an apology for accepting your invitation in the first place. But I would be a horrible person if I began a nonprofessional relationship of any kind with you right now."

"Who said anything about a relationship, Richard?" Pam threw her wood-handled chopping knife into the sink.

"What I mean to say is that my focus right now has to be on helping you achieve the health and fitness lifestyle you're seeking. If we deal with each other outside those bounds, then we risk compromising our professional relationship. Now, once we end that relationship, that's a totally different story, and I'd be the first one to—"

Pam sucked her teeth. "Just save it, Richard. The last thing I need is pity flattery."

"It's not pity flattery, Pamela," he said softly. "I'm very fond of you. More than you realize. That's why I'm trying to give you the respect you deserve."

"Richard, thank you for calling me at *seven-thirty* to tell me you won't be able to make it after all. Good night." Pam slammed the telephone down and leaned back against the kitchen counter, closed her eyes, and rubbed her forehead. She was embarrassed. As if she'd showed her belly button to a boy she believed would never laugh at it, but he had.

She was ashamed of herself. Disgusted with her behavior. Overwhelmed with the reality that she'd have to stay in her skin and live this thing out. Here she was, fifty-two years old, just beginning to fight a fatal disease, trying to start up something with her nutritionist, only to be rejected. She looked at the spread she had laid out on the table, waiting to be eaten by two people, and almost choked on her tears.

What made this pill even harder to swallow, though, was the truth: it wasn't that Richard didn't want to have dinner with her because she'd lost a breast and wore a wig. She knew Richard well enough to know better than that. Rather, the truth was that it was inappropriate. Inappropriate for Pam to have offered to entertain him and inappropriate—or so it would have been—for him to have taken Pam up on her offer. He was her nutritionist, and she was his client. And with that truth, Pam could not convince herself she was a victim of anything. Or even that her belly button had been laughed at. Much as she tried, Pam could not rationalize hating Richard and writing him off. She was left to deal with herself.

Chapter 20

ANDRUW JONES HIT a home run, and everyone in Turner Field was on his feet. The Braves and the Mets were fighting it out for first place, and at the top of the fifth, the Braves were leading.

"That brother is *bad*!" Lazarus grabbed his arms behind his head. He was a lifelong Braves fan and an Andruw Jones fan in particular. Marley knew little about baseball, except that the Braves-Mets face-off was a game almost all her colleagues, young and old, had been trying for weeks to get tickets to attend. And here she was, seated over the dugout, taking it all in. With Lazarus, no less.

"You having fun?" he asked. The anticipation in his eyes reminded Marley of a little boy, waiting on his mama to say he could stay outside an hour longer.

"I'm having a ball," she said, a wide grin across her face. And she was. The excitement of the fans, the smell of roasted peanuts and the sound of them crunching beneath the feet of the spectators, the lukewarm air and the midnight blue sky, the energy from the field below and the bright lights adding to it—all of it had cast a spell on her, causing her to feel as if she were in a dream, one from which she never, ever wanted to wake.

"Me, too," Lazarus said, his eyes smiling at her. "And not just because I'm watching my man Andruw play," he added, squeezing her lightly on her side.

Marley smiled and rested her chin in her hands. She stared at the stadium lights and then closed her eyes.

"You look like you're deep in thought," he said.

"Not really. Just thinking about things."

"What kinds of things?"

"Honestly?"

"Always."

She reclined in her seat and stared at the field. "Trains of thought are amazing, how they start in one place and end up somewhere completely different. First I was thinking about how happy I was being here with you, and how I really value the friendship we have."

"Mm-hm." He smiled.

"Then I started to worry about how I would feel if we stopped being friends. If all of a sudden we stopped hanging out. Then I started to think about my father and how it felt when he stopped being a major part of my life. And I realized that part of the reason I stayed with Gerrard for so long was because he was staying with me. He wasn't going anywhere. He wasn't going to leave me."

"Hm."

"Isn't that twisted?"

"No, it's not twisted. You are so hard on yourself, Marley. That's a human tendency. You were looking for fulfillment from a person, and a person can't give you that. The most committed person in the world will still fail you sometimes because he's not perfect. But now you're looking above for that fulfillment, and that's something you can count on to be with you forever, no matter what."

"I know it. I just have to live it."

"Yep," Lazarus said.

"You're gonna have to be patient with me, Lazarus," Marley said, looking at him.

"Only if you promise to be patient with me, too."

A vendor approached their aisle. "Light wands for sale! Get your light wands while it's dark!"

Marley looked at the magnificent colors of the light wands, fluorescent pinks, greens, and yellows, and remembered her childhood. She'd used to love those things, even though their batteries lasted no more than three days. They'd reminded her that she had been somewhere where her only responsibility was to have fun.

Lazarus waved a few bills at the vendor and passed them down the row. He pointed to a yellow light wand and the vendor sent it up to him.

Lazarus grinned sheepishly at Marley. "I used to love these when I was a child." He handed her the light wand. "I kept them in my bed and slept with them whenever I was scared of something." They both laughed.

"I want you to keep it," he said, touching her hand, "to remind you that the light of the world is always with you."

Marley let loose a huge grin. "You are so sweet, Lazarus. Thank you." She looked at the light wand. "I'm kinda psyched about having one of these again!" They laughed, and she cheered the Braves on, waving her light wand in the air.

During the bottom of the seventh, when the bases were loaded and Harvey Whittaker was at bat, Pam called Marley on her cell phone. Even Marley found it difficult to tear herself away from the action long enough to answer the phone.

"Hi, Mom," Marley yelled over the cheering crowds. "Is everything okay?"

"Um, well, no, not really. I need a few things from the store, but

I'm not feeling too well. I was wondering whether you wouldn't mind picking them up for me."

"Ah, sure," Marley agreed. She frowned, eyebrows furrowed. "You sure everything is okay?"

"Yes, mm-hm," Pam said.

"I can be there in about an hour. Is that good?"

"That's fine."

"I'll call you from the car to find out what you need. I'll see you in a bit."

"All right, honey. Thank you so much."

Marley hung up and stared blankly.

"Everything cool with your mom?" Lazarus asked.

"Doesn't sound like it. She said she's not feeling well and wants me to pick up some things for her."

"Do you need to go now?"

"Oh, no, not right now. I told her I'd see her in about an hour or so."

"By the time we leave the game and I drop you off at home, it will be way past an hour. Are you sure you don't want to leave now?"

"No, Lazarus. Thanks for offering. But we're going to finish watching the game, then we'll leave."

"If you say so. But I'll completely understand if you need to go. Moms are moms."

Marley tried to lose herself in the game again but could not. Her mother needed something. Marley doubted it had anything to do with items from a store.

To everyone's disbelief, Harvey struck out. The crowd booed him terribly. *Where was their loyalty?* Harvey seemed to wonder as he glared into the stands and stomped off the field.

Lazarus hopped to his feet. "Man, you can't be doing that against the Mets!" he yelled, hands cupped around his mouth, as if Harvey could really hear him. He raised his arms in the air as if to ask, "What's up?" and stared at Harvey until he disappeared from sight.

Marley tugged on his arm. "Lazarus," she began.

He looked down at her. "You ready to go?"

"Yeah. I'm really sorry," she said, her eyes searching his for understanding.

"Let's roll," he said, extending his hand.

"I wonder whether she feels bad about the way she treated me on the phone the other night," Marley said as they left Kroger with Pam's items.

"You mean the night she cooked dinner for her nutritionist?"

"Yeah."

"Maybe so. This time, though, you might want to communicate with her the way a friend would, rather than the way a daughter would."

Marley sucked her teeth. "Even as a friend, I would have told her she was tripping. She's been through a lot. Now is not the time to try to cultivate a relationship with a man, especially a man who's her nutritionist."

They reached the house and Marley climbed out of the car.

"I'm going to stay out here," Lazarus said from the driver's seat.

"Oh, no, you don't have to do that. Come on in."

"This would be my first time meeting your mother, and if she's not up to company right now, then—"

"Lazarus, I insist. Come on inside. It's time she met you."

He got out of the car reluctantly and followed Marley to the front door. "I don't know, Marley," Lazarus pressed. "It really may not be a good idea. . . ."

"Shh," Marley said, winking an eye and covering her lips with a finger. "It really is okay," she assured him as she opened the door.

"Mom," Marley called from the foyer, "it's me."

"Hey," Pam replied from upstairs. "Be right down."

"Mom, I've got someone with me."

"Oh?" Pam said, then paused. "Okay."

Marley took the bags into the kitchen and put them in the refrigerator. On her way upstairs, she leaned over the banister. "Have a seat, Lazarus." She skipped up the last few steps and went into her mother's room.

"How you doin', Mom?" Marley sat on the edge of the bed. Pam was pulling a T-shirt over her head.

"Fine. Who's downstairs?"

"Oh, that's my friend Lazarus. I really want you to meet him. He's a nice guy," Marley said, trying to sound casual.

Pam adjusted her wig and began to brush it.

"What's wrong?"

"You're dating? Already?" Pam's words were crisp.

"Huh?"

"I said," Pam emphasized, turning to face Marley, "you're *dating* already?"

Marley laughed uncomfortably. "Mom, I didn't say Lazarus was my new fiancé. I said he was a friend of mine. What's wrong with having friends?"

"Oh, nothing. Except it's such a *fragile* time for you right now, and I'm sure you *barely* know this man." She brushed past Marley and went downstairs.

She's tripping, Marley thought. Maybe the cancer was bothering her. Maybe she was going through "the change." Something was wrong, that was for sure. Marley tried to shake it off. She said a short prayer to God for patience and understanding, then went downstairs.

"Yes, ma'am, I was born and raised here in Atlanta," Marley heard Lazarus say.

"Mm-hm," Pam nodded, seated in her Queen Anne chair. "You attended college in the area as well?"

"Yes, ma'am. Right here at UGA."

"Any graduate course work?" Pam grabbed her spectacles from the coffee table and put them on.

Lazarus smiled. "Yes. I got my MBA from Emory."

"I see." Pam glanced at her hands and pulled at a splintered nail. "And what are you doing now?"

"My brother and I own a commercial food supply business. We've got an office downtown, and we're hoping to expand soon."

"Hm," Pam said. "Wonder if I've ever heard of your company. What's the name?" she asked, looking at Lazarus.

"Reap the Harvest Food Services. Typically we service contracts with large companies."

"I see." Pam leaned forward to pick up a glass of water from the coffee table. She looked at Marley, who had seated herself on the love seat opposite Pam, and smiled. She looked at Lazarus's glass and realized it was empty. "You've finished your water. Can I get you anything else? Anything to eat?"

"No, thanks, ma'am. Thank you anyway."

"Well, let me take your glass."

He handed it to her, and she retreated into the kitchen. He and Marley looked at each other and chuckled softly.

"Are you all right?" Marley whispered.

"Oh, yeah," he said and nodded quickly. "She's just being a mother, Marley—that's all she's doing," he reassured her.

"All right. Excuse me for a minute. I'm going to talk to her in the kitchen, and then I'll be ready to go."

"Take your time," he said, waving her on and fishing out *Black Enterprise* from the magazines sprawled across the table.

Standing in the kitchen, Marley glared at her mother's back. "Mom, could you have been any ruder?"

"What do you mean?" Pam turned, and her face was quizzical.

"What's with the third degree on where he was raised, where he was educated, and where he's employed?"

"Marley, I don't know him. Those are perfectly legitimate questions to ask someone that you don't know from Adam." Pam opened a cabinet door to retrieve a salad bowl.

"Mom, you know what I mean. You were interrogating him!" Marley peeked around the corner to make sure Lazarus wasn't listening.

"I thought we were having a perfectly normal conversation." Pam took spinach salad from the refrigerator and put a helping into her bowl. "He seemed to think it was a normal conversation, too. You're the only one who has a problem with it."

"All right, Mom. I'm not going to go back and forth with you about this. I *know* you know what I'm talking about." Marley peeked around the corner again. "Your carrots and the other produce are in the refrigerator. Kroger was all out of fresh blueberries."

"Thank you very much," Pam said rosily.

"Is that your dinner?" Marley asked, pointing at Pam's salad.

"Yes. I'm not very hungry this evening." Pam whisked by Marley on her way to the living room.

"Do you have family in the area, Lazarus?" Pam put a forkful of salad into her mouth. She had seated herself in her Queen Anne chair again and by all appearances was fueled up and ready for round two.

"Yeah, I've got—"

"Lazarus, I need to go," Marley interjected, standing near him. "It's getting late, and I need to head home."

"Oh, okay." He sounded disappointed.

"So soon?" Pam asked, still consumed with her salad.

"Yeah, Mom. We're gonna head on out now. I'll give you a call tomorrow."

"Okay, honey. Thanks so much for coming over. Lazarus, it was my pleasure to meet you."

"Mine as well, Ms. Shepherd. Hopefully we'll be able to continue our conversation." He walked over and shook her hand.

"Good night, Mom." Marley kissed her mother on the cheek.

"Good night, honey." Pam heard the door close. She continued to eat her salad until the lump that had formed in her throat made it impossible for her to chew. She put the bowl on the table and covered her face with her hands.

"I'm really sorry about that," Marley said, once they drove off.

"It's cool. She didn't know I was coming with you, so I think she was caught off guard. But it was fine." Lazarus glanced at Marley. "She was just checking a brother out, making sure I'm legit," he joked.

"Yeah, but all those questions about where you went to school and what you do for a living? Goodness! What if you hadn't gone to school anywhere? She just can't get the concept of Gerrard out of her head. All she can see is paper statistics, and she, of all people, should know that a good education and a good job does not make a good man."

"I'll bet you twenty dollars you'll be asking your daughter's male friends the same kinds of questions." He grinned at her and offered his pinky.

Marley pondered Lazarus's comment. She couldn't help but smile at the suggestion that he might be around to know what she would say to her daughter years from now. "All right, then," she answered, wrapping her pinky around his and pulling it firmly, "it's a bet."

"*Cool,*" Lazarus sang. "It's on."

Chapter 21

LAZARUS AND PAUL sat next to each other at the small round mahogany-veneer conference table they'd purchased from a used office furniture store. The space in their office suite was tight, but it didn't matter. They had promised each other, when they'd drawn up the business plan for Reap the Harvest, that plush upgrades would wait until the business's balance sheet had been in the black for five consecutive years. The first two years' numbers had hemorrhaged off the pages of the balance sheet, but the last four had exceeded even their greatest expectations.

"I think we should end our fiscal year in October rather than June," Lazarus said, rubbing his temples as he surveyed the mounds of accounting and financial records strewn across the conference table.

Paul chuckled, then sipped his coffee. "You're just saying that because you don't feel like crunching the numbers. But duty calls, my man." Paul placed his mug on the table, pushed his glasses up on his nose, and began to review records.

Lazarus reclined in his chair, folding his arms behind his head. "I spoke with Colin, the new brother over at Finks & Finks."

"Oh yeah," Paul said, turning to face Lazarus. "Their newest analyst. What'd you think?"

Lazarus nodded slowly. "I was impressed. He's extremely knowledgeable. Just finished a two-year stint at one of the Big Five firms and was able to cut his teeth on some large accounts while he was there."

"Good, good," Paul said, stroking his chin. "So he'll be working with James on our audit?"

"Yep. He's already up to speed on our financial history, knows about our prospective service accounts, and has some really creative ideas about how to best showcase our assets and downplay our liabilities."

Paul raised his eyebrows. "Interesting. What does he have in mind?" He reclined in his chair.

Lazarus leaned forward, resting his arms on the table and shifting a paperweight between his hands. "Well, he mentioned using a pro forma approach to account for earnings, rather than using GAAP."

"Pro forma?" Paul laughed. "You've got to be kidding, Laz. Do you know how misleading pro forma earnings are?"

"That's the thing, though—it's not what I thought it was." Lazarus sat up straight. "I used to think pro forma was a neat little way of hiding nonrecurring expenses, but there's more to it than that. This approach can really highlight our gains and diminish the impact of our onetime expenses."

Paul shook his head. "Man, we've been using GAAP since day one. I don't know why we'd change course now. For what?" he asked, lifting his hands, then dropping them on the table. "We're not about to go public, and we're not a tech firm. We've always given *full* disclosure and it has never hurt us. I'm not down with switching gears midstream, man."

"Oh, come on, man—I'm not in favor of anything less than full disclosure either," Lazarus said, leaning forward and looking at

Paul. "But I'm definitely in favor of using whatever accounting tools are out there to present the strongest financial picture we can. The big boys do it *all the time,* man. Meanwhile, we sit by, twiddling our thumbs, thinking we're being honest Johnnies when what we're really doing is shooting ourselves in the feet unnecessarily."

"Laz, it does *not* sit well with me. Straight up, man." Paul shook his head. "Our financial outlook has been strong for the past four years, and we have not used pro forma. There's just no reason to use it now."

Lazarus sighed and rubbed his temples again. He folded his hands and looked at his brother. "Paul, the airline is about to decide whether to sign on with us for a multiyear contract. This is a big deal for us. I think we need to be aggressive in our presentation. We need to sell ourselves as best we can, man. To me it's the difference between *showing* someone you're an Olympic competitor versus giving them an essay about your athletic ability and hoping they'll piece all the information together and come up with the conclusion that you can win the gold. I mean, *come on,* man."

Paul was quiet as he traced the rim of his coffee mug with his finger.

"I would never advocate anything dishonest, Paul. You know that." Lazarus looked intently at his brother. "I just want us to be as sophisticated in our approach as possible. I don't want our numbers to be any lower than they have to be, and I want our prospective clients to have full confidence in our staying power. This is a critical time for us, and I just don't want to blow it."

Paul removed his glasses and rubbed his eyes. "Lazarus," he began, replacing his glasses and folding his hands, "don't ever forget who we are. Don't ever forget what we believe. And don't ever, ever forget who our source is. We don't need pro forma when we have God working on our behalf."

Lazarus shook his head. "Paul, let's not get so spiritual that we can't function in the natural. *Listen* to me, man: I am *not* advocating dishonesty. Period. I'm advocating savvy accounting. I know who our source is, and last time I checked, the Bible didn't say, 'Thou shall not use pro forma accounting.' "

"Lazarus—"

"No, man, I'm serious," Lazarus said, cutting Paul off. "This isn't about doing anything outside of God's will. You know me better than that. You're absolutely right—we can never forget who our source is. At the same time, we need to use everything we've been given to build the enterprise we've been called to build. We have to use our knowledge, and we have to use our resources. That's all I'm saying."

Paul sipped his coffee and grabbed a stack of papers. He looked at Lazarus. "Let's pray on it, man, and then we can talk about it again. Right now, we've got a lot of work to do."

Shortly after eleven that evening, Marley's phone rang. Even without caller identification, she knew who it was.

"Hi, Lazarus," she said, grinning as she placed her book on the nightstand.

"Hey there," Lazarus said. "It's good to hear your voice."

"Yours too. Tired, huh?" she asked. His voice was flat, lacking its singsong bounce.

"Yeah, it was a long day."

"Well, things should slow down once you guys get through the audit, right?"

"Yeah, yeah. Not much longer. How was your day?"

"Fine. Same-old same-old. I'm working with a woman partner on a new employment discrimination case, and I'm pretty excited about it."

"Good," Lazarus said, sounding genuinely enthused. "No more Bob?"

"Well, at least not for the time being. Bob's case hasn't gone away, so I'm not completely off the hook. But a hiatus is better than nothing." Marley chuckled.

"I hear you." Lazarus sighed. "Man, what a day."

"Everything okay? You sure you're just tired?" Marley could swear she heard discouragement in Lazarus's voice; it was foreign turf.

"Yeah, everything's okay. Had a little discussion with Paul today, and it's still sort of on my mind."

"What was the discussion about?"

"Well, I spoke with a guy at our auditing firm, and he told me about a different approach to reporting earnings than what Paul and I have traditionally used. I thought the approach made sense, and so I told Paul about it, but he wasn't too impressed. That was fine, but then he started to imply that I was advocating less-than-full disclosure, gave me a speech on remembering God, and all sorts of stuff."

Marley raised her eyebrows. "Really? What kind of approach are you talking about?"

"Basically, it's a way of reporting earnings that excludes a lot of onetime expenses and strengthens your bottom line as a result. Even though our onetime expenses are nowhere near as great as they were a few years ago, they still exist. Lots of companies use the approach."

"But why would you want to exclude *anything* from your report?" Marley asked, trying to sound calm. She didn't like the sound of this.

"The expenses aren't erased from the books, Marley, they're just not accounted for in certain categories, and as a result the picture of the company's present earnings is more accurate."

"Mm." She was quiet. "I don't like the way that sounds, either."

Lazarus sighed. "Why not?" he asked, sounding as though he really didn't want an answer.

"Because there's nothing inherently wrong with onetime ex-

penses. How can it hurt you to account for those the way you normally would?"

"It's not that accounting for the expenses will hurt us; it's that
they don't necessarily help us, and when we're facing major contract acquisitions and renewals, we need to *help* ourselves as much
as possible."

"Have you used this approach before?"

"No."

"Hasn't the company been profitable?"

"Yes."

"Then why change?"

"Because the stakes are *higher* now, Marley. We have a major airline contract on the line. We're being compared with other food
service suppliers, and I want us to put our best foot forward."

Marley sighed. "I don't know, Lazarus. Seems to me that things
will work out as they should without you changing the way you do
business."

"All right. Thanks for your opinion, Marley."

Marley cocked her head to one side. "You don't sound too thankful for it."

"Yeah, I'm a little frustrated right now. Listen," he said, sighing,
"I need to take my shower and get ready for bed. Need to clear my
head. I'll give you a call tomorrow, okay?"

"All right," Marley said, barely able to hear herself.

"All right. Good night, Marley." Lazarus paused. "God bless
you," he said, then hung up.

When Marley walked through the door at Mickey's to meet Ashley
and Deanna for lunch, her face was so long that her chin could've
swept the floor. She didn't even bother to try and hide her disappointment.

"God, did the cat drag you in here or *what*?" Deanna asked, eyeing Marley. She pulled Marley's chair out for her and then continued to stare at her. "What's wrong?"

"Hello, hello, hello," Marley said, half waving at Deanna and Ashley as she sat. "How are you? Fine? Good." She picked up her menu and pretended to engross herself in it.

"Oh, come on—it can't be *that* bad," Ashley said, chuckling. "What's going on?"

Marley sighed as she placed her menu on the table. "Lazarus. He's a crook."

"What?" Deanna exclaimed. "What in the world are you talking about? Does he have a record?"

"No, no, nothing like that. I'm being facetious," Marley said, looking at Deanna and then at Ashley, who was frowning. "I guess you can say we had our first disagreement last night, and I'm disappointed in him."

"Why?" Ashley asked quietly.

"Well, it has to do with his business. They're preparing for their audit, and he wants to use some pro forma accounting method that leaves out certain expenses and enhances the overall financial picture for the company. His brother thought it was misleading, and so do I."

"Okay, so what else happened? What was it that upset you?" Deanna asked.

"What *else*? That's it. That's enough, isn't it? Goodness, did you hear what I said? I said he wants to exclude expenses from his reporting. How dishonest can you get?"

Deanna looked at Ashley and shrugged. "Maybe it's just me, but that doesn't sound criminal. Do other companies use this method he's talking about?"

"Yes, but—"

"I can't imagine Lazarus wanting to do anything covertly," Ashley added, shaking her head. "Did he come up with the idea of using this method?"

"No, their auditor recommended it."

Ashley and Deanna looked at Marley incredulously.

"What? Why are you looking at me like that?" Marley asked.

"Marley," Ashley began, touching her hand lightly, "if their auditor recommended it, then why are you blaming him for considering it? I mean, don't you think you're being a little too hard on him?"

"Yeah," Deanna added, reclining in her chair and folding her arms across her chest. "You've been hanging out with Lazarus long enough to know he's not a dishonest person. Maybe he wants to be aggressive. And maybe Paul's upset because aggressiveness is not the best thing for their company right now—the heck if I know. But it seems to me that you're being extremely hard on the brother, calling him a crook."

"I agree," Ashley said. "I don't know enough to have an opinion whether this accounting thing he's talking about is good or bad, but I certainly don't think he's a shady character for considering it. *I* think," she said, leaning forward, "that you've expected him to be perfect and you're suddenly realizing he's not."

Marley twisted her ring. After the waiter came to take their orders, Marley leaned on the table. "You're right," she said, looking at her hands. "I can't even argue with that. But I've been through a lot, and I refuse to overlook any flaws—even the small ones—in a man. That's what got me into such a mess with Gerrard. I'm not falling for the same nonsense twice."

Deanna smiled. "Marley? Honey? What would happen if Lazarus refused to overlook your flaws?"

Marley sat up. "Wait a minute, Dee, I'm not saying—"

"No, no, just answer my question. What would happen if he held you accountable for all your flaws?"

"Look, Deanna, I know where you're going with this. No one's perfect. I'm not suggesting I am. And I admit that I've been holding him to a very high standard. But that's partially because he's set the standard himself. He's different from any man I've ever known.

He's grounded, secure, strong in his beliefs. And he's good to me. He *demands* a high standard."

"And that's good," Ashley said. "That's great. But he's still a man, and he's still flawed. Your job is to decide whether his flaws are the kinds you can live with or not. That's it."

Marley was quiet.

"I just have one question," Deanna said, resting her hand on Marley's arm. "How did the conversation end?"

"What do you mean?" Marley asked, looking at Deanna.

"What was the last thing he said to you? Did he say 'God bless you'?" Deanna grinned, eyes wide and teasing.

Marley looked down. "Yes," she said, trying not to blush.

Ashley and Deanna looked at each other and smiled. Deanna patted Marley's arm and said, "Ten points for consistency, minus one point for considering aggressive accounting strategies, equals nine points for Lazarus. He still wins."

Chapter 22

"HELLO," MA GRAND half mumbled into the telephone. She was in the middle of sizing up the outfit Katie Couric was wearing on the *Today* show—in particular whether her skirt was long enough to cover her knees. The ringing telephone was an unwelcome interruption.

"Hey, Gran," Marley said.

"Hey, how are you?" Though she had not yet caught the length of Katie's skirt, Ma Grand was by far more interested in talking to her granddaughter. Marley was willing to trade gossip with her and, on occasion, was even willing to trade gossip about Pam.

"I'm fine. Got the Monday blues. Sitting here at work, rewriting a paragraph in a motion to dismiss for the fourth time."

"For the fourth time?"

"Isn't that ridiculous?"

"It most certainly is. You need to give up on that paragraph and move on to something else."

"I wish I could," Marley chuckled.

"Why can't you?" Ma Grand's tone rebuked the notion that Marley could not do whatever she wanted to do.

"Because I won't be able to write the rest of the motion until I finish this paragraph. It's like a critical piece in a puzzle."

"Oh shoot, child." Ma Grand sucked her teeth. "You better forget about that paragraph and start on something else. You can go back to it later."

"Okay. I'm gonna put my boss on the phone. I want you to tell her why I can't finish her project and that I'll return to it another time."

"Certainly. Where is she?"

Marley laughed. "You'd really do it, huh?"

"Of course I would. How's that mother of yours?"

"Ugh. I guess she's okay."

"I been telling you for years now that something's not right with your mother. She has run herself into the ground, working so hard and carrying on. She's tired, and she needs more help than she'll ever admit."

Marley rolled her eyes. Ma Grand was right about one thing. For as long as she could remember, there had rarely been a conversation in which Ma Grand had not told her that something was wrong with her mother and the likely problem was fatigue from working too hard. She wished Ma Grand could see deeper than that. Pam was not tired. At least not from working too hard.

"Gran, Mom is only working four days a week now. She was supposed to return to a five-day workweek at the beginning of June, but she didn't. If anything, she's closer to going crazy from having too little to do with her time."

"Don't need to have a lot to do with her time. Sometimes it's good to just sit still and be quiet and listen to yourself."

"I think she's been doing that."

"Well, she needs to do it some more. I keep telling you-all. You-all think I'm crazy."

"I don't think you're crazy, Ma Grand," Marley said automatically. "Anyway. I'm gonna spend a few days at Mom's this week. I was calling to see whether you wanted to go with me."

"You are? That's really nice."

"You gonna go with me?"

"Oh, I don't know about that."

"Gran, why not? It would be good for the three of us to be together."

"Yeah, well, you-all work my nerves too much when the three of us are together. I just got my blood pressure back down from that last devilish encounter."

"Ma Grand, that was months ago. And that was between you and Mom. I didn't have anything to do with that."

"Yeah, well, I'll have to see."

"What do you have to see about, Gran?"

"I've got to pay my bills. And I might have a doctor's appointment this week. I need to double-check on that."

"You can do all of that from Mom's house. You don't have to be at your house to pay your bills or go to the doctor, and you know it."

"It's how I like to do things, Marley."

"Gran, I'm going to pick you up sometime after seven o'clock tonight. Just be ready when I get there."

"Does your mother know I'm coming?"

"Yeah," Marley lied, "she knows."

"How I let you get me entangled into these various messes, I will never know. I have more sense than this."

"See you tonight, Ma Grand."

"Good-bye."

Marley hung up and immediately dialed her mother's number.

"Hello?" Pam said.

"Hi, Mom," Marley replied quickly.

"Hi. How are you?"

"Good. How are you?"

"I won't complain," Pam said.

"Good, good. You've got your three-month follow-up appointment tomorrow, don't you?"

"Mm-hm."

"When will the doctor be able to give you the results of your lab work?" Marley tried to sound as casual as possible, but these were important results. They would let Pam know whether the chemotherapy had stopped the cancer from spreading throughout her body.

"Usually I would get them in the office the same day. But it's going to take a day or two longer because of the Fourth of July holiday."

"Oh, okay," Marley said, making a futile attempt to sound casual. They both knew that news of the test results was no casual thing. "You up to having some company for a few days?"

"Um, yeah, I guess so. That would be nice." She didn't mean it. She had already made plans to remain in the self-pitying rut she had dug for herself. These days, she liked it there. It was safe. It was known. It accepted her the way she was, and it always justified her feelings.

"Okay. Gran and I will be over tonight."

It was quiet on Pam's end.

"Mom?"

"Yeah, I'm here."

"Is that all right?"

"Yeah, that's fine."

"Mom, you and Ma Grand need to work things out. Really. We're fortunate that Ma Grand is still living, and we need to take advantage of the time we have together."

"Marley, she's my mother. You don't need to tell me that. I *am* thankful for her. But I know her in ways you'll never know her, and every day is not always a good day for us to spend time together. Sometimes we do better with a little distance between us."

"I understand. But you said it's okay for her to come?"

Pam sighed. "Yeah, it's all right."

"Good. We'll see you tonight, then. Love you, Mommy."

"You, too."

Ma Grand waited until ten minutes before seven to begin packing her bags for her stay at Pam's. It wasn't that she had forgotten that Marley had asked her to be ready by seven o'clock. Her memory was as sharp now as it had been fifty years ago, and on days when she needed it most—maybe to disprove some twisted recollection of her daughter's or granddaughter's—her memory was even sharper.

No, really the delay in packing was purposeful. And multifaceted. First off, she was not one to be told what to do. She would pack and be ready when *she* decided she would pack and be ready— based on her internal time clock and not someone else's rigid schedule. She needed to pace herself, and no one was going to rush her along. Second of all, this whole slumber-party-at-Pam's was Marley's grand idea, and Ma Grand still wasn't completely certain she wanted to have any part in it.

But more than that, she was worried. She knew Pam would be getting her test results back by the end of the week. And she knew that a negative report could mean Pam would have to fight to stay alive through the end of the year. The thought that she would survive her only living child charred her heart like a burning stake, smoldering the single flame that kept her alive.

Ma Grand folded a few cotton shirts and placed them in her overnight bag. Long as that flame was burning, she had time. Time to begin to do the things she knew she had not done. Not all of the things, because that simply didn't make sense at this late stage, nor was all of it necessary. But some of the things she could do. She wanted to do. With everything inside her she desired to tell Pam she loved her. Lord knows she felt the urge, quite often, to tell her. But she had not raised her children that way, on a whole lot of empty talk. She wanted her actions to be her mouthpiece. She would feel right silly talking 'bout some love to her full-grown child. Pam had made it this far without all that outward emotional mess, and she was just fine.

For the most part. To herself, Ma Grand could not deny that she had wondered on many occasions whether Pam's marriage to Silas had been nothing more than Pam latching on to the first show of love she'd gotten, because she needed it. And whether if she had made more of an open show of love to Pam, Pam would have made different choices in life. Her daddy had loved her dearly, that was for sure. But even Ma Grand knew that a father's love is a father's love and a mother's love is a mother's love, and the two are as distinctively jointed as the caterpillar and the butterfly. If one was missing, then you prayed for, at best, a partial foundation and hoped to God the environment would be kind enough to let you eke out the rest of what you needed to blossom and fly.

And more praise. These days Ma Grand wondered whether she should have praised her children more. She prided herself on making her children earn her commendation and open admiration. She didn't dole it out like candy at Halloween. She guarded it, hid it even, believing a child's search for it would impart more strength and character than any group of feel-good words she ever could have heaped on them. *You're so pretty. You're so smart.* Ma Grand had watched more fools raised on those words than she cared to remember. Pretty and smart fools, who now were either scratching and clawing to survive or miserable and trapped inside a world that being so pretty and so smart had ushered them right on into. Ma Grand knew this to be true. Still, she did sometimes wonder.

She stood in the middle of the floor in her bedroom, bathrobe and slippers in hand, feeling suddenly paralyzed. What it all meant was that her daughter might pass on to the afterlife without ever having gotten some of the love she either wanted or needed. In either case, to Ma Grand, today it felt as though she had given formula to a newborn sucking in search of her mother's milk. The corners of her mouth began to twitch. Her throat became dry. Her forehead wrinkled, and the rest of her face followed suit. Tears of doubt, fear, and uncertainty, which for years had been bottled inside, rushed through Ma Grand's eyes like emptying wells.

Chapter 23

BY FRIDAY PAM'S doctor still had not called with the test results. By Friday Marley had chewed so much of the dead skin off her cuticles that a manicure would have been a waste of money. And by Friday Pam and Ma Grand had driven each other into a silent craze from the words they had not said.

Earlier that week, Marley had told Lazarus she would not be able to go with him to the Fourth of July cookout his parents were having on Saturday afternoon. She figured she would need to hang around her mother and grandmother that day, regardless of the outcome. By Friday she had changed her mind. She needed a change of atmosphere. But she also missed Lazarus. She wanted to look at him with new eyes, eyes that expected and made allowances for imperfection.

That Saturday morning, she left her mother and grandmother in the kitchen, nibbling on the last of their cheese grits, scrambled eggs, sausage, toast, and fruit, and made her way upstairs to shower and dress for the cookout. While guilt had accompanied her up the stairs, excitement had taken its place by the time she started to run the water. She was going to meet Lazarus's parents. Lazarus *wanted* her to meet his parents. This was big.

She thought about the prayer he'd prayed before they got off the phone last night. *Lord, we also want to take time to thank You for the beautiful friendship we've found in each other. We know You've brought us together for a reason, and Father, we trust in You and pray that Your will be done in our lives. Thank You, Father.* In a matter of months, she'd shared a level of intimacy with Lazarus that she and Gerrard had not developed in all their years together. She had fallen in love.

She knew it was love because the feeling reduced what for thirty years she had thought love was to a bundle of obsessions and compulsions twinged with occasional mania and depression. She knew it was love because she didn't *know* him. Not as she had known Gerrard, or others in the past, with the kind of knowledge that you can force out of the hallways of your mind but that takes irreplaceable treasures with it. She knew only his strength. His conviction. His backbone. She knew the God in him. And she loved him.

It was a scary, naked, vulnerable feeling, knowing she was in love. It meant she would miss him if he ever left. It meant he would see things in her that might make him want to leave. It meant he would do things she would die to forget and struggle to forgive. It meant that, to each other, they would become real, mortal, and messed up.

But in the midst of such a heavy reality, Marley felt a peace she had never known. It was a peace that her human mind simply could not comprehend. She felt assurance. She did not proclaim to hear much from God, but she knew enough to know that only the Lord could be the source of the assurance, the blessed assurance, she was feeling.

Marley let the currents from the shower gently massage her back. She rolled her head from side to side and let the water and steam loosen the tight grip stress had on her body. She pictured

Lazarus's face and smiled. She was ready for all that was to come with him—the good and the not so good. She would not force him to carry the baggage Gerrard had given her. Lazarus's hands were free—to hold her close and guide her along whatever path they would travel together.

The doorbell rang, and Marley's eyes shot up from her toes, which she was touching up with red polish, to the clock on the nightstand. It was half past one, the time Lazarus had promised he would pick her up. He was always on time—and in the midst of her shower and her daydreaming, she had completely lost track of it.

She heard her mother answer the door and panicked. She was not only still getting ready but also forcing Lazarus, again, to navigate the waters of Pamela Shepherd, this time ably assisted by none other than Ma Grand. How could she have allowed this to happen?

Marley walked into the hallway and peeked around the corner to get a glimpse of the foyer. She heard her mother welcome Lazarus inside and tell him to make himself comfortable while Marley finished dressing. Pam started up the steps and Marley scurried back into her room.

"I completely lost track of time," she said hastily, pulling the towel off her body. "Let him know I'll be ready in about ten minutes."

"He doesn't look like he's in a rush, sweetheart." Pam smiled. "Just slow down and take your time. He can wait."

"Mom, just so you know, Lazarus is a really nice guy. Hopefully we'll be able to spend some time together soon and you can get to know him for yourself."

Pam nodded. "I don't doubt it, honey. I know you wouldn't waste your time with someone who wasn't worth it."

Marley looked at her mother and then continued to dress. She yanked her black linen sundress off its hanger and stepped into it. It flattered her figure without sticking to it like paint.

"I owe you an apology for the way I've been acting lately," Pam said, sitting in the chair across from the bed. "It's just that I've, well, I've been dealing with a lot of personal issues. It was wrong for me to take my frustration out on you. I want you to know that I'm sincerely sorry."

Marley buckled her sandals and walked over to her mother. "Mom, it's okay." She reached out to hug her. "Now, why don't you tell me what's been going on? I knew something was wrong, but I didn't think you wanted to talk to me about it."

"We'll talk about it. Not now, though. You go on and get ready. Just know that I'm fine and I'm sorry, hear?"

"Okay. Thanks, Mommy."

"What are you going to do with that hair?" Pam said, looking askance at the curls scattered across Marley's head.

"I was hoping my roller set would last another day, but I'd be pushing it if I wore it down, huh?"

"That roller set has died. No question about that," Pam said matter-of-factly. "Pin it up and go on about your business."

Marley grabbed a handful of bobby pins from a container and dropped several of them onto the dresser. She slowed herself down. Her mother was right; Lazarus was not in a rush. He never was.

"See you downstairs," Pam called out as she left the bedroom.

Marley finished her hair, grabbed her purse, and was on her way out of the room when she stopped. Turning around, she sat on the bed, folded her hands, and closed her eyes. *I've got to remember to do this,* she thought.

"Dear God, I just want to thank You for this day. Thank You for waking me up this morning, blessing me with good health, and surrounding me with a loving family. I have so much to be grateful for. Lord, I pray that You will keep my loved ones and me safe this day. I pray that You will take care of all our needs. I pray that You give my mother peace today. And I pray that our lives are pleasing to You. In Jesus' name, amen."

She rose from the bed and walked toward the door. "Oh," she said, squeezing her eyes shut, "and thank You *so* much for Lazarus. Thank You, thank You, *thank You!*"

"Lazarus, are your mom and dad hosting the cookout?" Pam asked, seating herself in her Queen Anne chair and reaching for her mug of green tea. She had finally found the Japanese sencha Richard had recommended she start drinking on a daily basis and had woefully replaced her daily cup of java with it.

"Yes, ma'am," Lazarus said, leaning forward. "My mother has been battling arthritis for a while. She finally found a solution that stops her swelling and inflammation, so now she's a busybody and it seems like she and my dad are either going somewhere or entertaining at their house every weekend."

"What in the world is her solution?" Ma Grand asked skeptically. "I sure would like to know it 'cause I could've been taking whatever it is for the past twenty years."

Lazarus began to speak, but Ma Grand interrupted. "And if it's that estrogen cocktail, that ain't no good. It works at first, then it starts to bloat you such that your clothes don't fit right anymore. No sir, that's no good." Ma Grand shook her head.

"Actually, swimming is what helps her," he replied. "She's tried just about every medication on the market, as well as a lot of the herbal remedies, but she found that swimming really reduces the inflammation and relieves the pain in her joints. The pain was so bad that she had developed a slight limp. But since she's been swimming regularly, her walking is normal again."

"Humph. Well, I have to leave that swimming to your mother and keep on suffering," Ma Grand said. "Feature me in a swimsuit." She laughed.

Pam smiled. "I'm glad your mother is feeling better. There's nothing like being so ill that you stop doing the things you love to do."

"Yeah. My mom is pretty steadfast, and usually even the worst of things won't slow her down. But this arthritis really had her vexed," Lazarus confessed. He looked down at his folded hands. "I think she let it shake her faith a little bit."

"Happens to the best of us," Pam said, staring at nothing in particular. She placed her mug on the table, then reclined in her chair and looked at her hands. "I'm struggling with cancer right now—I don't know whether Marley has mentioned this to you or not." She studied Lazarus's eyes.

Ma Grand shot Pam a glance that suggested she had no business sharing the details of her sickness.

"Yes, ma'am, she has."

Ma Grand rolled her eyes.

"Well," Pam continued, "I would say that my faith has been pretty strong over the years. I grew up in church. I'm active in my own church now, where I've been for years. And I study the Bible—not as often as I should but enough that I know how to find a scripture when I need to. But I tell you, when this cancer surfaced, I got the wind knocked out of me. It was as if everything I knew, everything I'd learned over the years—all of it just flew out the window and I began to face my problems like someone totally on my own."

"And that certainly didn't make any sense 'cause you have never been totally on your own," Ma Grand snapped and rolled her eyes again. "No sir, not ever."

"I mean, of all times to stop praying, that's when I stopped. I think I felt like God had let me down somehow, and so for a while, I was too angry to talk to Him."

Lazarus smiled. "I know exactly what you're saying."

"Oh, shoot, you-all don't make no sense," Ma Grand interjected. "All of us face trouble in our lives, and it ain't got nothing to do with the Lord letting us down. It's a part of natural life. Part of His plan."

"Mama, please." Pam's eyes pleaded with her mother, and then she looked at Lazarus. "Anyway, I can relate to your mom's experience."

"Like you said, it happens to the best of us. Thank God we live a Christian walk and not a Christian sprint. We'd all be passed out on the sidelines by now," he said.

Pam laughed easily at Lazarus's words. "Yeah, well, I wasn't even on the track, honey."

"You know," Lazarus said, "I've got a really good tape in my car that I think you would enjoy listening to. It's one of my pastor's sermons, and I think you'd like it."

"Uh, okay." Pam wasn't big on hearing a lot of rigmarole from other pastors; you never knew who and what you could trust. At least she knew the evils that surrounded Reverend Watson. With everybody else, it was like playing Russian roulette.

"He's a good teacher. I wouldn't recommend it if it hadn't already blessed my life in some way. Just check it out and see what you think," Lazarus insisted as he stood and walked to the door.

Ma Grand watched the storm door close behind him, and she smirked at Pam. "He's something," she said, then looked away. She refolded her hands.

"He is. He's refreshing." Pam got up to refill her tea.

Marley hustled down the steps, then quickly slowed down before she reached the landing. She looked at Ma Grand and frowned. "Did he leave?"

"No, child. He went outside to get a tape he wants your mother to listen to. Says it's going to *bless* her."

Marley sat on the couch next to Ma Grand. Ma Grand peered at Marley's knees, exposed beneath her sundress. Then her eyes traveled upward to take in the full view of her granddaughter.

"You look nice," she offered suspiciously.

"Thank you," Marley said. She leaned on Ma Grand's shoulder playfully, and Ma Grand waved her away in pretentious fuss.

"What perfume are you wearing?"

"Summer Madness," Marley responded slyly.

"Yeah, that smells like some madness in the summer, too."

"It smells wonderful," Pam said, sniffing the air as she returned to her seat. "Where'd you find it?"

"At Parisians. It was on sale, too."

"Mm. I need to pick up a bottle of that," Pam said, sniffing again. She grabbed her daughter's arm and put her nose to her wrist. "Mm-hm."

"Pick me up some, too," Ma Grand said.

Marley looked at her and burst into laughter. "What you gon' do with it, Ma Grand? Huh? You got a boyfriend you want to impress?"

"Don't worry about me and what I'm doing. You don't know who I know and who knows me. Just mind your own affairs." She folded her hands.

Lazarus returned from the car with the tape and handed it to Pam. "Let me know what you think. Honestly. Good or bad, I'd be interested to know."

"I sure will. Thank you very much, Lazarus."

He turned and looked at Marley seated on the couch.

"Hi, Lazarus," she said softly, looking up at him.

"Wow. You look beautiful." He offered his hand to help her up. "With your permission, I'll be escorting this lovely lady to my parents' house now. I'll have her home before the streetlights come on."

"That sounds reasonable," Ma Grand said. "We'll be sitting right out there on the front porch waiting for you."

Pam walked them to the door. "You-all have a good time. And thanks again, Lazarus. I'm going to listen to the tape tonight."

"Good," he said, looking back and smiling at her. "You have a good evening, too." He opened the passenger door to his car and helped Marley inside. He waved at Pam before he climbed into the driver's seat.

Lazarus's parents owned a brick rancher on a hilly lot off Niskey Lake Road in southwest Atlanta. Encircled by dogwoods and ancient oaks, whose curved trunks seemed to sap forth their own histories, the Jacobs' house was humbly captivating.

"This is a beautiful home, Lazarus," Marley said, looking around. "The landscaping is incredible."

"This is Daddy's pride and joy. He works in the yard every day, even when it rains."

"Hm. It shows."

Lazarus stopped to purge a wilted leaf from one of the rhododendrons growing along the driveway. "This house is pretty average compared to a lot of the other ones in the neighborhood. But to Daddy it's a castle. He's never owned so much land in his life, and good stewardship is his motto. So he tends to the yard like an employee. We tease him about it and tell him The Man isn't staring over his shoulder anymore. And Daddy says, 'Yes, He is. The Big Man. And it all belongs to Him.' Then we feel all *stupid*," Lazarus said, laughing.

A humid breeze began to blow. It felt like a moist kiss against Marley's cheeks. "I can't wait to meet him," she said.

As they approached the wooden fence that separated the front and back yards, they heard loud keyboard strokes. Marley looked at Lazarus, her eyes widened. "Your parents hired a live band to play at the cookout?"

"Naw. I forgot to warn you about Beanie and Isaiah. Remember when I was telling you they're sort of trying to find themselves?"

"Yeah," Marley said, still puzzled.

"Well, right now they're feeling like they want to be musicians. Supposedly they've started a two-man band. Called 'Brothers.' Is that original or what?"

"Lazarus, you know you should have helped them come up with a better name," Marley said, laughing.

"When it comes to this music thing, these brothers are helpless, I'm telling you. Paul and I can't tell them anything 'cause they think we're trying to be know-it-alls. With us having our own business and everything. And they're older than me, so they *really* don't want to hear what I have to say."

The tunes from the keyboard continued to fill the air. It sounded as if the keyboard player was warming up or playing scales of some sort.

"You're in for a treat," Lazarus said, ushering Marley through the gate.

Marley was surprised at the number of people in the backyard. There had to be at least forty or more of all ages, seated, standing, and walking around. Young children chased one another around the perimeter or swung in the swings stationed in the far right corner. Two older gentlemen played checkers on a small wooden table. A circle of older, grandmotherly women whispered and chuckled to themselves. Husbands rehashed scores from championship games and knockout punches from boxing matches dating three, five, and twelve years back. Wives shared stories about their children's latest and most outrageous transgressions.

And there, just a few feet from the long porch that wrapped around the back of the house, were Beanie and Isaiah, known as the Brothers. They looked like twins, except that Beanie was tall and light and Isaiah was short and dark. Both had Lazarus's deep, penetrating eyes and wide mouth. They were remarkably handsome and, like Lazarus and Paul, athletically built. Immediately, Marley began to matchmake in her mind, figuring she could get her girls together with Lazarus's brothers and just let the chips fall where they might. Then she remembered that Beanie and Isaiah were "finding themselves" and thought it best not to direct a tornado toward a china cabinet.

"There's my baby," a soothing voice came from behind Lazarus and Marley. They turned around to face Mrs. Jacobs, a short but large-boned woman with stunning gray hair and walnut-colored skin.

"Hey, Mama." Lazarus squeezed her shoulder. She smiled as widely as he did, and immediately Marley saw the resemblance.

"I was wondering what was taking you so long," Mrs. Jacobs said, her brows wrinkling, "but because you've got such a beautiful young lady with you, I'll cut you some slack." She winked at Marley.

"Thank you very much," Marley said.

"Mama, this is Marley, my friend I've been telling you about." He beamed, even stuck out his chest a little.

"It is so nice to meet you, sweetheart. Lazarus has been talking about you for so long, I was starting to think he had made you up. He's the baby, you know, and the babies are the ones who tend to have imaginary playmates and so forth. When Lazarus was three years old, he had these two imaginary playmates named—"

"Mama," Lazarus said and put his hand on her shoulder.

"Oh, Lord, there I go again. Telling all his business too soon. But it's all right, baby. I keep telling him there's nothing wrong with children having imaginary playmates. To this day, I believe it's the reason why he is so accepting of people for who they are. He realized early that the human beings walking this earth will never be all that we hope or wish for them to be."

"Thank you, Mama," Lazarus said, still sounding embarrassed.

"I'm glad I'm finally able to meet you," Marley said. "I didn't think I would be able to make it at first. My mother has been sick."

"Yes, yes," Mrs. Jacobs said, compassion suddenly flooding her face. Her cheeks seemed to redden with empathy. "Lazarus told me all about it. I've already fixed her a plate of food for you to take back with you. And I baked an extra pound cake this morning, so you take that back home with you, too," she instructed.

"Oh, Mrs. Jacobs, you really didn't have to—"

"Hush, now. I'm happy to do it," she insisted. "I don't know your mother, but you tell her that the Good Lord is watching over her. *I can feel it*. And you tell her she's blessed. And tell her to eat several pieces of cake whenever she wants to."

They laughed, and Mrs. Jacobs patted Marley on the shoulder. "Lazarus, go on and fix you and Marley a plate while there's still some food. You know we've got some folks here who act like they're at a soup kitchen. I'm honestly wondering when they last ate. Luanna and Amos have already asked for aluminum foil to take stuff home with 'em, and they just got here." She winked at them and walked away.

"She is wonderful, Lazarus," Marley said, her eyes wide. "What an angel."

"Yeah, she really is." He watched his mother mingle easily with the older women seated on lawn chairs.

Suddenly two loud voices, backed by frantic keyboard strokes, permeated the air. "All right, all right, all right, party people, get *rea-daaay*!" the Brothers yelled into their microphones.

"Which one is Beanie?"

"Beanie's the rapper," Lazarus mumbled. "Thirty-seven-year-old rapper. Compares himself to Kurtis Blow."

"Is he married?"

"We don't really know. He and his wife have divorced each other twice, but they're still together. My niece and nephew over there are his children," Lazarus said, pointing toward the swings. The boy was making race car noises and shoving his car into the dirt. His hair and face were ashen with dust, except for his lips, which were candy-apple red from repeated lip licking. His sister was singing "Mary Had a Little Lamb" and bobbing her head from side to side, forcing her ponytails to swing in the air as she pushed herself gently on the swing.

"What about Isaiah?"

"He's not married. Been dating Geneva, his girlfriend, since high school. He's thirty-three now. I told Geneva she should move on. She told me it takes some men longer than others to figure out what they want. Whenever my mother asks her what she's going to do if Isaiah ends up figuring out that she is not who he wants, she just smiles and shakes her head. Poor thing."

"They've been dating since high school?"

"Can you believe that? Ain't that much indecisiveness in the world. Geneva's been around for so long, though, that she's part of the family. It would be like divorce if Isaiah started to date someone else."

"All right, all right! Everybody wave your hands in the air! And wave them like you just don't care. Come on now!" Beanie yelled into the microphone, pacing across a small patch of grass as he tried to rev up the crowd. Most of the guests just stared at him in bewilderment. Isaiah continued to bang frantically on the keyboard.

"We got something for the old-timers today, so we gon' take y'all way back, and we gon' do a little *somethin' somethin'* for you. We got something for everybody," Beanie chimed and began to clap his hands.

"Oh, no, you don't," a deep voice bellowed from the side of the yard. The owner of the voice limped as fast as he could to where Beanie and Isaiah were stationed. "Not in my backyard you won't." It was Lazarus's father, and he had an attitude.

Mr. Jacobs stood directly in front of his sons. "Now, Beanie, I told you when you first started talking this band mess that it was foolish 'cause you can't sing and your brother can't play the keyboard. And I told you when you asked me whether you could play today that I have rules. I have rules at this house. No ungodly music. You boys been knowing that for more than thirty years, so don't come out here with that 'party people' rapping and talking. You see these folks sitting out here in this yard? Do they look like party people to you?"

"Dad, you didn't even give us a chance to get started!" Beanie whined, sounding thirteen rather than thirty-seven.

"I know, Dad," Isaiah joined in. "You don't even know what songs we're going to play, so how you just gon' call them ungodly?"

"What's the first song you're going to play, Isaiah? Just tell me the name of it, son." Mr. Jacobs' hands were on his waist.

"It's an Isley Brothers song, Dad. You probably don't know nothing about it," Isaiah whined. "Come on, Dad!"

"Boy, I knew 'bout the Isleys before you knew how to walk. Which song?"

" 'In Between the Sheets,' " Beanie mumbled.

Mr. Jacobs' face, which was the same almond color as Beanie's, grew beet red. "Boy, if you don't cut that mess out, you'd better! Now I'mo tell you one more time. No ungodly music! Pick something positive that you won't be embarrassed if your children repeat, and I'll let you play. Those are the rules. Otherwise, pack this stuff up and take it inside, and come on and sit out here and be with your family like two grown men ought to do. You hear me, boys?"

"Yes, sir," Beanie and Isaiah mumbled in unison.

Mr. Jacobs began to walk away slowly, his limp less apparent. He stopped, closed his eyes briefly, and mumbled a few words, then turned around.

"Now, sons, I love you. You know that. And there's no one way to achieve success in life. As long as you're responsible for your environment and everybody in it, and as long as you honor the good Lord, then I'm with you. No matter what. You understand?"

"Yes, Dad," they said.

"Good, then." Mr. Jacobs patted them on their backs. He turned to walk away, then said over his shoulder, "How about playing a nice nursery rhyme for the children?"

"Dad, come on!" Isaiah exclaimed.

Mr. Jacobs chuckled and waved his hand at them as he walked away. He spotted Lazarus and Marley and walked over. "Hey, son," he said, hugging Lazarus.

"Hey, Dad. Let me introduce you to Marley, my friend I told you about."

"Well, well, well! This is Miss Marley!" Mr. Jacobs extended his hand. "It's nice to meet you."

"Nice to meet you too, Mr. Jacobs."

"We're a colorful bunch, Marley," Mr. Jacobs added. "We've got food dealers, struggling musicians, and even underwater photographers. Did Lazarus tell you about Jacques Cousteau?"

Marley laughed. "You must be talking about Jeremi."

"Boy's been a swimmer all his life. It all started in the bathtub. Boy stayed in there till the water was cold and brown. Layla and I used to have to drag him out every night. Lord knows I had no idea he'd become a scuda man."

"Scuba, Dad. Scuba. He's a scuba diver."

"Yeah, right, well, anyhow, now they got the boy going out to the Caribbean every summer, teaching those tourists how to dive."

"That's incredible," Marley said.

"Yeah, it really is. Dad's got some of Jeremi's underwater photography hanging in the den. I'll show it to you a little later on," Lazarus said.

"But now, here's the thing," Mr. Jacobs said, eyes wide, hands open. "Do you know that the boy has got to wear a tank on his back to do all that? He's got to rely on a rubber tube and a metal box to help him breathe in depths of the water where can't no man breathe? You ever heard of such? Boy thinks he's a fishy."

Lazarus and Marley burst into laughter.

"But that's okay. They're my sons just the same. Different colors of the same rainbow," Mr. Jacobs said, looking past Marley and Lazarus. "Listen, it was nice to meet you, Marley. You'll have to come over for dinner sometime soon. I'll make some of my fried turkey."

"Fried turkey? I've never had that before."

"Oh yeah, fried turkey. It's so good it'll make you talk to yourself."

Marley laughed. "I'll look forward to it."

"Good, then. Lazarus, you tell your mother when you're gonna bring her back over, hear?"

"All right, Dad, I will."

Mr. Jacobs patted Lazarus on the back and went to visit with the older gentlemen who were still playing checkers at the wooden table. He bent down and spoke into one of the men's hearing aid. "Now, Johnny, you lost that game fifteen minutes ago. It's time to get on up and let somebody else play, man."

Lazarus took Marley's hand. "Come on, let me introduce you to the rest of the folks here." She squeezed his hand, large and warm, and it grasped hers tightly, leaving no room for fears or insecurities. His hand held hers as if it would never let go.

He took her around the yard and introduced her to just about everybody in attendance. Then he pulled up a chair for her next to Sheila and left her with a plate of food while he consorted with the husbands who were debating whether it really was Charles Smith's fault the Knicks had lost the Eastern Conference Championship to the Bulls in 1993.

"How have you been, Marley?" Sheila asked, smiling and fanning herself.

"I've been doing really well. How about you?"

"Sick as a dog, but other than that I can't complain."

"Really? What's wrong?"

Sheila looked around sheepishly and leaned closer to Marley. "Promise you won't tell Lazarus, because we're going to announce it today and he hasn't heard it yet."

Marley gasped. "Are you—"

"Pregnant," Sheila whispered. Her eyes beamed.

"Oh, my goodness, Sheila!" Marley hugged her, and they giggled. "That is so wonderful!"

"I know. Isn't it exciting? Girl, we've been trying for so long. Finally we just gave it to God and figured He'd bless us with a child whenever He got ready to do it. As soon as we stopped trying, bam!"

They laughed. "Isn't that always how it happens?" Marley said.

"Yes, indeed. You should've seen me—taking my temperature every morning, charting my cycle, raping my husband on ovulation days—it was madness! You'd think we'd know by now to let God do things in His own time and stop trying to regulate everything ourselves."

"That's the truth. Sheila, I am so happy for you and Paul. You-all are going to make wonderful parents."

"Thank you, Marley." Sheila couldn't stop smiling.

The girls wrapped themselves up in baby talk. Across the way, Lazarus and Paul had separated themselves from the husbands and, as usual, had begun to talk shop.

"I didn't expect Johnston and Dumfries to renew their contract so much earlier than the expiration date. And I certainly didn't expect them to renew for more than one year," Paul said, sipping punch from his plastic cup. Johnston and Dumfries was the oldest, and by many accounts the most prestigious, black law firm in Atlanta. The firm had given Reap the Harvest its first contract and had also proved to be its toughest customer.

"Tell me about it," Lazarus agreed. "Those brothers love to keep us guessing until the last minute. It's always so hard to get a read on whether they're pleased with the food or not."

"I know. But I think we can finally accept this as a vote of confidence."

"Congratulations, brother." Lazarus gripped Paul's shoulder.

"Same to you, my man. You deserve it."

Lazarus stared at Paul. "Listen, man—about the audit. I just wanted to say that—"

"Don't even sweat it, man," Paul interjected. "You were raising a valid option for consideration. Nothing wrong with that."

"Yeah." Lazarus looked around the yard. "And honestly, I still think it's an attractive option. But I've been thinking about where the business is now and where we're headed, and I'm cool with staying the course." He extended his hand to Paul. "For now, at least," he added once Paul had taken his hand.

They laughed. Paul stared at the trees. He sipped from his cup and turned to face Lazarus. "You're all right with me, man. Always did have that backbone." He patted Lazarus roughly on the back. "As the godfather of my first child, I expect you to pass that trait on," he said, grinning.

"You know it," Lazarus said, slapping Paul's hand. "I can't wait."

"Well, you've only got about seven more months to wait."

Lazarus stared at his brother blankly; then his eyes widened with realization. "*Whaaat?* For real? Oh *wow!*" He hugged Paul and pounded his back vigorously.

"Yeah, man," Paul said proudly. "We just found out about a week ago. We're going to make the announcement today, but I wanted you to be the first to know."

"I am so happy for you, man. Wow!" Lazarus rubbed the back of his neck. "You're going to be a wonderful father."

"Thanks, man. Sometimes I wonder. But I figure if God is sending us this child now, then He's already equipped me with everything I need."

"You know it."

Hours later, after the sun had begun to set, Lazarus and Marley sat alone on the swings in the backyard. Most of the crowd had dispersed, and a few family members and close friends were inside the house congratulating Paul and Sheila and eating the last of the chicken wings, potato salad, and peach cobbler.

"Did you have a good time today?" he asked.

"I did." She smiled. "I really needed this."

"I'm glad you came. It wouldn't have been the same without you." He stared at her.

"My day wouldn't have been the same without you, either." She stared back.

"I really appreciate you, Marley. I appreciate who you are, how you think, and what you believe in. I want you to know that."

She grinned. Patting his knee, she said, "I wanna hear all about this appreciation the next time I give you my opinion and you don't like it." They laughed, and she carried on.

"Seriously. Instead of 'Thanks for your *opinion,* Marley,' I wanna hear 'Marley, baby, you're exactly right. I'm wrong. I value your opinion *so* much, 'cause I just love who you are and what you believe in. You're the *bomb,* Marley.' "

"Full of jokes today," he said, shaking his head, still laughing.

They swung slowly, their feet grazing the ground. They shared a silence drawing them closer than hands could have; Marley nestled her mind inside its grip.

Today she had joy to spare. She was so happy she felt guilty. For a fleeting moment, she couldn't remember the grief she'd used to carry around with her. And she couldn't remember the fear that had begun to root itself in her mind and cloak her thoughts whenever she thought about the call her mother was expecting from the doctor. But the moment did flee. She saw her mother, at home, pretending to watch TV as she tried to outrun the demons chasing her mind. Marley stopped swinging.

Lazarus stopped, too, and held one of the chains on Marley's swing. "What's wrong?"

"I was just thinking about my mother. Feeling a little guilty because I'm so happy sitting here with you, but I can only imagine what she's going through right now. I'm sure the doctor's call will come on Monday." She paused. "It could go either way, you know." Marley's voice cracked, but she didn't try to contain herself. "I don't know what I'm going to do if I lose her, Lazarus."

He took her hand and squeezed it. "It's all right," he said softly. His reassuring words and his gentle touch made Marley feel safe to cry, to scream, to say things that made no sense, to say nothing at all.

"I remember," Lazarus began, "when my father lost part of his leg at the manufacturing plant where he used to work. He was out of a paycheck for quite a while because the plant had done some legal maneuvering and determined he wasn't eligible for workers' compensation. Anyway, the infection in his leg got worse, even after the surgery, and my mom had tapped just about every financial resource she could. She was working two jobs, our church had taken up a collection, and Beanie had finally given in to the guilt trip my grandma laid on him about being the oldest son and needing to cut grass or rake leaves or do something to help the family out. Little by little, I watched as my family began to give up things we loved. We sold the car. All seven of us moved into a two-bedroom apartment. I was only eight then, and I remember being an angry little knucklehead. I was angry with my father for losing his leg and angry with my mother for being willing to clean people's houses. Even the houses of people we knew.

"It was so embarrassing. I couldn't understand why we didn't just have money automatically, like other folks seemed to have. And I remember thinking about all the stuff we heard in church every Sunday, about how good God is and how He'll pick you up when you're down and He'll save you when no one else can. And I thought, 'What's up, Lord? Last time I checked, my family had reached the bottom and couldn't sink any deeper, so don't we qualify for some assistance right about now?' "

Marley grasped his hand more tightly, hoping to absorb some of his peace.

"My mother told me that one night, when I kneeled down to pray, I made a deal with God. She tells the story so often that I remember the prayer like I prayed it yesterday. I said, 'Dear Heavenly Father, everyone tells me You're the greatest. My mommy told me that You found some friends to write the Bible for You. Miss Rosamond at church school says the Bible is Your own very special book of promises. My daddy told me that in Your promise book You said Your children won't suffer. I think I'm Your child. And my mommy and daddy say they are Your children even though they are not kids. My daddy is sick, and my mommy is tired and poor. It's five of us in one bedroom, and I have to sleep with Isaiah and he pees in the bed, God.' "

Marley looked at Lazarus, and they both began to laugh.

"I said, 'It's not fair, God. If we love You, why do we have to suffer? Dear God, please keep Your promises that you made. I believe You, God. God, if You come through for me, I will stay loving You forever and ever and ever. I trust You, God.' "

Marley looked at Lazarus, who was staring off into the amethyst sky. She imagined what it must have been like for him to suffer that kind of lack. Her own childhood had been far from perfect, but she certainly had never wanted for any material thing.

"Well, we made it through the storm. My father had always been good at plumbing, so when the plumber at our apartment complex quit his job, my father applied and got the position. He did an excellent job, and all the neighbors loved him because he fixed other things in their apartments even though he didn't have to. Eventually, he became the grounds maintenance manager, and when he got that job we moved into a three-bedroom apartment and lived rent-free. My parents started saving like crazy, but we continued to live off one income since we had done it for so long and had gotten kind of good at it. Anyway, time passed on, and—"

"Wait a minute!" Marley looked at Lazarus, her eyes wide. "Is this the same apartment complex that your father owns today?"

"Yep. Daddy ended up buying the building." Lazarus laughed. "Is God good or what?"

Marley stared at Lazarus, then looked away. She shook her head. She was coming to know God's goodness. But still, sometimes she marveled at how readily, and easily, the impossible became probable with God. "God never ceases to amaze me," she said quietly.

Lazarus got up from his swing and sat on the wood chips covering the ground in front of her. He took both her hands and held them and searched her eyes.

"Marley," he said softly, "I promise you. God is real. If you truly love Him, and you give Him every ounce of trust you have and just put everything in His hands—all your fears, all your worries, all your concerns, all your cares—and just wait on Him, He will come through for you in due time. Go to Him with the word, and He will keep His promises."

Chapter 24

P AM LEANED AGAINST the headboard on her bed and clutched one of her tasseled pillows. She couldn't get her mind off the sermon she had just heard on the tape Lazarus had loaned her. It was as if the message had been prepared especially for her.

More than anything else, the sermon made Pam miss God in a way she never realized she could miss Him. She hadn't been to church in quite a while, mainly because she was tired of the nosy questions and the pitying smiles and stares. But by avoiding the questions and the smiles and the stares, she had shut off one of the major vehicles through which God nurtured and sustained her: His church.

The sermon also gave Pam a revelation. All her life, she'd had difficulty reconciling God's will with personal prayers of healing. Never had she felt comfortable praying that her friends or relatives would be healed from their physical infirmities, because she had no way of knowing whether it was God's will that someone be healed or whether God needed them to go through a physical infirmity for a specific reason.

It never occurred to Pam to check the scriptures to see what

God's word said about health and healing. She had never heard a sermon from anyone on the subject. But the tape that Lazarus had loaned her was loaded with scriptural references that she had no idea even existed. James 5:15 said that a prayer of faith will save those who are sick and the Lord will raise them up. Matthew 8:17 reminded her that Jesus had already taken away her infirmities and borne her sicknesses. And 2 Corinthians 12:7–10 assured her that even in weakness God had given her strength and that often God will use times of weakness to show forth His grace and power. Pam had a right to pray for healing. And she had to have faith that God would work His will, in His way, in His time.

She heard Marley's keys unlock the front door. Pam hopped out of her bed and walked out to the hallway. "Hey," she whispered from the top of the stairs.

Marley looked up quickly and put her hand on her chest when she realized it was her mother. "You scared me." She tossed her purse on the couch. "Ma Grand's sleeping?"

"Yeah. Been asleep since about nine o'clock."

"Good. She needs the rest." Marley bolted the front door.

"What's in the bag?" Pam asked.

"Oh, Mrs. Jacobs sent this to you. It's food from the cookout and some pound cake she baked for you." Marley walked toward the kitchen.

"My goodness," Pam said, walking down a few steps, "how sweet of her." She touched her cheek. "You've got to give me her telephone number so I can call and thank her tomorrow."

"I will," Marley said, returning to the foyer.

"Did you have a good time?"

Marley smiled a toothy grin. "Yeah," she said slowly, dreamily, and scurried up the steps and into Pam's room. Pam followed and closed the door behind them.

Marley threw herself on the bed, arms behind her head. "Mom, he is so special. I'm serious. He's not like anyone I've ever known. He's *gorgeous,* obviously, but what makes him even more attractive is that he is a true man of God. I never knew a man of God before."

Pam smiled and listened. She leaned against her dresser, her arms folded across her chest. "He seems to be a very peaceful man."

"And, Mommy, he's so gentle. And so caring and considerate in all the right ways. Do you realize we've been dating since spring and we haven't . . . well, you know. The anticipation is *killing* me, but the excitement about waiting until the time is right is even more tantalizing!"

They both laughed open-mouthed, silent laughs. "You're a crazy child," Pam joked.

"I'm serious. He promised God that he would not have sex again until he gets married. How many men do you know who could honor that kind of promise?"

"Not very many." Pam's mind raced back to Richard. She had come to admit, at least inside, that his decision to restrain himself was indeed honorable. She was planning to call him next week to get back on schedule with their appointments.

"It's just another example of God's power, I tell you," Marley continued breathlessly. She sat silently for a moment. "I really think I love him. Can you believe that?"

"Yes. But only because the relationship is not physical. If you had become intimate with him, I would say that your judgment was clouded and you wouldn't know whether you loved him or whether you were strongly lusting after him."

"You're right," Marley said. A mischievous grin edged out of the corners of her mouth. "I can't lie, though. I've sho' 'nuff had some lusty thoughts about him."

They laughed easily and loudly, then heard the bed in the guest room creak under the weight of Ma Grand's shifting. Pam put her index finger over her mouth and shushed her daughter.

"You're a woman. A human being. It's natural for you to have those thoughts. In fact, I'd be concerned if all you had was a whole lot of spiritual attraction and no physical attraction. That could be just as problematic down the road."

"I know. Mom, I feel like I have an opportunity with Lazarus to do something completely and totally right in God's eyes. I feel like I can let this relationship develop exactly the way God tells us to develop our relationships. I know it's not going to be easy. But I also know that God doesn't ask us to do anything He hasn't already given us the power to do."

"I want to go to church with you tomorrow," Pam blurted out. She stood straight, then turned around and began to organize the bottles of perfume and tubes of lipstick that were already organized on her dresser.

Marley's eyes widened. She caught a glimpse of herself in the mirror and changed her countenance. "Okay," she said, trying her best to sound normal and unaffected. "Great." She looked at her mother, then looked down and tried not to smile. "That'll be really nice."

"The early service," Pam stipulated, looking at her daughter in the mirror.

Marley paused. She and Lazarus had agreed they would meet at the later service, and the only way she was going to be able to go to sleep that night was because she knew she would be able to see him the next morning. But her mother was making a major step at a critical time in her life. There was no way she could refuse.

"Okay. We'll go to the eight o'clock service."

"We'll get Mama to go with us, and we'll treat ourselves to a nice breakfast afterward," Pam added. She looked at Marley, but Marley was looking away. Pam relaxed her shoulders, thankful that Marley had not made a big deal out of the situation. Asking to go to church was hard enough.

"Sounds good." Marley stretched her arms above her head and yawned. "On that note, I guess we'd better get ready for bed."

"Yep. Sleep well, honey."

"You too, Mommy."

On the way to the bedroom, Marley poked her head inside the guest room where Ma Grand was sleeping. Lying across her chest, secure in her hands, was one of the numerous magazines Ma Grand subscribed to. Marley tiptoed inside the room and gently removed the magazine. She was about to place the magazine on the nightstand when the title of the article on the open page caught her eye. It was called, "It's Never Too Late to Love Your Children Correctly."

Marley looked at her grandmother. Every line and crease on her face seemed to represent stories or struggles that, like the lines and creases, were all interconnected somehow. She kissed her grandmother on her forehead and wiped a few wisps of gray hair out of her face, turned off the lamp, and went to her bedroom.

Once inside, she closed the door and hurriedly sat on her bed and dialed Lazarus's telephone number. She felt like a high school girl sneaking to use the telephone, way past her bedtime, to call the guy she had sat next to at the basketball game that night. Only now she was a woman eagerly anticipating the sound of the voice of the man whom she was starting to love, just to hear him say "God bless you."

He answered on the first ring. "You're not asleep yet, Miss Shepherd?"

She blushed. Obviously there were no other women calling him at that time of night. "Not yet. Wanted to make sure you made it home okay."

"I did indeed," he said. "I'm going to sleep like a baby tonight, I'm so tired."

"Good. You've been working way too hard lately. You need to get some rest."

"Can't wait to see you tomorrow morning."

"Bad news," Marley said softly.

"What?"

"Well, it's good news, actually. My mother wants to go to church with me. And Ma Grand is going to go with us, too. They want to go to the early service, so I told my mother that—"

"That's wonderful news, Marley. Wonderful." Lazarus sounded excited. "As much as I want to see you, I know that you need that time with your family."

"Thank you for being so understanding." She meant it. Because a part of her had been scared that if he had insisted they all go to church together, she might have tried to accommodate his desire. She'd been that kind of woman not long ago. Thank God Lazarus was not that kind of man.

"I'll call you sometime tomorrow afternoon to hear how everything went."

"Okay. Sleep tight. Don't let the bedbugs bite."

"You either," Lazarus said. "God bless you."

"God bless you, too," she whispered.

"I love you, Marley."

A lump formed in her throat. A tear, mixed with the salt of joy, cascaded out of the corner of her eye. "I love you, too, Lazarus."

"God has brought us together, Marley. We're going to follow Him every step of the way, and the reward is going to be unimaginable."

"I know," she whispered.

"Get some rest, sweetheart. Good night."

"Good night."

Marley hung up the telephone and sat, dazed, on the side of the bed. She wiped her eyes and covered her mouth in shock. She started to smile, then she laughed. She went to the bathroom to brush her teeth and wash her face, and when she finished she was still smiling. She got down on her knees and prayed to God, and when she finished she was still smiling. She climbed in the bed, called Ashley, and told her about the first "I love you," and afterward she was still smiling. She drifted off to sleep, and she was still smiling.

Chapter 25

FROM PAM'S FRONT porch, Ma Grand, Pam, and Marley observed as a soft breeze rustled the leaves on Pam's chestnut tree. The sun had set on what had been a fulfilling day for all of them, and they were lingering outside just a while longer in hopes of savoring the last satisfying drops of what Sunday had bestowed. They didn't know what Monday would bring.

"I still can't believe that woman had the gall to wear that six-inch feathered hat to church today," Ma Grand said. "Not only were the feathers so tall that folk couldn't see beyond them, but the hat had the nerve to be hot pink." Ma Grand shook her head. "Some folk just don't have good sense."

"There should be a law against hats like that," Pam added. "I mean, women have to know that they're obstructing other people's vision when they wear those hats."

"Sure, they know," Ma Grand snapped. "They're trying to get attention, that's what they're doing. Ought to be 'shamed of themselves."

Marley stretched her arms and sat up on the plastic chaise longue. "Didn't you used to have a feathered hat like that, Ma Grand?" Marley swore she recalled seeing a similar hat in her grandmother's closet years ago when she used to search for clothes to play dress-up.

"I certainly did not. No, ma'am. I can't stand feathers. They're sleazy. Plus, they make me sneeze."

"I think you did have a feathered hat, Mama," Pam said. "A beige one, with brown feathers, that you wore with your cream Ultrasuede suit."

"Pamela, you have lost your mind. I did not own such a thing. You-all need to get your brains checked out—the both of you. You're too young to be so senile."

"She had it," Marley said to her mother. Pam nodded.

They shared the silence. Pam rocked back and forth on the rocking bench. It was just like her mother's, and it was the last gift her father had given her. "From my hands and my heart," he'd said, his voice raspy from a cold that had blossomed into pneumonia and snuffed his life out.

Pam wished the conversation had not stopped; for that brief period of time, she had forgotten about tomorrow.

"It sure was a beautiful day," she offered.

"Yes, indeed," Ma Grand agreed.

"The breeze is still blowing," Marley added. Pam and Ma Grand nodded.

Silence again. Now each of them was hoping to strike up something of a conversation, anything to make tomorrow's heavy possibilities take a backseat.

Marley gave up. She was sleepy, for one. But she also realized that these were the times when she needed to trust God the most. She was tired of worrying about things that God had told her to release to Him. She was proud of herself for remembering God at a moment like this.

"Well, ladies, I'm going to head on inside."

"Yeah, you need to get in the bed since you've got to go to work tomorrow," Ma Grand said.

"Actually, I'm taking off tomorrow."

"Why?" Pam said suddenly. Did Marley know something about the test results that Pam didn't know? Why did she need to take off from work?

"Because I just filed a brief on Friday, and I have some downtime that I want to take advantage of. Days like this don't come around often," she said, standing.

"Mm," Pam mumbled and continued to rock on the bench.

"Well, good, then. You can make us some of that fancy fake beef sausage and some of those fake eggs for breakfast in the morning," Ma Grand said. "Can't believe I didn't vomit after I ate it the other morning."

"Mama, those were real eggs, just minus the cholesterol. And if you're asking for it again, you must have enjoyed it."

"It was all right. It's still fake food. But it's all right, I guess. I'm willing to *broaden my horizons,* as Marley says I should do."

"I'm gonna go on inside." Marley opened the storm door, then paused. "Do you mind if I say a prayer first?"

"Uh, no. Not at all. Go ahead," Pam said. She looked at her mother.

"Go on," Ma Grand agreed.

Marley approached the two women she loved most in life. She took their hands in hers. She closed her eyes and felt the strength and power of their blood, running like currents through their veins. She clutched their hands tighter, hoping to absorb the staying power that only time and trials had earned them.

"Heavenly Father, we come to You in the name of Jesus. First, we want to thank You for the beautiful day You have allowed us to experience. We realize that each day is a precious gift from You and that it's only Your grace that has allowed us to be a part of it. Thank You, Father."

Marley paused and closed her eyes tighter. She blocked out her surroundings and continued.

"God, right now we come to You with special needs. There is something on each of our hearts, Lord, and we know that You said for us to cast all our cares upon You. We lift up my mother to You right now, God."

Pam began to sniffle, and Ma Grand's hands began to shake.

"Lord," Marley continued, her voice beginning to crack, "there is a disease that has afflicted my mother's body. Its name is cancer."

Pam's sobs grew louder, and it was becoming hard for Marley to hold on to Ma Grand's shaking hand.

"But God, the name of cancer is beneath the name of Jesus. Jesus is the name that is above every name. Cancer has no power over the name of Jesus. So we lift up the name of Jesus right now, Lord, and we thank You that Jesus has already healed us and made us whole. We thank You that You created us in Your image and in Your likeness, and we know that there is no disease or sickness in You, so it cannot be Your will that disease and sickness should prevail in us."

Pam cried openly and tears rolled down Ma Grand's face. They held on to Marley's hands.

"So we stand firm in the knowledge of Your word, Lord. We thank You for Your word, and we thank You that You are faithful to it. We thank You right now that all my mother needs is a mustard seed of faith to rise above the sickness that has afflicted her body. We know that she has a purpose for being here, Lord, and that she has not finished fulfilling that purpose. So comfort her in the way that only You can comfort her, Father. Assure her in the way that only an omnipotent God can assure her. She has faith, God. She trusts You. She loves You. Father, take that faith, that trust, that love, and multiply it. Remind her that she is the child of a king, and that if she follows You, You will make sure that only goodness and mercy follow her all the days of her life. We pray this in the matchless name of Jesus Christ, our Lord and Savior. Amen."

The three women cried, Marley standing while Pam and Ma Grand remained seated. Pam opened her arms to Marley, and Marley fell into them like a child. Pam rocked her daughter back and forth across her lap.

Ma Grand sat next to them, still sniffling. She wanted to reach out to them so badly, but she just didn't know how. She hated herself for being scared to express her emotions. Too scared to put a loving hand on her daughter's shoulder. Or to stroke her daughter's hair, which she hadn't had the joy of touching and feeling in her hands since the last ponytail she had braided for her more than forty years ago. She felt Marley's hand cover her own, and it made her angry. What was wrong with her?

Marley stood up. She wiped her eyes and looked at her mother and grandmother. "I love you both so much. Everything is going to be all right. It really is."

Pam nodded. "You're absolutely right. I believe it." Pam stood. "Thank you for that prayer, Marley. I'm ready to go to sleep now, because I know I'm not alone. God will be with me tomorrow to face whatever it is I have to face."

"That's right," Marley said.

"Come on, Mama. Let's go inside."

"You all go on. I'll be in shortly."

"You sure, Gran?" Marley asked, her brows raised.

"Of course I'm sure. I sit on my own front porch by myself all the time. I'll be fine. You go on inside."

"Okay. Good night, Gran." Marley patted her hand.

"Good night."

"Good night, Mama," Pam said. "Don't forget to put the top lock on when you come inside."

"I won't."

Ma Grand watched them go inside. The bench had stopped rocking when Pam got up, so Ma Grand moved her feet and caused the rocking to continue. She could not think clearly; she was hurting so much on the inside. She didn't know what she could do to make herself feel better.

"Cast all your cares upon Him," Pastor Woods had said during his sermon that morning. Ma Grand's mouth began to twitch. She squeezed her eyes shut and rocked faster. In all her years, and through all her pain, she had not cast her cares upon *anyone*. She had had no time for that, when there were children to feed; a job to hold down; a body to outwit and a husband to satisfy; a city to desegregate. She had simply blotted her cares out of her mind, pushed them into oblivion, repaved the path that led to them. She had simply denied them.

But the pain she carried today would not be denied, for she was not its object. It refused to move. It pitched itself a hole into Ma Grand's consciousness and sprawled itself across her heart. She had to cast it somewhere. So she caved in and said, "Dear God . . ."

Chapter 26

AFTER BREAKFAST ON Monday morning, Marley and Ma Grand returned, almost by force, to the front porch. Any room in the house would have been too encroaching.

Marley heard the telephone ring inside and almost dropped her glass of orange juice. She looked at Ma Grand, and Ma Grand glared at her.

"Child, get yourself together," Ma Grand whispered. "You can't be spilling things and breaking things every time the phone rings."

"Hey, Ava," Marley heard Pam say inside, and Marley sighed. "It's Ava," she informed Ma Grand.

"It is?" Ma Grand asked, pretending she couldn't hear.

From the front porch, they listened to the entirety of Pam's conversation with Ava, and it wasn't until Pam hung up that Marley sipped her orange juice. Ma Grand had been holding a few grapes in her hand, and she didn't eat them either until Pam's telephone conversation ended.

Both wondered what Pam was doing inside and whether she would join them on the front porch. Both secretly hoped she would not. It just seemed easier that way.

The telephone rang again, and this time Ma Grand jumped in her seat. She cut a sideways glance at Marley to see whether she had witnessed her reaction and quickly folded her hands in her lap. "Doggone phone rings too loud," Ma Grand mumbled.

"Yes, you can go ahead and fax the standard estimate to them," Pam said to her secretary.

"It's her secretary," Marley said.

"I can hear," Ma Grand snapped.

"Oh." Marley drank her juice.

"You mean to tell me she's trying to work from home on a day like today?" Ma Grand whispered to Marley.

"She probably thinks it will keep her calm."

"Humph."

They heard Pam conclude her telephone call with her secretary and walk toward the front porch. They straightened themselves up in their seats and attempted to relax their facial expressions.

"You-all sure are quiet," Pam said through the storm door.

"Just enjoying the morning." Ma Grand began to rock on the bench.

"It is beautiful," Pam said.

"You gonna join us?" Marley asked.

"Not just yet. I want to straighten up a few things in the kitchen first. Then I'll be out."

"Okay," Marley said quickly.

"See you then," Ma Grand said as Pam walked away.

Marley looked at her grandmother strangely. " 'See you then?' " she whispered. "And you told me to get *myself* together?"

"Oh, hush."

The telephone rang again. Marley's stomach dropped. Somehow she knew this was the call. Ma Grand's body stiffened in her seat, and she stopped rocking.

"Yes, hello, Doctor," Pam said. She left the kitchen and walked somewhere, and Marley and Ma Grand could no longer hear. If

Marley could have stopped breathing in order to hear the conversation, she would have.

Ma Grand shut her eyes and began to rock on the bench. She clasped her hands together and mumbled a few words Marley could not make sense of.

Marley closed her eyes and said a silent prayer, her third that morning.

Several minutes passed, and they had not heard or seen Pam. Marley began to worry. Another minute passed, and she turned to face her grandmother.

"Do you think we should go inside and check on her?"

"Yes." Ma Grand's face was contorted.

Marley held the door open for Ma Grand and followed her inside. They heard a noise upstairs and began to climb the steps.

Marley saw her mother lying across her bed. She was crying, and her face was covered with pillows. Marley's heart dropped. Ma Grand mumbled inside the doorway.

"Mom," Marley said as she walked toward the bed. She put her hand on her mother's back and began to rub it. "Was that the doctor?"

"Yes." Pam's voice was muffled.

"What did he say?" Ma Grand asked from the doorway.

Pam sat up and wiped her eyes. Her face was red and puffy. "The doctor said," she began, and cried again.

Marley continued to rub her back. She steeled herself on the inside and promised herself she would be the strongest one in the room, for all of them.

"He said there's no sign of cancer in my body."

The room fell silent. Marley looked at her mother and screamed. She hugged her so tightly that they both fell back on the bed.

"Oh, my Lord. Oh, my Lord," Ma Grand said and paced the floor back and forth. "Oh, good Lord above," she repeated over and over.

Pam and Marley sat up on the bed. Pam wiped her eyes again.

"God has been so good to me," she said, weeping. "So good. I just don't deserve it."

"He's got a plan for your life, Mommy." Marley wiped tears from her cheeks. "You've still got work to do here."

"I know, I know," Pam agreed, wiping her eyes.

Ma Grand stared at her daughter from across the room until the vision was a blur from the tears that had formed in her eyes. She hobbled toward Pam, breathing heavily.

Ma Grand placed her shaking hands around her daughter's face and stared down at her. "He answered my prayer," she said and began to cry.

Pam looked up at her mother with the glassy, hopeful eyes of a child. She grabbed her mother's wrists, as if to make sure her mother would not let go. It felt too good, too comforting, too necessary for her to let go.

Still holding Pam's face in her hands, Ma Grand bent down. She kissed her daughter on the forehead and stroked her hair.

Marley stared at the wondrous image of love beside her, an image she had longed to see for some time. Everything felt complete.

Marley said, "Thank you, Father."

Chapter 27

Thanksgiving, Seven Years Later

MARLEY WIPED THE sweat from her brow and removed an oblong baking dish from the oven. There, in her hands, was her pride and joy: her macaroni and cheese, made from scratch. She'd done it without referring to Ma Grand's recipe, without calling her mother for quick clarification, without measuring the ingredients. She'd done it on her own merit, her own wisdom, her own instincts.

"Mommy, Mommy, Steven's *bothering* me!"

Marley had barely placed the dish on the stove before the tiny, sticky, Magic Marker–stained hands of a four-year-old gripped her legs and shook her balance. "He's taking the rabbit out of the cage, and he's letting it run around, and he's, he's also *touching* me with it, a whole *lot,* and—"

Marley looked down at the little body that was attempting to push its head between her legs. "Hannah, what did I tell you about tattling, huh?" Marley frowned. "What did Mommy tell you about that?"

Hannah's eyes widened and moistened. "That, that, that I shouldn't *do* it." Pouting, she looked down.

"And why not?" Bending down, Marley gently placed her hand on the back of Hannah's neck.

"Because, because, because it's not *good* to do." Hannah wiped her eyes. "Because, because I should talk to Steven first, and *I* should handle it *first,* and then I should tell *you* after *that.*"

Marley stroked Hannah's head. "And did you do that, sweetie? Did you talk to Steven first?"

"Noooo," Steven said from the doorway. "She never does," he said, shrugging as he walked off.

"Steven, get back in that kitchen," a deep, firm voice said from the dining room.

"But Dad, I didn't *do* anything," Steven fussed, passing a race car back and forth between his hands.

"In the kitchen, son," Lazarus repeated from the dining room as he placed folding chairs around the table. "Now."

Across the ceramic-tiled foyer, in the family room, the soft tunes floating from the stereo were drowned out by a heated NBA Live video game in progress. "Boy, you ain't *seen* a dunk till you see what I'm 'bout to put on you," Beanie shouted, pressing buttons and leaning sideways as he attempted to score. He missed, and Isaiah laughed. "Take that mess somewhere else, man," he said as his player captured the rebound and headed down the virtual court.

Mr. Jacobs and Jeremi carried more folding chairs down the hall. Hearing the commotion in the family room, Mr. Jacobs walked to the doorway, peeked inside, and narrowed his eyes. "You cannot *tell* me," he began, voice low, face red, "that you can't find a way to be of some help to *someone* in this house right now." He glared at his sons. "Now get yourselves *up* off that floor and go find somebody to help. You plan to eat, don't you?"

Isaiah looked as if he'd been punched in the face. "Dad, why are you always—"

Beanie elbowed Isaiah and paused the game. "Don't say nothing, man, just don't say nothing," he advised his brother as he hopped up off the floor, brushed past his father and Jeremi, and left the room. Isaiah followed, shoulders slumped and face long.

In the dining room, Pam leaned against the mahogany china cabinet. "I don't think we can fit another thing on this buffet," she said, looking down, hands on her hips. "Not another thing." She shuffled the collard greens and sweet potato soufflé but failed to find more space.

"Don't worry about it," Mrs. Jacobs said. "I'm gonna move the cranberry sauce and stuffing over here, next to the turkey, and that should do it."

Pam watched Mrs. Jacobs' maneuvering and agreed. "Mm-hm. That does it." She massaged her temples. A mild headache had begun to surface.

Mrs. Jacobs glanced at her as she moved dishes. "You all right, sugar?"

"Oh yeah, I'm fine. Just a little tension headache." Pam smiled, her eyes closed as she continued the massage.

"The radiation going all right?" Mrs. Jacobs asked softly.

"Mm-hm. Two more weeks and I'll be done, thank God." Pam slid her body into one of the upholstered chairs—a cream-and-burgundy print she had recommended.

"Well, honey, that haircut is the sharpest thing I've seen since sliced bread. Makes me want to go out and do the same thing, only my head is too round for that."

Pam touched the side of her closely cropped, barely there hair. "Oh, I think it would look wonderful on you, especially with all that gray you've got. It would be stunning." Pam ran her hand through her layers and shook her head. "It's a shame that it took the threat of losing my hair again to make me cut it all off. Should've done this a long, long time ago."

"Doesn't matter," a male voice said, approaching from behind.

"You were beautiful then, and you're beautiful now." He stood behind Pam and massaged her shoulders.

"Lord, Lord," Mrs. Jacobs said, hands on her hips as she stared at Richard. "Every woman deserves a friend like you. You sure you're not some angel disguised as a human?"

Richard laughed and winked at Mrs. Jacobs. "I'll never tell." He looked down at Pam. "You feeling all right?"

Pam looked up and smiled. "I'm feeling fine. Thank you," she said, patting his hand lightly.

"What has Anne recommended for the headaches?" Richard asked, his brow furrowed.

"Nothing, really," Pam said.

"Peppermint is what you need. I'll pick some up for you tomorrow." Leaning down, he whispered, "You owe me for all this free advice I'm giving you."

Lazarus poked his head in the dining room. "Everything ready?" he asked, surveying the scene. Candles burned around the room, steam rose from the food in the uncovered dishes, and jacquard gold plates stood high in a pile, waiting to be filled.

"All set," Mrs. Jacobs said, winking at him.

"Where's my fried turkey?" Mr. Jacobs roared playfully as he entered the room.

"Right over there, baby," Mrs. Jacobs said, pointing to the buffet.

"All right, everybody, let's gather around the table," Lazarus called.

Mr. and Mrs. Jacobs joined hands. Isaiah stood beside his mother, still pouting, and Geneva stood next to him. Beanie's wife— whom he'd married for the third time last Christmas—held Geneva's hand, and their children stood between them. Jeremi held Beanie's hand, and Paul, Sheila, and their twin sons stood next to one another. Pam and Richard stood by Lazarus and Steven, and the circle was almost complete.

"Where's Mom?" Steven asked, still holding his father's hand as he looked around.

"Here we come," Hannah said from the foyer. "Move, Steven," she said from the doorway, pushing him as firmly as she could manage.

"Mom!" Steven shouted, and Lazarus yanked his hand.

"Move, *stupid,*" Hannah persisted, cutting her eyes at Steven and turning to point at the wheelchair behind her.

"Hannah, stop it *now,*" Marley snapped. She took a deep breath and bent down. "Dad, do you want to stay in the chair, or do you want me to help you up so you can stand in the circle?" Her head was near Silas's, and her hand was on his shoulder.

His sightless eyes seemed to stare ahead, his head tilted slightly. "Ah, I, ah, I think I want to stand," he said, his voice gravelly.

Marley helped her father out of the wheelchair and into the circle, where Pam and Richard made room for him. Pam gripped Silas's hand firmly, and a tear cascaded down his face.

"It's all right, Dad," Marley said quietly, rubbing his back before she took his hand. She looked at Lazarus and winked. He grinned at her and then bowed his head. "Let us pray," he said.

"God, You're so good that we don't know where to begin," he said, and amens and yesses filled the air.

"We come to You in the name of Jesus Christ. It's Jesus who loved us enough to take our sins to the cross and die for us. It's Jesus who covers us with His blood, and it's His blood that allows You to see us clean, whole, and new. We're nothing without Jesus—just a bunch of flesh without purpose or direction—and so, on this day of thanksgiving, we put first things first and we thank You for Your son. Thank You, Father."

"Thank You, Lord, thank You, Lord," Mr. Jacobs said. Mrs. Jacobs shook her head and rocked from side to side.

"God, we thank You for family. You've taught us how to bear with one another, to make allowances for one another, to forgive one another. You've told us that the only way we can love You is by loving one another. Thank You, Lord, that we have one another to forgive. Thank You that it's not even *hard* to forgive, because all we need to do is remember the new mercies You extend to us on a daily basis, the sins You forget, the grace You bestow when we're so undeserving. We're here today, holding hands, and God, we thank You for it. We don't take it for granted, because we know that tomorrow is not promised. So Lord, help us to live each day as if it's our last. Help us to love one another. Help us to be thankful for one another."

Tears streamed down Pam's reddened face. She closed her eyes as tightly as she could. Through blurry eyes, Marley glanced at a portrait of her grandmother hanging over the head of the table. It was their first Thanksgiving without her. Marley stared at her grandmother's eyes, as she often did, willing her to speak strength. Ma Grand's eyes seemed to stare right back, commanding Marley to look within.

"And finally, Lord, we thank You for the food. We know that there are many who are hungry today. There are many who don't know where their next meal will come from. Let us search our hearts for ways to provide for our brothers and sisters in need. And let us be thankful for what You've blessed us with. Stop us from putting too much food on our plates and wasting it. Let us live on less so we can give more. Let us always remember that You are our source—not our paychecks, not our pensions, but You, God."

"Yes, Father," Paul said, nodding his head vigorously.

"We thank You, God. We praise You. And we lift this prayer up to You in the name of Jesus Christ, our Lord and Savior. Amen."

"Amen, amen!" Mrs. Jacobs said.

"Amen," the children mumbled obligingly, brushing past the adults and dashing for their plates.

*   *   *

In the middle of a bid whist game, the doorbell rang. Marley sat up, stared at the door, and smiled. "That's her. That's gotta be her." She jumped out of her seat, leaving her hand on the table.

"Saved by the bell," Paul said, arranging his jokers next to his ace, king, and jack of spades. " 'Cause this is an uptown you'll never forget," he chuckled. Sheila winked at Paul, and Lazarus shook his head. By the sight of his own hand, he knew Paul was right.

Marley swung the oak door open and screamed. Deanna fell into her arms. They rocked back and forth, laughing and hugging, not letting go of each other. Ashley and Pablo stood on either side, grinning at the reunion they knew Marley and Deanna had been longing for.

"Girl, look at you! You look fabulous!" Marley said, stepping back to take Deanna in. Her blond twists were swept up, revealing rock-size diamond studs and a matching pendant. Her two-piece cream cashmere outfit enhanced the glow from her suntanned, coppery skin. She brought a dose of July to November. Happiness spilled out of her eyes.

"I am *soooo* happy to see you!" Deanna squealed, then hugged Marley again. "Can you believe it's been two years?"

"I really can't, Dee. God, it is *so* good to see you!" Marley beamed. She looked at Pablo and tapped her forehead. "Forgive me for being so rude—I got caught up in the moment." She laughed as she gave Pablo a hug. "It's good to see you, too."

"And you," Pablo said, smiling.

"Hey, girl," Marley said, quickly kissing Ashley on the cheek. "Here, let me take your coats. Come on in and see everybody."

Stopping in the doorway of the family room, Marley poked her head inside. "You all remember Deanna and her husband, Pablo?"

"Hey, Deanna," everyone said.

"Where's my autographed *ball,* Pablo?" Steven asked from the floor, forcing his battery-operated racing car to jump off the track and crash into the wall.

"Girl, if you don't get over here and give me my hug, I don't know what I'm going to do," Pam said, standing and opening her arms.

Marley returned from the coat closet and walked over to Deanna. "Y'all have fifteen minutes to talk to her, then it's girl time upstairs," she said, resting her hand on Deanna's shoulder.

"Me too, Mommy? I'm getting to go to girl time, too?" Hannah asked from the floor, surrounded by Barbie dollhouses, cars, swimming pools, and barbecue grills.

"No, sweetie. Big girls' time. Just the big girls for a few minutes, then Mommy'll come and get you, okay?"

Hannah stuck out her lower lip and frowned. She made Barbie trip over her motorcycle.

"Come sit on Grandma's lap and have girl time with me and Aunt Sheila and Aunt Geneva," Mrs. Jacobs said quickly, patting her knees.

Hannah jumped up and accepted the offer. Mrs. Jacobs winked at Marley, and Marley mouthed her thanks.

"Look what you've done with this *room*!" Deanna marveled as she walked around the master bedroom. The wood-burning fireplace was framed in tile and topped with a maple mantelpiece, and a chaise longue sat across from it. A Turkish rug with muted earth tones covered the center of the room, and the cherry king-size bed was adorned with damask pillows that matched the window treatments.

"You know Pamela Shepherd did this," Marley said, climbing on the bed and folding her legs beneath her.

"Incredible. Absolutely incredible," Deanna said, kicking her shoes off and hopping on the bed. Ashley was stretched out at its foot.

"I'm sure it's nothing compared to the showstopping palace you and Pablo just bought in California," Marley teased.

"Really," Ashley said, lifting her hair off her neck. "When are you gonna fly us out to see it?"

"Girl, I'm never there. We barely have a bed to sleep in. I have *got* to hire somebody to pull that house together." Deanna looped her necklace around her finger. "I'm on the road with Pablo so much that I feel like home is whatever hotel we're staying in."

"She's all the way across the country, yet she still knows more about what's going on in Atlanta than we do. Tell her what you told me in the car on the way over here," Ashley said, nudging Deanna's leg.

"Girl, girl, girl," Deanna began, hitting the bed with her hand. "You will never, ever, *ever* guess who I saw at the airport in Chicago."

"Who?" Marley asked, brows raised.

"Gloria Shore."

Marley's heart dropped. "You're kidding. Gerrard's mother?"

"Yes, girl. Looking thirty years older. It was awful." Deanna shook her head.

"Did she remember you?"

"Oh, yeah," Deanna said. "Knew I had married Pablo and everything."

"Well, that's just like her," Marley said flatly. "No local news skips past that woman." Marley stared at Deanna, uninterested in playing the stalling game. "So? How's he doing?"

Deanna pursed her lips and shook her head slowly. "Not good. He's going through his second divorce, and some woman from Arizona slapped him with a paternity suit."

"Mm-mm-mm," Marley said, shaking her head. "I am genuinely sorry to hear that." And she was. Life had been too good to her to leave room for hard feelings. Rarely did Gerrard cross her mind; when he did, she simply remembered to pray for him.

"Yeah," Deanna said. "Of course, I told her all about you and how well you and Lazarus were doing. Showed her a picture of Steven and Hannah, which she stared at forever. Said they were the cutest things she'd ever seen. Poor woman."

"I know. A victim of circumstance," Ashley said. She looked at her hands. "I think about women like her, and I remind myself it's not so bad being alone at thirty-seven. Better this than that."

"Yeah," Marley said, picking at her toenails, "but you don't have to hook up with someone like Mr. Shore, Ash. Just remember that."

They heard a light rap at the bedroom door.

"Hannah?" Marley asked, hopping off the bed. Just that quickly, she had forgotten her promise to include her daughter in girls' time.

"No, it's Jeremi," he said from the hallway. "Dad needs some peroxide, and Laz told me to ask you where I could find it."

"Oh, sure, come on in," Marley said, opening the door. "We have some in our bathroom—I'll get it."

Jeremi poked his head inside the door and waved. "Hey," he said.

"Come on in, Jeremi," Deanna said, beckoning with her hand. "We won't bite your head off."

He smiled. "I'm cool. Feels like a lioness's den up in here."

Deanna and Ashley laughed.

"How you been?" he asked Ashley, looking directly at her. "Haven't seen you since, what, last Christmas?"

"Fine, fine. Doing the same old thing. What about you?"

"Same old thing." He stared at her, nodding slowly. She smiled, and then looked down.

Marley returned with peroxide and a handful of cotton balls. "In case he needs these, too," she said, stuffing the items in Jeremi's hands.

"Thanks," Jeremi said. "All right, ladies. If I don't see you before you leave, then good night and all that good stuff."

"You too," they said.

He looked at Ashley. "Let's try to see each other before the next holiday," he said, nodding in her direction, and walked away.

Marley closed the door and laughed silently, mouth wide. Deanna made faces at Ashley and poked her in her ribs.

"Y'all are worse than kindergarteners!" Ashley said, twisting in laughter.

Lazarus forced a salad plate into the already overstuffed dishwasher, closed it, and leaned against the counter. He glanced around the kitchen and exhaled. "I didn't think this room would ever get clean after today."

Marley chuckled as she wet a dishrag.

"You outdid yourself, baby," he said. "Everything was wonderful."

"Thank you, sweetheart," she mumbled, walking to the stove. She wiped grease stains off the knobs. "So Dad didn't mind riding home with your parents?"

"No, not at all. Kept thanking me for picking him up and including him in Thanksgiving dinner. I think he's still in shock that you've embraced him the way you have, after all that's happened."

"Yeah, I think so too." Marley applied pressure to a stubborn chunk of dried stuffing that wouldn't loosen its hold on a knob. "You never could have told me he'd end up blind and crippled. I mean, you hear about terrible car accidents all the time, but you never expect that one of your own family members will become a victim." She shook her head. "Anything can happen. I'm just glad he wasn't too proud to let us help him."

"Oh, no," Lazarus said quickly, shaking his head. He rubbed his chin thoughtfully. "Silas has a good heart. I heard him telling my parents at least three times tonight, 'They've got me in the best assisted-living facility in the city.' And then he'd start tearing up, you know?"

"Yeah." Every now and then, that old streak of silent rage would creep up behind Marley and tap her on the shoulder, just when she was looking at Silas with compassionate eyes. Usually she shook it off like a wool sweater on a summer day. But every now and then, it would hang around, refusing to be shaken, insisting to be worn. "Yeah," she said again, abandoning the stove's knobs for the burners.

Lazarus watched her as she lifted the burners and wiped in the crevices. He loved watching her as she worked, loved the way her arms, shoulders, back, and legs worked rhythmically to complete the most minor task. He watched her—the woman who'd been made to walk through life with him, the woman he'd been made to serve—and he smiled at her and at his longing for her. He gently grabbed the waist of her pants and pulled her to him.

"Want me to run you a bubble bath?" he whispered into her ear, kissing it lightly.

She closed her eyes, smiled, and tossed the dishrag on the stove. She let the weight of her body rest against his and snuggled into his embrace. "Are Steven and Hannah asleep?"

"They will be," he promised, tracing the side of her neck with his nose.

She turned to face him and pressed her forehead against his chin. "Do you know how much I love you?"

"Yep," he whispered, rocking her from side to side in his arms. "And after this bubble bath, you're gonna know how much I love you, too."

She giggled. "All right, Mr. Jacobs. I'm going to take the dirty linen to the laundry room, and then I'll be upstairs. The water better be hot when I get there," she teased, backing out of his arms and out of the kitchen.

"Oh, it'll be hot all right," he said, smiling wide as he folded his arms across his chest.

Marley made brief stops in every room before she went upstairs. She fluffed the pillows on the couch in the family room, rearranged the vases on the coffee table in the living room, and opened and closed the curtains in the dining room. She felt pieces of her husband's and children's spirits in every corner, and she smiled. This was home.

She stopped in front of Ma Grand's portrait and touched it softly, her fingers tracing the creases in her grandmother's forehead. She smiled with misty eyes. "Wasn't the same without your butter beans." She laughed, wiping her eyes. She looked at Ma Grand's folded hands. "But my macaroni and cheese was incredible, if I may say so myself."

Marley twisted her ring. "Dad was here. He's going through a lot right now. It's hard sometimes, but honestly, I'm glad he's back in my life. And he and Mom are like the best of friends—you'd be amazed." She looked up at her grandmother. "But if you had been here, you would've cursed him from here to Biloxi, so I guess things have a way of working themselves out.

"Well," she said, hands on hips, "I'm happy, Gran. Really, really happy. Life is good. God is good. I'm blessed. And I'm truly, truly grateful." Marley walked to the doorway and turned off the light. "Happy Thanksgiving, Gran. I love you." She went upstairs, the weight of her heart lightening with each step. By the time she reached the top, saw the candlelight flickering down the hall, and heard the soft music playing, she was smiling. Her man was waiting.

With a chenille scarf draped around her neck, Pam sat on her front porch and rocked on the bench. The night was so still, so quiet, so peaceful that she could hear her thoughts. They were loud, as usual, disregarding one another as they competed for center stage. But she'd learned to tune them out, handpicking her mental companions instead.

At the moment, she chose to think about her life. The past didn't scare her anymore. Cancer had been a toothless panther; its mouth had done no more than grip her forcefully, all to carry her over hurdles with a speed and agility she'd never possessed. Oh, the things it had helped her achieve in seven short years! There were the tangibles: she ate more healthily, walked more, complained less. But the greatest achievements, the most marked strides, lay in the daily scriptures she absorbed and the meditations she offered, the emotional weights she'd dumped like the sewage they were, the peace she'd claimed as her God-given right.

The future didn't scare her, either. The tumor was there, right on her lung, and no one knew whether radiation would shrink it away or not. But who cared? Life was about the here and now: forgiving instead of harboring, laughing instead of questioning. It was about picking up the bat, swinging at the ball, and not being afraid to strike out—because the bat was hers to swing and the ball was thrown for her to hit or miss. Life was about being grateful for the game. And what a blessing it was to play on the team, with God as the coach. What a blessing that winning or losing was *her* choice, a choice that began and ended in her mind.

She peered through the portals of the present, and all the signs of victory were there. She loved her family for who they were. She appreciated her friends for what they could give. She cared for those who hadn't always cared for her. It had taken almost sixty years for her to find this space, stake it out, and make it home, but she'd done it. Twenty more years of life anywhere other than this was not life. It was not living. It certainly was not winning.

A light breeze shook the leaves on the chestnut tree. It trickled over to her face and brushed her cheek. Pam closed her eyes and smiled. She knew this breeze; it had befriended her three days after her mother had gone home to glory. It showed up at the oddest times, when normal breezes would be blowing their wisdom somewhere altogether different; but then, it was just like her mother to negotiate a divine understanding, to get a holy permission slip, to obtain an anointed hall pass, enabling her to blow as she chose. It was just like her mother to find a way to speak when she no longer had a voice. And it was just like God to give Pam spiritual ears to hear what the wax of life had blocked out of her natural ones.

"Happy Thanksgiving, Mama," Pam said, wrapping her arms around her shoulders. The breeze circled about the porch, jingling the wind chimes, rustling the leaves of hanging ferns, and finally settling near Pam. She smiled wide. "I love you, too."

Acknowledgments

THE BEST THING about being republished is that I get to thank more people for the support and encouragement they've given me. Thanks to Djana Pearson Morris, Robin Rolewicz, and Melody Guy for appreciating my talent and helping me share it with others.

I hold a special place in my heart for those who were there in the early days, cheering me on, supporting my self-publishing efforts, and praising the book as if it were a *New York Times* bestseller. You know who you are, but just so the rest of the world knows, too:

The booksellers who took a chance on an unknown writer and were kind enough to do more than place my book on a shelf: Simba, Yaw, and the crew at Karibu Books; Robin and the crew at Sibanye; Carl and Angela at Sounds of the Times; Tracey and the People's Community Baptist Church bookstore; Scott and the crew at Reprint Bookstore; Mrs. Betty and Ligorius Bookstore; and Lecia and Basic Black Books. A very special thank you to Trina Banks and those who labor in love in the From the Heart Church Ministries bookstore— your efforts helped to bless souls and sell books at the same time. Thanks, also, to Nati at African World Books for buying in bulk on faith alone.

The book clubs, fellowships, and groups that welcomed me into their circles and found my book worthy of reading when they could have chosen a million other novels to read: Lisa Cross and the Sistah Circle in Dallas; Jeanne Wells-Jessup and STARZ; Hillary and Verna Woodson and the Literary Ladies; Kizzie Bozeman, Charrise Tucker, and the Dream Circle; Veronica Gipson and the Sistahs in Chicago; Alita Wingfield, Ma (Brenda) Shirland and her Delaware book club; Kaye Braxton and Regal Book Club; Patricia Oliver and the Singles Fellowship at Judah Temple A.M.E. Zion Church; Dr. Diana Cherry, Rev. Willette Wright and the precious, bright, and beautiful life-givers at From the Heart Church Ministries Christian School; the Homemakers Ministry at First Baptist Church of Glenarden; Meilyn Marino and T.I.L.I.I.; Kanika Raney and the Book Nook of Delta Sigma Theta Sorority, Inc., Northern Virginia Chapter; Portia Moore and Dear Sistah; Tiffany Davis and Daughters of Isis; Tanya

Upthegrove and A Sista's View; Cassandra Moore and A Room Full of Sisters; Shari Slate and her California book club; Rhonda Waller and Third Sunday and Leona Williams and Sista Chat; Terrie Jones and the Healthy Babies Project; Sarita Lyons and her Delaware book club; and Sonya Dean Walston and her Atlanta book club. Thank you so much, ladies (and gentlemen)!

The journalists/periodicals and others who found my book and me newsworthy: Hamil Harris and Natalie Hopkinson at *The Washington Post;* Melita Myles at *The Philadelphia Tribune;* Judith Upshur at *The Bowie Star;* the *Spelman Messenger* (special thanks to Eloise Abernathy-Alexis and the Office of Alumni Affairs); the *World of Faith Family Worship Center* newsletter; and Tracy Baskerville, the Baltimore Office of Promotions, Cheron Porter, and WMAR-TV in Baltimore.

The friends I've made in the publishing industry who've given freely of their advice and support and who've never hesitated to reach as they climb: Sharon Ewell Foster; Nicole Bailey-Williams; Nancey Flowers; Kwame and Stephanie Alexander; Tonya Marie Evans and Susan Border Evans; Brian Egeston; Tracy Price-Thompson; Maurice Gray; Kevin Johnson; Gloria Anderson; Yolanda Callegari Brooks; and Pamela Walker-Williams. Thanks, also, to Marina Woods and the Good Girl Book Club for featuring the book; to Tee C. Royal and Zane at R.A.W.S.I.S.T.A.Z. for reviewing it; and to Phyllis McLaughlin and Circle of Friends II for making room for it at the annual event that I was too pregnant to attend.

Taydra Kennard, a talented young sister who chose me and this book as the subject of a book report that earned her countywide honors—I'm so proud of you! And to Bernadette Kennard, Taydra's mother, for standing in the gap, raising an exceptional child, and being a superwoman—God bless you.

My friends and family, who've *shamelessly* promoted and/or sold this book from school buildings, medical centers, office suites, college campuses, trunks of cars, and the like: Mommy, Daddy and Brenda, and Carole; Nadine, Dad and Caryl, and Rashida; Angie "Kat" Brown—thanks for connecting me with Simba; Cheryl Jackson; Toni Foxx; Vicki Preston; Pat Carter, my other mother in Atlanta; Benita Wynn, a true gem (How many sistahs would voluntarily take twenty books to sell the first time they meet you!); Rev. and Mrs. Porter Lawson; Mia Fuse Chidebelu-Eze; Romeldia Salter; LaQuita Taylor-Phillips; the staff at Hillcrest Heights Elementary; Tia Shabazz, Tanya "Journey" King, and Kimberly Hines; Monica Davy; and Rita Collins, Kirsten Hadley, and Monica Dean—always, always there.

Every institution and person that has influenced my spiritual development: First Baptist Church of North Brentwood, Maryland, for introducing me to the Lord Jesus Christ and teaching me His ways, and its pastor, Rev. Perry A. Smith III, for being my father in God in the truest sense; and From the Heart Church Ministries, Inc. in Temple Hills, Maryland, for teaching the uncompromising word of God each and every Sunday, and Pastor and Mrs. John A. Cherry, for being committed to exalting the name of Jesus in word and in deed, all the time.

My husband, Malik—my best friend—whose unwavering love and support provide the fuel I need to keep going. I'm so thankful we're journeying this life together.

Finally, a humongous thank you to all the unnamed people who've spread the word about the book—whether by sharing it with a friend, posting a review on Amazon, sending an e-mail, recommending it to a book club, or reading it under the hair dryer at a beauty salon. Word of mouth sells books. Thanks for the words you shared on my behalf—and, ultimately, on the Lord's behalf.

God bless.

A Conversation with Jamellah Ellis

Q: What motivated you to write *That Faith, That Trust, That Love*?

A: Several things. The impetus for Pam's character, and in particular her battle with breast cancer, came from the fact that breast cancer had hit so close to home with me. My great-aunt died from breast cancer in 1995. My mother-in-law was diagnosed with it in 1997, and my aunt died from it that same year. But my grandmother is a thirty-plus-year breast cancer survivor! There are so many ways to approach illness, and I wanted to use an identifiable character like Pam to show that faith in God and belief in His word are the most powerful weapons a sick person can have.

As for Marley, her journey of spiritual rediscovery is a lot like my own. I wanted to reach other women, especially my younger sisters, and tell them that their issues with churches and religion are so valid and so real. I wanted to let them know that God is not part of the hypocrisy or the wholesale spiritual extortion going on in the church today. Despite it all, God is real and Jesus saves, and I wanted to impart that message. For every corrupt church there is a church that teaches the unadulterated word of God.

Q: Gerrard and his family are at the top of Atlanta black society, and it seems that Pam is anxious for Marley to have the security and status that membership in those circles would provide. What did you hope to convey about class issues in your novel?

A: Nothing in particular, except that blacks are not monolithic. We're poor, we're rich, we're well traveled, we're limited in exposure. Our literature should continue to reflect that.

Q: What other authors have influenced you?

A: Because my writing is in its infancy, I can't say I've reached a point where the "influence" of other authors is apparent yet. But I admire so many: J. California Cooper, Diane McKinney-Whetstone, and Zadie Smith are some of my favorite contemporary authors. Zora Neale Hurston is one of my favorite classic authors.

Q: The book deals extensively with dynamics of the mother-daughter relationship, both through Marley and Pam and also with Pam and Ma Grand. They're family, yet the two relationships are very different. Why?

A: Because in real life no two mother-daughter relationships are the same. There are no hard and fast rules about how mothers and daughters should relate or express their love. Some are like best friends, talking all the time and sharing deep secrets, while others are like acquaintances who happen to share blood. Yet you can't judge either type, because there's history behind both. In the case of Pam and Ma Grand, I tried to show how Ma Grand's traditional Southern upbringing by parents not far removed from the psychological vestiges of slavery had a direct impact on how she raised and nurtured her children. Pam, who was raised with lots of exposure to culture and little exposure to emotional expression, took a different path when she raised her own daughter.

Q: What is the primary message you want people to come away with when they read your book?

A: Life is filled with challenges, and when things get tough we tend to get anxious, abandon what we know, and fight battles with our own hands. If we can remember during tough times to stand still, seek God, have faith, and trust that things will work out as they should, then peace will surround us and crowd out the chaos.

Reading Group Guide

The following reading group guide was created to enhance your group's discussion of *That Faith, That Trust, That Love* by Jamellah Ellis, the story of one woman's spiritual awakening and journey to life with God.

1. The contrast between Marley's relationships with Gerrard and Lazarus is unmistakable. What is the key difference between the two? Even before she knew of Gerrard's infidelity, Marley knew there was something wrong with their relationship. Why couldn't she do anything about it? Why didn't Marley trust her instincts?

2. Ma Grand prides herself on speaking the truth, but it is her pride that hinders her ability to see the truth about herself. Why? Has pride kept her away from the truth of God?

3. In Pam's eyes, her daughter has a chance to have the successful marriage and love she never had in her own life. As a result, Pam is almost more excited about Marley's engagement than she is. Why is Pam living through her daughter? What does she realize in the end that enables her to let go of her disappointments with her own life?

4. One theme of *That Faith, That Trust, That Love* is making a decision to accept God into one's life. How does each of the characters reach such a decision? What makes them resist?

5. Marley thinks church is a good idea but is usually disappointed by the messenger or the message when she does attend. How common is this among young people today? What is the difference between Gilead's Balm and her previous experiences with churches?

To print out copies of this or other Strivers Row Reading Group Guides, visit us at http://www.atrandom.com/rgg

6. Marley's spiritual awakening leads to greater peace in other aspects of her life—in her work and in her relationships with her family and friends. Why does this happen? How does a relationship with God affect one's relationships with others?

7. When Marley begins to attend church at Gilead's Balm she feels as if the sermons are meant directly for her. Why does this happen here and not elsewhere? What allows her to open her ears and heart?

8. The verse from Luke 12:27 that opens *That Faith, That Trust, That Love* talks of how God's power and the promise of faith are evident everywhere in life, even in the smallest things. How do we see this in each of the characters in the book?

9. Among the three friends, Ashley is the most secure in her relationship with God and her idea of what she wants in a man. Yet she remains single while Marley and Deanna eventually marry. Why is this?

10. Pam blames her mother for not showing her enough love as a child. Is she right in placing this blame on her mother? Is her mother's disapproval the reason her failed marriage haunts Pam's life? How much do parents affect their children's choices or lives?

About the Author

JAMELLAH ELLIS is a graduate of Spelman College and Northwestern University School of Law. She left the practice of law in 2001 to pursue a writing career and focus on her family. She and her husband, Malik, and their sons live in Maryland. She is the author of "Chasing Horizons," a short story in the anthology *Proverbs for the People*. This is her first novel. You can contact her via her website: www.jamellahellis.com.